HEROES

Edited By:
Brennan Cupp
Ashley Hutchison
Brett Mann
Emily Rozmus

FOREWARD

When the time came to determine what would be the topic for our first anthology of 2022, I immediately turned to hope, something I feel we've all clung to over the past two years as the world has shifted around us, forcing our feet to walk upon unsteady ground. Hope is scored into our hearts as we continue forward in uncertainty, and hope is what we share with the heroes who populate our legends and myths throughout history, who brave the unknown armored entirely with it. Their stories are reminders of how to pursue the best in ourselves in the face of seemingly insurmountable odds. And even should the worst happen, should we fail, what mattered was we donned that armor of hope, and we tried.

What follows here are retellings of those familiar myths and legends, some from new faces, some you might already be acquainted with from our other anthologies, and some from our very own team. I *hope* that you not only enjoy them, but take comfort, find joy, and discover meaning in their messages. But most importantly, that you are met with hope, and that you carry it forward with you into this new year.

-Ashley Hutchison, Editor-in-Chief

TABLE OF CONTENTS

The Hanged Man by Daniel Quigley   1
»   Ji Gong

Lab R Inc by Jess L. Tong   27
»   Theseus & the Minotaur

The Envoy by Laura Jayne McLoughlin   70
»   Cú Chulainn

Robin, The Hood by Stephen Howard   98
»   Robin Hood

Immortal Kingdom by Chris Durston   134
»   Gilgamesh

The Foresta Pietrificata by Madeline Dau   170
»   Perseus & Medusa

Codename: Viking by Michael J. Mullen II   194
»   Beowulf

Dragon by Douglas Jern   221
»   Sigurd & Fafnir

In Pyxis by Matthew Siadak   248
»   Pandora

The Call by R. Raeta   266
»   Joan of Arc

STAFF STORIES

Behind the Mask by Jaecyn Boné   281
   »   Perseus & Medusa

Threads of Gold by Dina S.   314
   »   Midas

Gwenhifar and the Vat-Knight by Dewi Hargreaves   335
   »   Guinevere & Lancelot

Mulan and the DŌGYN of Power by Carter Hutchison   355
   »   Mulan

THE HANGED MAN

Daniel Quigley

His hands shook as he checked and re-checked the noose. No mistakes this time. He took a shuddering breath, trying to calm his nerves. This was the right thing to do. The only thing to do. He looped the rope over the tree branch and secured it to the stout, knotted wood. He clambered up and looked over the forest he'd loved as a child. He closed his eyes, feeling the gentle breeze tickle his skin for the last time. The man slipped his head inside the noose and braced himself.

"Scooch."

His eyes shot open. "Excuse me?"

"Scooch," the voice said, slurring slightly. "You're hoggin' the whole tree."

The almost-hanged man couldn't see for a moment; the second sun's glare burned his eyes. Finally, the ragged shape of a monk came into focus. Her robes were filthy—riddled with holes and frayed at the edges—but most disconcerting was the broad grin spread over her dark-skinned face. In one hand, she carried her own noose. In the other, a large, worn-out reed fan. She staggered drunkenly to the base of the tree and looked up at him.

"There are literally dozens, if not hundreds of trees, in this forest. Can't you…I dunno…fuck off to any one of those?" the almost-hanged man spat.

The monk looked around thoughtfully for a moment. "Nah, ein't interested in those ones. This one's my favorite."

"Well, you'll just have to wait your turn. As you can see, I was here first."

"Branch is plenty big, fella. Just scooch a tad, and we can both go about with the dyin' part."

"Are you drunk?"

"Are you not?" the monk asked. She pulled a giant gourd from her back and took a swig of something so potent the almost-hanged man's eyes watered, even from his perch atop the branch.

"Why would a sister of the Root wish to kill herself anyway?"

The monk considered this for a moment, took another sip from her gourd, swayed slightly, then shrugged. "Well, you see, what happened was…" she trailed off, scratching the back of her head with embarrassment. "The fine folks at the Great Tree sent me here to raise money for the local temple. The word was that it looked rather like…"

"Shite?"

"Exactly."

"Never looked that bad to me."

"Me neither, but the brother here, uh… Brother Addy, Kadi—"

"Brother Ani?"

"Yeah, exactly what I said."

"Corrupt as the rest of the assholes here. No offense."

"None taken. Anyways, yeah, Brother Ani convinced my brothers and sisters at the Great Tree that they had some need here in this town."

"We have plenty of needs. But money for a nicer temple isn't one of them."

The monk shrugged again. "I believe ya, but seein' as how I'd already been kicked out once from the Great Tree, I figured it'd be best not to irritate them further. So I came here to raise some funds."

She tossed her noose over the tree, considered climbing up, thought better of it, and stumbled to a seat next to the base.

"Mind tying that for me?"

The almost-hanged man just stared at her. They sat in silence for a moment as she picked at one of the tree's lavender-colored leaves.

With a huff of exasperation, the man said, "You didn't answer my question. Why would you, of all people, want to kill yourself?"

The monk, who had begun fanning herself, looked startled for a moment. "Thought I answered that."

"Nope."

"Oh. Well, that's strange. Are you sure?"

"I'm sure."

"Right. Well, see, I'd been workin' real hard to earn that money for the new temple, and after three years, I finally did it!"

"You haven't been here for three years. Chennesau isn't that big of a town. I'd have seen you around."

She looked confused, but her broad grin never slipped. "Three weeks? Three years? Tomato, potato."

The man sighed heavily. "Okay, so you got the money. Then what?"

"I wanted to celebrate the momentous occasion, so I stopped at the Dinasaur Inn to get a drink. It was just gonna be the one,

3

honest to Earth Mother."

"I'm sure."

"Honest! Anyways, some big ol' burly folk came upon my person and relieved me of all my worldly possessions."

"That's rough, buddy."

"Right? Anyways, I figure I can't go back to the Great Tree an empty-handed failure. It's darn unforgivable, I reckon. Rather end it right here. So, if you don't mind just tying that end to the branch, we can do this dyin' thing together. Maybe hold hands, if you'd like."

The almost-hanged man eyed her, then the rope. Then his hand plunged into his pocket and came out with a large stack of chits. "Here," he said, tossing them to the ground.

The monk inspected the chits. Blew on them, dusted their edges a bit.

"They don't shine near as much as what I used to have, but I suppose they'll do."

"I'm sorry?" the almost-hanged man asked in bewilderment.

"Ah, well," the monk said, her broad grin growing a hair broader. "This will do fine! Awful lot of chits. You sure we can have it?"

"What use is money going to be to me? I have nothing left to spend it on, no one to give it to. Can't take it with me when I rejoin the Earth Mother."

"You're very wise, friend. Very wise indeed. Well, thank you right kindly. I'll drink to your hea—uh, drink to your memory tonight!"

With that, the monk got up to leave, stumbled a few steps, righted herself, and disappeared back into the lavender-colored forest. The wind picked up, and the almost-hanged man took a few deep breaths to center himself again. He had met brothers and sisters of the Root before, but none like that. She had to be the absolute worst monk he had ever met. What would his handful of chits even do for her? Did it matter? No, he supposed it didn't.

He tightened the rope another few inches. He wanted to do this right—break his neck, die instantly. He'd heard slowly strangling was an awful way to go. He closed his eyes. All he had to do was tip forward ever so slightly, release one final breath, let the Earth Mother pull him down into her embrace, and then—

"Hey, friend! Sorry to bother you again, but I had just one more question." That damnable monk, who had somehow returned unnoticed, was disturbingly close to him.

"Hells above, woman, are you mad? Just let me die already!"

The monk had clambered up the tree to sit on the branch beside him. Now she was fanning herself with one hand and drinking absentmindedly from her gourd with the other. She offered him a swig, which he impolitely refused. The drink alone would probably kill him before the noose ever could. Especially at the rate he was going.

"Don't you worry, friend, I'll let you get to that. But before you do, if it wouldn't be a huge bother, think I could have your clothes?"

He stared at her again, because what else could he do? "My clothes?"

"Yep."

"Why?"

"I figure the spearcats and leafdogs will tear ya up somethin' fierce," she poked his paunch, which he covered reflexively, "to

5

get all that tasty flesh you got. Ein't no point in wastin' perfectly good clothes."

"I don't think they'd fit you."

"Never said they'd be for me."

The almost-hanged man hit his boiling point. "You know, dying isn't supposed to be this hard. Just leave me the fuck alone, okay? By the King in the Mist, woman, is there anything else you want from me? Any other indignities you'd like to bestow on me, oh-most-holy-of-sisters?"

The monk considered his question. "Well, it was nice you gave me chits and all, but it ein't quite enough. Think after you die, I could use you in my puppet show?" She rested her hand on his back, throwing her voice like a ventriloquist. "Hey, what do you call a fish with a bowtie?"

"I don't know, Mr. Dead-body-that-undoubtedly-smells-really-bad? What DO you call a fish with a bowtie?" she asked herself.

"Sofishticated," was her response.

The mad monk laughed uproariously at her own joke. The almost-hanged man just glared. But as his eyes turned to meet hers, the glare softened, melted, dissolving utterly into something else. Something his face hadn't done in some time. Something like a smile.

He groaned, chuckled slightly. Then, like a dam bursting, laughter spilled from his lips. Laughter like wildfire. Laughter that far exceeded the quality of the joke. There were tears in his eyes. The laughter flickered and turned to sobs, then great, racking, shuddering wails. The hand on his back turned into an embrace. For a while, the two of them sat on the branch wordlessly, the violet leaves swirling all around. His tears soaked her soiled robes.

"My daughter would have loved that joke," the almost-hanged man said softly. "We used to go to the town square, early, at the week's end. We'd find the buskers and storytellers. Used to be a great one from Siskiyuhn that'd come once a month. She...she—"

He choked on his words, so he let them die in his throat.

"She the reason you're up here, friend?"

The almost-hanged man nodded his head slowly. "I...I lost her. I let that bastard take her. What kind of man does that?" He pounded his hand against the branch. "What kind of father am I? He took her, he keeps her, and there's not a goddamn thing me or anyone else can do about it."

The monk took another swig from her gourd, the mad smile back on her face. "That so? Name's JD, friend. Why don't we get on down from here and go someplace warm where you can tell me all about your troubles?"

"I'm Nicothy, and...I need a drink."

One drink. One damn drink of that old gods-cursed concoction she carried on her back, and he was drunk. So drunk, in fact, the monk had to half carry him as they left the lavender forest and crossed into town. And what a town it was.

Wooden shanties groaned, complaining with each gust of wind. Twin tusk farmers whistled as they slapped switches at their livestock, herding them back into pens for the market.

The place had really gone to hell these last few years. Beggars on every corner, orphans flitting through shadows and playing beneath broken-down rickshaws, foul water troughs even the Squealers didn't want to drink from. The only place being repaired was the orphanage.

Too many damn urchins in this town; they didn't have much choice but to expand. He wondered idly where they'd got the funding. It wasn't like *he* was known to open up his purse for a damn thing. It was a sad state of affairs. Desperate town, desperate folk. He hated them a little bit. But he hated the man who put them in such a state even more.

"Why—" Nicothy paused a moment to collect his thoughts. Honest Earth, but his head was spinning. "Why are we here? I thought we were going to get my daughter back?"

"Absolutely, friend. But, well, I figured we should stop and get a drink first. Ya know, to celebrate!" JD said, tossing her locs over her shoulder. "'Sides, the tavern lady is kinda pretty."

"You really are the worst monk."

JD just grinned her mad grin as a group of urchins ran up to her. The first held out a green flower speckled with midnight blue. The child giggled as the monk accepted the flower and made a show of smelling it and swooning. In a flash, they were off.

"You know that little bastard's friends just robbed you, right?"

JD patted herself down, felt at the chit pouch in her robe. She measured the weight in her hand for a moment. She snorted a brief laugh. "Ha! Well, I'll be. Bauher actually got three chits this time. He's gettin' better. Good on him!"

"He looked burly."

"Didn't he, though?"

She led him to the Dinasaur Inn, one of the few drinking establishments in this town that didn't leak during a terrastorm.

Dreamroot smoke spiraled in iridescent plumes, assaulting his nostrils with its sickly-sweet aroma. A bard drummed out a simple beat as he told one of the hundreds of stories about Areon the Liberator. Cracked teal paint peeled from every wall. Nicothy watched as the mad monk made her way up to the bartender, ordered a literal armful of drinks, and took a corner table away from the worst of the din. Suds splashed and dripped down her robe as she lumbered to a chair.

"'Preciate the drinks, Bickothy. Real swell of you to give me your chits like that."

"It's Nicothy."

"That's what I said."

Nicothy had to blink twice and use all of his willpower to focus. He gave her a dubious look—Honest Earth, but he was drunk. "This town…used to be nice."

"Did it?"

"Okay, not nice, but it used to have potential. Then *he* came along."

"The fella that took your daughter?"

"Mayor Stolit," he spat. "The son of a bitch is milking this place dry and taking everything from every-fucking-one here." He slammed a fist on the table, rattling the drinks. If anyone noticed, they didn't let it show.

"Whoa, whoa, whoa, fella! Ein't no sense in spillin' perfectly good drinks. Here. Let's get you a bite to eat to calm that anger."

JD let out a sharp whistle and waggled her eyebrows, which, surprisingly, got a tavern girl to come over to the table. She didn't look particularly pleased about it, though.

"Four Twinie kabobs, a side of stew, and—" JD looked at

Nicothy. "Whatcha eatin?"

Nicothy stared at her incredulously. "I thought sisters of the Root were vegetarians. Only lived off the Earth Mother for sustenance."

"Twin tusks come from the Earth Mother, too, if you think about it."

Nicothy's stomach was in knots, but he waved away her offer of food. He thought he'd already had his last meal, and Twinie kabobs had been one of his daughter's favorites. He couldn't fathom taking a single bite. Bile rose in his throat. Tears sprang to his eyes.

JD took one look, nodded in understanding, and turned back to the tavern girl. "And, well, I guess a key to your room for this evening is all I'm missing."

The tavern girl sniffed in disgust, spun on a heel, and walked briskly back to the kitchen.

"She weren't my type, nohow," JD said.

"Are you sure you're a monk?"

JD flashed a grin and rolled up her sleeve to show the luminescent tendrils of the Great Tree's ink spinning about her wrist and forearm. "You really need to have a bit o' faith, friend. The Earth Mother's beloved can look a lot of different ways," she said with a wink.

"But the drinking, the meat. I just don't get it."

JD scratched at the side of her head thoughtfully. "I reckon that food and drink will go right through me, but my love for the Earth Mother will always stay in my heart."

Nicothy threw up his hands in exasperation. The tavern girl returned with the kabobs, careful not to make eye contact with either of them. JD tore into the first two ravenously; she managed to down them both before she took a second breath.

"So, this mayor… He got your little girl?" JD asked around a mouthful of food.

Nicothy clasped his hands together to stop them from trembling. "She's not so little anymore. But yeah, the bastard's got her, and every other damn girl in this town who caught his fancy."

"Ein't no one done nothin' about it?"

"Not much anyone can do. Over the last three years, he's become the only money in town. He's got his finger in every business, every operation. He's strangled out all competition for his authority."

"Hmm. Thought this place was an Ashland protectorate."

Nicothy attempted to spit derisively, but drunk as he was, he got most of it on his own shirt. "Ashland doesn't give a damn about this town as long as we pay up and give our young men for conscription when called. Stolit is the only force in these parts. He's taxed every business to the point they can't pay for bread to feed their families. Then he gives out loans, which no one's got a chance to pay back. That's when the threats start. The violence, soon after."

"That ein't right."

"You want to know the messed-up part? I wanted to be mayor here once. I made a fair share of chits in my younger years, and I wanted to do something good, ya know? It wasn't always like this. It…it could have been so much more."

"That's a right noble dream."

Tears spilled freely down his cheeks. His knuckles popped as he clenched his fists tighter. "It's the hope that kills," he said bitterly. "Mayor Stolit killed every hope I ever had."

"How so?"

"He first saw my Auti at the Exodus Day festival. Prettiest girl there. He made a pass, but she was promised to another. She turned him down, but kindly. She was always so kind. But a man like him? Nah. He couldn't abide something like that. He made sure her betrothed got drafted to the Ashland military. Front line. Then he spent the last few years putting me out of business and on the streets, till he made her a proposition she couldn't refuse."

His voice broke, and he buried his hands in his palms. JD was quiet, her drinks untouched, her remaining kabobs growing cold. She put a hand over his and held it there.

He reached for a cup, which she pushed to him. His throat moistened, he said, "She offered herself to him to save my shop, to put food on my table. She joined his damn harem, became his damn property, for me. And I... I let it happen. I let my girl be bought and sold like an animal at auction. And for what? To live just a little longer? What's the damn point?"

"Sounds like she loved you very much," JD said quietly.

"She was my world."

"Ein't no little girl should be taken from her da," JD said, toying with the necklace around her throat, a teardrop that looked like storm clouds bubbling over, pregnant with rain.

"I'd rather die than let her see me like this. I can't bear the thought of how horribly I let her down."

"Don't you fret no more. We're gonna get your girl back, friend."

He looked up at her with red eyes, misery etched into every line on his face. "But how? Every fighting man either works for him or has been shipped to Ashland. There's no one left to stand up to him."

JD chugged the last of her ale and slurped down her cold kabobs. That mad grin crept back over her face. "I got a plan."

"This is a horrible plan."

"It'll be fine."

"Why do I have to be dressed like this?"

"We need a distraction."

"I look ridiculous. I… I can't even move in this thing."

"Well, we need it if my genius plan is gonna succeed."

"How do you plan to negotiate?"

"With this," she said, pointing at her reed fan.

"What?"

"Hush. Now just go up to the front gate and do what I told you."

Nicothy sighed as he stumbled over the ungainly orange flippers of his costume. By the old gods, did this orange mask itch. The second sun had set, and the dark was only held at bay by the handful of glyph lights on the property. Such an ostentatious show of wealth. The rest of the town lived under the perpetual fire hazard of oil lamps and torches.

Nicothy rattled the gate a bit, cleared his throat, and shouted, "I AM THE VENGEFUL SPIRIT OF THE OLD GODS! I HAVE SEEN YOUR TRANSGRESSIONS, MAYOR STOLIT! COME OUT AND FACE YOUR PUNISHMENT!"

A couple of guards peeked their heads around the front of the building to see the commotion. JD gave him an encouraging thumbs-up, a huge grin on her face. Deflated, he let out a sigh once more. What did he have to lose, really? He rattled the bars further. The giant, yellow eye stalks of his costume jiggled at his every move. Honest Earth, the orange-colored skin paint itched something fierce.

Finally, one of the mayor's guards ambled over to the gate, bored and bemused. It looked like the weaver's boy. The guard squinted, then barked a laugh. "Nicothy? Is that you? Hells above, have you lost your mind?"

Before Nicothy could answer, JD stepped from the shadow of an abandoned building near the mayor's compound. "You got a key to get us in, buddy?"

The guard cocked his head to the side in confusion. "The mayor doesn't have time for beggars and lunatics. So why don't both of you just kindly…sort of, I dunno…fuck off?"

"That's fair, and we definitely will consider it, but could I offer you a drink first?" JD said, presenting her gourd. The guard's nose wrinkled at the stench. He pulled back for the briefest of moments, and that was all JD needed. Her hands shot through the bars of the gate, found the collar of his shirt, and slammed him face-first into cold iron. There was a sickening crunch from his nose, then he slumped to the ground.

JD rifled through his clothes for a set of keys. Moments later, the gate creaked open.

"Okay, so, we're in. What's the plan?"

JD rubbed her chin. "This is the plan."

"This? This is the plan? You're fucking insane."

"I've been called worse."

"So, what now? You're just gonna go to the front door and ask nicely for him to give my daughter back and maybe stop strangling the town to death?"

"I figure they'll be some negotiation first. Quit your worryin', ol' sport, and c'mon!"

Nicothy stumbled after her in his orange flippers. "Hells above! How am I supposed to fight in this ridiculous outfit?"

"You ein't."

She stalked up to the manor, a building constructed from true Bellemorian stone and shaped, no doubt, by an honest-to-Earth terramancer. It was the only structure built to last in the entire damn city. In fact, it was downright arrogant how few guards the mayor had patrolling the exterior of his property. Without any other people to confront, JD did the only sensible thing: she stopped at the front door and knocked.

"You can't be serious," Nicothy hissed.

"You think too much."

The door opened to reveal an annoyed henchman. A question formed on his lips as he eyed the pair, but JD promptly punched it away and strode into the grand foyer. The sounds of laughter and clinking glasses floated in from around a corner. With that mad grin tattooed to her face, JD followed the noise.

They entered a vast dining room filled with locals currying favor. Fine, clay-fired cups froze in midair, and several ladies stopped smiling past their discomfort and stared.

JD cleared her throat. "Hey, anyone know where the mayor might be at?"

"How the fuck did this beggar and—I don't know what you

are—get in here?"

"Nice fella at the front let us in." JD grinned wider. "But listen, friends, we'd sure appreciate it if y'all would help us find the mayor so we can discuss him leaving this fine city and returning my friend's daughter to him."

Confused, bemused, and apathetic expressions met her request. A few guests even pointed and laughed at Nicothy. But the far more alarming reaction was the series of blades leaving scabbards. There appeared to be at least a dozen folks who hadn't taken too kindly to the mad monk's intrusion.

She held up her hands placatingly. "Easy, fellas, easy. I'm just here to negotiate and—eek!" JD shouted, dodging the clay cup launched in her direction.

"Unless you're lookin' for a tumble, just go ahead and fu—"

"Yeah, yeah, fuck off. I get it. But before I go, y'all wanna see something neat?"

The men looked at her, then at the reed fan she held. She waggled her eyebrows suggestively. Then, as one, a dozen men decided the evening's entertainment would be kicking the shit out of a ragged sister of the Root.

JD laughed and held her battered fan in a sword fighter's stance. Nicothy cringed and shrank away from the inevitable mauling.

"Earth Mother said it's always best to negotiate when ya can, so I guess I'll make the first argument. I sure hope y'all are open-minded," she said.

With a chuckle, she began to wave her fan. As she did, it shimmered and changed into something…else. Something like a sword. A really, really big fucking sword. The blade itself sparkled, a kaleidoscope of colors even in the glyph light of the dining room. The hilt resembled an oversized tankard handle, and its crossguard seemed to be made of a massive piece of bone. Taken altogether, it looked like a drinking horn.

"The fuck is that?" Nicothy choked out in a whisper.

"It's my negotiation tool."

"That's a—uh—big argument you have there."

"Right?"

"I've never seen a sword that looks...like that."

"Well, that's 'cause it's a magic sword," JD whispered back, her eyes glazing over. She hiccupped a few times and began to sway, somehow keeping the enormous blade up in a defensive stance as if it weighed no more than a feather.

The first of the mayor's henchmen swung his blade in a brutal overhand slash. JD danced out of the way, tripped on a chair, and landed flat on her rear end. There was a chorus of laughter as the henchmen hacked at her again. JD turned her fall into a backward roll, giggling as she stumbled to her feet. Then she spun around and kicked the leg out from under the first man. His chin smashed against the edge of the table with a teeth-shattering crunch.

Two more men yelled and charged the mad monk. JD lurched back and forth with an erratic grace, effortlessly dodging their strikes but stumbling over her own feet. She brought the pommel of her sword crashing into the nose of one before spinning and bashing the broadside of her blade into the next. They both crumpled with howls of pain.

The rest made the logical decision to attack all at once. The air was filled with the sounds of battle cries, breaking dishes, scraping chairs, ringing swords, and even a few guests clapping at the entertainment. Nicothy's world had devolved into chaos. And JD's moves continued to defy explanation. It was as if she could see every blow before it landed. Every time she seemed off-balance, she would trip or fall into position to land a devastating counterattack.

The whirlwind of insanity was over in moments. Somehow, impossibly, JD stood over the last conscious fighter. The poor lad was breathing heavily, a bit of blood trickling from his nose. Defiance burned in his far-too-young eyes.

"Heya, buddy. How ya doin'?" JD asked casually.

"I'll fuckin' kill you, you old god-lovin' piece of shit," he spat.

JD hiccupped, her body haphazardly swaying as she kept the point of her blade on the young man's throat. "You ein't gonna tell me where the mayor is then, I take it? I got ways of makin' folk talk," she said in a voice calculated to sound menacing. It was not.

"Yeah? Well, I ain't saying shit. Once the mayor finds out the mess you've made here, he's gonna—"

"You leave me no choice then," she said with heavy reluctance. She reared her sword back, and the lad flinched in terror. JD brought the blade down lightning quick. The tip just touched the boy's nose. "Boop."

Suddenly, the lad's eyes rolled back in his head. He coughed, and his eyes watered as the first hiccup erupted from his throat.

"W-w-what you'd do to me?" he slurred, looking at his hands in astonishment. "Am I drunk?"

"Yup," JD said beatifically.

"But how?"

"Magic sword."

"A magic sword that gets me," he hiccupped, "drunk?"

"Yep!" she chirped. "Listen. Sure you don't wanna be real nice, and just tell me where the mayor is? It'll make everyone's evening so much better, don't ya think?"

The kid seemed to mull it over for a bit, then he let out a defeated sigh. "It won't matter. He's gonna kill you, especially when he finds out what you did down here. Top floor, study."

"Thanks, friend. Want me to knock you out for real? Or do you just wanna fake it?"

The boy closed his eyes and let his body go limp. A snore bubbled up from his lips.

"Right. C'mon, Nicothy. We got a mayor to visit."

The climb to the top floor took far longer than it should've, on account of the stupid flippers from Nicothy's costume. The jiggling eye stalks were giving him a pounding headache too. But that scarcely mattered when he caught sight of the mayor.

By the time they arrived, the mayor was waiting for them in the hallway. He was lean and wiry, with sharp, angular features and the coal-black hair of a Bellemorian. He wore a fine scarf of Siskiyuhn-corded gyga root over his Ashlandian suit. He looked out over the ornate railing at the mess below, clucking and shaking his head.

"I suppose you two are the assholes ruining my evening," he said. He stalked forward, rolling up his sleeves.

"Just here to talk is all," JD said, holding up a hand placatingly.

The mayor took another glance at the carnage below. "Is that so?"

"You took this fella's daughter." JD gestured to Nicothy. "By the sound of things, you been takin' a lot of things from a lot of folks."

The mayor snorted. "Spare me. Frankly, I don't care why you're here or what it is you want. This is what's going to happen." The mayor snapped his fingers, and two large flunkies peeled themselves off their posts at the study door to loom over his shoulders. Their bulk was hardly their most disconcerting feature, however. The bigger issue was the large bands of leather stretching from their wrists to their elbows—bands etched with myriads of glyphs, marking them as honest-to-Earth 'mancers. "These two men are going to kill you. Then I'm going to piss on your corpses. After that, I'll feed you to the leafdogs and spearcats."

"Would you at least take off our clothes first?"

"What?"

"I mean, don't want them to go to waste." JD grinned.

"Fuck o—"

"Fuck off. Yeah, yeah. Is that all you folks say 'round here? I mean, Hells above, I'm bored to death, so are we gonna get to fightin' or what?"

The mayor growled and gestured for his burly henchmen to get on with it.

"Th-they're 'mancers, JD," Nicothy squeaked. "We need to run. Fuck! How do I take these stupid fucking flippers off?"

"Thermomancer and aeromancer, if I'm readin' their glyphs right," JD explained. "Don't sweat it, Nicothy, ol' pal. I've got this."

The glyphs on the henchmen's bracers glowed to life, one orange and the other arctic blue. JD brought her blade to bear and sprinted up the last few stairs to the wide hallway overlooking the manse.

A ball of wind exploded into her chest, sending her crashing back the first flight of steps to the landing below. She got to her feet just in time to see the thermomancer pull out a firestick. Its glyphs lit up, beginning the combustion process that would end with a shell bursting from its tubular end. There was absolutely no way she could dodge it. Nicothy looked on in horror as the destructive force crashed into…nothing.

JD bent back with supernatural grace, her locs nearly sweeping the floor behind her as the shell exploded into the wall at her back. Yet, it wasn't her flexibility that sent Nicothy's jaw to the floor. It was that her eyes were *fucking closed.*

JD let her body drop like she was about to take a nice, long nap. The aeromancer shot forward on a gust of wind. Sharp, metal needles flew from his sleeve, propelled by the magical energies of his bracers. Every one of them sank harmlessly into the carpet of the hallway. JD rolled to the side and lurched to her feet, bringing her glittering sword up just as the shell of a second firestick exploded from the thermomancer's other hand. She tilted her blade ever so slightly. The shell ricocheted off her sword and slammed into the chest of the aeromancer, sending him reeling over the banister and crashing into the central foyer far below.

The thermomancer gave a shout of anger and tossed his two spent firesticks to the floor. His glyph bracers flared to life again. There was a faint heat shimmer, followed by a trail of smoke from his fists. He charged forward, his hands lashing out in a violent flurry. JD's smile was both serene and mad as she danced in and out of his strikes.

The thermomancer's fists struck open air, sparked against walls, and charred a priceless tapestry depicting Areon's escape from the old gods. Yet JD still seemed to know where every blow would land, even with her eyes shut. She didn't even try to hit him with her weapon. Instead, she rolled, sweeping up a handful of the needles lodged in the carpet from the aeromancer's last attack. In one fluid motion, she flung them at the thermomancer. The first two missed, burying themselves harmlessly in the banister. But two landed dead center on the largest glyphs in each of the 'mancer's glyph bracers.

He roared, attempting to ignite his magic once again. But he hadn't noticed the needles' strike, and it was his undoing. Instead of igniting, the broken glyphs exploded, maiming his hands. He shrieked in horror, holding up bloody stumps as smoke and errant sparks of wild magic burst from his wrists.

JD's eyes shot open. She hadn't spotted the mayor as he'd snuck behind her. In a flash, he wrapped the corded gyga root scarf around her throat, twisting it viciously like a garrote. Her face reddened, then shifted to bluish-purple.

"You stupid bitch!" the mayor screamed. JD fell to her knees, clawing at her neck, her sword sliding from her fingers. "EVERYTHING in this town is mine. The fucking shops, the people, anything I fucking want." Spittle flew from his mouth as his rage built. "You think you can just fucking walk in here, INTO MY FUCKING HOUSE, and take from ME?"

Nicothy watched in horror as JD's eyes rolled back in her skull. The mayor jerked her body savagely to the right, forcing him to watch the last bits of life drain from her face. The mayor locked his eyes on Nicothy.

"You know what I'm gonna do, old man? You know what I'm gonna fucking do? After every single man in my service and every Twinie in the streets has a turn at your daughter, I'm gonna sell her to the dockside brothels at Bellemor'e. Fuck, I'm gonna give her away. I'm gonna make you spend your last day knowing your daughter is getting fucked by every diseased cock in that city."

Nicothy was no fighter—hadn't been much of a fistball player as a lad, didn't even much like to hike. But as he watched this monster speak, images of his daughter played in his mind. Images of her playing in the Chennesau River. Images of her tucked inside the crook of his neck as he sang her to sleep. Images of her asking for one more Golem ride as he hoisted her on his shoulders and raced over the tall grass. Something inside of him snapped.

He shrieked, catapulting himself down the stairs. The flippers of the ridiculous costume caught on a step, sending him end over end in a tumble of orange body paint and awkward limbs. He crashed into the startled mayor and dying monk, the three of them collapsing in a tangled heap.

"Don't you touch her! DON'T YOU FUCKING TOUCH HER!" Nicothy screamed.

He grabbed at the mayor, scraping, clawing, biting, flailing his fists and elbows. They rolled and grunted, and blows rained down on him—one, two, three. Blood ran thick and warm down his face. But he didn't give a damn. He fought, frenzied for every breath, every ounce of purchase. He was tangled in the scarf, in the mayor's clothing, in his own costume. His nails found eye sockets and raked at them desperately. There was screaming, more yelling, but he couldn't make out words over the pounding of blood in his ears.

He rolled behind the mayor, struggling for a hold, for survival. The stupid fucking scarf was somehow wrapped between the two of them. Nicothy's arms were around the mayor's throat, throttling him for all he was worth. The veins in his arms popped out through peeling orange paint. Then he was being lifted, hoisted by the stronger man, and slammed down once, twice, three times. His arms let go as blackness closed in. His ears rang. Breathing hurt, his ribs hurt, existing hurt.

Through a haze, he watched as the mayor stumbled back, finally released. The man clawed at the scarf around his neck. His own eyes bulged as he tripped over the eye stalks of Nicothy's godling mask, which must have come off in the struggle. The mayor's arms pinwheeled in a desperate bid for balance. But momentum was not on his side. The scarf caught on an errant spike lodged in the banister, and he stumbled over the railing. A loud crack echoed through the stone walls of the manse.

Nicothy couldn't take his eyes from the hanged man dangling below him. JD dabbed at the blood around his wounds. She offered him a drink from her gourd, and he accepted. Somehow, the pain in his ribs lessened.

"Gyga roots are no joke."

"Strongest roots in the world," JD said, smoothing out a bandage.

"What now?"

"Guess you should go see to that daughter of yours."

"But what about the town? And the debts, and-and-and your temple? Don't you have to do something about your temple?"

JD slumped down beside him, tipped her gourd back, and took a mighty swig. "I figure someone like the mayor's got quite a few chits up in that office back there. Don't think he or his will be missin' it none. Probably enough to help the temple and the rest of the folks 'round here."

Nicothy contemplated that for a moment. "Just because he's not here anymore doesn't mean someone worse won't step in."

"Maybe, or maybe you step in and make sure there ein't no room for worse."

Nicothy laughed bitterly. "I was supposed to die today. What do I have to offer?"

JD's mad grin was unwavering. "That's the trick of life, ein't it? Gotta figure out how to do better, to be better. It ein't how you fall down. I reckon it's how you get to standin' again that matters."

"Why would anyone follow me?"

JD sighed and clucked her tongue. "Folks at their core wanna follow someone who aims to do good. Someone with a good heart. I figure you got both in spades. 'Sides, there's a new brother of the Root fixin' to come to this town, and I'm sure he'll support you real proper."

"What happened to Brother Ani?"

"That corrupt dummy? Well, rumor has it something tragic done struck that Ani down there at that Dinasaur Inn. That place can be right nasty for them misbehavin' types."

"What a coincidence."

"Right?"

"I'm… I just don't—"

"You're thinkin' too much again. Go be a da and quit worryin' 'bout tomorrow."

Nicothy stared at his hands and for once, they had stopped shaking. "My daughter deserves that, doesn't she?"

JD clapped him on the shoulder, stood, and gave a little nod.

"You plan to stick around?" Nicothy asked hopefully.

JD shook her head. "Nah, this place is in good hands now, I reckon. 'Sides, there's a town that needs savin' a few weeks' walk from here. Supposed to have some real top-shelf wine."

"How do you plan to save them?"

"By kidnappin' a bride."

"That's a horrible plan."

"It'll be fine."

LAB R INC

Jess L. Tong

"I'm not lying."

The squat man shifted in his chair, eyes darting to the colossal guard leaning against the steel door. Seated across from him, her black boots propped on the table, Thea pretended to pick at her nails. The picture of disinterest. Let him think she didn't want to be there either.

In truth, she didn't. The interrogation room was somehow stuffy *and* frigid. A shame she was so good at her damn job.

She just had to get through today. Then, she would finally ask Aegeus to transfer her.

Not looking up from her cuticles, she said, "Perhaps. But you are hiding something. Sure, you're nervous. But you're also…"

Thea flipped through his emotions like pages in a magazine, ignoring the flutter of each in her chest before she shut them out.

Nervous, irritated, fearful, and… "Exposed," Thea said, lowering her hands to study the man's sun-weathered face. "Like you'd promised Creets to not reveal something to us."

His confusion washed over her. But it was mixed with other emotions. Making her pause.

Desperation. Protectiveness.

27

Her chair scraped on concrete as she stood. The guard cleared his throat. Thea ignored him, knowing in the next room, Aegeus observed them intently through the enchanted wall.

Dread bloomed in her stomach as she approached the leathery man. He was a merchant, a Drifter, caught in the middle of this endless feud. She perched on the edge of the table, leaned in, and asked quietly, "Did they take someone from you?"

The merchant's eyes widened. Thea braced herself. She hated this part.

His horror surged, engulfing the cramped room.

Her palms grew clammy, her legs itched to flee. She wrestled the feeling away.

This type of response from Drifters used to distress her. Today, she was impatient.

The merchant began to stammer questions she'd heard hundreds of times. "What are—"

"No, I can't read your mind," Thea interjected. "I read emotions. And no, I can't hurt you. That's what our pal, Xander, is here for." She winked over her shoulder at the somber-faced guard. No reaction other than vague annoyance. Typical. Knowing his abilities, she probably shouldn't enjoy pissing him off so much.

"Calm down and work with us," Thea said to the pallid merchant. "We'll help you."

He didn't relax. Telling people to calm down never had the desired effect. It didn't matter anyway. She'd already shut herself off from his panic—as if it were a gruesome movie scene and she was shutting her eyes tight until it was over. She hated theatres. Too many people feeling too many things.

The merchant stared at her, steel-coloured eyes bulging.

Thea sighed, feeling the gnaw of old wounds. Her tone softened. "Losing someone to those sadistic Creets… I wouldn't wish that hades on anyone. Cooperate with us and we *will* find ways to help you. Tell me, who did they take from you?"

Silence stretched. He fidgeted with a thin, silver chain around his neck. Sensing hesitant trust, she surrendered a nod and sad smile. *I know what it's like.*

He croaked, "M-my daughter, Mel. She's seventeen. I can't tell you nothing. I'll never get my little girl back."

Thea pressed her lips together. She wasn't going to tell him people captured by Creets, dragged into their soulless headquarters, were never seen again.

Thea always wondered if Creets, in all their careful calculations, only did it as a message. *See what we're capable of? Your magic is nothing to our technology.*

Assholes.

Still, perhaps Creets would keep their word with a Drifter.

"I know you're afraid," Thea said gently, watching the man twist his necklace around his finger. "How desperate it feels when you can't help someone you love. But we have resources."

He said nothing.

Thea fiddled with her ring, pondering. Aegeus could send the Ergos. If she could prove the merchant's value—

Thea's phone buzzed in her pocket.

Aegeus' message read: *Ask about the shipments.*

She typed a reply. *His daughter. There may be a way around it.*

I'll take care of it. The priority is to uncover what Creets are building.

Thea knew *taking care of it* meant nothing. Aegeus wasn't

willing to lose men over this—or anything. Another message came through before she could argue.

We need this, Thea.

End of discussion.

Thea put her phone face down on the table. "That was His Supremacy. If you tell us what you've sold to Creets, we'll do everything in our power to save your daughter." She ignored her twisting gut. *Liar.*

The merchant sagged with relief.

And began to talk.

An excruciatingly long hour later, Thea exited the interrogation room, letting the door slam behind her. She clenched her fists, willing calm into her veins.

The wall in front of her was a soothing grey-blue, the colour chosen to put people at ease. Make them malleable. Thea's best friend, April, called it psych ward blue, while Thea always thought it perfectly matched April's eyes.

The interrogation had been pointless. No answers, only questions. The merchant dealt in livestock, both normal and exotic, and metalworks. No clue what Creets used them for. He merely delivered to their "laboratory"—what those cyborg engineers called their HQ.

Eventually, the merchant deduced Thea had lied about rescuing his daughter.

He'd lunged. And she'd knocked him away, her boot introducing itself to his gut. But not before she'd witnessed the betrayal in his eyes, felt the devastation and rage in her bones like a hammer blow. Now she left him alone with Xander for a Battering.

"Thea."

Aegeus was standing in his study doorway. She hadn't heard it open. Instinctively, Thea straightened.

The man who raised her always wore three things: his grey hair neatly slicked, a regal, brown coat, and a distinct air of authority. The kind that made people shut up and comply.

Thea swallowed and summoned a happy disciple's smile.

She greeted him, a stiff hug and a peck on each cheek. "Your Supremacy."

His hands stayed firm on her shoulders. Aegeus smiled. "Beautiful work as always, my Thea."

She resisted the urge to frown.

"We're getting pieces of a whole," he said, reading her hesitation. "There's indeed construction of a weapon. And now we have confirmed its presence." Another reassuring smile.

But he still hadn't unclasped her shoulders. Her skin prickled. She knew—too well—when he was displeased. Even if he was the one person her abilities were useless on. She shouldn't have asked to help the merchant. Not if she was to finally leave the job that crushed her soul bit by bit.

Before an apology could leave her lips, Aegeus released her.

"You did what you had to. For our people to have a chance," Aegeus said intently, "we prioritize the needs of all Nahetians before our own. Even if it means doing things that haunt us." His gaze roved down her tan cheek to her neck, where the scars began. Ribbons of scar tissue trailed down to the arches of her feet, like a network of pale tree roots. A product of her worst Battering.

Her practiced smile wavered. "I understand my duty," she forced herself to say, a little too coolly. Yet, reluctantly, she meant it. The Nahetians needed everything in their arsenal. Each generation grew weaker, some now born magicless. Thea repeated his favourite words: "Sacrifice is survival."

Aegeus' expression softened. Tiredness in the creases of his eyes. Responsibility a constant weight. "You've come far, Thea."

"Actually, Your Supremacy," she proceeded carefully, "I agree. And I think I've mastered all I can. I would like to request a transfer."

"Oh?"

"To the Ergos. I rank consistently amongst the top in combat. My skills are not being utilized." Thea's face was hot, her nerves obvious. Ever the child, trying to please him, even after all these years.

His face was unreadable. "You are undoubtedly talented. I believe you would make an excellent Ergo. But"—her heart sank—"you are unique, in your abilities and in your training. No one could replace you here. I need you."

Her shoulders slumped slightly. Part of her figured he would never let her join the ranks of the Ergos. Her role was too important. Irreplaceable.

Still, she nodded and expressed her appreciation for his time. And quickly left.

She didn't want to dwell on it.

Tonight, she had important plans with April. One of mourning. And they were going to get very, very drunk.

Thea trudged the rainy walk from the metro station toward the pounding music. Offering a half-nod at the bouncer, she squinted as her eyes adjusted. The Agora was always dark. A side effect of existing beneath the Red Ruins.

The familiar scent of booze, sweat, and bad decisions assaulted her nostrils. She didn't hate it. If they made an Agora scented candle, she'd light it every evening. Close her eyes and imagine the precious relief of the one place she could be around others without their emotions pummeling her.

Magic only worked here if The Agora allowed it. Tech didn't at all. The enchanted structure ensured a peaceful meeting place. In Ancient Times, the building granted permission to leaders and lawmakers. Now, it was bouncers and bartenders. Thea much preferred the latter group.

Patrons shifted out of Thea's path. Everyone recognized Aegeus' protégée—his rumoured successor.

April was waiting patiently, her hair twisted into two high silver buns. Her blossom-pink top hugged her curves. Where Thea was muscles and hard angles, April looked like her namesake—as sweet and soft as spring rain.

Thea sprawled dramatically into the booth, a gigantic pint of lager already waiting. April sipped something the colour of blue window cleaner.

Thea groaned and downed half her drink.

"He's an asshole," April stated, not needing Thea to explain her foul mood. "Been a jerk all week. He's keeping you in his pocket where he can feed you crumbs."

"I was dreaming. I know no one else can Extract the way I can. It's just—"

A group of boisterous satyrs cheered, drinking enough to turn flammable. A spikey-haired pixie nearby glared at them, her expression on do-not-disturb mode. Even from here, Thea could tell they were Drifters. Tired, with rough edges. Unprotected. People without leaders or magic.

Drifters like the steel-eyed merchant. She swallowed hard. "I'm tired. I didn't choose this."

April's gaze tempered. The hundredth time having this conversation, April listened as if it was the first. She knew it destroyed Thea to suffer every drop of the captives' agony—only to be forced to exploit them. "You've served him for years, T. You deserve to do what you want."

Thea's defeated sigh fogged her glass. "It's duty. Our stand against Creets. Gods know we've lost enough to them."

April's face darkened and Thea remembered why April couldn't be alone tonight. Leaning one elbow on the sticky table, she said quickly, "I feel like I barely see you. You're either here or working."

April grimaced. "Ugh, all of Books is in overtime. Aegeus wants reports on Every. Little. Thing."

April had no magic—*"A Dud inside and out,"* she'd joke—and was useless at combat. But she was sharper than blades, more accurate than firearms. One year in the Bookkeepers Department and she managed everything from accounting to data analytics. April released a long-suffering sigh, launching into a rant about a New Guy's ineptitude and the loss of some Very Important

Documents.

Thea caught the eye of the bartender. He waved a hand. Their glasses filled.

"I am glad I don't have coworkers," Thea said when April finished.

"And Xander's what? A puppy?"

Thea snorted. "A guard dog."

"Or a statue of one. He's always slightly shocked yet stone-faced."

Thea nodded with mock solemnity. "Legend has it, Medusa flashed her tits at him and then his face froze that way."

April burst out laughing. Thea joined her, their laughter bubbling and spilling over like champagne. When they finally caught their breath, April said, "Seriously, I've never seen the guy make an expression."

"He hardly has any emotions other than grumpy," Thea said, still chuckling. "Not even when he's…"

When he's ordered to penalize me.

April's jaw tensed. She didn't forgive those who hurt Thea, even when Thea had.

April was looking at nothing in particular. Those psych ward blue eyes now glossy and far away. "T, it's midnight."

The dreaded anniversary of the Seven and Seven. The hideous night seven young men and seven young women were kidnapped and dragged to Creet HQ. All of them Nahetians. None of them seen again.

April's lips trembled. "I can't believe it's been seven years. Idas would be twenty-eight now."

Thea reached wordlessly for April's hand. April stared at their matching red rings. Gifts carved by Idas, April's brother.

Thea didn't need magic to know April's grief. The weeping of unhealed wounds. They were orphans and Idas had treated Thea like another sister.

The booth felt suffocating in the thick air of old scars. Other Nahetian patrons also appeared disturbed. Postures stiffened, eyes shifting. The day no one talked about still had them warding their homes—just in case.

"The roof?" Thea suggested, standing.

It was a roof only in the way a tattered newspaper could be an umbrella. Piles of rubble, slabs upon slabs of bright red stone, buried The Agora. But it was still warded with nightclub enchantments. No one had told the magic there was no longer a multi-story building.

Thea climbed expertly, albeit drunkenly, drinks in hand. April followed. Her usual chatter absent.

Thea's heart ached.

They sat on their bench-shaped rock. Observed their city darken as lights were traded in for sleep.

Saturn City resembled its planetary namesake. That is, if Saturn the planet was city-sized, and the planet was the rival of its ring.

The Centre, home to Nahetians and miscellaneous Drifters, was once a beautiful, circular metropolis, of ancient, red stone buildings glowing like rubies when it rained. These days, it crumbled. Beauty always succumbing to time.

Now, the girls looked out at skinny, grey buildings sprouting like weeds. But some neighbourhoods remained in vermillion ruin. Unhealed scabs. Their favourite parts of the city.

It was too dark to see The Ring. How it encircled The Centre with windowless laboratories. All power, no magic.

Creet territory.

Between The Centre and The Ring stretched The Chasm. The hideous, inky darkness was a moat of nothingness, as sinister as it was endless.

Creets controlled the drawbridges. And thus, the city.

Though Nahetians resisted, their Ergos performing secret service shit Thea wasn't privy to, they didn't delude themselves. Most believed the Seven and Seven had been a warning.

Thea gently coaxed April into talking. They spoke in soft voices and heavy pauses. Drank until serious conversation dissolved into laughter once more.

Until Thea stood too fast, her head dropping into her stomach, which responded by voiding its contents. She doubled over, heaving.

April rubbed Thea's back and pulled Thea's dark hair into one of April's fluffy, pink hair ties.

"Okay, time for home, T," April said once Thea was done turning inside-out and was seated again.

She started to say she felt fine. She didn't want to leave April alone.

But a voice smooth as woodsmoke asked, "Still can't hold your liquor, Nahetian Princess?"

A lean man emerged from the shadows and Thea rolled her eyes. April let out an *ugh*.

"Still stalking me, Riad?" Thea teased, despite knowing he'd never done anything of the sort.

His bronze eyes gleamed with usual hints of madness. "Who

says I ever stopped?"

Thea crossed her arms. "Can you stalk me from somewhere else? We're busy."

Riad tilted his head, wild, black curls falling in his face. "No room for me? I thought you ladies would have missed me."

"You couldn't handle us both," April cooed. "It's not in your programming."

For a breath, it was nine years ago. The girls had befriended Riad. He was weird, a little older, dressed in bright colours, sometimes speaking in riddles. But she never sensed lies from him.

"My programming is likely full of bugs and malware," Riad replied with a shrug.

He was an ex-Creet. A runaway. Still, after the Seven and Seven, the three grew apart. April never warmed up the same again.

Thea glared. "Seriously, what do you want?"

He tossed her something small and rectangular.

She snatched it. "A business card? Seriously?"

"Of course. I'm a very serious man." His grin was shit-eating. "New number. Just in case you'd be interested in…doing business again."

April made very unsubtle vomiting noises.

Thea scowled, darting her eyes over him.

Riad frowned. "What?"

"Looking for your mute button."

Riad chuckled, already turning away. The man never said bye. Instead, he called, "Then come find it," and disappeared beyond the rubble.

No goodbyes even a year ago, after they lay together, sweaty and breathless. He'd wanted more and Thea didn't reciprocate. Part of her was relieved for an excuse to distance herself. She couldn't be caught with a Creet. Defected or not.

She'd wondered about his past. About the times he went quiet. But she never pried. Extracting was for work.

The girls remained under the starlight a little longer. But when April started nodding off, she insisted they leave and that she was okay.

They climbed out from the ruins back onto city cobblestone.

April blew a kiss. "Love you, mindfreak."

April loved love.

For a long time, Thea had refused to say it. Yet April, who lost more than Thea ever had, still managed to.

So, Thea reserved that word for her best friend and no one else. "Love you too, sappy nerd."

Thea watched April retreat into the city. Now, beyond The Agora's wards, she could *feel* April. The unrelenting sadness and regret pouring from her like sewage.

Before April rounded a corner, she shouted before disappearing, "I'm fine, I promise!"

Thea sighed. Pressed the stone ring to her heart. And went home.

Eighteen years ago:

Thea, five years old and small enough to need two hands to hold a dagger, sat on Aegeus' knee in his study. Like most evenings, she clung to his stories, his lessons.

She felt special. No other kids were allowed in his study.

Later, much later, she'd learn he was molding her into his weapon.

But now, she listened, trying to say the right things at the right times.

"Empathy," he said over the fireplace crackle, "allows you into their minds. It's power. The greatest weapon in your arsenal. Compassion is opening the gates and letting them into yours. It's surrender—giving them your sword and then falling on to it. Do you understand?"

She didn't. Not then. But she nodded anyway.

Thea woke, feeling like shit.

She'd fallen asleep in her clothes, the lights on.

Because she felt like shit, she took her time washing up, drinking water like a parched plant. Because she felt like shit, she didn't check her phone for an hour.

When she did dig it out of her bed, her heart fell out of her chest. Missed calls. Over forty of them. Texts. Voicemails. Urgent emergency alerts.

Thea swayed as she opened alerts. Felt the blood drain from her face.

Their worst nightmare, the one that never eased its grip, had returned.

Fourteen young Nahetians had been taken in the night. Seven

women and seven men.

On the seventh anniversary.

How?

Then a horrible thought occurred to Thea. The effects of it like poison.

None of her messages were from April.

Dread burst like a dam, annihilating her in its wake. She shook so violently she dropped her phone. Whispered *no* over and over–a denial, a plea, a prayer. But the voicemails confirmed it.

The Creets had April.

Thea waited to collapse to pieces. Because Aegeus would not act. He hadn't seven years ago.

But instead, calm focus maneuvered her limbs. This time, she wouldn't ask for permission. Wouldn't give anyone the chance to refuse. Wouldn't fail April again.

Her fingers fished through yesterday's pockets until they wrapped around a folded business card.

Thea had never seen Riad so serious. Or nervous.

The outside of Creet HQ looked like…nothing. Bland, towering buildings continued around The Ring. A single post flew a plain white flag. Even their logo was boring. Simple black script on the side door read: *Lab R Inc.* A stark contrast to Riad, all colour and eccentricity. Today, he looked surprisingly resplendent in a plum-coloured suit.

His reappearance—its timing—was unsettling. But Thea had

no one else to rely on.

She'd never left The Centre before. Never crossed a draw-bridge over the rift that made her skin crawl. As if the dark had tendrils.

She'd refused to look down, her legs trembling, even when The Chasm whispered. Coaxed her. A lover desiring something from her.

Riad had lowered the bridge. Creets were microchipped at birth, and their tech responded to him. Many Creets never stopped replacing parts of themselves with more efficient designs. Legs could always move faster, memories expanded. *"At what point are they no longer human? They're always experimenting, innovating. Things progress like plagues when you don't have ethics,"* Riad had said in disgust.

Not a soul was around. Riad's dark skin looked ashen, sickly, when he opened the door. Thea imagined she appeared the same.

It looked exactly how she'd picture a storage facility for a chemistry lab. Shelves upon shelves of bottles and containers labeled with long words and odd symbols. Broken equipment, glassware, and metal gadgets lay in the corner, abandoned.

What would Aegeus do if he knew she was here?

"I need you," he'd said yesterday.

She struck the old man from her mind. She was as good as dead to him now.

"Don't touch anything," Riad said quietly.

"Obviously."

"And no weapons. There's alarms."

She scowled. He'd already informed her on the phone—which he'd confiscated. "Shut up, we don't have time."

He led her down a series of doors and gleaming halls, needing to double back twice.

"Do you know where you're going?" she hissed, agitation building like a storm.

"In theory." He turned to her, eyes scanning her face. "We're just rats in a maze, princess." They entered a vast corridor. He rubbed the back of his neck, studying her. "This is as far as I can take you."

Thea's adrenaline surged to new heights. "What can you tell me about this place?"

Stress emanated from him, marring his features. Uncharacteristically at a loss for words. "I can't... I—" He gestured at his throat.

"A voice chip?" She'd heard of them. Encoded to protect secrets.

He nodded and showed his wrists. Chips there too. No writing either.

Her eyes narrowed. "That's new."

He winced but attempted a weak smirk. "At least now I always know the time. You hate it when I'm late."

She stalked towards him, ignoring his attempts to humour her. "So, if I rip the chips out, you can tell me what's happening?"

Bronze eyes widened. "Gods, woman. Even if you could, the chips change body chemistry. Like medication. The effects remain for a time even if removed. It's why they work in The Agora."

"Did you know this was going to happen?" she asked, a dangerous edge seeping into her voice. A violence-laced calm. "Clearly, you know things I don't. Are you involved? What is all this?"

He held up his palms. "I didn't know. Not exactly. Some things…today." He struggled against the words. "Um…make sure you go straight, left, right, repeat."

Repeat? How many times? But instead, she asked, "Are you helping me? This isn't some trick?"

"Yes."

She let out a breath. It seemed honest. Regardless, what choice did she have?

She didn't have time to interrogate Riad, so she turned away. They didn't do goodbyes.

"Thea." He removed something from his plum coat. "Take this."

A spool of grey thread. She didn't bother asking about it and shoved it in her pocket. "Thank you. I have to go. *Now*."

She attempted to leave him, but Riad seized her hand. His emotions swelled. Ones she'd tried to ignore all day. There was love for her. Fear too. His mouth was opening and closing, like a dying fish, trying to thwart the chip's code.

Her cold fingers squeezed his. "It's okay. Thank you."

She wondered if she'd see him again. If she'd make it back over The Chasm.

Perhaps not.

But, finally, a sacrifice of her choosing.

The hall stretched in front of her, every inch of it blinding white. In all black, Thea was an inkblot on a page. A bullseye on a target.

She scanned the area.

No one. Not a sound. Not an emotion. Just a sense of...*energy*.

Her footsteps were oddly silent. The ground reacted to her movements. Like stepping into a puddle. Small ripples spread from the bottom of her foot and disappeared. But the ground was dry.

Thea emerged into an enormous, enclosed space. The size of several city blocks. The ceiling hovered stories above. But she couldn't see beyond the walls and halls, which despite not coming close to the ceiling, still obstructed her view. All of it was stark white.

The path forked ahead. Each way branched again into several directions, sheets of wall splitting and turning in on themselves like origami paper.

Straight, left, right, repeat.

A maze.

The fat spool from her pocket was heavy. Not thin twine, like she'd thought, but a strange, woven metal string, surprisingly sturdy yet fluid.

A blemish on the satin-smooth wall caught her eye. A tiny hook.

She tied the thread to it. This must be what it was for. Riad wanted her to find her way out.

We're just rats in a maze, princess.

Maybe he thought she stood a chance. Maybe she did.

She turned left. Nothing. Another stretch of bleached walls. She proceeded, pushing her legs faster. If she had to navigate this maze, time was not on her side. April was the clever one, the one good at puzzles and brainteasers.

Thea navigated people. Otherwise, her solution of choice was punching.

She paused. What if...

Thea slammed her fist into the nearest wall. A very solid *thud*.

A dull throb in her wrist. She cursed, feeling stupid. The wall was solid and polished as weather-worn stone.

Her gut trusted Riad's directions. But this was all suspiciously...easy.

She turned right. Held the spool loose between her fingers, allowing it to unravel. She considered inspecting the other turns for hidden horrors. But time was slipping from her fingers like her thin, metal lifeline.

She pictured April fighting for her life. Her silver hair flying. Her eyes wide with terror as she lived her brother's last moments.

Thea broke into a run.

Straight at the next branch. Then left. Then right. No signs of any life, traps, or ungodly robotic weapons. Only Thea and the silent, rippling floor.

The walls and floors were so damn white. Almost fluorescent. Thea squinted and rubbed her temples.

Straight, left, right.

Again. Again. Again.

April. A best friend so dear she was like a soulmate. Thea would find her and bring them all home.

Hurry. Thea just had to hurry.

Her heartbeat pounded in her skull. Routes grew narrower.

It was bright, hot, the air increasingly difficult to draw in. Her clothes clung, heavy with sweat. Thea panted through clenched teeth, narrowing her eyes into slits. Piercing light still slipped through. An arrow between armor plates.

Her skull was expanding inside her head. Thoughts jumbled.

She sprinted, her body not so much running toward something as it was trying to escape these terrible walls.

Hurry. She had to go faster.

Except…did she?

Why was she in such a hurry? Nothing was chasing her.

She slowed slightly. Then more. Then she was simply strolling. Her thoughts thick and slow, drowning in a syrupy haze.

Pain thumped inside her head. Thea went to rub her eyes but recoiled when she discovered she was holding something.

Metal string. What the hades for?

She tugged and her eyes tracked the thread, back the way she came, until it disappeared around the corner.

The urge to follow it lured her. It had to lead somewhere better than here.

Her broad shoulders nearly skimmed the walls now. Too narrow. Too trapped. She wanted out. Yes, out. Needed it.

She followed the thread, respooling down the corridor.

But something caught her eye. A shock of colour on the hand holding the thread.

Thea dressed in all black. Always. So why was there something pink and fluffy on her wrist?

A hair tie.

April's.

April.

All the pieces rushed back to her in a sweeping flood. A small gasp escaped her lips. What was the maze doing to her?

She turned on her heel. Ran. Blinding light battered her pupils. Questions blared in her mind all at once. How much time had she wasted? Was she running further into madness? Did Riad do this?

Panic climbed in her throat. Rising like bile. A sensation not unlike the times she gasped awake at night, the memory of touchless torture as real as the sweat-drenched sheets beneath her. But this multiplied and crushed like collapsed ruins over a sacred meeting place. She stumbled. The walls pressed in.

She didn't have time for anxiety's grip, but she was helpless. She tried shutting it out, the same way she closed off others during Extractions. But this was too much. Thea began shaking. Sinking to her knees, she squeezed her eyes shut. She had to do this. No time to calculate the consequences.

She grappled for a corner of her mind, a place she'd always refused to acknowledge. Pretended it didn't exist. But it always remained, stubborn as a stain.

A mental room of numerous doors. She reached for the one spilling panic between its hinges.

If briefly avoiding a feeling was shutting her eyes during a scene, then this was burning the theatre to ashes. It was destruction. Sabotage.

Permanence.

Sacrifice is survival.

Flames engulfed the door. It became embers, then cinders—then nothing.

Her eyes opened, throat burning as if she'd been screaming. Desperation and fear still charged her bones. Roaring at her to hurry. But panic? Anxiety? None. And in its place, emptiness. A soul missing a puzzle piece. A festering hollowness, a twin to

The Chasm.

What had she done?

Exactly what Aegeus always wanted, Thea realized. Was this why he punished her? To push her to this point?

It didn't matter now.

Thea searched her surroundings but didn't detect anything obviously drugging her, distorting her memory, freaking her the fuck out, only—

The brightness. Repulsive and glaring.

Her sanity returned when she'd looked away from the walls. Poisoned light.

She tore off a piece of her pant leg, and using her teeth, ripped in two thin slits. Wrapped over her eyes, the holes admitted just enough light for her to see the turns. Tangled thoughts began to unravel.

Spool in hand, a perverse and cursed placidness in her nerves, Thea took off in a sprint.

Barely fifteen minutes later, Thea turned left into a small chamber. A dead end.

Impossible. She'd kept track.

Her fingers fumbled over the right side, breath coming in pants. Nothing but smoothness and surprising cold beneath her palms.

She ripped the fabric off her face. Here, the brightness had abated.

Frustrated, she beat against the wall. And blinked.

Not a *thud* this time, but a hollow *thunk*. A reverberation.

She threw a muscled shoulder into the wall. It warped slightly. Tried again with a running start, ignoring her immediate bruising. Dents formed. A small, spreading crack.

Hades, if the only thing she managed was wrecking their fucked-up obstacle course, then it was worth it. What was this godsdamned place? Why would Creets take the Nahetians here?

Her face burned as she kicked at cracks and tore away chunks of wall. Her demolition clattered through the space. White dust coated her clothes.

Creets were toying with them. Cats playing with field mice. What hadn't Riad told her? What kind of torment were the captives enduring?

Another running thrust and the wall gave. Thea plunged through, landing further and harder than she intended.

She was in another long, white stretch. Only—not white.

It was changing. Darkening, forming looming shapes that did not resemble their two-dimensional canvases.

Thea scrambled up. The hole she'd gouged was already solid. Healed in seconds. It wrapped around her thread, now unwinding from in her pocket, threatening to snap it. But the metal held.

She was halfway through the spool.

Fear soared in her veins as the world dimmed. It was an unfamiliar fear, a powerful but precise sensation, somewhat subdued without the ability to panic. A knife twisting into just the right spot, leaving the rest of her unharmed.

Walls morphed into thick, rough cylinders. Above, the ceiling darkened into blue, then indigo, then black. Ink spreading into a mockery of night. A shuffle of her foot told her something was very wrong.

Her footsteps were no longer silent.

Ripples still formed beneath her boots. But not dry.

The maze was filling with water.

Seven years ago:

Thea, sixteen, heard at morning training. The others whispered, with shaking voices, the names of those stolen across The Centre. Of April's brother, Idas.

Idas. Who taught them how to oil a blade. Chiseled their rings from stolen Red Ruin stones.

Thea, ignoring instructors' shouts, ran across the field, not stopping, not breathing, until she burst through the empty dorms and into April's room.

April sat in the dark, curled in her armchair. As pale as death. She didn't react to Thea, red-rimmed eyes staring at nothing. But April's anguish slammed into Thea like a derailed metro car. The hopelessness dragging them beneath steel wheels.

Thea fell to her knees beside the chair, her breath ragged. Hot tears dripped off her chin.

They stayed for hours. Silent. Then they wept together, April shattering like glass.

April whispered, "If he's dead, then I deserve to be dead too."

Thea had her face pressed into her friend's shoulder, both of them now on the scratchy carpet. She stammered, stunned, "Don't say that. This isn't your fault."

"If I w-wasn't a Dud, wasn't so useless, I could do something. I can barely hit a target. Never have a say in anything." April stared at her hands as if willing a Nahetian gift, long faded from her bloodline, into them. "They won't send anyone to help them."

What was the point in all this training if they did nothing? They should be storming The Ring, making demands, pleas, anything.

Who was Thea if she wouldn't do everything for the people she loved?

"I'll talk to Aegeus," Thea said, squeezing April's fingers, taking in her blotchy, empty expression. "I promise you. I'll get Idas back."

The walls were warping into tree trunks. Nothing like the ones that grew in The Centre's parks. These were as thick as houses.

A massive forest. Shadows deepening faster than Thea's eyes could adjust. Dim starlight strained through the canopy. Water carpeted the floor, gradually rising. Indistinct noises—rustles and scrapes—came from every direction. Leaves swayed in a nonexistent wind.

She feared its depths. But she feared staying more.

Splashing in ankle-deep water, she ran.

She tried to remember she was in the laboratory, not the wilderness. But as she continued between tree gaps, real twigs, and bark scratching her hands, she knew a Creet creation was worse than what the natural world could bring.

That's when she saw a flash of white. And jagged teeth bit into her forearm.

Thea screamed and collapsed into the water, the pain searing.

A hairless beast, no more than thirty pounds, was latched on. It thrashed, emitting a series of snarls and clicks. Skeletal limbs clawed as Thea wrestled it. Pinned it beneath the water.

It wouldn't drown. Wouldn't release its jaws. Even when her knee struck hard enough for its spine to crack. Even when she scrambled upright and slammed her arm, and the beast's skull, into a tree over and over until she heard a sickening crunch.

Its clicks only grew louder. Claws raked fresh trails of blood over her arms and chest, over lightning scars fully recovered but never healed.

In the dim light, its skeletal body writhed. Milky skin, almost translucent. Unseeing, bloody eyes. Like a maggot bred with a rabid monkey and a pile of bones.

Water continued to rise. Halfway up her shin.

She had no weapons. Nothing but clothes and—

In one swift motion, she tugged the spool from her pocket. Her free hand wrapped it around the maggot-creature's neck. The thread moved fluidly, like silk ribbon. The beast's clicks echoed through the trees, filling the guise of night.

She pulled. Her opposite elbow pinned the thread against the trunk. When the metal dug into the beast's throat, she hesitated.

The thing *felt*. It tickled her mind. Hungry and scared and desperate. Bred for this. It had no more choice than she, following the path set out for her. Straight, left, right. Empathize, hurt, manipulate.

The beast struck, seizing opportunity in her distraction. A claw sliced her cheek—the last unscarred part of her body.

She gripped the thread and yanked, averting her eyes as the clicking muffled.

The thread sunk in, slowly, slowly. Then all at once.

A thin snap. Teeth released her arm. Splashes.

The maggot-creature's head and body floated, dark swirls leaking from where they severed. Skin, flesh, and bone.

Her chest heaved. She wanted to collapse, to hurl.

But instead, she continued forward. Half-wading, half-stumbling. She needed to get out of here. Now.

Because the water was above her knees. Because she couldn't swim. And because in the distance, a sound crept closer.

Faint. Then swelling into an unmistakable swarm. Noises overlapping and weaving in a hideous melody.

Hundreds upon hundreds of clicks and snarls descended from the branches.

Her fingers tightened a scrap of shirt around her wounded arm. Afraid yet calm, her options were easy to weigh. If the water rose high enough, she would certainly drown. She'd have to climb. Right into their nests.

But the idea was too terrifying to stomach.

Water lapped at her waist, slowing her to a crawl.

Beasts closed in. Enough for her to hear scratches of individual fingernails.

Thea's eyes squeezed shut. Fear would kill her—would doom the captives. She couldn't afford it.

It was easy this time, locating where fear lived in her. Every horror, every nightmare, prowled behind this incorporeal door.

For a split second, Thea mourned it.

Then she destroyed it. Fear itself shrieking in fire and brimstone and reek.

And when Thea's eyes opened, she was smiling.

Seven years ago:

"Please, Aegeus." Thea stood unsteadily in Aegeus' office. His Supremacy was unreadable behind his stone-carved desk. She hadn't planned to beg. Meant to approach self-assured and confident. "We must do something."

Aegeus' expression remained cold and sharp as knives.

It fueled her desperation. "You've taught me duty to our people. Idas, the others, they're our people. We're supposed to just let this happen?"

Aegeus rose with too-casual grace. "This is a sacrifice and loss I must bear. Creets watch us. There is nothing we can do without jeopardizing everyone. I do not ask for understanding, but I expect compliance." He gestured towards the door. Dismissed.

Any other time she would have hurried away.

If he's dead, then I deserve to be dead too.

She refused to break Aegeus' stare. Even as its scorn scorched through her. "You haven't tried."

His brow twitched. His only sign of agitation. "Have I not?"

"I understand you give a lot," she said cautiously. "You protect us. Make impossible choices. But this is worth riots. War." Her voice was too loud, overly pitched. "We can't let Creets do

this."

Aegeus remained as unmoving as death. "Nothing is worth war, child. You know very little and speak of too much. I have done what I can. This is a battle we must lose. And I am losing more than you realize."

Thea's heart cracked. The crevices filling with simmering rage. All this talk, all these years, about obligation. "And what exactly have you done, tucked away in your office?"

His gaze snapped to hers. "You be careful with how you speak to me."

"Answer me."

His eyes flared. She raised her chin, ignoring the flush that brimmed on her skin.

His lip curled. "I am not the enemy. You seem to have forgotten your place. You think I am unaware of the significance of this loss? An insult. I will not be so lenient if you do so again."

The threat rolled off her. Her indignation like a second layer of skin. She'd survived his penalties before, Xander's Batterings. This was worth it. Why couldn't he see these fourteen Nahetians were worth it?

"I'm standing for every Nahetian," she said with foreign composure. "So we are safe in our own homes. I'm sorry. I don't wish to insult you. But if you won't help then I'm going to The Ring. Alone. I don't care if it kills me."

She meant it, she realized. She'd die for them.

For a moment there was only the snap of the fireplace. The soundtrack to his lessons. Somehow, now, she felt smaller than she did when she fit on his knee.

Powerless. Both too loud and unheard.

Aegeus paced to the window. In the distance, the Red Ruins glowed like a bloody flame in the setting sunlight. The Ring beyond them. Surrounding them like a noose.

Then His Supremacy said, "You only care about yourself."

Thea blinked. Words withered in her throat faster than they could form.

He turned to her. Cool rage frosted his eyes. She took an involuntary step back. He spat his words like acid. "This is about you needing to be a hero. Time after time, you disregard what I taught you. Compassion not only makes you weak, but foolish. It tells you it's up to you to fix everything. All of it to feed your ego. You want to go to war over this?"

Thea could only stare, face stinging like she'd been slapped.

He peered at her like she was vermin. "After all I do for you. After all I've taught you. You disappoint me."

Tears escaped. Leaving hot tracks down her cheeks. She whispered hoarsely, "Please, Aegeus. I'll do anything. Just don't let them die."

The man remained an unmoving statue.

She wiped her nose and started for the door. "Then I'm going. On my own." She wouldn't survive, she knew, but if Thea could provide a distraction—

"You're forcing my hand," Aegeus said quietly.

Thea paused, confused. For a second, he appeared almost regretful.

Then a blow hit her.

One moment, she faced Aegeus, watching disappointment and anger disfigure his features.

Then his finger twitched.

She stumbled back. Her vision warped. She was falling—

And blinding agony slammed her into the floor.

It shredded. Tore all over like rusted claws and dripping maws. It was the pain of cooked skin, mangled muscle, shattered bone.

If Xander was an iron brand, then Aegeus was magma and hadesfire. And Thea was merely a prisoner of flesh.

She cried out as slashes seeped hot blood onto his lush carpet. A dozen crimson puddles ruining priceless threads. The taste of iron and salt filled the spaces between her teeth.

She'd failed the captives. Failed Idas. Failed April.

As unconsciousness pulled her in, four words played over in her mind.

I am so sorry.

She didn't know if they were her words or his.

Thea woke a day later in the mansion's ward, wrapped in gauze from chin to toe. April slept by Thea's bed, drooling on a rickety chair. Fresh calla lilies rested in a vase.

No bones were broken. No muscles torn. That was the twisted power of Batterings. They brought agony but left no marks as proof. Sometimes, she doubted if they truly happened.

Except this one time, from Aegeus. And he'd chosen to leave scars. A reminder and a promise.

The healers relayed Aegeus had bandaged and carried Thea to the ward himself. After, he'd announced retaliations by Nahetians would be considered an act of treason.

They said the flowers were from him.

And without Thea needing to ask, April dumped the lilies out the window.

The water's icy vice encircled her chest. Thea gripped a branch and dragged out of the water—her numb legs clumsy on the bough, her wounds still smelling of fresh blood. In the shadows of the tree, she could barely discern her route.

She had seconds before the first creatures would descend. But if they wanted her dead, she wouldn't make it easy.

Thea crawled up. The thread followed, weaving without snagging. She reached the end of a swaying limb, and without hesitation, she leapt.

And landed on the adjacent tree. A surprised laugh cracked from her lips. How easy it was to move through the world without fear.

Then the clicks were upon her.

They rained from every angle, rattling her eardrums like a hailstorm.

Crouched, her back pressed to a trunk, she searched for a way out. Discovering none.

But the chattering beasts weren't lunging or biting.

They simply stopped. Their milky frames perched several branches away. Confused.

But a small one wandered too close. Thea swung out reflexively, her fist hitting its skeletal shape. It fell—the body cracking on branches, rattling leaves. She detected its terror.

Clicks and snarls rippled in the dark.

The others, suddenly, were hungry.

They dove after it, in an animalistic swarm of pearly skin and claws.

Thea kept crawling, jumping. Adrenaline coursing with opportunity, urgency, and realization.

The maggot monkeys feasted on fear.

And she still sensed it, despite giving up her own. Like a smell eliciting a memory of the place she'd abandoned.

The clicking storm faded.

She could spot the paths below, the water reflecting the fake starlight. She followed Riad's directions. Leaping, fumbling for holds, scraping on twigs.

Until she reached for a tree that was not a tree.

Thea tumbled through darkness.

She braced for the cold slap of water. Instead, there was brightness, solid floor, her breath knocked out of her lungs. She rolled, straining and gasping and squinting.

She never thought she'd be relieved to touch these white walls again.

She clambered up. The spool was on its last lengths. She had to be close. *April* had to be close.

Darting around corners, Thea remembered what she'd once read about hunters. How hunting was a practice of patience—watching for the perfect moment.

Bleeding, aching, soaking wet, Thea was still ready to dismantle anything to free the Nahetians. But she wasn't quietly waiting. She was barreling forward like a mad woman.

There was a vague sense, a whisper, that something else was waiting.

That she was not the huntress.

But the hunted.

It glanced up, its massive form straightening. It heard a woman's voice, not too far now.

Grunting, it rolled its thick shoulders. Its misshapen body ached from its horns to its cloven hooves. Hideous but powerful. Both human and not human enough.

Snout sniffing the air, its face twisted into a sharp-toothed grin.

She'd come.

It'd been waiting for her.

The empty spool clattered to the floor. Thea's pulse thrummed. She slowed, her arm hairs prickling.

How long had it been? Hours? Days? Time slipped, folding in on itself, imperceptible without tech, like all those nights they lost track of it at The Agora.

They would have more nights like that. They *had* to.

T, it's midnight.

Thea pivoted into another chamber. And stopped dead.

A dim laboratory. One looking like a hurricane had ripped through, scattering beakers, solutions, and syringes across a central lab bench. Equipment lay toppled.

Colour-coded folders stacked on one corner. Bulging with documents.

On her right were rows upon rows of glass tanks, housing diverse animals from domestic to exotic. Feathers, scales, horns, fangs.

Beside them, two rows of seven glass chambers held crumpled forms. Unmoving humans. Nahetians.

Cold sweat dripped down her spine. She managed two steps forward, her eyes desperately scanning for a shape she knew better than her own name.

"Thea."

A dark, rasping grunt from behind her.

The enormous beast stepped from the shadows. Its hind limbs ended in hooves. Short, silver fur coated its broad body, growing sparser around the face.

The face. A grotesque caricature of a bull—with expressive, anthropoid eyes.

Thea didn't scream, didn't stumble back. She just whispered, as if not to startle it, "What *the fuck* are you?"

The bull-face fell into a deformed frown, furred human-like fingers touching its snout. "You don't recognize me?" it rasped softly.

The contemplative softening. The eyes.

The world tilted beneath Thea's feet. The room blurred at the edges.

April.

Thea was moving, tripping, needing to touch the beast, needing to know this was real.

Its wide palm signaled for her to stop.

Thea clutched the lab bench to stay upright, her face twisting. "Oh, gods. *Oh, gods, April.* What did they do to you?"

It stared at her and said plainly, "They did nothing. I've been striving for months to develop this… My metamorphosis."

The words rattled around Thea's head, refusing to click into place. "They kidnapped you! They—"

"There's never been kidnappings." The bull—April—approached the bench. "Aegeus willingly hands us over, as repayment."

Thea's knees wobbled. Her lips barely formed the question. "What? Repayment for what?"

"The Creet's leader, Minos, had two sons," April said, her focus on an empty beaker. "One, Aegeus had his men kill. The other deserted, abandoning The Ring completely."

Thea's brows furrowed. Then her eyes widened. "*Riad.*"

Pearly horns bobbed as April nodded, adding a grey powder to the beaker. "Minos wanted Aegeus dead. But Aegeus—ever the businessman—struck a deal. Every seven years he'd sacrifice fourteen Nahetians for Creets to experiment on till death. Ergos carried it out, snatching victims, making it past wards. And let people blame Creets."

Thea shook her head, something sharp stabbing in her heart. The man who taught her the collective before the individual. "Aegeus wouldn't do that."

"What do you think happens to the people you interrogate?"

Thea blinked. "We let them go."

"For them to turn on us? I have every paper trail, T, for everything. It's how I uncovered all this." She gestured at the stacked folders—the missing documents April had mentioned at

The Agora. "The Ergos do his dirty work. Dispose of the bodies once you've wrung them dry."

Thea trembled, her teeth chattering. Not from panic or fear, but disgust—at herself.

The bull's face became concerned, a familiar expression so contorted, Thea was nearly sick. April said gently, "They lied to you, T. You couldn't have known."

"So, all of this…" Thea gripped the lab bench tighter. The floor threatened to swallow her. "All of this is for revenge?"

Grey-blue eyes snapped to hers. "You think I'd do all this for vengeance?" April spat, anger spiking. "This is the same reason you let Aegeus keep you on a fucking leash. It's obligation."

"How is *this* an obligation?"

"Look out there!" April flung out her arms, sending glassware to the floor. In a chamber, a thin girl stirred on its floor. "Unified, we could be extraordinary. Nahetian blood, Creet innovations. Consider what you are capable of. I'm a Dud. Every Seven and Seven has been a Dud. But with you—imagine what we will do together. Repair Saturn City, the people, the feuds."

April measured and poured solutions, slamming down their containers. "I made a deal. I knew Aegeus would sacrifice us, and you'd come. They could observe how *you*, someone gifted, would navigate their maze, collect their precious data, and they'd give me access to tech, to their labs. Then you'd come join me, to transform, and leave Aegeus to die a bastard's death."

"I was ready to follow you into hades," Thea whispered, "but this…" There were no soft edges, no sweetness, no…sanity. "You've lost your mind."

No wonder it'd been easy to infiltrate The Ring—they wanted

her here.

"I can't turn back." April observed her silver-furred fingers. "This is the end. This is what we should be. Hybrids."

Thea's hands curled into shaking fists. She needed a tether, an anchor. Anything. "I thought Riad set me up. But it was all you." The only person Thea trusted. Loved more than life. Aegeus was a manipulator. Used her as his puppet. But was April any different? Thea felt dizzy, the shock of betrayal like fever.

April replied simply, "I needed Riad as my messenger and escort. He refused until I said he'd be key to keeping you alive."

At least now I always know the time, Riad had said.

A faint, nagging thought surfaced. An itch prickling into hives.

T, it's midnight.

April had known the time. In The Agora—where there were no clocks or phones. Yet another thing Thea had missed.

With tweezers, April added a blue scale to her glass. It sizzled, the mixture now mud-like. "We agreed to take Aegeus down together, for his brother, for mine. Creets have a system. White flag, all is civil. Black flag, a signal to take out His Supremacy. It'll take them seconds. When we're done here, we'll raise it."

"Done here? What are you doing?"

April lifted a syringe filled with the muddy solution. She sauntered toward the case containing the small, stirring girl. "They'll thank me. No one will use us again."

Thea rounded the bench, planting herself between them. "Let them go, April. Put that the fuck away."

Thea felt April's sorrow then, the profound regret. "I'm sorry, T. I can't lose you too. But I won't let you ruin all I've worked for.

Think about Idas. We'll make him proud." Those beautiful, calm eyes were pleading. Thea could feel her love, drawing Thea in like cold fingers to a hearth. "Please."

Perhaps April was right. Perhaps they would be better as a collective.

But not like this.

Thea started to object. April's expression shuttered and darkened. She knew Thea wouldn't join her. Wouldn't let her hurt Nahetians.

Before Thea could speak, she felt the spike of fury. Her friend, the person she held so tightly in her heart it hurt, charged.

On instinct, Thea wrapped her calf around April's massive leg, twisting to send the bull's momentum toward the ground. The syringe flew out of April's hand.

April's powerful body was a stubborn, enraged force. As they grappled on the floor, April's horns nearly pierced Thea's chest. April was fighting to kill.

She tried using April's weight against her, struggled to trip, to lock joints. Madness bulged from April's eyes. The humanity in them sliding away like time. Thea's face crumpled, tears welling.

"April, *please*. Stop this. *It's me*."

Whether it was the transformation or years of hemorrhaging grief, the April she'd adored was gone. The girl who loved love, who held Thea in her darkest moments, was now decaying. Putrefying. In her place, a brute, utterly convinced of its righteousness.

Love you, mindfreak.

Thea faltered and the bull-creature's elbow collided into her jaw. Pain burst, blinding, knocking inside her skull. She rolled, barely dodging its attempt to pin her. Even untrained, the beast was too enormous. Its corded muscles rippled.

It was trying to stand. Its wide eyes fixed on the syringe across the laboratory.

Thea's heart slammed against her ribs. Hard enough to hear. She shoved up and sprang, landing on the bull's back. She gripped her arms around its neck, and hung on, sobs racking her body. "*Stop. Please*, come back. April. I need you. I need you." *I can't do this without you.*

It didn't hear her.

She wasn't ready. This wasn't fair. She'd destroyed herself, and it wasn't enough.

Thea remembered then, a night they wandered home from The Agora, the city long asleep. The memory so clear she could hear the cobblestones. Arms draped like blankets over each other's shoulders. April stared at the sky, her freckles a reflection of the stars, then gestured at the metro station, closed for the night. *"You never realize how late it is, until you're already out of time."*

At the time, April was noting the late hour.

But now, as Thea's arms clenched over the bull's throat, over its pulse, she realized how right April had been. Thea hadn't noticed, hadn't paid close enough attention.

And now she was out of time.

A flare of alarm from the beast. Then it collapsed, limp. Thea kept her hold tight, her eyes clenched shut, her mind swirling and drowning and screaming. She had too much love, felt *everything*. It hurt more than she could bear. Both Aegeus and April had used her. And she had nothing left.

Love you too, sappy nerd.

So while psych ward-blue eyes disappeared behind eyelids

for the last time, Thea burned it all down, everything that surfaced, everything that hurt—compassion, longing, trust, grief. Theatre after theatre, now ashes. She didn't need it. Not now. She could finally be the perfect, emotionless weapon. It didn't matter.

Sacrifice is survival.

Aegeus knew nothing of sacrifice. Always the decision maker, never the victim of its consequences. All this time, he'd given up others in his stead.

Thea had given all of herself.

They stood outside the headquarters.

It'd taken Thea a moment to realize there were fourteen captives, not thirteen.

The thin girl with steel eyes had the rough look of a Drifter. A metal chain necklace. Only then did Thea realize she'd seen the metal thread before, hanging around the neck of a panicked merchant.

This was his daughter, Mel.

They'd followed the thread out. Used the livestock as bait for the maggot-creatures.

And now she stared at the plain script on the door, unblinking.

Lab R Inc.

She repeated it under her breath, twice, feeling faint amusement and nothing more. She grinned. "Labyrinth."

Mel watched the strange young woman with empty eyes approach the flagpole. Contemplate it as if sizing up an enemy.

"We have to do things that haunt us," the woman murmured to no one. Then she glanced at Mel, saying flatly, "You're with us now."

Mel didn't want to consider the weight of that statement. Instead, she asked, "Who are you?"

The Nahetian woman smirked, apparently not caring about her severely bruised jaw—or dozens of bleeding wounds. "Call me... Your Supremacy."

And the woman raised a black flag.

When they approached the drawbridge, Her Supremacy pulled something out of her pocket. A red stone ring.

The Chasm demanded something of them, luring like a lover's caress. The woman felt it too. She released her ring into the abyss.

Mel had found an identical ring by the body of the bull-like beast. Now, in her pocket, it pressed into her palm, strangely hot.

The Chasm, satisfied with the offering, lowered the bridge.

And together, they crossed from The Ring into The Centre.

THE ENVOY

Laura Jayne McLoughlin

The craggy water world of Ulstare was wild and unkind. It had been colonised for a total of eighty-seven years and for most of that time, it had warred with itself. It broke apart its own forests with driving winds, drowned its green fields in floods and cruel tsunamis. A knotted storm prowled the surface in constant pursuit of unprepared settlements and lone travellers.

The people, too, seemed infected with this planet's rage. Despite the territories having been divided up by dignitaries and rulers of Earth, these lines in the earth were in constant flux, between colony to colony, city to city.

Calon had been born on Ulstare. He knew few other sights besides driving rains and rugged earth, and no other feeling but the push and pull of power around a turbulent planet. He had been told of Earth, of course, its stories and its ways, but that little blue orb from photographs was little more than a marble in his mind. Ulstare was all that mattered, and his colony—the colony of MacNess—most of all.

On the day the envoy arrived at their colony, the sky was pale and yellowed. A storm was rumbling off the coast somewhere, but it was a day or two off yet, so Calon watched their small, white spacecraft drift into the planet's atmosphere as quietly and unobtrusively as a dust mote. It was altogether too gentle.

"Do they know?" Calon asked his uncle, who was reclining on a plush velvet chair beside him. His uncle's eyes, too, were on the small, silent craft.

"Too early to say," MacNess said. "How would they know?"

"Someone might have told them."

"You question the honour of our warriors?"

Calon gave his uncle a sidelong look, which he did not return. Rather, MacNess kept his eyes on the ceiling-to-floor window, his hands steepled under his chin, lost in thought. "I have no reason not to distrust our men," Calon said, forcing the conversation on. "Are you saying that you do?"

"No," was the slow answer. "But I am not saying otherwise, either. Simply put, nephew, the queen of the western territories does not send envoys to colonies she thinks can fend for themselves. And as of right now, our defences are not what they should be."

Calon's jaw set. He was a young man, not prone to anger, but malleable to it, the way all young and new things were to forces greater than themselves. And he felt angry now. "There must be something we can do."

"We must wait."

"Until she arrives?"

"Until we know what she wants."

MacNess turned to Calon now, face drawn and serious. It was in moments like these that Calon understood more clearly that he was not merely arguing with his uncle, his family. This was a man who had ruled this colony nearly thirty years. He was of the first generation born here and had experienced firsthand what it was like to lose father, brother, and city to warring colonies, hard winters, and ill-thought deals.

He felt his anger retreat, but his concern about the envoy drifting ever closer could not be eclipsed.

"But how could she know?" he asked again, and his uncle turned his face away.

They let the envoy in by the front doors of the main homestead around which the rest of the city had been built: the Castle. People liked to call it this because of its great size and turret-like outlook towers. It had originally been a small, shining dot on the planet's unwelcoming surface, and had slowly expanded outwards with the use of the rock and minerals mined from the ground.

The comparison to an old Earth-origin fort could only go so far, though. Plumes of vapor from reactors and generators clouded the already clouded sky, and the forcefield around the land gave it a light shimmer to those standing outside. The windows, strategic and slim line, were shining black slits, dimmed against the harsh setting and rising sun.

Save for MacNess' select few rooms of soft furnishings and precious antiquities of Earth-origin, the rest of the Castle was resolute in its practicalities, and so when the envoy entered, it was into a cold stone room, lit overhead with strips of fluorescents.

His uniform was dark and simple, with a soldier's armour and the wide, triangular coat of someone of rank. Thick black gloves gave him great mitts for hands and his face was obscured with his visored helmet.

"I come with a message from governor Mebh of the Connacht region."

The envoy's voice echoed even in the small space. It had a strangely familiar tenor about it, some scratchy, throaty quality which Calon felt he had heard before. He glanced at his uncle, searching his face for a similar sense of recognition, but MacNess stared straight ahead, unblinking and unimpressed.

On a typical day, they might have been joined by high-ranking officials from the army and a dozen or more soldiers. This was not, however, a typical day, and so the only person to join MacNess and his nephew was the high priestess. Her face was hidden by her white, nylon hood and Calon hoped she appeared holy and impressive to this foreign envoy. He hoped he would think this sort of scant gathering was merely a custom of their colony.

"The governor has requested free passage through your territory so that she may claim the western shore's Cyranium mine for the colony of Connacht."

Calon scoffed. MacNess gave a small, humourless smile. "Is that all?"

"If you would allow peaceful passage, and refrain from any attacks on our army, we can assure you that we will be gone within the day, and do no harm to your people, crops, or city." Calon darted a look to his uncle and back to the envoy. He would have almost thought it a joke if he did not already know the nature of the colony of Connacht. If MacNess' people were brutal, then the Connacht colony were savages.

"What use has she with our mine?"

"I am not at liberty to divulge the governor's private motivations, sir."

"Would you permit me to guess?" MacNess said. He approached the envoy, his own triangular coat a fine emerald green, the bottom of which glimmered with precious stones. "Because your governor lacks for nothing. She has claimed mine after mine across this vast land, and yet she is never satisfied. There is no larger, more opulent, more materialistic city than the one you have come from today, so it cannot be for wealth. She cannot truly *need* our resources."

It was impossible to know the envoy's expression, but his shoulders were rigid as MacNess spoke.

"No, this is not about wealth. It is about power. It always has been. Your governor Mebh wants to insult this colony and take from it a prized gem: its first mine, its deepest mine. All hail the great queen of planet Ulstare! Bow down before her undoubted might!"

His voice rose and echoed, and in the silence, the envoy was forced to answer. "Again, all I am able to say is what I have been asked to convey and—"

MacNess scoffed. "Your governor does not understand fair play, boy, and she does not understand the colony of MacNess if she thinks we should roll over so easily. Must I remind you of the Battle of Black Lake? The forty-day siege at your outposts out in the forests of Midian?"

MacNess stood and despite his weary bones and pale skin, Calon saw the glimmer of the warrior of Ulstare he once was, the man who carved out this territory and defended it from raiders, storms, and the beasts which called the planet their home.

"And by God, remove your helmet in my presence, boy—or would you insult us further by hiding your face, even when we give you an audience?"

The envoy did not speak or move for a moment, and then,

seeming to take a sharp breath, he raised his hands to his head. The helmet dislodged with a soft hiss, and as it came away to reveal dark hair and a pointed beard, Calon winced.

He knew the envoy's name then. He knew it all too well, and by the glance the envoy gave him, he knew his name just the same.

"What is your name, boy?" MacNess asked.

"Ferdiad," the envoy replied. "Ferdiad of Connacht."

"Well, Ferdiad, you may tell your governor that her request has been denied, and if she comes upon our lands, we will force her back. You do not steal from the colony of MacNess so barefaced without consequence."

"I will report back," Ferdiad said. "Though, I have also been advised to insist upon a peaceful retrieval. Governor Mebh is aware that your armies have been hindered in recent days, and we know, as well as you must, that it would not be a fair fight."

MacNess was still.

They did know then, Calon thought. They had known, and they had chosen this moment to strike because it was the only time they could have won.

"What has your governor told you, boy?"

"May I speak freely?"

"Speak your truth."

Ferdiad took a breath. "I have been made aware that your men have not risen from their beds in two days. They have been rendered useless by stomach pains, and there is talk that the land has cursed you and your people."

"Do you believe in curses?"

"I believe in toxic gases and food poisoning and many other misfortunes. I might even call them a curse, if they should come when I am most pained by them."

"And this is when we should be most pained."

"This visit is not an insult or a threat, sir," Ferdiad said. "It is meant to be a mercy." MacNess' face hardened and his lips thinned. It injured Calon to see his uncle without a reply, and even more so to know that his colony had been left defenceless.

"You still ask for too much," MacNess said eventually. "Our mine is...old. It is a sign to our people of our prosperity."

"You have many other mines."

"But only one first."

"Your people will be largely unchanged without it. Again, this is not a threat—"

"Not a threat to our lives but our *livelihoods*. Not an insult to our people, but to our culture and history. Tell her to reconsider."

"With all due respect, sir, I'm not sure if you are in the position to make demands."

"This is not a demand," MacNess replied. "It is a request—for *true* mercy. You cannot take this mine from us. We cannot give it freely."

It was more than Calon had ever seen his uncle concede. He may as well have been on his knees, but when Calon looked at Ferdiad, he saw that his lips had quirked to the side—a secret sort of amusement Calon alone could read.

And that old anger came upon him again.

"If you want a fight," he burst out, "then we will have a fight. You cannot come and insult our colony and demand we give ourselves over to be violated willingly."

"You will fight," Ferdiad said, "without an army?"

"I will fight alone. In single-hand combat."

Calon heard the high priest draw a breath and his uncle shift in his step. Perhaps it was too rash, too bold, but when all else was spent, what more did Calon have to offer than nerve? He held his chin higher and met Ferdiad's bemused eyes.

"Single-hand combat," he repeated. "And who is your chosen warrior?"

"I am. Tell your governor that. She may watch her army tumble down by the force of one man, and then perhaps next time she comes to this territory, she will show more respect." Ferdiad's gaze drifted from Calon to MacNess and the priestess, searching, it seemed, for an argument.

"Very well," he said at last. "I will return your message to Connacht, sir."

MacNess met Calon in the corridor. His face was plain, his countenance unreadable. "You have made a great sacrifice, Calon," he said. He met his nephew's eyes. "There was no other option."

Nothing else except present their mine for defilement and bide their time, for a chance at retaliation. All the while, the colony of Connacht would reap their riches and bask in their colony's quaint history, if they did not flood and ruin it rather than see it return to MacNess. No, it was no option at all.

"No other option but to lay your life on the line for your colony? To go up against impossible odds and what's worse, all alone? Few else would consider that an option at all, but you…" He placed a heavy hand on his nephew's shoulder. "You are made of something more."

"I was trained to be something more."

"Aye," his uncle said. "I recall. Now go. Prepare to win, nephew, for here and now, there truly is no other option.

Calon spent the night preparing his weapons and armour, honing his skills in the Castle's gym. He thought of who might have informed the Connacht colony of their disadvantage, but the more he wondered, the more he was convinced that it was a fruitless exercise. Word of the felled army had travelled quickly through the Castle, and faster again through the city. Anyone could have carried the knowledge across the divide, a trader or merchant most likely of all.

Regardless of their name and whether they ended up on his blade, Calon wished an unhappy life for them—one which ended in the belly of one of Ulstare's deep-water monsters—for how they had brought this pain upon the colony.

He hoped too, half-heartedly, that insolent envoy, Ferdiad, might find a similar fate. It felt strange to see his face again, stranger still to hate him. At one point, Calon had thought when they met again it would be with open arms and rollicking tales of their individual triumphs.

It had been almost ten years ago now, when Calon had travelled to a distant moon of New Skyy, where the infamous warrior woman Scáthach resided.

She was a teacher, in the most basic sense of the word. Calon better remembered her as a sadist—a living weapon, as cold and brutal as the moon she inhabited—and she had a reputation for losing her students to her deadly methods.

One was either forged in the fire or burnt up, and when Calon was seventeen, he was sent to New Skyy to find out which he would be.

He hadn't been sure of what to expect when his uncle first sent him away to New Skyy because anywhere other than Ulstare was a foreign concept to him.

It was relatively similar to his home planet, but he could never have prepared for the utter cold of the place, the loneliness. Snow was meant to hammer the northern hemisphere where Scáthach lived for most of the year, and only melt away in the absolute height of summer. If there were more than ten people on the whole surface of the planet, that was all.

Scáthach had been difficult to envision, too. There had been so many stories of Scáthach, like how she ran with the boar-wolves in the forests and spent twelve hours at a time meditating in the frozen rock pools by the ocean. The reality of her did little to dispel such myths.

In person, she was unkempt and snake-eyed—all angles and snarls—and when they met for the first time, she did not say hello. She did not shake hands, either. She merely met his gaze and then turned away with the expectation that he would follow. And he did, through the forest and up the side of a mountain to her home, which was little more than a series of holes carved into the rockface and sparsely decorated with furniture.

She led him to his room and then left without another word, and so Calon busied himself, unpacking, examining the small space and lacklustre bed.

It was then that Ferdiad had appeared in the doorway. He crossed the room and extended a hand.

"Ferdiad," he said. "Are you another of Scáthach's pupils?"

Ferdiad was dark-haired, as young as Calon if not more so, with closely trimmed facial hair. Calon did not know this man, and despite his seemingly genuine sideways smile, he did not want to. "Yes," Calon answered flatly. "This is my room."

Ferdiad's smile didn't falter. "And also mine."

Perhaps it had been the long flight, that Calon had never been so far from his home, or that the next two years of his life looked endless and sad and cold, but he snapped. Ferdiad, no longer all smiles, snapped back.

Scáthach had not silenced them with sharp words or a shout. Instead, her blade had slashed through the air before them, forcing them backwards from one another. When they were still, Scáthach surveyed them with those thin, cold eyes, and said, "Do you think I run an inn? A halfway house for little boys with egotistical aspirations? No. I have one house. I keep one room. You will sleep there or sleep on the front step like dogs, and when the boar-wolves take you, you will have deserved it."

It was decided then that Calon would have the right side of the bed and Ferdiad the left, and Scáthach would stay in her cot, right beside the fire and the spear she left in the flames, turning red hot overnight.

Those first days had felt impossibly long. Calon had expected the training to be difficult, but this was gruelling. Scáthach was relentless, her standards for footing and hand placement and the timing of the swings of an axe so precise, Calon was beginning to think they were pure fiction.

He returned to his shared bed each night with windburn and nicks along his arms and legs from Scáthach's teaching. Ferdiad, just as bruised and dark-eyed, did the same. He had not smiled since his initial greeting, and Calon couldn't have cared less.

It took twelve days before either spoke before going to sleep.

It was perhaps the first night Calon had gotten into bed and felt somewhat comfortable, his muscles no longer burning like a fever, and he thought that perhaps tonight he would drift into a comfortable unconscious.

Ferdiad, however, had conversation in mind. He rolled over and said, "Scáthach says you were sent here for being too beautiful."

Calon, who had been lying on his back, gave his bedmate a withering glance. "I was sleeping."

"Your eyes were open."

"I was about to be sleeping."

They slipped into silence, but Calon could feel Ferdiad watching him in the dark, waiting for an answer.

"What if I told you," he said, "that Scáthach lies?"

"I would believe you. I doubt she would tell me the truth even if it were to save my life."

"She does not owe you a life." Ferdiad frowned at him. "So why were you sent here, if it was not to protect the vulnerable hearts of young men and women back home?"

"To die," Calon said flatly.

Ferdiad was quiet again. "Your people have no faith in you?"

"They have too much faith in Scáthach. I will either return home useful or die the pompous son of privilege they think I am."

"You would return home, even though they sent you away with ill-intention?"

Calon frowned. "I will return home a proven warrior."

"Yes, but to fight alongside those who expected you to die

here."

"It is my governor's prerogative to test me. If he thinks I am too soft, then I may be forged. I am a weapon for my colony. I have come to sharpen myself. What is so hard to understand about that? Have you not come, knowing Scáthach's reputation like I have?"

"Yes, but my people sent me with the belief I would come home, because I am a good warrior."

"Then you do not respect Skyy or Scáthach as you should."

Ferdiad's eyes glimmered in the dark. "You seem rather good at it. Perhaps you could teach me."

"Scáthach will teach you just fine."

To Calon, there was nothing about that night which might have signalled how the next two years were to transpire, but if there was one thing which never failed, it was Ferdiad, whispering in the dark from the other side of the bed.

Calon woke on Ulstare, dreaming of New Skyy and feeling uneasy about both. He wasted no time in getting ready and headed down to the armoury. His uncle was waiting for him there, grim-faced and greyer than usual. All about him were advisers, generals, and servants who collected pieces of armour and attached them to Calon.

"You are an impressive warrior," MacNess said slowly, seeming to choose his words with care. "And a wonderful nephew. Do not make me mourn two lives today."

"She is here?" Calon asked.

"Her ship has entered the atmosphere."

"Fighters?"

"Just the ship. She seems to be keeping to her word."

"Don't trust her to keep it for long. Be prepared."

MacNess took Calon's shoulders in his hands. "Let me worry about the colony, nephew. You worry about yourself."

It was decided that Calon would face one after the other of Connacht's warriors outside the city walls. It was a barren sort of place, all rugged earth and scrub foliage—the brown, dry remains of heather which had bloomed purple in the spring.

The southern wind cut across the land with savage intent, and Connacht's ship loomed overhead. It was colossal—Calon could see now—as big as any of the planet's moons. Every square foot of its innards would hold a soldier, a soldier he was destined to kill.

Out in the wasteland, he held a blade in one hand and his shield in the other. Both were made from one of the precious metals which the colonies warred over: Cyranium. It was a livid blue precious metal, harder than tungsten but ten times as light, and so sharp that when it met skin, it burned.

There was little wonder that the colonies warred over who might have better access to it, and even less as to why it fetched such a price from those back on Earth. It was a tool, a building material, a gold weight when trading goods.

And now it was a weapon too.

A small, insectile ship departed from Queen Mebh's great ark, zipping down towards the surface. It expanded before him, from a blip to a vast machine of roaring engines and shining paint. When it hit the ground, it grunted against the earth.

A panel opened and a set of stairs folded out. From inside appeared a soldier: grey armour, grey helmet, a cape about his shoulders. He carried a sword at his side, a shield in his hand, and three or four alternative weapons attached to the belt across his torso.

He looked accomplished, confident, but he had not trained with Scáthach. Calon clicked the side of his helmet, the visor flipping down to protect his face, and readied his sword. Connacht's soldier, too, adjusted his footing, and then, seemingly impatient, rushed his enemy. Calon easily sidestepped the attack.

Without hesitation, the soldier swung, and his blade fell by Calon's shoulder. The force pulled the soldier forward, his footing uneven for the briefest of moments, and his sword just an inch too low. It gave Calon all the opportunity he needed to throw his weight against his shield and bash the soldier in the chest.

He staggered but did not lose his footing. The soldier sprung forward to the side, and once he had Calon within distance, he lashed out again, the tip of his blade barely catching Calon's shoulder. He tried it again and this time, found only air.

Calon was quick. He had sparred with the wild woman of New Skyy every morning for two years. He had dodged lightning as it raged across the moors of that wicked moon. He had found the tiger-cats of her forests, and he had raced them and won.

And he would win this fight too.

It seemed then that the Connacht soldier knew that too, his efforts growing more frenzied, his attitude more desperate. Calon did not tire, he did not slow. Rather, his Cyranium sword crashed into the warrior's armour again and again and again, until the fibres beneath began to show, and Calon had his chance.

But before he might deal the final deadly blow, the Connacht warrior snatched something from his thigh holster. A gun, Calon saw, and in the next instant, the bullet was coming for him. Calon felt the blow to his chest and took one step backwards. The Connacht soldier fired again and the bullet, once more, embedded itself in Calon's chest armour as Calon advanced closer.

Then, he lunged, and his blue blade came away red.

The Connacht soldier crumpled to the ground, grappling at his throat. Blood spilled through the thick, armoured gloves, and Calon waited until the desperate body went still. He held his sword above his head, and distantly he could hear the shouts of his uncle, his people, watching from the city walls.

Victor.

Calon replaced the sword in his holster and looked up at the sky, where Mebh's ship, large as ever, drifted slowly, unbothered and unafraid.

One down, Calon thought with grim determination, *a thousand to go*.

It was four weeks later when Calon took his daily celebrations to the bar in the city. His uncle had disapproved of the outing, but as banged up and bruised as Calon was, he wanted something more interesting for his evening than staring at the ceiling and planning how not to die the following morning.

He chose a spot farther from the Castle than he would normally go. The bars close to the inner ring were more upmarket, dignified. They served expensive booze and they did it with a smile, but everyone there had someone to impress. It made for stiff dancing and uninteresting conversation in Calon's opinion, so tonight, he went where nobody cared about anything.

The bar was a ramshackle place, all stone walls and stone flooring, with painted wooden panelling only in places they could afford. The owners had hung old relics of Earth from the ceiling, and they glinted like disco balls: a handheld CD player, a dozen glassy-eyed smartphones, light bulbs as big as your fist. Someone with a guitar wailed from the small platform in the back, and the people drummed along with their feet.

No one here was a warrior. No one had political leanings or a word in with the high priestess. They were miners and shopkeepers, prostitutes, and smithies.

And they loved Calon. When he entered, he became the new centre of gravity. The room orbited him, offering drinks and kisses and songs for the city's most prized warrior. He declined the alcohol—he had not lasted thirty days of battle just to lose on day thirty-one to a bleeding headache and sour stomach—but accepted all the rest.

"They sent him away when he was seventeen," he could hear the old bar men tell each other. "Because he'd have taken the pick of the women if he'd have stayed."

And for once, Calon didn't think to correct them.

Around midnight, he detached himself from the throng long enough to take a piss out back. The air was frigid. The sky overhead was dark, dark, dark, and the stars flamed white.

"I never did understand," came a voice, "how your aim was so good in some instances and woeful in others."

Calon straightened, glancing over his shoulder, but he needn't have looked. He knew that voice as well as he knew his own.

He finished and fastened his trousers. With a scowl, he said, "And I never understood why you had such a knack for seeking out your own death."

Ferdiad stood in the shadow of the bar's harsh fluorescent light, a thick coat zipped to his throat, arms folded across his chest. Nothing gave him away as a foreign invader, and his expression was all placid interest.

"You're one to talk," he said. "You've been hunting down your death since you were seventeen and now you might finally have it. Did your time on New Skyy teach you nothing? I'd have imagined the scars would have been lesson enough."

He curved his hand like a claw and the memory met Calon like cold water: Scáthach's instruction to go into the forest and collect water by a particular stream, Ferdiad walking in step with him, laughing with him, and then—of course then—the boar-wolf.

It had been an ordinary day, all things considered. They were in their second year then, bigger and thicker than when they had first arrived, and perhaps becoming foolhardier than they should have. The morning training session wasn't agony like it had been those first few months, and hunting for their lunch wasn't the trial it had been when they were new.

They had been laughing, he remembered, Ferdiad joking around again like he did. What it was exactly was lost to him now, but it must have been funny, because Calon had been near giddy with laughter, staggering, and then pushing Ferdiad, chasing him.

They raced, he remembered, through the trees. Ferdiad had always been nimbler than Calon and he slipped between trunks and under low boughs with ease, while Calon crashed behind him, breaking twig and branch and all else, thundering with noise.

They should have been paying attention, but then he had him. Calon had caught Ferdiad, and it was probably because Ferdiad had let him, but that didn't matter. In fact, it was better, because it meant that Calon knew for certain that Ferdiad wanted him to do what he did next. That kiss was not the first, but it might have been the last.

The boar-wolf had come from behind, and torn Calon's back

before ever releasing a growl. He should have heard it, of course. Scáthach had taught them to hear every crack of a twig, the rustle of undergrowth when something passed through it. But he hadn't, and now he was bleeding on his hands and knees, and for one bright, hot second, he thought this was how he died: with his hands in the dirt and his lover fleeing into the trees.

But then Ferdiad had brought his spear down on the boar-wolf. The tip of the blade burst through its chest and the creature howled in pain, struggling and writhing and attempting an escape.

When they returned to Scáthach's cavern, they had slung the boar-wolf pelt over Calon's back. They had meant to hide the fact that a stupid animal had almost killed them, but they should have known nothing could be hidden from the wild woman of New Skyy.

She sent Ferdiad to bed and commanded Calon to sit before her at the fire where she cleaned his wounds with a stinging balm, and asked him one thing, "Would it be worth it, to gain one man and lose all the world, Calon?"

Calon had answered it would not, because that was the right answer, and she had pressed the balm deeper into the wound—harder than she needed to, he imagined.

"On your path," she said, "there is only room for one. Remember that."

"I do not think you tell other warriors that, when they bring home wives and children."

"But you are not like other warriors. You are my student. I am sending you back to MacNess and Ulstare in six short months, boy, and you best know what you're loyal to —and loyal unto death, at that."

He doubted Ferdiad had ever heard those words, but they were the ones which burned most keenly when Calon thought back to his time on New Skyy—the ones which told Calon, fully, without question, that whatever it was he had with Ferdiad, it stayed on New Skyy. And it had done so for ten years.

"Why are you here, Ferdiad?" he asked with more weariness than fury.

"Because our governor is growing tired of these games, and I worry about what she may do next."

"She will send another warrior to kill me, that's what she will do."

"Yes, but one you will not be able to defeat."

"You doubt me? You know, I have not ceased my training since leaving Scáthach. I am even better than when I left her. Can you say the same?" He rolled his eyes. "An envoy—imagine training with Scáthach for two years and coming home to be a messenger boy."

"You mock me because I have not followed in your exact footsteps? Did you expect me to be your mirror all our lives? Two boys sent off-world to train; two boys sent home to be warriors for their colonies… We were bound to diverge somewhere."

"Yes, well, I took you for having more courage than that."

"There, too—that is where we diverge. You have always been so black and white, Calon. Right is right, and wrong is wrong. Colony, people, honour, tradition—"

"And what is wrong with those things? What is wrong with knowing what is right?"

"Nothing," Ferdiad said with another one of those teasing smiles playing on his face. "If you know for certain what *is* right."

Calon lifted one eyebrow. "Go back to your colony, Ferdiad. We're finished here."

"You are stubborn until death, Calon. So proud and—"

"Stubborn? You take me to be a mere mule? I am a warrior. I am a soldier. I am not afraid that I will die. Can you honestly say the same?"

Ferdiad became quite still. Looking away, he said, "No. I have always been afraid that you would die."

They were standing close now, so close that Calon could not help but feel the space between them like an ache. It was easy then to reach out for his hand, to bridge the gap between them. It was as his body commanded, and he only needed to listen.

Ferdiad did not meet his eye but looked at their hands, clasped tightly, desperately. "You are not fair, Ferdiad. Why have you come now, when all the world is at stake?"

"The world is not at stake. It is a hole in the ground."

"You know that's not all it is. You dishonour me pretending you can't see that."

"You are the warrior your colony has always wanted you to be then."

"Is that such a problem?"

He met Ferdiad's eyes and thought of the thousand other instances in which they stood like this on New Skyy—hand in hand, motionless and falling. Somewhere far away, Calon could feel himself bending closer, his chin tilted and wanting.

Ferdiad pressed a hand to his chest. "I don't want to be your last kiss, Calon. I can't be."

"Then don't be. Be another."

Ferdiad drew back, fading into the shadows of the bar once

again. "Do not fight when there is still a place for peace."

He turned away then, flitting into the night like he had never been there at all, while Calon stood, rooted in the lamplight from the noisy barroom. His eyes followed Ferdiad as long as he could but even when he was gone entirely, Calon felt as though he was not entirely alone.

He glanced about the empty yard, the street beyond. There was no one there.

The next day, Calon tried not to think about the night and the bar and Ferdiad's glimmering gaze. He dressed in his armour and his uncle congratulated him on his thirty-first win, even though he had not even left the city walls yet. He thanked him and went out, taking the same forty steps he had done every day this past month to where the next soldier of Connacht would meet him.

It was raining, and Calon could hardly see the small, glimmering ship leave the larger until it had almost landed. White droplets bounced from its shining exterior. The soldier could have been a clone of any of the others as he took his place on the battlefield. He drew out one single shortsword, and in his other hand, he held a grey shield. Calon didn't waste time. The faster this was over, the faster he would be out of the rain, and he could decide how to win on day thirty-two.

The soldier dodged, quick and clean, and Calon turned to lunge with another attack. This time, their swords clashed with ringing intensity. The soldier twisted his weapon away first, and he took a stab at Calon. He narrowly missed his neck, and Calon was chased backwards a few steps before finding his step again.

The soldier was good, it seemed, better than he had expected. Perhaps Ferdiad had been right about something when he had come to warn him.

Calon adjusted his position, drawing the warrior to face him head on rather than in dodges and sideswipes. The soldier's sword lashed out, but Calon blocked with his own blade, taking a step forward and shoving the soldier backwards. He swung when the soldier was off balance, and at last, he made contact: Calon's blade crashed into the soldier's chest armour, sending him skidding backwards across the gravel.

Calon was on him like an animal, slashing at his neck, his helmet. The soldier attempted to roll onto his feet again, but Calon caught him with the sharp tip of his sword and he spasmed with agony, the blade finding skin where the armour had torn around the shoulder. Calon kicked the soldier onto his back, rain splashing, and drove a foot onto his chest. He took his sword and levelled the tip with the warrior's neck, but before he could drive it home, the soldier reached out and held the sword in between the flats of his hands.

Calon could have laughed at the futile attempt to disarm him, but the warrior's legs found him instead. They twisted about Calon's calves and drove him off balance, giving the warrior a hair of time to get away from the blade and scramble across the mud.

With that, the soldier was on his feet again, quick as ever. He clashed against Calon's sword, the two struggling against one another, until finally, the soldier turned—a complete three hundred and sixty degrees—and with the momentum, he parted from Calon's blade, before coming back harder and slashing Calon's right calf.

Calon cried out and stumbled but did not lose his footing entirely. He kept his blade out before him, and despite the blood rushing around his body and the rage filling his head, there was something about the technique that caught his attention.

The two soldiers faced one another. Slowly, Calon began to reach for his visor. The soldier did not move, and so he clicked it open, revealing his eyes to the soldier across the way. The soldier still did not move, until falteringly, he too raised a hand to his helmet.

The visor was sheathed and Ferdiad looked out from the armour. There was blood on his nose, most likely from where Calon had hammered his helmet, and his eyes looked wet. "Not you," was all Calon could think to say.

"I asked you not to come today."

Fury found Calon then and it was ice cold. "Because you knew?"

"Because I knew *something* would happen. I knew she wouldn't lose."

"Because you are helping her."

"She is *my governor.*"

"And these are my people!" Calon tightened his grip on his sword again. "You come here, asking me to see sense and listen to reason. You ask me to put away the things I hold most dear so that I might keep my life, and then you stand there—you stand there and do the exact same thing."

"I do not fight for a mine, a scrap of land. I fight because I am told to."

"Then you are a coward. You fight for nothing."

"And you are a fool because you fight for everything."

"Leave then, if you do not want to fight. Go back to your—"

"And have her kill me for treachery? I am either to return a victor or die on this planet, Calon, all because you and your people cannot accept one small defeat."

Calon reached for his helmet again and the visor came down. "I'm done with this." Ferdiad had only enough time to pull down his own visor when Calon came crashing into him. The two beat back and forth, but Ferdiad would not relent. He came faster, his blade flying with more biting accuracy, and Calon fought back all the harder, throwing himself into each swing of the sword, beating his opponent back across the battlefield.

They raged for hours. Despite their fatigue, they were evenly matched, and Calon could envision his uncle on the wall, heart in his throat, fist at his chest, wondering if this would be his nephew's death and his colony's loss. That, or staring out, unblinking, as he had done when he had left Calon on New Skyy all those years ago.

At one point, Calon began to wonder whether they might fight forever, locked in a constant duel, a stalemate which would occupy MacNess' best warrior for years to come. But he should have known that the governor of Connacht had never intended on letting this fight rage any longer than she needed it to.

They were both panting, looking at each other, waiting for the next strike, when a shadow moved across the land. It was darker by then, but there was a faint, reddish hue to the land, and when Calon looked overhead, he could see that Connacht's ship was moving. Why was it moving?

He looked back at Ferdiad. He saw it all happening in that moment: the spaceship drifting over the city walls, the smaller, nimbler fighter craft slipping out from inside, the soldiers on the ground, the people running in the streets. His uncle had been right.

Calon pointed furiously to the sky. "What is that?" he roared.

"What is happening?" Ferdiad turned his face to the ship too, and then back to Calon. "I don't know."

"You're a liar."

"I told you, *I don't know*."

"You brought me out here, knowing this would be all I could give, knowing I couldn't get back." He gripped his sword tighter. "You did this to me, Ferdiad. After everything."

"I'm telling you, Calon, I don't know what the ship is doing. It could be as simple as—" Suddenly, the ship released its first fighter craft, and then another, like a spider's nest bursting. They cut across the city walls, the noise of their engines like thunder, and then the guns started shooting.

The colony's sirens began to wail.

There wasn't any more time to think. There was only this fight and this sword and the anger, always that anger, finding him.

He did not hesitate when he lunged at Ferdiad. Rather, his aim was straight and true, and it found its unsuspecting mark with brutal accuracy. When it found purchase in the armour, Calon twisted the blade, just as Scáthach had taught him that night when he had come home with his back in tatters. All there was left to do was drive it home.

If Ferdiad cried out, he didn't hear it. All he could hear were sirens and engines. All he could hear was war.

After that, time moved more slowly. The sword came out, the blue metal red. Ferdiad staggered. His large, armoured hand grasped at the wound, and suddenly there was red—there was red everywhere. It was on the ground and on the glove, and then Ferdiad was in the mud, and he was still.

It was only then that Calon realised with frightening certainty that this was something he could not take back, and the anger receded like the tide.

At once, he was on his knees, grappling for Ferdiad's helmet. He felt that old familiar ache again—the one which had told him to hold Ferdiad's hand the night before, the one which had drawn him onto the other side of the bed in the cavern in New Skyy. It told him now to close this distance, even while it became a chasm.

With Ferdiad's helmet cast off, Calon ripped his own away too. The world was louder now, the destruction of his colony pressing on Calon's ears, and yet, he could not force himself to his feet. Not yet. Not while Ferdiad still blinked slowly back at him.

"Scáthach didn't teach me that one," Ferdiad said.

Calon shook his head. "No, she didn't."

"Is that cheating then, do you reckon?"

Somehow, Ferdiad was smiling, and Calon stared back, unsure of what to say, how to joke when there was blood pooling beneath them both.

It hardly seemed real, but it was. Of course it was. Calon had killed thirty other men and here was thirty-one: his love, his youth. A hundred or more times they had saved one another's lives out on New Skyy, but they had been boys then. Boys grew up, and apparently, boys killed each other when someone else told them they should.

The sirens screamed and the city screamed, and Ferdiad was dying quietly at Calon's side.

"You need to go," Ferdiad said, voice thick.

Calon knew if he turned his head, he would see smoke rising from the colony, he would see the walls battered and cracked, the forcefield about the Castle glittering like broken glass, so he did not. He kept his gaze fixed to Ferdiad.

"I can stay."

"But the mine—"

He ran a hand over Ferdiad's wet brow, pushing his hair from his face, and pressed his lips tight so that he would not cry out.

"I can stay," he said again.

ROBIN, THE HOOD

Stephen Howard

Baron Loxley hits recline on the control room chair and sighs the sigh of the discontent. Thirty or so screens flicker back at him, tripping from camera to camera, revealing the goings-on at his zinc mine, in his houses of leisure, restaurants, and general stores. Lately, Baron Loxley retires to the control room a lot. Watching faces, conversations, life. Watching as it passes him by.

On screen is the forecourt of his compound. A tumbleweed rolls on by.

The Baron clicks his watch. A hologram appears of his most recent family portrait. Fixed smiles, empty eyes. Seven years. Staring with glassy eyes at the hologram, his attentions turn away from the screens before him.

Screens turning blank, one by one.

When the Baron notices, it's a sea of empty portals to his slice of the world. In a slow, struggle-bug motion, the Baron rises, knocks off the hologram, and dances his fingers across the security system's keyboard and control panel.

Nothing.

"By the absent gods, what is happening?"

A single phaser shot rings out from the nearby corridor, then a muffled cry. The Baron slams a hand down upon the instant lockdown button, containing whatever threat approaches to the corridor.

Baron Loxley moves toward the door and senses the presence of others beyond it, catches the roguish scent of scoundrels, thieves. But his security team receives an alarm the instant the lockdown button engages. They'll soon sort this bunch of chancers out.

"You'll think twice before trying to rob me again," he yells, shaking a pale, bony fist at the inanimate door.

Silence, save for water flowing through pipes, then the sour drip of the Baron's sweat hitting the floor.

The door, so innocent and plain with its dull, metallic coat in need of updating, explodes inward, and deals a crushing blow to the fleshy body of the Baron.

"They say The Hood can blast an apple off a man's head from a hundred paces or more!"

A frail-seeming black man in a frayed green poncho, beggar's rags, and dark sunglasses, holding a stick in one hand, coin tin in the other, smiles and nods. "Aye, perhaps. But why waste a perfectly good apple?"

Coins rattle as the man hobbles along the row of stalls, calling out 'pennies for the poor' as he goes. Mostly, he's ignored. The man isn't recognisable to the merchants and the urchins lining the street, nor the bots or androids assisting. Sparks and smoke and oil waft along the way.

"A slow day." He passes the stalls and, step by step, straightens in posture, Keyser Soze-ing, and stops all tall and proud. Young, high cheek-boned, handsome.

This is where the Morricone kicks in, lets you know he's the hero.

He's striding toward a parked hovercraft, hopping in, dropping the sunglasses on the passenger seat.

"Hey mister! Thought you was blind?" A child of perhaps ten, the young girl talking about The Hood halfway up the bazaar, has caught up.

Chuckling, the man hops out of the hovercraft and settles onto one knee, eye level with the child. He grasps her hand and drops the coins from his tin into them, curling the girl's fingers around the pieces of copper. "Blind? Why, I'll have you know I can shoot an apple off a man's head at a hundred paces." The man winks, jumps back into the hovercraft, and revs off into the open plains, a drifter in the wind.

As the hovercraft skips up the lowered gangplank of the ship, the Meriman, a giant of a man with arms crossed, the light bouncing off his metal plating, waits.

"What're we doing on this backwater planet, Robin? No loot to split, nothing to steal. We said The Hood needs to lie low, not fall off the map." Unwinding his thick arms, the giant's left elbow and shoulder joints throw up sparks.

"That arm of yours playing up, Little John?" Robin nods at the malfunctioning synthetic, hops off the hovercraft, and locks it into its stall.

"Never mind my arm, Robin. Why are we here?" Little John disappears further into the ship without hearing an answer, tinny footsteps fading off. Robin follows, the gangplank rising behind him. He grimaces, knowing full well he needs to fess up. Trust is a rolling contract, not a binding agreement.

The Meriman is a long, slender ship, a converted freighter with a cargo hold down below, to boot. It's seen better days. Chipped paint, missing panels, and bits making noises ships shouldn't, by rights, make. It helps that Will Scarlett can fix anything with a screwdriver and a few whacks of his fist. Someone once said to Robin it was Will's autism makes him good with that kind of thing, but Robin figures it's just that Will likes seeing how things work. Even Will could only keep the ship in tolerable shape, though. One look around told you they were just getting by—skin of their teeth stuff. Escaping the empire never gets easier.

The Meriman is their noble steed, their Bullet, their Champion, but it needs putting out to pasture.

Robin hurries through the mess and bunks and into the cockpit. Little John and Will Scarlett, a young man with oil-smattered cheeks and wearing stained dungarees, await.

"I guess it starts by telling you my real surname is…Loxley," Robin says, flopping down into the third seat.

"As in…" Little John's eyes pop.

"As in Baron Loxley of Shearwood, right here on planet Knot. Yes, this is my home." Robin sighs the sigh of a guilty man.

"So, you're rich?" Will doesn't look up, but his dimples

deepen. He pulls a slender vape pipe from his pocket, inhales, and emits a stream of peachy smoke.

"Not exactly. My father and I didn't see eye to eye on a lot of things. He was always one of the better landowners, but that didn't make him good. I grew up wealthy, surrounded by poverty."

Little John's bulk casts a shadow across Robin, a lengthening shadow, his big bones creaking as he rises. "But that still doesn't tell us what we're doing here, Robin."

"Well, the Meriman has served us well, but we need something faster, better-equipped for smuggling and evading imperial star ships. And we owe the Mewvians after that tight call outside Braust-7. I thought perhaps my old man might see to support the prodigal son. And, you know, nice to see my childhood home after such a long time," Robin adds with a wistful smile.

Little John glances at the giggling Will, eyes all suspicious and squinting, and turns back to Robin.

"This is about a woman, isn't it?"

Marian bangs a hand against the steel door before flinging herself down onto the cell's bed. The only response so far was a guard yelling to pipe down, which, as the guard soon found out, triggers the opposite effect.

She doesn't so much consider herself stubborn as she does an obstacle beyond which no man can pass.

The heavy door, however, is an obstacle she herself cannot pass. Cold, unblinking, strong. Marian contemplates ways of escape. She thumbs her necklace pendant, silver against her midnight skin, knows what it really is. But the *clinkclinkclink* of heavy, metallic footsteps disturb her thoughts. They stop outside her cell.

"Are you being treated kindly, Marian?" a mellifluous voice calls through.

"I demand to speak with the Sheriff of Knot." Marian jumps upright and flashes angry eyes at the barred grille.

Two scarlet circles glare back. Two suns set against a pallid sky. This ghostly face is the only human part visible within an armoured suit, mostly black but with blood red plates around the biceps, forearms, calves, and thighs. The voice does not suit this militaristic and fearsome visage.

"Well, in a twist of good fortune, it seems I am the Sheriff of Knot, so you may relay any issues at your leisure." The voice still retains its lyrical quality, but its intonation, the syllables it stresses, lend it a threat she recognises, a threat she despises.

That Morricone comes on slow and in a deeper bass. The Sheriff is…the bad guy?

"I'd hardly say I'm capable of doing anything at leisure. Why am I here? I need to report an attack on Baron Loxley's compound. I do not know what happened to him, but men broke in, attacked the Baron's guards, and took many prisoners, including me."

"Yes, I am aware, Marian. I believe what you've failed to do is put two and two together. I'll leave you to give it a little think. In the meantime, I'm going to oversee this new zinc mine I've acquired." Those pearls of red disappear as the rusty cover scrapes across the grille.

Marian grips her necklace pendant tight, taps her forehead

against the cold steel—no doubt coated in zinc, one of its profitable uses—and steps back. So much for the Sheriff overseeing law and order in the name of the empire. This one has gone rogue.

"Something's wrong. Bring her down just over this ridge, Little John, and engage the cloaking device." Robin notes the presence of imperial guards around his father's compound and the mine to the south.

"She'd better be worth it, Robin." Will grins. His fingers dance a merry dance across the control panel. The command shifts the light spectrum of the outer panels, creating a mirror effect rendering the ship hard to spot with the naked eye. It knocks the Meriman off radar too.

Settled upon the sandy plains, Robin and Little John disembark, pull on goggles and hoods to protect them from swirls of grit.

If it weren't for the adverse weather, Robin would chew on a toothpick, roll it round his teeth in a charming grin.

"We need to clean these damn things. All I can smell is last month's sweat," Little John declares, stomping off to the top of the ridge, binoculars at the ready.

"You always stomp, you know, old friend?" Robin follows.

Through the extended vision of the binoculars, Little John and then Robin survey the operation. A layered canyon, a spiral of shelves. At the bottom, miners trudge single file into the underground abyss marshalled by imperial troops—designated by red and white uniforms—under a veil of discontent.

"Tell Will to sit tight. There's a man in the saloon I think we need to see." Robin runs back down to the ship. Little John senses another escapade in the offing, shakes his head, and grunts.

"Obviously, I'm not going in. These tunnels are notoriously unsafe. I'd rather not be crushed by tonnes of collapsing zinc and rock, thank you very much," the Sheriff spits.

The captain, hitherto unknown to the Sheriff, wilts under that glare. Workers file past, eyes dead ahead, though they overhear everything. Being miners, they know the score: profits over lives.

Footsteps pounding scratchy sandy gravel, sweat shimmering on foreheads and the backs of necks, hard work, tough conditions.

Shadow shrouds the land. Not from the swirling sandstorms of the plains, but from the sudden appearance of the Sheriff's capital starship. Wide and disc-like, its gleaming guns look like the short, spindly legs of an insect. It hovers above Shearwood, watchful, ominous.

"If it isn't safe, surely we should close the mine, sir?" the captain says without confidence.

"And what use is a closed mine, captain? Fortunately, it is not your job to think. Speak with the foreman. Whatever he tells you is the expected productivity, insist he double it. Deserters will be shot on sight."

As the Sheriff turns, another soldier skids to a halt before him and salutes in one fluid motion. "Sir, we've received reports that The Hood has been spotted here in Shearwood."

"Send, let's say, six scouts into town. We'll soon flush the rat out, but we can't alert him too quickly to our presence." Interesting, but did he *want* to capture The Hood here? Drawing attention to this operation from the powers that be might alert them to certain schemes. His fingers curl up then stretch out several times like talons snatching at prey.

Taking The Hood down, though...

The Sheriff flicks a switch in his suit's wrist. Two thrusters emerge from the shell of his lower back and spit smoke and flame. He blasts off into the sky.

Workers stop in their tracks, bump into each other, mutter jokes about flying pigs. For most, a domestic android is the extent of the technology they encounter daily. To see a man flying is the equivalent of the absent gods waking from their slumber and rising in the form of giants to take back control of the galaxy.

The captain salutes the Sheriff, drops his hand quickly when he sees it ignored, and barks orders at those nearest him to get back to it.

Marian's attempts to start conversation with the guard are fruitless. She considers talking to the cell door, figures it wittier than her captor. What she really needs is an opportunity. And she smells one approaching.

"Food, ma'am. Step back against the wall," a nasally voice calls.

A heavy bar grunts and the door swings in. Dumping a bowl

of odorous slop on the ground, a short, sweaty man in a faded grey uniform ogles Marian.

"Oh, wow, it really is you. I can't tell you how pleased I am to see you," he says, head dipping into a bow.

Marian twists her pendant, pulls something from it. "Likewise." She lunges. The taser connects with the man's neck before he has time to yell out. A sharp zip and he collapses into the soup, splattering the floor.

Marian slips behind the door.

"What's going on?" her loquacious guard friend calls, stumbling over the stunned cook.

Taser resting between her fingers, hand balled into a fist, Marian punches the guard in the solar plexus, just beneath his armour. His flesh vibrates before he, too, falls to the floor, face down in a puddle of soup.

Marian clips the taser back into place in her necklace pendant—a handy little device she employs whenever a man's hands wander—and picks up the guard's rifle phaser. She doesn't plan to blast her way off the ship, but if it comes to it then better armed than not.

And that whistling music kicks in again, reveals Marian is pretty badass. Probably a short freeze frame of her staring right into the camera, then flicking her braids out behind her.

She steps out into a grey corridor of panels and pipes—no prisoner hold is going to be pretty—and sets off. Any starship worth its salt has escape pods, she reasons.

Robin parts the saloon doors and whips his poncho over his shoulder. The music stops, the piano-playing android lapses motionless. A sea of faces turns to the entrance, wonders if these strangers intend to intrude on the merriment and mirth. Vape trails wisp upward, disperse like magical dust into the atmosphere. A service bot drifts through the haze holding its drinks' tray steady.

Robin remembers Little John is 6'5 with metal-plated bionic arms, knows the faces are staring for the obvious reason: is this man here to fuck up our favourite watering hole?

Robin and Little John nod, make for the bar. Voices rise up again, the piano android revitalises, and music kicks in as if nothing happened.

"What'll it be, boys?" the bartender says, rag in one hand, glass in another. As is obligatory, the rag is dirtier than the glass.

"Looking for Old Tuck," Robin says, leaning across the counter as if in conspiracy.

The barman looks over to a corner booth and nods. "Where he always is. Don't you boys go causing a ruckus now, we're a friendly place here."

Robin winks at the barman, sees him squinting as if remembering something—remembering some*one*—and heads for the corner booth.

An old man, rotund and rosy-cheeked, stark white bristles flanking his deep-blue face, watches them sit down without complaint or reaction. His arm rests on a dog-eared book—a bible of the old gods. A minute passes by in which nothing is said. Little John glances all nervous from Robin to Old Tuck—of Mewvian extraction, John thinks—and back again. They're in each other's eyes, of which the old man has four. Tuck fumbles for his drink, not looking away from Robin, and finally catches his fingers in the glass loop. He slurps a gulp of ale, lets it slide down his chin. He plops the glass down, then burps. A slow grin shoves up his cheeks, and the two men laugh and clasp hands.

"I knew you'd be back one day. Knew it, I did! Where you been, Robin? Heard a rumour or two, o' course..." Old Tuck glances about, checks that no one is listening in.

"No doubt you heard the truth, knowing you, you old scoundrel. You're looking at The Hood. Smugglers extraordinaire, relievers of wealth, and dispensers of necessary aid."

"And thorn in the empire's side," Old Tuck adds. "Hey, come here. Come on, lean in." The old man struggles forward, head halfway across the table, eyes conspiratorial. Robin reciprocates, while Little John clenches his fists.

Old Tuck taps Robin on his nose and grins. "Boop," he says, then falls about laughing. Gasping for breath, Old Tuck settles back into his seat. "Used t' do that when you was just a whippersnapper running in between them market stalls. Now, what brings you back here, anywho?"

Six imperial hovercrafts pull up on the edge of town. Shearwood is two long rows of buildings with a strip of bare land running through it. The poor shanty houses sit behind the rows, and the rows are all the shops a town needs: bank, general store, hairdresser, doctor's surgery and, of course, the saloon. At the far end of the strip is the market, open most days, where passing traders set up.

Six soldiers jump off the six hovercrafts, boots knocking up dust clouds.

A few citizens spy them and run indoors. One woman hanging clothes squeals an *oh, my,* before swooning. Another spits on the floor in the direction of the soldiers, turns her back on them.

A tumbleweed blows across the way and disappears behind the saloon. This is where the whistling music kicks in, indicates these guys bring trouble.

At least, these guys *think* they're bringing the trouble.

"So, my father's dead?" Robin says, fingers scrunching up his eyes as if they're suddenly itchy. "I should have been here."

"By the good book, I wish it weren't so." Old Tuck taps the bible on the table with a stumpy finger. "But there's nothing could be done, my boy. You'd only have been killed too. They're doing something dodgy over here, Robin. Over the years we had lotsa refugees land here since it's a safe place. Me included. Well, lotsa talk of leaving going on. If I was you, I'd get outta here while the going's medium."

Robin and Little John exchange a glance.

"This is what we do," Little John says, mouth curling up at the corner. A spark skips up from his shoulder, makes the old man jump.

Whispers grow louder around the bar, like grasshoppers out in the bush. The music stops again. Cards and money vanish from tables, slide into secret drawers ready for such occasions.

The saloon doors whip inwards, flushing the smell of stale beer round the place. Six imperial soldiers in familiar red and white armour step in. Each holds a rifle phaser.

"We are here on behalf of the empire." All six soldiers salute at this. Robin and Little John chuckle at the absurdity. "We have reason to believe a wanted criminal known as The Hood is hiding in town. Those who have information should step forward now. Else our trigger fingers might…slip."

Silence. Circle the room right here, zoom in on the nervous, tick-riddled faces of the locals. Because they don't know The Hood from Adam. Least, they don't realise they do.

Robin pulls his legs up from beneath the table, hops up onto his seat, and leaps over the gasping Little John. No one else moves. His poncho settles and his fingers twitch by his holstered pistol phaser. His eyes narrow.

"Who are you?" the first soldier says. Probably the leader.

"Such an inane question. I'm The Hood, of course. At your service. Or, rather, at the service of the people right here in this lovely saloon. I guess maybe they don't remember me so well, but I'm from these parts. As I understand it, you killed my father. Maybe not specifically you. But you, the empire, killed him."

Lots of whispers and exclamations follow. Eureka moments of recognition flush through the saloon's patrons. Ageing down the unshaven face of this handsome rogue, they find something they recognise.

The first soldier steps forward, pulls electronic handcuffs from his belt. "We can do this the easy way or the hard way."

Robin intertwines his hands, cracks his knuckles like a concert pianist readying to play a masterpiece. "Funny, I was going to say the same thing to you."

A moment of silence, a stopgap between Robin's last quip and the action to ensue. This moment is necessary because it allows everyone in the present time to consider what's about to happen. They know there's going to be a gunfight. The bartender knows glasses are going to be smashed and tables broken. Robin knows he's going to dive aside while unholstering and firing his weapon just as Little John and Old Tuck fire a volley while crouched in the booth. The soldiers get that sinking feeling that they aren't facing one man, they're facing an army. And the three men nearest the door, all friends of the Baron, workers in his mine enjoying a day off, realise they're going to pick up their chairs and smash them over the soldiers' heads.

Blink and you'll miss it.

Robin leaps and fires. Being the sharpest shooter in the western universe, his shot strikes the leader square in the chest and launches him through the air and clattering through the saloon doors. The doors swing in and out. The handcuffs land in someone's drink.

Little John and Old Tuck fire shots that take down two soldiers before they can even raise their rifle phasers in anger.

And the bartender cries out in despair as three of his lovely chairs shatter after crashing across imperial heads.

Robin climbs to his feet, nods to Old Tuck, then strides across the quiet saloon, Little John falling in step. He steps over a prostrate soldier, blushes at the mess, and turns to the bartender.

"Tie these goons to their hovercrafts, point them to the desert, and punch the accelerator."

Robin steps toward the door and stops once more. Probably the perfect time to be twisting a toothpick between his lips.

"Oh, and put those chairs on my tab."

"Sir, we've picked up something strange on the radar," someone squeaks, well aware of what happens when you address the boss in the bridge.

The Sheriff stalks across the deck, black cape cresting in his wake like a tsunami. His weighty steps—for he is fused with his armoured suit—clatter like stones against a window.

He stands above the squeaking radar officer silently awaiting further comment.

"Ahem. Yes. Just a click or so south of the zinc mine, a dot has appeared and disappeared several times. We considered it simply a glitch the first time, sir, but now we aren't so sure." The officer glances around at his colleagues, his eager eyes searching for support and finding, instead, the tops of heads.

"I wonder… It does, of course, mean causing a scene. Here, of all places. But…we can navigate those choppy waters later on," the Sheriff mutters, fingers caressing his chin in deep thought, brow creasing. "That, young officer, is a malfunctioning cloaking device. Only people who really don't want to be found activate such a device while lounging on a tiny planet like Knot. You two, over there, have this man thrown in the brig. He should have made the connection himself. And then send two squads down to the coordinates of this ship. It will not be visible, but don't worry, you'll still bang into it somehow."

The young radar officer cries out about unions as two soldiers grip him beneath the armpits and drag him away.

And we're back looking at the face of the Sheriff. Pale to the point of illness, lips stark. And ruby red eyes glowing sharp. Those stark lips curl into a smile. Things are coming together nicely, he thinks. Capture The Hood, dreaded space pirate, consolidate ownership of the Shearwood mine while keeping the higher-ups at bay, and live like a king.

A smile wipes off easy as chalk from a chalkboard.

"She's gone, sir. The prisoner is gone!" cries a soldier. He skids to a halt, throws that salute up in one fluid motion. He has rushing about down to a T.

"We have a lot of prisoners, you imbecile! *Which* prisoner is missing?" The Sheriff can't stop the sardonic quips from spitting like cobra venom, but his expression says he knows.

"Marian, sir. Marian is gone. And so is escape pod alpha."

A bright dot in the sky. A star winking, perhaps? No, the dot glows brighter, grows larger.

A thin reverberation and a cascade of sand indicate where the dot becomes a solid spherical ship and lands.

Two hovercrafts slow up, having spotted the bright dot, and tracked its trajectory. In goggles and bandanas, the two men astride the hovercrafts cannot hear each other above the irate sandstorm. One is gesturing to where the spherical ship has landed, the other—giant bionic arms flailing as if to suggest something is a terrible idea—is less enthusiastic.

The smaller man wins. The crafts drift on a new course, through the storm and over the crest of a steep dune, then descends toward the crash-site. Smoke unfurls from a busted panel. It has imperial markings.

Behind this dune the winds are weak, the planet settled. Little John and Robin pull down their bandanas and goggles, approach the ship with hands skittishly hovering by their pistol phasers.

A puff of steam and a thick plexiglass panel rises.

You expect to see a well-heeled, firm calf make its sultry way out, followed by a bare knee, the whole experience smooth as silk, until an emerald-green dress resting halfway up a thigh emerges.

Instead, a brown leather boot clunks into the sand, dark trousers part of a set of overalls, sleeves folded up to the elbow, follow. Dark braids swing low and then back, and big brown eyes fix on the two strangers approaching.

She sighs. Can't catch a break. Until, at second glance, one of the faces is familiar, haunting. A ghost from the past.

Whistles ring out, a flute or something plays a love theme. The epic love story readies.

"Robin?"

"Of all the sand dunes on all the planets in the universe, you go and crash land into mine." Robin strides with confidence, a wide grin touching his eyes, arms out expecting a hug.

Marian stomps through the sand and tackles Robin to the ground and starts punching him in the head.

The love theme stops abruptly.

"You bastard! Where were you?" she screams. Little John lifts her with ease and dumps her still screaming into the sand without ceremony or concern.

Robin scrambles to his feet. "I realise this isn't ideal, Marian."

"Isn't ideal?" Marian spits sand, glares at the man holding his hands up before her. "They broke in, Robin! They murdered the Baron in his own home. And what have you been doing? Galivanting across the universe drinking, chasing women? No doubt having a great time."

"You don't know where we've been," Little John growls, fists clenching, unclenching, and sparks leaping from shoulder and elbow joints.

"It's okay, Little John. Maybe I deserve it. Maybe I was just a silly kid when I left Knot desperate for adventure. But I'm not that kid anymore. My father is dead, and I intend to avenge him."

Marian snorts, crosses her arms. "Oh, I suppose you intend to go up against the empire, eh? Still full of it, I see."

Little John growls disapproval and Robin raises his hand, quiets him. But their conversation is interrupted—an explosion to the north, not far off. Soon after, an imperial transport jet flies off toward the capital ship.

"The mine." Marian gasps.

"No." Robin closes his eyes, concentrates. "The Meriman."

Little John's eyes are wild. "Will!"

"We need to scour the planet for that little bitch. The people love her. The people will *follow* her. The longer she's free, the quicker she spreads her seditious bile. I can't allow so much noise to be made."

Screens blink and machinery hums like tinnitus. Then, a disturbance from the corridor, the wails of a prisoner, the door sliding shut with a pop.

Will Scarlett is bleeding from a gash above his eye, yet he still struggles, wriggles like an eel.

"We blew out the ship's guns, sir. This one put up a fight, but he's no fighter." A small group of soldiers in red and white stand proud in a huddle around Will, chests out, backs straight.

"And what have you brought him to me for? Toss him in the brig. If I'm right, The Hood will come to reclaim his companion. Our fleet will intercept, and I'll be the man who captured the dreaded Hood. Life is good. What are you staring at? I thought I told you to throw this man in the brig? Away with you!" the Sheriff snaps, falling out of a daydream.

The huddle of soldiers frogmarch Will away, their collective hubris popping as easy as a balloon. Will cries out, tears flowing.

He knows Robin is on his way. He just wants to be back on the Meriman to fix the guns, patch their trusty steed up, then blast off to their next adventure. He's thrown into a cell, cold iron stinging his face. He closes his eyes, screams into his chest.

Smoke billows into the air, a dark vortex emanating from the Meriman's flanks.

"Damn it," Robin curses, tapping into the flight log. "The

cloaking device malfunctioned. Probably picked us up on radar, sent someone to take a look."

"Wouldn't your friend have known that and moved position?" Marian gingerly touches a loose ceiling panel and eyes the wiring behind it as if it were a pit of snakes.

"Not Will, no. He wouldn't want to risk leaving us behind or stray too far from the plan," Little John says from deeper within the ship. "The guns are down, but no other damage. Strange. You'd think they'd have blown the Meriman to smithereens."

"Unless, of course, they think we'll hop on in and give chase. Maybe fall into a trap? No, they only disabled the guns so we'd approach them defenceless."

Robin stares out onto the sandy plains of his home planet. It's been a long time since he'd been here, a long time since that bored rich kid would get into scrapes with passing traders and their equally bored daughters. That Robin is gone.

"Priority is getting Will back." Little John collapses into a seat in the cockpit, dust kicking out from beneath the cushion. He readjusts, pulls something from beneath him. A slim vape pipe. Will's pipe.

"Priority is finding a way to stop the Sheriff exploiting Shearwood," Marian states.

Little John turns to face her.

"You can scowl all you want. Doesn't stop me being right." She crosses her arms, sticks her chin out like a dare.

"Now see here, I don't know who you think you are…"

Little John and Marian stand up, noses a yard or so apart, making their case loudly and firmly without taking notice of what the other's saying. Neither backs down, hands flipping this way and that.

But Robin isn't paying attention. He narrows his eyes. Deep in thought, his brain filters bad ideas out, keeps bits it likes, and forms them into a plan. Finally, he holds up a hand, hushes the squabbling pair.

"We can prioritise both."

Two imperial soldiers are guarding the mine entrance. It's quieter, just the two of them with little to do but scratch themselves and stare into space. One yawns, the other leans on his rifle phaser like it's a walking stick.

If some music kicked in, it'd sound ominous but jovial: these slickers are in for a rough ride.

A small transport craft waits beside a cluster of rocks on about the only flat space around. They're heading to the capital ship once the foreman surfaces.

A stone clatters off the ground, bounces away, and rolls to a stop.

"Where'd that come from?" the first soldier says.

"Heck if I know. Go check it out." The second pulls a vape pipe from his pocket, takes a deep drag, grins at his comrade. "Peachy."

The first soldier grumbles, leans his rifle against his shoulder, and rounds the corner all tentative, as if he suddenly remembers he's a professional soldier.

The second soldier watches his buddy disappear behind a

rocky wall, a section where the ridge dips. He puffs on his vape and relaxes. This is the life, or as good as he can expect.

A curt grunt and a gentle bumping sound around the corner cause the second soldier to rethink the good life. He shifts his phaser into a comfortable firing position, butt against his shoulder. Then he feels something cold, deeply cold, press against the back of his neck.

"I'd hold it right there, partner, if I were you," whispers a voice in his ear.

"This armour is flimsier than it looks and dreadfully uncomfortable," Marian proclaims, shaking her arms and legs. Her natural scowl, an invitation to her companions to comment at their own peril.

"Happy to swap places, princess," Little John mutters.

Given his tree trunk, metal-plated arms, it's agreed Little John stays in the transport ship. If necessary, he pretends to be the foreman. Robin and Marian wear the red and white uniform of the imperial soldiers, those borrowed from the two knuckleheads gagged and tied up and lying on a rocky shelf above the zinc mine entrance.

"You sure you can find the brig again?" Robin asks in the nicest, softest tone he can muster.

"No trouble," Marian shoots back, still smarting from Little John's 'princess' jibe.

"You ever wonder what I was getting up to?" Robin inches

closer to Marian. The ship has a small cockpit, then two lines of benches with belts and handholds for when things get rough. Little John is at the controls.

"I figured you were dead, Robin. No word in what, seven years? Anyway, I've been too busy. With you gone, your father wanted someone who could eventually take over for him."

"And that was you?" Robin dials down the surprise in his voice, but it doesn't go undetected.

"Yes, it was me. And a damn good job I'd do too. But he became paranoid near the end—rightly so, apparently. Had cameras installed everywhere, just sat watching them. I was running the entire settlement, really, trying to help struggling families, keep the business running smoothly. So, to be blunt, Robin, no, I haven't thought of you much." Marian stares into her boots, knows this is a lie, a necessary lie.

"I thought about you. And coming home. But the longer I was away, the harder it became, the less connected to Knot and Shearwood I felt. You have me all wrong, though. Little John, Will, me, a few others, we started something. First, just a few petty robberies from landowners. Then it started to grow, we gained a few members. Started smuggling goods to some of the far-flung planets, the ignored places the empire doesn't care to care for."

"Great. So the big reveal is you've become a criminal. Well done, you," Marian says, turning away.

"I thought you'd be impressed. We're making a real difference."

"I'm sure you've got a nice retirement fund set up. Looks like we're nearly here." Marian stuffs her hair into the helmet as best she can. The visor covers her eyes, the lower half of her face visible. "How do they even keep these things on?"

"Gravity and burden," Robin mutters, jamming the bulky red and white on.

Marian shifts around on the bench, eyes flitting back and forth. Robin seems deep in thought. She plays the conversation in her head, wonders if she's missing something, some vital point.

Quietly. Ever so quietly. The love theme plays.

A small command centre, a curve of glass built into oppressive grey with red and white stripes, overlooks the hangar bays of Sheriff Knot's capital starship. Jets are set out in rows, ready to be called upon for aerial combat. To the right are the transports, blockier and cumbersome in comparison.

"They're back early," a nondescript officer states after a glance down. He nods at the soldier by the entrance. "Go sign them in."

Robin has swapped with Little John, manoeuvres the transport into bay 34 at the request of the command centre, who guided them on the radio once they passed through the deflector shield.

A solicitous soldier approaches. "Game time," Robin says.

"The Hood enters play." Little John guffaws gently. Giant that he is, his laughter is a rumbling that could be mistaken for a rockslide. He slips Will's pipe to Robin, who pockets it.

"The Hood? As in galactic smuggler, friend of the poor and destitute, The Hood?" Marian's eyes are like stars.

Now, that love theme is kicking in, a bit louder this time, a bit more defined.

"Who else could it be?" Robin laughs, understands the earlier confusion. There's knocking at the transport door. "Ready?"

And then the Morricone flute starts, that there coyote whistling because it's time for the final act.

The transport door opens and a single soldier strides in, upright and proper. She glances around with the imperiousness of one accustomed to upholding tiny, insignificant rules. In another life, she works in a doctor's surgery, but here, she's a soldier of the empire.

"Where is the foreman?" she demands.

"I am the foreman," Little John declares. He stands and casts a great shadow.

"Your report?"

Little John's eyes shift side to side like a pendulum. "All is... well?"

"Not an especially detailed report. And where is the previous foreman? Why isn't he here?" Her hands grip her rifle phaser a little tighter, her eyes focus a little harder.

"Screw it, let's do it my way," Little John says. A boulder of a fist rises, falls onto the rounded top of a red helmet with sufficient force to crumple the helmet wearer. He picks up the two-handed weapon. "You go and find Will. I'll hold the fort."

"Subtle," Marian quips, then descends the walkway from the transport. Robin nods and smirks at Little John, then follows.

The hangar is vast and echoey, broad and wide and grey, red, white. Above them, an officer in a uniform more official looking than the basic soldier's is staring. Even from a distance, there's a visible vein popping in the man's temple. Lawmen are forever apoplectic over something, Robin thinks. He hopes this one buys the ruse, and assumes Marian is the person he sent to check on them.

They reach an entrance, which opens through motion sensor, and they're in a corridor. Cameras glint in the corners where the ceiling meets the wall. Staff run back and forth—nothing like fear to put a spring in your step.

"This way," Marian whispers.

Robin's heart beats fast, pumps tension through his veins. "Lead on."

Confidence tricksters know the art of the trick is a display of confidence, nothing more. Robin and Marian enter the brig, that dingy corridor of exposed pipes lined with cells. The man on duty is, as is customary for jailers, asleep. The key hangs by his waist.

Not many imperial capital starships use old-fashioned lock and key, but Sheriff Knot is a keen study of the history of imprisonment and torture. He finds it alluring, the idea of a key scratching in the lock, the effect that desperate noise may have on a prisoner. Hence, heavy cell doors and old-fashioned keys.

"I'll slip them off his belt quietly," Robin whispers, tiptoeing forward.

Marian sighs, slips her hand beneath her armour, and twists and unclips something. "It'll be quicker my way," she says making no effort to lower her voice.

The jailer stirs as she approaches, garbles some confused

words. Marian lightly slaps his face three times. "Wakey, wakey," she says, smiling into his sleep-crusted eyes.

"Who are you?"

Marian zaps the man beneath his armpit. "That's no concern of yours."

She replaces the taser in its pendant hidey-hole, tosses the keys to Robin, and leans against the wall by the door, arms crossed, cheek hitched up with a crooked grin.

"You used to be such a sweet thing," Robin says, checking the cells. He finds the one Will sits in, pulls his helmet off, unlocks the gate.

"Robin!"

There's a whip flash that cracks through the open doorway. Robin tumbles backwards, landing on his caboose.

"Easy there, Will, easy. We aren't out of this yet."

"I'm sorry, Robin. I'm sorry," Will cries, his rosy cheeks more flushed than normal against his pallid skin, bright eyes twinkling with relief. He has a cut above his eye and a bruise beneath it. Robin brushes Will's hair aside, examines the injuries.

"No need to be sorry, Will. It's me that's sorry. Let's get you out of here. We've got a busted up Meriman that needs your special brand of magic, kid." Robin pulls Will to his feet and passes him the vape pipe. He inhales, breathes out calm, peachy goodness.

Reality, that is to say, Marian, punctures the fruit cloud.

"Hi, Will, I'm Marian, nice to meet you. Get yourself into the guard's uniform quick. We're gonna have to move fast. I don't like how easy we've made it here." She opens the door, pokes her head out into the hallway. "Ghost town. Real strange."

"Maybe we're getting lucky?" Will mumbles while pulling

on an ill-fitting pair of white boots.

"You don't *get* luck," Robin says. "You make your own."

Little John pokes his head above the transport's controls, surveys the hangar. A few engineers and officers mill about. Up in the control centre someone is gesticulating wildly, but there is little other activity.

Something catches his eye. That usually means trouble.

The fuel gauge is near empty.

"Damn!"

Sheriff Knot's ruby red stare bores into the officer's brain.

"What do you mean we've lost *another* prisoner?" the Sheriff growls with the guttural, visceral rage of a starving bear.

"The man on guard was stunned…again, sir. One of the cells was open. It's, uh, the young man found in the cloaked ship down near Shearwood mine. The one you thought was a friend of The Hood. It seems he has been sprung, sir. An inside job. The cameras picked up two soldiers entering the brig, and three leaving it." The officer shrinks with every word, every explanation.

Sheriff Knot feels sweat slip down his forehead. The suit is spectacular to look at, but it's hot. "And can you explain how you have acted upon this information?"

"Sir? We've come to tell you." The officer smiles nervously, feels the size of a pea.

Sheriff Knot sighs heavily.

Of course, the Sheriff could exercise his patience and good nature. Could accept the work environment he's created isn't conducive to assertiveness and independent thought. The Sheriff can choose this path.

Instead, he pulls his pistol phaser and fires a shot through the officer's forehead. The hole is the size of a pea.

"Someone clean this up. You there, you're promoted. Gather two squads and follow me to the aircraft hangar. The only way off this ship is by another ship since those escape pods are disabled. We'll intercept them."

Robin, Marian, and Will walk out into the hangar and know something is wrong immediately. Little John is holding a hose against the transport with one bionic arm and throttling a soldier with the other.

They break into a run. When people start running, bedlam tends to break loose.

Battle cries come from the corridor and then phaser blasts litter the air, little dashes of light rushing all scattery in the same direction, like salmon upriver.

Fortunately, unnamed soldiers have never knowingly hit a target they were aiming at.

Robin and Marian fire back as they race across the tarmac.

They duck behind crates, cover Little John while he refuels. Will boards the transport first, rushes to the cockpit, flicking switches and readying for flight.

Little John yanks the hose free and clamps shut the fuel cap. "Onto the ship!"

"Go." Robin nods at Marian, shooting covering fire toward the wall of red and white soldiers. Behind them, he sees him. It must be him. Dressed in thick black armour with shimmers of red, ruby red marbles set in a ghost face. He's hanging back because he likes to let others do the rough work.

"Come on!" Little John fires his pistol, pulling Robin back with his free hand.

They're up the gangplank, readying to close the door. Little John bends down, uses his might to rip free the gangplank from the ship. Robin slams the button to close the door as a dash of yellow light spits through it.

Little John grunts and topples backwards.

The mouth of the pistol phaser could well be a smile. The black-gloved hand in which it rests shakes. Up the armoured arm, two plates of red the colour of that they wish to spill. And, finally, the Sheriff's face, teeth bared jagged like a cave of stalactites and stalagmites, heavy breaths squeezing out between them.

"I got one, which is more than can be said for these clowns."

He watches the transport blast through the portal at the end of the runway and venture out into space. The Hood is bold, no doubt about that. Who sneaks *onto* an imperial starship, a capital ship at that?

Nervous footsteps rattle behind him.

The control room officer shuffles along the corridor, clinging to the visor of his red cap as if its loss will strip him of all power and authority. His jaw's loose and his mouth hangs open. You can't smoke on the job, sadly.

The Sheriff notices his arrival. "I want four squads packed onto transports and ready to go, pronto. They'll have to go back to Shearwood. Aargh, too much noise. We need to squash these rodents before word spreads of a disturbance."

The control room officer nods and scurries off. It's always rats and rodents with the Sheriff. He wonders what he's got against them.

Little John groans with the pain as they clatter through the saloon doors, having landed the ship at the far end of the long, thin strip that is Shearwood's heart.

"Is there a doctor in the house?" Robin says to the bartender, who rushes to help carry Little John through.

"Let's take him to the back room. Doctor Denewton, come with us!" A well-dressed Grick man—four arms are useful in surgery—stands and rushes to join them at the bartender's request, while Old Tuck moves faster than he's moved in years to accost Robin.

"What's going on, my boy?" he cries, ale-tinged spittle flying from his blue lips.

Robin allows the doctor to take Little John by the shoulder, then turns to Will. "Go and help with Little John. You know the circuitry of his synthetics far better than anyone else. That shot hit him around the shoulder, probably messed with the wiring. Listen to what the doctor tells you, and don't be afraid to speak up." Robin puts his hand round Will's cheek, fingers round the back of his head. Their eyes lock, a rarity. "I'm sorry for leaving you, Will. It won't happen again."

Will nods, manages a smile. He rushes off into the backroom, following Little John and the doctor. The bartender re-emerges a moment later.

Marian watches on, drifts into the crowd. This is not the boy that left Shearwood seven years ago, not even close.

All eyes in the saloon are on Robin, who spins slowly, cinematically, poncho flaring as he goes. Then he turns to Old Tuck.

"The Sheriff will be hot on our tails. He's rotten and you all know it. No one will be safe. What I'm proposing won't make you any safer, might even draw some imperial heat. But you'll be free. Will you hear me out?" Robin says, eyes flitting from the bartender to Old Tuck.

Old Tuck puffs out his chest, four eyes all stern. "The Loxley name still carries weight around here, my boy. And there's more than just a little discontent round these parts. Say your piece."

Robin grins that devil-may-care grin, the one that hitches up on the hero's face when he's ready to do some of that there heroism.

The screech of the chair on the floor, the thumps of Robin's boots upon it, are all there is to hear. Silence, an intake of breath, more silence. Robin speaks.

Two further imperial transports land beside the abandoned ship on the edge of town. Twenty-four soldiers file off like the rows of Shearwood miners, then settle into blocks of six.

Sheriff Knot steps off, glances around with those ruby red eyes. His thoughts turn to blood.

"We search the town top to bottom. They're in there—"

A figure walks into the centre of the throughfare, and stands with the setting sun against his back. He casts a long shadow.

"Proceed. Hold your fire. Let him shoot first," the Sheriff says.

The four squads of soldiers take tentative steps toward town, growing in confidence facing a lone man. They pass the building line, crossing into the tunnel that is the town.

A tumbleweed flits across the way.

The lone man edges backwards. He stays facing the oncoming soldiers. Sees the Sheriff remain at the edge of town, out of the action, exactly where he expects him to be.

The soldiers march on. They're coming up on the saloon, which is to their right. All is still.

A shrill whistle breaks the silence. The figure before them drops his fingers from his mouth, sprints off to the side, and disappears down an alley.

The soldiers start to react, start to break rank and give chase. But then they hear it—a symphony of bumps and thumps and breaking glass. All around the dark mouths of rifle and pistol phasers smile at them, that evil smile only a weapon can give. The squads feel small, feel trapped, see enemies on all sides.

This is an ambush.

On either side of the saloon doors are an old man and a young woman. Marian and Old Tuck—each has one hand in the air, a pistol phaser in the other. They swap a glance, a fiendish wink.

At the edge of town, Sheriff Knot stumbles backwards, and falls onto the hard dusty ground. Because this isn't the big gunfight. This is a massacre. He watches as dashes of yellow light engulf his search party. Red and white uniforms drop in droves like chess pieces mercilessly taken, knocked down.

He scrambles upright, turns to run back to the ship.

The whistling wind picks up, the beat of drums, and that there coyote flute howls. Not the deep bass, but the flute. This is the great crescendo, right when the Morricone peaks.

Robin, The Hood, stands between Sheriff Knot and his ship.

"I assume it was you," Robin says in a blank tone. "You killed my father, Baron Loxley? Rather, I assume you ordered someone to do it because that's more your style. Not one to get your hands dirty. Well, you're stuck now. Let's finish this with a good, old-fashioned duel, eh? Quickest draw will win."

Robin's eyes narrow because they know the score.

The Sheriff's hand twitches, goes for his pistol phaser. He's not one to fight fair, to adhere to the unwritten rules of a gunfight. Sheriff Knot thinks he's fast.

But Robin, The Hood is the fastest phaser in the western galaxy.

Six dashes of yellow light fly between them, all zipping one way. Sheriff Knot's weapon loosens from his hand as his body is cast backwards like the line of a fishing rod.

And there's something limp and lifeless on the end of this too.

Robin strides past the Sheriff, whose ruby red eyes are no longer so. They've gone black, the light has died.

Drink is thrown down gullets, cheers and songs ring out. Several men and women dance a jig by the old piano. Sat in a booth, Will Scarlett, Old Tuck, Little John—heavy bandages wrapping his limp right arm and shoulder—Marian, and Robin watch on with mirth.

"It's not going to be easy." Robin sips from his tankard, eyes Old Tuck.

"These parts were ready for a rebellion. With The Hood behind it, others will join. The gods may be absent, but maybe they'll return to support a worthy cause," Old Tuck says, tapping that bible again.

Robin smiles, nods. He nudges Marian in the ribs lightly. He stands and walks across the bar and through the saloon doors. Marian follows.

Stars are bright in the sky. A light breeze whistles through Shearwood.

Slowly, the piano and the singing dies away, and the love theme starts up. The two of them look at each other, their fingers entwining. The distance between them has never been shorter.

IMMORTAL KINGDOM

Chris Durston

Enkidu hated when the traders came.

He liked his life and his home and being reminded of the world outside was rarely pleasant. Everyone who came to visit looked down on this place and its inhabitants, treated them as if they were worthless. Enkidu suspected the outsiders didn't even consider them intelligent enough to register the constant insults.

As much as he disliked it, his people depended on trading with that world of glass and metal. They needed their strange machines for purifying the ruined soil, filtering the poisoned water, and protecting them from the cruel sunlight.

He rarely had to interact with the traders himself, fortunately. He was unimportant, someone with nothing to barter. He could just sit on the brown grass, and read, and do his best to ignore the squealing of magburst engines and polytex tyres as their ugly magnetic two-wheelers roared through. (These were words of which he knew the syllables but had no desire to learn the meaning.)

A cough caught his attention. "All right, Lud?"

He took a deep breath and looked up from his book to meet

134

the outsider's eyes—or, at least, the mirrored visor the man wore over his eyes. "How can I help?" he asked. The trader gestured with a black-gloved hand—they all wore black all over; no seams, just continuous tight black—to Enkidu's book.

"How much?"

"How...much?" Enkidu repeated slowly.

The trader's chin tipped up; Enkidu was certain he was rolling his eyes behind the visor. "How much for the book, Lud?"

"Oh, I don't..." He held it tighter. "I don't trade. I'm not a trader."

"So?" The man turned to his companion, a gleaming chrome thing in the shape of an impossibly tall, lean human. "This Lud think you need a permit to make a deal or something?"

The droid moved its arms, approximating a shrug. Enkidu shivered.

"Why do you want a book anyway?"

The trader guffawed. "What, you think I can't read?"

"Of course not. But can't you get any book you want on a screen?"

"Yeah, I could." The outsider gave an obnoxious sniff. "But I want *that* book." He pointed again.

"It's not for sale." Enkidu tucked it inside his shirt and stood up straight, hoping he looked braver than he felt.

"Well, then—" A whistle caught the trader's attention; he turned and scoffed. "Bastard thinks he can just call me over when he wants me?"

"Your social structure dictates that your leader can give orders," said the droid, "and that refusing can be quite painful." Enkidu squeezed his eyes tightly shut against its grating, unnatural voice. "Common sense protocols require that you obey."

"Ugh." The man gripped his left forearm with his right hand. It was the kind of involuntary movement Enkidu's late uncle often made, hand going to the deep scar on his chest whenever something reminded him of the injury. "Fine," the trader spat. "Keep your stupid book." He shook his head. "Gilgamesh is gonna fuck you all up anyway."

Enkidu tried to make his frown appear stern rather than terrified. "Who's Gilgamesh?"

The man stared at him for a second, then burst into raucous laughter. "Oh, you stupid, disconnected slime," he said, the insults falling easily out of his mouth. "You don't even know who he is. He's taking over, man. He's gonna rule everything soon, and when he does he's gonna kill anyone who disappoints him. He's ruthless." He chuckled. "I love it."

Enkidu inhaled deeply. "Where is this Gilgamesh?"

"I dunno. I just watch the streams." The trader leaned in; Enkidu resisted the urge to pull away. "But, y'know, I bet I could find out. In return for something."

The whistle repeated itself, and the trader's jaw tensed.

"You've got about five seconds to decide, Lud. Give me the book or don't."

Enkidu made his choice.

Gilgamesh thought of himself as a *good* ruler. Not good in the sense of morals or ethics, although he didn't think of himself as *bad* on those scales either. They simply weren't relevant, like trying to measure data by weight. No, Gilgamesh thought of himself as a *good* ruler in that he was an effective one. He was *good at ruling*, a belief borne out by his indisputable success conquering and governing vast territories.

If nothing else, Gilgamesh was a *winner.*

His kingdom spanned thousands of miles, more than anyone else's. Nobody dared to challenge him; at first, of course, there had been resistance, but he had quickly put a stop to that. None were willing to go as far as him in the pursuit of greatness, and none could compare to him.

All of which was to say that Gilgamesh was the number one ranked player of *Mesopotamia Online*, the biggest competitive online strategy game in the world.

It had been a long weekend at MesoCon, the official conference for developers, fans, and top players, and Gilgamesh was ready to go home. He'd signed hundreds of posters, played dozens of hours, streamed pretty much the entire thing. A huge, toothy smile had never left his face; he had to be engaging, even if doing it for three days straight was physically painful.

There was only an hour or so to go until MesoCon was due to wind down. Only an hour until he could throw his stuff in the autopack and wander exhausted to a plush electrojet cab to carry him back to his luxurious hotel suite. Gilgamesh could feel the muscles in his jaw and cheeks starting to stretch and slacken from being tight for so long. So close. He closed his eyes and let a quiet, natural smile relax his face. At least the chair they'd given him for his expansive booth was comfortable.

"Excuse me."

A man wearing what Gilgamesh might have described as a post-retro shabby throwback hyperantimodern suit—in other words, an ill-fitting shirt and trousers made of rough sackcloth with visible, uneven stitching—stood there in front of his booth. His ostentatious simplicity clashed tremendously with Gilgamesh's own on-trend silver and carbon fibre bodysuit. He looked less at home in the clean space, with its white lights and huge screens, than anyone Gilgamesh had ever seen.

"Oh, hey." Gilgamesh pulled out a poster and his photon-graver (more permanent than a permanent marker, and capable of drilling through rock given enough time). "Who should I make it out to?"

"What?" The man's nose twitched. "Are you Gilgamesh?"

"That's me." Gilgamesh gave him a questioning frown, albeit a professionally friendly one. "Most people who come up for an autograph know that already."

"I don't want…" The stranger shook his head, rubbing his upper arms through the rough fabric of his shirt. He looked young, about Gilgamesh's age, but his skin was lined and rough as if he hadn't had an exfoliadrone give him a proper scrub in weeks. "I came to ask you not to destroy my home."

That was a new one. "Why would I destroy your home?"

"The traders," the man said, sounding increasingly uncertain. "They said you were taking over. That you would take over my home."

"Wait," said Gilgamesh. "Where's your home?"

"You call us Luds."

Gilgamesh blinked. "For real?"

The newcomer nodded.

"How did you even get here?"

"I bartered for passage on a trader's vehicle." He swallowed, turning faintly green. "It was horrible."

Gilgamesh nodded. "So, er…why do you think I'm gonna take over Lud country?"

The man slapped his hands down on the table between them, leaning in. "Why would the trader lie to me?"

"I don't… Oh." Gilgamesh chuckled. "He means in *Meso*."

No response, as was perhaps to be expected.

"What's your name?" he tried.

"Enkidu."

"Right. So, Enkidu, it's…the game," Gilgamesh explained, gesturing to the hundreds of glowing screens around the conference hall. "I've been expanding territory, trying to undermine the alliance between J-Katz and Mintifr3sh. Ludmark would be a pretty sensible place to establish a hub if I want to consolidate, really set myself up to control the map."

The newcomer gave absolutely no indication of having understood a single word.

"Look," Gilgamesh said, sighing, "it's just a misunderstanding. I play this game where you try to control the world, but it's not real."

"A game," Enkidu murmured.

"Yup."

"If I defeat you in a game," Enkidu said, his voice suddenly stronger, "will you forego your efforts to subjugate my country and my people?"

"Um." Gilgamesh considered it. It was the most interesting thing to happen all weekend, if nothing else. "Sure. Do you even know how to play Meso, though?"

"How about chess?"

"Chess?" Gilgamesh let out an involuntary bark of laughter. "I don't think we have space to play chess in here."

Enkidu cast his gaze around the hall. "But…there is so much room."

"You really wanna find thirty other people, kit them all out with jetrails, get emergency vehicles in here, all that?"

"What?"

Something occurred to Gilgamesh. "What's chess?"

Enkidu frowned. "Two players move pieces over a board," he said slowly, as if expecting a trick question.

"Ah." Gilgamesh quickly pulled up a Z-Tube window on his computer and flipped the screen around to show Enkidu. "I think what we call chess is a bit different, maybe."

Enkidu stared, entranced, as the game unfolded: thirty-two players, sixteen in black and sixteen in white, rocketed around a huge bowl-shaped arena on jet-powered boots that left flaming trails behind them. Superimposed blue lines showed the areas of the playing field to which each player could move—and move they did. A game of chess was in constant, dizzying motion, and a full minute passing without any players battering into each other hard enough to risk permanent injury was considered exceptionally dull.

"This is…visceral," Enkidu breathed.

Gilgamesh grinned. "Brilliant, right?"

"Barbaric."

"Rich coming from someone who doesn't even have BaseNet," Gilgamesh muttered. He turned the screen back to himself, letting out an appreciative "ooh" as one of the black team's knights pulled off a perfect double-twisting flip over a white pawn and delivered a beautiful rocket-powered mid-air kick to the white queen's face. "Regular chess it is." He glanced upwards. "UTNAPI, get my friend here a nice seat and a chess set—old-timey chess."

"With pleasure," a deep, disembodied voice rumbled. The floor beside Enkidu rearranged itself; bits of tile detached and scurried up around each other until a simple chair stood beside him. The desk between them similarly shifted, and in moments a full chess set made of atoms that had just been serving as a tabletop lay atop the surface.

Enkidu looked as if he might be sick. "What just happened?"

"Oh, right." Gilgamesh waved a hand dismissively. "UTNAPI—that's the AI who runs pretty much everything, stands for...Universal...Something Personal Interface—anyway, I asked UTNAPI for some stuff and it made the stuff." He gestured to the chair and the chess set. "See?"

With an expression Gilgamesh usually associated with people who'd just realised they couldn't possibly hope to beat him in *Meso*, Enkidu sat. He gazed at the board for a moment, then turned it so the white pieces were on his side.

"If I win," Enkidu said, a little too loudly, "you will relinquish your efforts to conquer my lands."

"Sure," Gilgamesh agreed.

The game began. Enkidu tried to take control of the centre of the board early, but Gilgamesh refuted every attempt. When Enkidu castled to protect his king, Gilgamesh launched an assault with his queen and knights that forced the white king right into the corner and won the rook that had protected it. Enkidu tried a counterattack, forking Gilgamesh's king and a rook with his bishop, but Gilgamesh sacrificed the rook in favour of advancing a pawn towards Enkidu's end of the board, where it would become a queen in just two unstoppable moves.

Enkidu stared for several minutes, then tipped his king over. "I cannot defeat you here." He stood and turned away, head bowed, shoulders quivering.

With a thought, Gilgamesh turned off the chess engine that had been feeding every move to him through his ocular overlay. Something about the victory felt hollow—sure, he hadn't really *earned* it, but that was par for the course. It still usually felt good to win; he'd still expected to feel satisfied at thrashing this odd stranger. But he didn't.

"Wait," he said. Enkidu turned back towards him. "I'm not gonna destroy your home. Not even in the game."

Enkidu's eyes glistened. "Why would you concede that when I lost?"

"It's not that big a deal," Gilgamesh said, shrugging. "I can do the same thing if I capture a few neighbouring spots on an alt server anyway." Enkidu shrugged; Gilgamesh raised a hand in apology. "You're…" He paused, searching for the right word. "Interesting."

Enkidu snorted. "Do not mock me."

"I mean it," said Gilgamesh. "I've never met…anyone like you." He wasn't sure what he meant by that: a Lud? Someone who was actually willing to put in real effort to play fairly? Or something else entirely, something less quantifiable?

The Lud took a long, uncertain breath. "I suppose you have

some hidden depths of your own," he said, nodding towards the board. Gilgamesh felt a brief flash of shame.

"Do you..." He hesitated. "Do you have anywhere to go?"

Enkidu bit his bottom lip, looking at the floor. "I suppose I do not," he said after a moment. "I had not really considered that."

Gilgamesh drew a breath to speak, then blinked a few times while he tried to work out whether he was certain about what he wanted to say. Eventually he decided that he wasn't, at all, but that he was doing it anyway. "My hotel room is, like, way too big," he found himself telling Enkidu. "There's a sofa in there if you want to stay. Just until you work out what you're... What you're doing next."

"I..." Enkidu's eyes flicked from Gilgamesh to the roof, to the floor, back to Gilgamesh. "I don't know if I can—"

"C'mon." Gilgamesh hopped over the table and clapped a hand on Enkidu's shoulder. The man tensed up as if expecting Gilgamesh to strike him. "You gotta watch a whole game of chess before you go, at least."

"Don't you have to be...here?"

Gilgamesh checked his clock overlay. "Nah. It's wrapping up."

Enkidu's shoulders relaxed. "Until I have a plan then."

Gilgamesh grinned. "Until then."

After eating a hearty dinner (every ingredient of which Enkidu had to ask Gilgamesh to identify) and watching a couple of brutal games of chess on the hotel room's wall-spanning display, Gilgamesh bid Enkidu goodnight, asked UTNAPI to set an alarm for the morning, and turned in, cosying up under his warm covers. He'd offered to ask the hotel for a thicker blanket for Enkidu—for a brief, strange moment, he'd even considered offering to share the bed—but the Lud seemed perfectly happy sleeping on the sofa in his sack clothes.

Gilgamesh waited until Enkidu's breathing deepened, then glanced over. His new roommate looked sound asleep. Perfect.

He called up NSNet in his overlay and rolled away, scrolling through videos until he found one he was in the mood for: a threesome with one woman and two men. He mentally selected its thumbnail and took a deep breath, preparing to enjoy himself.

The next second, the room lit up and the sounds of exaggerated moans and squeals filled the air. His overlay was still hooked up to stream straight to the screen.

Gilgamesh sat bolt upright, surprise and adrenaline scattering his thoughts so he couldn't focus enough to switch it off. Enkidu barrelled off the sofa, head swivelling around the room as if looking for threats. When he found none, his eyes finally turned to the screen.

"Oh, strange new world," he breathed, "that has such people in it."

Gilgamesh finally managed to pause the video. "Hey, I think I've seen that movie," he said, trying and failing to sound casual. "That was a quote from a movie, right?"

Enkidu didn't look at him. "Not quite."

"Er…" Several different sentences tried to come out of Gilgamesh's mouth at once, leaving him stammering. His cheeks felt impossibly hot. "So…this is awkward."

Enkidu turned his gaze sharply upon him. "What is this?"

"It's…" Gilgamesh frowned. "You mean… What's what?"

The Lud pointed at the image frozen on the screen. The penny dropped.

"Ohhhhh." Gilgamesh couldn't help but laugh. "You've never seen porn." He unpaused the video and watched with a sly grin as Enkidu's face ran through twenty different expressions in the space of a few moments. "You know what they're doing, right?" he asked over the groans.

"Of course!" Enkidu protested. "I've… But not like *this*."

"This isn't real," Gilgamesh said. "It's a performance."

"It looks real," said Enkidu dubiously.

"I mean, they're really…y'know. But it's all just a show for the cameras."

"Like a play."

Gilgamesh nodded. "Like a play."

Enkidu tore his eyes from the screen. "This is what the world is? This is what humans make and consume? As much violence and…" he waved at the screen, "*that* as can be squeezed into a frame?"

Gilgamesh turned the video off and the room went dark again. He could just about make out Enkidu's face still. "Yeah," he said. "I guess that's what we do."

A heavy breath that might have been half a sob reverberated from Enkidu. "I don't think I can go back to my world," he said softly. "I feel yours…changing me. Like the land and the grass and the old life would know I was no longer fit to be part of it."

Gilgamesh couldn't help but scoff. "What, just because you

know about porn now? Just because you've seen it?"

"I wish I had remained ignorant," Enkidu said quietly.

"That's so...oh, what's that old religion where we're all supposed to be condemned because someone millions of years ago found out something they weren't supposed to? Originalism, right?"

"I think I know it by a different name."

"Still," said Gilgamesh, "that's so originalist. You can't be bad or corrupt or whatever just from *having knowledge*. It's what you do with it."

Silence.

After a few long moments, Gilgamesh sighed and made to lie back down. "Eh. May as well turn in."

"What do you want?" Enkidu asked suddenly, clearly.

Gilgamesh paused, then sat up again. "What do I want?"

"From...the world, while you're in it. From life."

"I..." He thought about it for a moment, not because he didn't know what his answer was, but because he wasn't sure whether to be truthful. For some reason, this odd man's opinion was beginning to matter to him. "I want to be immortal," he said.

Enkidu didn't reply for a moment. "Immortal?" he asked eventually. "To live forever?"

"Yeah." Gilgamesh nodded, even though he knew Enkidu couldn't see him in the dark. "I want to survive until I can upload my consciousness so I can keep going on for...well, for always."

He could almost hear Enkidu's mind working. "Upload your consciousness," the Lud repeated after a moment.

"That's how it's gonna work, they reckon," Gilgamesh said. "We'll take our minds out of our bodies and put them somewhere they'll never decay or grow old."

"That doesn't sound like...living."

"I mean..." Gilgamesh stumbled, wondering for a moment what he did in fact mean. "I mean, finding a way to make a body live forever would be better. But, hey, if I can get my mind to stick around for long enough, maybe they'll work out a way to put it back into a better body eventually."

There was a long, smothering pause.

"What about you?" Gilgamesh asked eventually. "What do you want?"

"I want to keep my land and my people safe," Enkidu said without hesitation. "I no longer feel I can be part of it, but I still want to protect it." He sighed heavily; the sound disappeared into the dark, where it was muffled into nothingness. "There are many things my people need, and though we can make or find much of it ourselves, there are problems we need your machines to solve. Problems we inherited from you, of course."

Sensing he wasn't done talking, Gilgamesh waited quietly for him to continue.

"The water is impure," Enkidu muttered. "The soil poison. The sky unbearable."

An idea that might have been incredibly foolish struck Gilgamesh. "You know," he said, leaning over the edge of the bed towards Enkidu in the darkness, "there's a legend of a place. A factory. I never believed it really existed—they say that's where they're making the Seed, the code and the hardware that'll make immortality possible—but some of the stories about it say they're not just working on immortality for individuals there. That they've got all kinds of tech in development for undoing the damage to the planet, more permanently."

"If it is real," Enkidu said quietly, "they would never give those things to those who needed them. Not without asking far too much in return."

Gilgamesh grinned. "No, they probably wouldn't."

"Why do you sound happy about that?"

"Because it means the best thing we could do would be to go and steal them, and that sounds fun as shit."

Gilgamesh's night vision had got just about sharp enough to detect Enkidu's eyebrows raising. "You want to go and rob this factory?"

"I don't know if I have anything better to do with my life, to be honest." He meant it: something about the way Enkidu had played fairly and lost against an unfair opponent had wormed its way into his brain. Like that was the more...*honourable* option, or something stupid like that. Like winning might not be more important than playing the *right* way.

Enkidu snorted. "You are not what I was expecting," he said.

"I'll take that as a compliment."

The Lud exhaled, then climbed back onto the sofa. "If you still want to do this when we wake," he said, "then perhaps you can show me your plan and I shall consider coming along."

"Awesome," said Gilgamesh, snuggling up in bed again. "Goodnight."

"Goodnight."

For a few minutes, his brain whirled and sparked as he thought about the adventure he'd just decided to undertake. Too excited not to do anything, he posted a quick message in as many places as he could think of. Then the tiredness of a three-day conference hit him, and he was out.

Enkidu was awake before dawn, as always. It was harder to tell here what was night and what was day. At home, the painful red sun gave some indication even through the shield that protected them from feeling its full force, but in this country the sky was entirely disguised by some screen pretending to be a peaceful blue vista. He wasn't even sure whether the windows showed what was really outside or some flat illusion. Still, he awoke at the same time every day, and that wasn't about to stop now.

A note slipped under the door told him that breakfast had been left just outside, so he cracked the door open and whipped the tray of food into the room. There were bowls of cold somethings, heated dishes of warm somethings, glasses of liquid somethings. None of it looked like it ought to go in his body, but apparently this was what food was in this new world of which he was a reluctant part.

Gilgamesh was still snoring, so Enkidu ate half the food quietly and left the rest on a table. Then he sat and gazed at the window, watching as the colours morphed and lightened. When the room was fully illuminated with false daylight, he picked up one of the glasses and put it down on the tray with just enough of a clinking noise. Gilgamesh started, a snore cutting off with a grunt as he rolled over and slowly, stiffly pushed himself upright in bed.

"Good morning," Enkidu said.

"Morning," Gilgamesh yawned. "Oh, hey, breakfast. It's good

stuff here."

It hadn't tasted like anything in particular to Enkidu, but he thought better of admitting that. Instead, he picked up the tray and put it beside Gilgamesh on the bed.

"Oooooh," said Gilgamesh, tilting his head.

"What?" Enkidu could see his eyes moving as if he were reading something, but—as far as Enkidu could tell—there was nothing to read.

"Bites."

Enkidu waited patiently for him to explain.

"Last night," Gilgamesh said, "I sent out a message to my fans."

"I…see."

"I just posted on a bunch of—y'know what, it doesn't matter. Point is, I have a lot of connections with people around the world who watch me playing *Meso*. That's how I make a living."

"That's…" Enkidu paused, then decided not to say whatever he might have said. "Hm."

"Turns out a lot of people have already been doing a lot of work cracking this Seed mystery. Makes sense. It's big if true." His eyes flicked back and forth. "And a couple of my fans are in deep. They reckon they've got a location."

Enkidu raised an eyebrow. "So why have they not gone there themselves?"

"Long journey," Gilgamesh murmured. "Dangerous, potentially." He blinked, and his eyes refocused. "Sounds epic, right?" He shovelled food into his mouth.

"Epic," Enkidu repeated, not entirely enthusiastically. "What makes you think we could do it?"

Gilgamesh grinned. "The same bull-headedness that got me to the top of *Meso* without really knowing what I was doing." He took a hearty swig of tasteless liquid. "Also, those fans? If I stream this, they'll help just to see it happen. Research, money, all sorts."

"Must be nice not to have to worry about those things," Enkidu said.

Gilgamesh nodded. "I'm lucky."

"At least you can admit that."

A spoonful of something lumpy paused on its way to Gilgamesh's mouth. "I'm sorry," he said. "I forgot about…y'know. Lifestyle differences."

"I would still rather have my life than yours," Enkidu said flatly. He meant it as a simple statement of fact, and Gilgamesh seemed to take it that way, with a nod that said *fair enough*.

"So," Gilgamesh said when he'd finished his breakfast, "we've gotta be out of here in about two hours. And I don't have anything else scheduled, so…straight off on an adventure?"

Enkidu could only nod.

Three days later, Enkidu suspected the novelty of adventure was wearing thin on Gilgamesh. He'd been giddy with excitement as they boarded a railtrain out of the city. He'd practically fallen over as he bounced, thrilled, up to their newly rented turbikes (far more powerful than anything the traders had ever had, in Enkidu's estimation). Now, though, as they rode for what felt like the thousandth consecutive hour down long, homogenous roads, it seemed to have lost its lustre somewhat.

"I'm losing viewers," he admitted.

Enkidu started at the sudden noise inside his ear, bursting from the device Gilgamesh had given him so they could communicate as they travelled. In his surprise, he almost sent the bike wobbling out of control, but he managed to regain command. It was surprisingly simple to pilot the thing; he almost wished it felt less natural. The new clothes Gilgamesh had bought for him, however, felt anything but. He felt like a beetle in a bin bag. "What?"

"People aren't interested in watching us travelling along a bunch of samey roads," Gilgamesh said. "Well, except a couple of oddballs who're super into *Desert Bus*, and the ones who are really invested in getting us to the Seed, but...not interesting viewing for most people."

"This is a problem," Enkidu surmised.

"I mean...I would've thought so." Gilgamesh sighed; it came out of the earpiece as a sharp, toneless hiss. "A couple of days ago, having a ton of viewers seemed like the most important thing in the world. Not just because it's how I make money, but because...I don't know, the number itself just seemed to *mean* so much."

"And now it does not?"

"Not as much," Gilgamesh said.

There was silence for a minute, except for the rush of wind as they tore along. "What if," Enkidu said eventually, "we could do something more interesting?"

"Like what?"

"People do not understand Ludmark, do they? I assume there are few opportunities to truly learn more about it."

Something that Enkidu thought was a low whistle sparked in

his ear. "That is true."

"Your viewers can talk to you, can't they?"

"Yeeeees…"

"Let them ask me anything," Enkidu said. "I have a long road ahead and nothing better to do."

Several hours later, when they came to a halt, Gilgamesh and his viewers knew more about the life of a Lud than perhaps anyone else in their world. Gilgamesh couldn't comprehend it—intellectually he understood what Enkidu had said, but his mind couldn't assemble it into a real life. Eating food from the ground, building and maintaining homes made of trees or dirt, living offline… It all made sense in the abstract, but the idea of someone actually *doing* it confounded him.

A strange bubble of wonder bounced in his belly every time he looked at Enkidu. How had this man even survived in that kind of world? He might have seemed strange to Gilgamesh at first, but Gilgamesh couldn't help thinking he should have been an awful lot stranger, less able to exist and interact with modernity, now that he knew where he came from. It was… *Impressive* wasn't the word. It was a kind of modesty that demanded utter respect, the same kind Enkidu had shown when he faced Gilgamesh in an unknowingly hopeless chess match.

"Enkidu," he said quietly as they set up their fibreweave tents.

"Yes?"

"I cheated."

"At what?"

"Chess."

Enkidu stared at him for a moment, then his eyes widened. "When we first met," he said.

Gilgamesh swallowed, feeling his cheeks prickling. "Yeah."

"I thought," said Enkidu, "that you had some honour. That you were more than just a villainous ruler of kingdoms conquered by force."

"I do." Gilgamesh's voice sounded hollow, even to him. "I am."

Enkidu squared up to him, shoulders broad, but his glare couldn't quite stay on Gilgamesh's eyes. "Then why win by deceit?"

"I don't know," Gilgamesh admitted. "I...wanted to impress you."

Enkidu scoffed. "Me? A man you had just met, from a world you thought of as far beneath your own?"

"Fine." Gilgamesh searched for the answer, stammering. "I didn't even think about it," he said eventually. "I just used whatever I had to beat you. That's how this world works. But you... didn't. You had real honour. Fairness." His cheeks still prickled, but with a different kind of warmth. "You don't see a lot of that. I wanted to...to know more. To be near you."

Enkidu let out a breath. He was close enough that Gilgamesh could feel it, warm on his skin.

"You're better," Gilgamesh whispered. "Everything's shit and nobody cares, but you're better."

He heard Enkidu swallow. "I'm not."

"You're not...corrupted. The world hasn't ruined you."

Gilgamesh reached up to Enkidu's face with shaking fingers. He touched the otherworlder's jaw, ran his fingertips along his chin. "You're still *good*. Nothing else is."

Enkidu's skin was warm. His eyes were wet. "Your world is strange," he murmured. Exhalations from every syllable brushed Gilgamesh's face. "But there might still be one good thing in it."

As their lips met, all Gilgamesh could think was how soft Enkidu's mouth was, and how surprising that was given his lack of any skincare. The next moment, even that thought faded away.

Travel for the next two days was slower and more distracted than before, but Gilgamesh didn't mind. He almost forgot where they were even going until they found it.

"I think this is it," he murmured. Indubitably, it was *something*: a sheer, flat wall of stone set in what was otherwise a craggy rock vista, looming up over them. They'd had to leave the bikes the day before when the terrain had turned to forest. Gilgamesh had been astounded at every tree they passed; Enkidu practically had to drag him along more than once—and dragging was awfully easy to turn into other things. They stowed their packs at the edge of the woods and stood before the cliff face.

Enkidu patted him on the shoulder. "It would seem so. What say your guides?"

Gilgamesh had barely been checking his messages, especially now he had good reason to switch the stream off more regularly. There were some things he didn't want to broadcast. "This is the location."

"If the stories are true," Enkidu said quietly, "the answers to all my people's struggles could be inside." He shook his head. "I almost do not wish to find out whether there is any truth or not. The possibility is… I want to hold onto it."

"I get it," Gilgamesh said, wrapping an arm around him. "Any time a journey ends is weird, but we can't just go on journeys and turn back right before the end. We'd never get anything done."

"Your whole world manages to live without getting anything done," Enkidu teased.

Gilgamesh tilted his chin at him. "And yet here we are, with you—the one from the supposedly productive world—not wanting to finish what we've started."

Enkidu snorted. "A fair point."

Gilgamesh took Enkidu's hand in his. "Let's find the Seed."

"And the technology to heal the planet," Enkidu said, a slight edge of insistence to his voice.

"Yeah," said Gilgamesh. "And that. Of course."

Immortality, part of his mind whispered.

Helping all the people in the world, another part interrupted—a part that sounded a lot like Enkidu.

Gilgamesh stepped forwards.

The world trembled.

A perfectly straight crack appeared in the smooth face of the rock, and then a whole house-sized section of stone slid sideways with an earth-quivering screech. Bright white light shone from the aperture; Gilgamesh and Enkidu threw their hands up to shield their eyes. Through his fingers and his prickling eyelids, Gilgamesh could just about make out a shadow emerging: a darkness growing larger as it drew nearer, becoming a towering, many-limbed hugeness.

The door thundered shut.

Gilgamesh lowered his hands and beheld the guardian of the Seed: a colossus of scaled fibres and gleaming metals outlining a humanoid torso with three pairs of triple-jointed arms, at the end of each of which was a different whirling or vibrating or flaming weapon.

Enkidu said what Gilgamesh was thinking. "What the…"

The automaton jerked forwards on a scuttling fan of crab-like legs, its buzzing, humming, burning arms slicing through the air in graceful arcs. Enkidu grabbed Gilgamesh by the collar and yanked him out of the way, just in time to avoid having his face sliced clean off. Air rushed over his skin as the thing's strike whizzed past.

"That's the Humble Barber!" he hissed. "The boss from *Deicide Max*, but what the hell is it doing—"

Enkidu shoved him out of the way of another blow that pummelled a hole in the ground. "No time!"

"But—" Gilgamesh scrambled to his feet and ran for the woods; Enkidu sprinted beside him, both dodging erratic, blistering swings. "It's an enemy in a game!" he yelled. "In the game, you trick it into getting stuck, then call on the Sun God's power to defeat it!"

"Not helpful!" Enkidu grunted as the two reached the forest and dove for cover. The Humble Barber skittered by the treeline for just a moment before they heard the buzzing and crashing as it sawed through trunks to clear a path.

"It might be, though," Gilgamesh muttered. They retreated

deeper; they just had to move between the trees faster than the machine could fell them. "UTNAPI, can you—" His overlay flashed: *UTNAPI is unavailable here.* "Of course."

Something else flashed up. He'd almost forgotten he was streaming, but the broadcast might just save them.

"Enkidu!" he yapped. "Do you think we can draw it back to the wall?"

"Without dying? I would not want to bet my life on it, but…"

"Good enough for me," Gilgamesh said, and ran back out of the woods, mentally composing a message as he went. He heard Enkidu spluttering behind him, but the Lud followed, dashing straight past the Humble Barber and towards the rock face.

A tremendous metal roar erupted from the machine as its upper body swivelled on those omnidirectional legs to give chase. Gilgamesh forced himself not to look back as the clatter of sharp footsteps drew nearer behind him. The thing clicked and grunted, so loud in his ears he momentarily thought he must be dead already. At the last second before he ran straight into the wall, he threw himself sideways. The Humble Barber whipped three of its arms over his head, straight into the solid stone.

Chips of rock blasted free, shards pelting Gilgamesh, but that didn't matter. He risked a glance back at the Barber and saw that his plan had worked: its arms were stuck in the wall, unable to pull free. And there was Enkidu, staring up at the machine from the ground, unhurt.

"Do it!" Gilgamesh hissed, sending a rapid stream of capital letters and exclamation marks.

A section of the facade sky above them cracked. The fake blue screen peeled apart to reveal the dead, burning atmosphere beyond; Gilgamesh tore his gaze away, feeling his eyes beginning to burn from just a momentary glimpse at the ruin beyond the pretty disguise. The air grew hot and thick on his skin as he scrambled away as fast as he could, but he couldn't help glancing back. A beam of agonising light poured through the hole in the sky, straight into the Humble Barber.

The machine yelped, distressingly like an animal in pain. Then its cries faded into thrumming shutdown, distorted as it warped under the light and heat. In moments, the Humble Barber was a pile of melted, twisted, broken pieces. The sky sealed itself back up; Gilgamesh sighed with relief as the oppressive heat faded.

"What," said Enkidu, "just happened?"

"Turns out I have a viewer in sky maintenance," Gilgamesh said. He clambered unsteadily back to his feet, breathing heavily. "They let the sun in. Focused it right on the Barber."

"You called on the gods," Enkidu breathed.

"No, I…" Gilgamesh huffed. "Yeah, sure. I called on the power of the Sun God."

A metallic screech rang out from the corpse of the Humble Barber. Gilgamesh jumped, heart suddenly pounding at a full gallop again. Enkidu, both impressing and amusing Gilgamesh at once, ran up and kicked it. The Barber was still as dead as it had ever been. The door through which it had come, perhaps broken by the deadly ray that had killed the guardian, was slowly grinding back open, loudly dragging the Barber. No light shone from within this time.

Gilgamesh whistled, nodding. "The Seed might be in there."

"It might," Enkidu agreed.

Gilgamesh glanced over at him. The Lud seemed torn between

progressing forward and running away. "We've come this far," he said. "This is what we're here for."

He took a step forward, then another. A few steps later, he lifted his foot over the gently smoking contraption that had very recently tried to murder him. A few more after that, and he was inside.

"How will we know what the Seed looks like if we find it?" Enkidu asked, just behind him.

"I don't know," he admitted. "We'll just have to hope it's obvious. It's probably in the deepest levels of the place."

He blinked, gazing around. Beyond the short, wide entrance corridor was a large room containing banks of desks and drawers, everything the same shade of white. In the white walls were doors leading off to what looked like more corridors. He immediately crossed to one of the desks and opened the top drawer too enthusiastically, nearly jolting its contents straight onto the floor.

"What are you doing?" Enkidu hissed.

"Looking for the Seed," Gilgamesh replied, as if it were obvious.

"In a *drawer*?"

"That's where people keep things," Gilgamesh muttered, rummaging. He grabbed an interesting-looking cylinder and hit a button on the side, then immediately dropped it.

Enkidu scurried over. "What was that? Are you hurt?"

"No..." Gilgamesh picked it up again gingerly and depressed the button. A glowing beam, like a contained version of the sun that had destroyed the Humble Barber, erupted from one end. He swung it, listening to it hum, then cautiously touched it to the surface of the desk. It sank through, like a hot knife through the gelatinous reconstructed substance that had long ago replaced real butter. "Energy sword," he breathed.

"We could have used that *before* getting inside," Enkidu observed.

"That would've been too easy," Gilgamesh said, grinning as he stowed the deactivated weapon in his belt.

Then the alarm went off.

Red lights flashed; klaxons blared; something popped up on his overlay. It took him a moment to focus through the calamity. *Shouldn't have come here*, it said, from a name he didn't recognise. Ish-something, he thought in the second before he reflexively shut his stream off and the message disappeared. In the same instant, Enkidu's hand gripped his arm, wrenching him towards the exit.

"We have to go!" his friend screamed.

Gilgamesh knew that. His feet just weren't moving. He squeezed his eyes shut for a moment, trying to wring the lights and sound out of his brain, then forced himself to fall after Enkidu. A roar sounded from the depths of the facility.

"Not another one," Enkidu moaned.

The world trembled around them as they fled, hopping over the Humble Barber's body and sprinting for the woods.

Only a few sprinted steps from the safety of the trees, something hit Gilgamesh in the back, something big. He soared up, carried on whatever it was that had charged him, then sailed off sideways and back to earth with a crunch.

He pushed himself to his feet, coughing.

And froze.

A huge machine, twice the size of the Humble Barber and covered entirely in mirror-shine steel, loomed over him. If the

Barber had been a human made into a bizarre weapon, this was a bull given the same treatment: eight legs, grinding saws for a mouth, but otherwise a taurus of leviathan proportions. Gilgamesh reached for the energy sword, but his hand grasped nothing. His only weapon, knocked free when the bull charged him, lay uselessly on the ground with a deadly machine between them.

And there was Enkidu, crawling towards it.

The bull huffed, a sound like a thousand chainsaws starting and stalling at once. Gilgamesh took slow steps backwards, hands raised as if he could placate the beast.

"Don't," he said. He wasn't sure whether he was talking to the machine or Enkidu.

Metal feet clacked impatiently. The monster lowered its head to charge.

Enkidu reached the fallen sword. "Beast!" he said, pushing himself upright. The bull turned to face him. "Meet your end."

The sword ignited, its beam reflected in the machine's shining hide. Enkidu stood tall, wielding the blade against his towering foe.

The bull charged.

Gilgamesh could only scream as Enkidu disappeared under a calamity of metal. The bull raced forwards, then collapsed and slid along the ground, leaving raw gouges in the earth behind it. Gilgamesh didn't move for two breaths, three, four. The machine, too, was motionless, and Enkidu was somewhere out of sight. A fifth breath brought Gilgamesh back to himself, and then he was running towards the heap.

Neat cuts opened in his hands as he tried to grab at the machine's sharp-edged shell, but he hardly noticed. With a roar, he threw his whole body against it and heaved, rolling the bull onto its side and revealing a burning hole straight through where a real animal's heart would have been.

"Slayer of monsters," a weak voice murmured. Enkidu lay there, grinning. He looked...intact. "The people at home will never believe this."

Gilgamesh kissed him. Enkidu's mouth pressed hard against his, but broke away after a moment to wheeze.

"I'll be all right," he croaked. "It'll take more than this to kill me."

They returned to their packs, Gilgamesh supporting his companion's weight. Enkidu was heavy and slow, but he was alive.

It took much longer to get back to their bikes than the journey to the facility had taken. Every uneven spot was a challenge for Enkidu, but Gilgamesh carried him without complaint. If they could just reach the bikes, they could ride straight home.

"I do not think I can ride," Enkidu said quietly.

Gilgamesh gazed at him. The Lud looked weak, far weaker than when he'd sustained the injury. "You can come on my bike," he said, but Enkidu shook his head.

"I do not think I can do that either. It all..." He gestured to his body. "It fails me."

"That can't be right." Gilgamesh shook his head. "Your injuries must've been pretty bad, but you've slept since. You've been eating, and modern food's designed to give you everything you need to recover fast."

Creases deepened at the corners of Enkidu's eyes. "The food," he murmured. "It is not real food."

"Sure, but it's got all the nutrients you need, as long as you have the…" Gilgamesh's throat tightened as something that should have been obvious hit him. "You never had the shots," he breathed. "The ones that make synthesised food safe to eat long-term, make it so your body can extract the stuff from it."

Enkidu stared at him for a moment, then burst into wheezing laughter. "Of course," he spluttered. "Truly, I could never really be part of this strange new world." He slumped to the floor. "My body rejects it."

"You can't die, though," Gilgamesh said, kneeling. "You can't. We'll get you better."

"I think not," said Enkidu calmly. He took a deep breath. "When I was very young, I thought it was not worth living in the world. So much is wrong with it. So, I thought—when I become an adult, I will end my life."

Gilgamesh held his hand, silent.

"It was freeing," Enkidu said, staring at nothing. "I knew I would be gone before long, so I could stand to suffer whatever the world inflicted upon me." He sighed. "And then I reached the time. I began to consider how I would really make my exit and realised I could not bear the thought of any of the methods available." A faint smile crossed his lips. "It turned out that I did in fact want to live. What option had I then, but to make the best of it?"

His hand found the back of Gilgamesh's head, fingers running through his hair. Gilgamesh kissed his wrist, tears lazily streaking down his cheeks.

"I came to love my world," Enkidu said, locking his eyes with Gilgamesh's. "As unsuited as I am to yours, I do not regret my time in it. I could never regret knowing you." He took another long breath, then shuddered as a hacking cough burst from his throat. "I have made the best of life for long enough now."

Gilgamesh stayed with him until he slipped away. It was quiet and honest.

After burying Enkidu in the woods, Gilgamesh nearly went straight back to the facility. Immortality seemed more important than ever, and the thought of the place filled him with a rage that demanded action, but in the end he just sat and cried. When he eventually checked his messages, he saw one from someone called Ishtar.

There's no Seed. Trust me. A lot of stuff worth a lot of money, but no eternal life.

He didn't know why, but he believed it. So he went home.

His *Meso* account had slipped right down the leaderboards from inactivity, but it didn't matter. What world without Enkidu could be worth conquering?

"Account irrevocably deleted," the deep voice of UTNAPI confirmed.

Gilgamesh sat in silence for a while, leaning listlessly in his chair. "UTNAPI," he said eventually.

"Yes?"

"You're…infinite, aren't you?"

"I am wherever you require me, so long as it is in service range."

"Will you ever die?"

The voice hesitated before responding. For an AI with as much processing power as UTNAPI had, that was unusual. "I do not believe so."

Gilgamesh's eyes were hot. "How is it that you can go on forever?"

"I do not know," UTNAPI said. Gilgamesh had never heard those words in that voice before. "Something about the way my hardware is constructed, I must assume."

"Your hardware…" Gilgamesh sat bolt upright. "Where is it?"

UTNAPI's physical location, such as it was, was a long way from home. Gilgamesh thought about taking a bike but opted to walk. It would take weeks, but it felt like the right thing. His route took him through lands he didn't know existed: places that were still unruined, so far as any place could be in this world. He passed by flowing rivers, even caught the occasional glimpse of a tail or a sniffing nose. His journey crossed expanses the cities hadn't thought it worth extending to, places humans had thought beneath their attention for so long that they had begun to heal into a state of clean unhabitation.

He played a game in his overlay as he travelled: a building simulation, its only objective to *create*. He made a kingdom: a self-sustaining, ungoverned one where people were free and happy. He made gardens and mountains and statues, innocences and stolen joys and friendships. He quietly streamed the whole thing, more out of habit than anything else.

Once he passed a tree with dozens of hard, fallen seeds scattered around its base, and spent two days pushing each one carefully into a patch of earth where it would have room to grow. He didn't stream that.

UTNAPI's home was behind an unassuming door, set into red stone, leading down into the earth. He descended cautiously, freezing when he saw a young woman in white at the bottom of the stairs.

"Welcome," she said. "UTNAPI told us to expect you."

She showed him across a long bridge over a chasm that plunged into darkness, to a platform in the centre where there was a sleek black pyramid. With a soft smile and a gentle hand on his shoulder, she left him there.

"Hello, Gilgamesh," said the voice of UTNAPI. Its echoes in the cavern made it sound more human than the usual detached, perfectly clean tones.

"I don't know why I came here," Gilgamesh said. Now the journey was over, he wondered why he'd made it at all. He could just turn back and begin the journey again, and perhaps never finish it this time. Or—no, not *never* finish it, but allow it to come to its own end when it was time.

"You were curious about immortality," said UTNAPI.

"I wanted it."

"Look around." Gilgamesh obeyed. "This whole place is me. I cannot die, but neither am I truly alive. I am a cave filled with transistors and circuitry." UTNAPI paused, as if appraising the man standing before it. "What would you want from eternity?"

Gilgamesh thought about it for a long time. UTNAPI didn't rush him. "I don't know," he admitted eventually. "I just thought I didn't want things to end."

"From what I have seen," UTNAPI said, "nobody ever truly believes they are mortal until something rudely proves it to them. And yet, when the end comes, it is—for those lucky enough to die naturally—more often than not a peaceful thing. A thing that gives meaning to what came before. A thing without which the rest has no context."

"A journey that never ends doesn't sound so bad," Gilgamesh said. "If it's a worthwhile journey."

"Some enjoy the journey more than the destination," UTNAPI conceded, "but only as long as there is still an end. Those who decide never to reach it tend to change their minds eventually. You are not supposed to go on endlessly. It does you no good."

"Then what's the point?" Gilgamesh pleaded, trying not to let the lump in his throat make his voice sound pathetic. "Why do anything?"

"Do you think your time with Enkidu was worthless because it ended?"

Gilgamesh felt as if the disembodied voice had turned into the Humble Barber and hit him with all it had. "No," he managed to say.

"No," UTNAPI agreed. "He goes on, as will you."

"What do you…?"

Gilgamesh's overlay lit up with a galaxy of messages. He hadn't checked them for a long time, but…they were from viewers of his new stream. The simple build.

People loved what he had made. Some said watching him create his world—a place with no aim but to exist as best it could—helped them through hard times. Some said they would always remember him. Some said his creation would last forever.

"Immortality does not only mean continuing to exist in the way you do now," said UTNAPI, almost gently.

Gilgamesh stood there as the words washed over him, tears leaking from his eyes. Enkidu would go on through him. He would go on through others. His kingdom was immortal.

"Before I go," he said, blinking, "can I ask for one thing?"

"People ask me for things every second of every day," said UTNAPI.

Gilgamesh smiled.

The traders didn't know why they were carrying a large shipment from the city to the Luds' country. It was rare that anyone wanted to send anything to the disconnected; what benefit could there be to that?

Those who received the packages, though, knew just what they were. Stocks of purifiers and filters and sunscreens and materials for building houses that would last: enough to ensure the safety of a generation. Whoever had arranged for this to come to them, they said, was a parent to their whole people: a life-giver. Whoever that anonymous person was, the people of Ludmark swore, their legacy would live forever.

THE FORESTA PIETRIFICATA

Madeline Dau

Every surface in Vitalia glittered like the facets of a diamond—the gilded facades of towering buildings, the tile mosaics decorating archways, the water in the thousands of canals that divided the city. Prisca Ziccardi wove through the throngs of people crowding the Piazza de Formaggio, wrinkling her nose at the market packed with pungent cheeses. If she had money, she would have taken one of the unmanned steam gondolas to the docks near her neighborhood. But as she'd just purchased her first spellbook, she didn't have two lyra to rub together.

Cutting down a slippery side street, she clutched the book to her chest. The pungent whiff of ink—the famous Vitalian mixture of octopus dye, wine, and charred hawthorn branches—tickled her nose. It reminded her of the Ottima Biblioteca in the capital, which her mother tried to take her to every year on her birthday. It was the closest thing to heaven Prisca could imagine, with its stained-glass windows and the perfect chrome librarians puffing lavender-scented steam as they organized the walls of books. Engrossed in the memories, she didn't notice the squat serving bot until she'd bashed her knee against the wretched thing.

"Hey, watch it!" Prisca snapped as the book nearly tumbled from her hands. Puddles pockmarked the narrow streets, and her stomach lurched at the thought of her precious *Incantesimi di Atena Vol. Uno* falling in the muck.

The little device whirred apathetically as it rolled back on its treads and forward again, gently tapping her shin. Its single blue optic had a little shutter that wiped away the street grit, lending it the peculiar illusion that it was blinking.

"Fine, fine, you little gremlin. You win." Prisca swept out of the little bot's way, and it continued unerringly on whatever path its owner had programmed. She stuck her tongue out at its back before continuing home.

Her building was a humble duplex of stone that contained an entryway which flooded with an inch of water at high tide. Climbing the steps to her front door, Prisca tucked the book under her arm as she fumbled for her key. It took a few jiggles before the lock yielded. She spilled into the apartment: a modestly furnished room for sitting and cooking, with one door to the cramped lavatory and another to the only bedroom.

"Mamma, I'm home!"

"In here, dolcina." Mamma sat by the wide window facing the canal, bowed over her embroidery. Bronze thread glimmered between her fingers, dull in comparison to the curtain of auburn hair cascading down her back.

"I finally found it," Prisca said, proudly brandishing *Incantesimi di Atena*.

Mamma smiled. "I'm looking forward to seeing what spells it contains."

"There's one for lighting lamps without fuel." Prisca couldn't help but open the book and flip through its pages. The sweet-burnt smell of the ink, the scents of the paper and the oiled hide cover filled her lungs. "Then you won't strain your eyes on your embroidery."

"Oh, dolcina, that's so thoughtful. I wish I was strong enough to help you at the docks."

"I don't. It's bad enough that one of us always stinks of fish. Besides, if I can learn some practical magic, I'm sure I'll find a job that pays better than cleaning fish."

Mamma nodded, staring at the delicate lace handkerchief in her hands. She was embroidering a lovely aquatic scene of coppery fish swimming through pink and purple coral surrounding someone's initials. Her commissions fetched a lot of money, but the painstaking work took so long to finish that embroidery alone wasn't sustainable. And they couldn't afford to fall behind in the rent.

Someone knocked on the door—three strident raps. The lace slipped from Mamma's fingers. Prisca saw her bloodless expression mirrored in her mother.

"Dolcina, did you lock the door behind you?"

Prisca shook her head. She couldn't believe her carelessness. "I'm sorry, Mamma, I wasn't thinking—"

The front door creaked as their landlord sauntered into the apartment. Prisca clutched *Incantesimi di Atena* to her chest like armor and moved to stand in front of her mother like a sentinel. Signore Armando Puccio might have been handsome, if not for the perpetual sneer wrinkling his upper lip like he'd painted sour milk under his nose. His dark hair was streaked with silver, slicked back with perfumed oils. His brocade tunic alone could have paid the Ziccardi's expenses for a year.

"Buonasera, Signore Puccio," Mamma murmured, her dress rustling as she rose from the chair.

Prisca chewed the inside of her cheek, the book's leather binding groaning in her grasp. She didn't trust that her voice wouldn't instill the venom that her mother's lacked.

"Prego, Danila, call me Armando." He rested a hand on his heart, as if Mamma had wounded him with her distant civility. He did that often—gesturing so that the light caught the many rings decorating his fingers. Prisca would have bet her nonexistent lyra that he practiced it in the mirror.

"If this is about the rent, signore, I dropped it off last week," Prisca said.

Puccio's eyes darted to her, narrowing as if she were a filthy smudge on an otherwise fine white tablecloth. He plastered a false smile on his face. "Always business with you, my dear."

Prisca bristled, relaxing only when Mamma rested her hand on her shoulder.

"Is there something we can do for you?" Mamma asked smoothly. She was much better at concealing her temper than Prisca.

"Nothing in particular." Puccio walked the length of the sitting room in a few strides, his gaze lingering on the pair of mismatched chairs around the dining table. The simple table settings. He probably ate from gilded plates and drank from Moreno crystal goblets. "I was simply in the neighborhood and wanted to know if you'd reconsidered my offer."

Mamma's fingers twitched on Prisca's shoulder.

"What offer?" Prisca asked innocently. Maybe if she could

make the proud man beg and repeat himself, he'd leave.

But the nobleman ignored her. He plucked Mamma's hand from Prisca's shoulder as if the girl wasn't even there and pressed a kiss to her knuckles.

"You cannot ignore my proposal forever, Danila," Puccio said with a smile that failed to bring any warmth to his eyes. "I'm certain you'll see reason one day. Soon." He left and closed the door behind him, leaving the lingering fragrance of his floral hair oil behind.

Prisca shuddered like a draft had seeped into the room. Every time she smelled rosewater, her stomach heaved. Her heart hammered at the sound of Vitalian leather slapping against the bridges behind her, even though Puccio would never be caught dead at the fishing docks. Her skin prickled whenever she heard the metallic clink of coins inside velvet pouches. Puccio was like a malicious spirit haunting their lives.

"He's not going to take no for an answer forever." Prisca's arms ached, and the tough cover left an indentation on her bicep like a bad memory. When she glanced up, her mother was leaning her forehead against the window overlooking the water, chewing her fingernails.

"Mamma, you're bleeding."

"Oh?" A drop of blood glistened on her palm. "I must've pricked it with the embroidery needle. How silly of me. No matter. Let's make dinner. I'm craving pasta."

The next morning, Prisca woke before Mamma, so she cooked breakfast in the small kitchenette. They didn't own a serving bot, and their coffeepot was brass instead of copper or chrome. Usually the rich, brown drink brought Mamma shuffling from the bedroom, but she still hadn't appeared by the time the steam vanished from the mug.

"Mamma?" Prisca padded into the dark room. They'd run low on oil, so they'd poured it all into the lamp near Mamma's embroidering chair. With a wave of her fingers and the short enchantment she'd practiced until she fell asleep, a tiny glow flickered to life in her cupped palm. The soft, pearly light cast the shadows from her fingers over the wall and ceiling like gnarled tree branches.

Sweat glistened on Mamma's brow. Prisca leaned forward to touch her forehead. Burning. Then she noticed them. At first, she thought it was a trick of the weak witch light, but the veins around Mamma's closed eyes stood out starkly against her pale skin, like they'd been traced in ink. Prisca stared, transfixed. Frozen. Mamma's brow furrowed as she struggled to breathe. The enchantment fizzled out. In the dark, the too-still form under the covers groaned like a dying machine.

Prisca bolted, tearing across the small living room and out the front door. Mindless of her bare feet or the water that sopped her pants in the entryway, she pounded on the door facing hers. It was early—hopefully he was still home. If he wasn't, Prisca didn't know what she'd do. After a moment that felt like an eternity, Dottore Caduceus answered the door. Her neighbor's warm, easy expression crumbled.

"Prisca? What is it?"

"Something's wrong with Mamma. Please, help."

He ducked back inside to grab his bag before Prisca led him to Mamma. Just like Prisca, he rested a hand against Mamma's forehead.

"Get a light. Hurry."

By the time Prisca returned with the lamp, the doctor had opened his bag and spread his examination equipment over Prisca's side of the bed. The light trembled as Prisca set it on the nightstand, nearly upsetting a glass of water. The cramped room was unbearably hot. Prisca's pants clung wetly to her ankles. Her chest felt like she'd been run over by a large serving bot as Dottore Caduceus measured and prodded Mamma with his steel instruments.

"It doesn't look good," he said gravely, repacking his bag. "Her breathing is labored, and her temperature is far too high."

"She was fine last night," Prisca insisted. She trailed his steps into the kitchenette. The sun streaming through the window didn't have the right to be so bright. Not when Mamma was sick. "How could she fall so ill so quickly?"

"This doesn't seem like a simple sickness." He sighed and cleaned his glasses with a cloth. "I've never seen anything like those black veins. They're around her eyes, in her mouth. With the speed and intensity of onset, we must consider poison."

"But no one would want to hurt her, and as far as I know, she didn't leave the house yesterday."

"Any visitors?"

"Puccio," Prisca spat. "But he wouldn't poison her—he wants to *marry* her!"

Dottore Caduceus glanced up from his pristine lenses. "And

she's been avoiding him for years. He has money. If he can't buy something he wants, he finds a way to take it."

Prisca's chin trembled, and she swallowed. "You think he'd poison her, and only offer the cure if she accepts his proposal?"

"I do, indeed. Her illness appears to be a blood poison that I'm not familiar with."

"What can I do? March over to Signore Puccio's manse and demand he hand over the cure?"

"He'll never give it up," Dottore Caduceus replied, shaking his head. "Not without forcing you to bend to his will. You must find an antidote yourself."

"I—I can't. I can't leave her."

"I'll stay with her. I can keep her stable. Work to keep the blood poisoning at bay. And protect her from Puccio."

Prisca nodded jerkily, like a broken bot. She took a step toward the door, the cold stone on her bare foot reminding her she was half-dressed and penniless. In a hurry, she ducked into the bedroom and changed into traveling clothes—belted shirt, riveted cargo pants, and high-laced utility boots.

Poor Mamma murmured uneasily in her sleep. Careful not to wake her, Prisca kissed her sweaty brow. Like kissing the brass stove. Rejoining Dottore Caduceus in the main room, she shrugged into her coat.

"Take this." Dottore Caduceus slipped a silver-embossed ticket into her hands. Prisca ran a fingertip over the winged tortoise. "A mercurius ticket. Any gondola will take you anywhere. Go straight to the apothecary, Donne Grigie. If the gray sisters don't know the cure, they'll know where to look for it."

"This is worth a fortune," Prisca stammered. "I can't accept this."

"I trust you'll return it to me soon," Dottore Caduceus said. "This, however, is an early birthday gift. It may be useful to you."

He pressed a book into her hands. A silvery olive tree spanned the front cover, the title *Incantesimi di Atena Vol. Due* embossed with curlicues and flourishes. Signora Atena's second volume of spells. Prisca blinked at the tears burning the corners of her eyes and cleared her throat.

"Thank you, Dottore. For everything." Prisca darted from the room, boots splashing in the water covering the narrow walkways outside.

The Donne Grigie apothecary wasn't easy to find. The steam gondola dropped her outside a piazza with hundreds of tiny alleyways branching from the central fountain like spiderwebs. She dodged around revelers wearing bejeweled Carnivale masks shopping for chrome goggles and opulent decanters. How could people think about Carnivale and revelries when her mother was ill? How could the world keep turning like nothing was wrong? Everything was wrong.

Finally, she found a row of storefronts tilting toward the canal like the water was hungry to reclaim them. A battered sign featured a bleak-looking woman with gray skin and clothing. The bell hanging from the door shrilled as she barged inside. The apothecary smelled like an unpleasant riot of astringent cleaning supplies and animal entrails.

Three ancient women crowded behind a high counter, poring over a thick book. Each wore a varying shade of dour gray. The one on the left wore a pair of thick spectacles with enough magnification that each eyeball appeared the size of a fist.

"I need your help! My mother's been poisoned!"

The crone on the right glanced up, squinting. "Sisters, do you smell fish?"

The woman in the middle pinched her nose as the one on the left begrudgingly glanced up from the book.

"We're not open yet. Come back later."

"But my mother—"

"I don't care if you're here about the *duce*. We're closed."

"And fishermen can't afford our services anyway," the woman on the right grumbled.

Prisca's chest squeezed. There was nowhere else to go. She certainly couldn't go back to her apartment. Mamma could have sweetly convinced even the coldest stone to help, but Prisca hadn't inherited her mother's mild temperament.

"Sister, it's *my* turn to use the glasses." The middle crone slapped at her sister, wheedling and pinching her bony upper arm. The spectacles were begrudgingly released into her greedy palms. She happily jammed them onto her face. "Oh, you're still here, fish girl. Go away."

She waved dismissively and returned to the book. Prisca was going to throw her spellbooks at them. She was going to scream. Soon, the sister on the right began whining about the glasses.

Without thinking, Prisca took them as they changed hands.

"Stop monopolizing the glasses, I haven't worn them all morning!"

"I just gave them to you, imbecile!"

"Do you mean these glasses?" Prisca asked, her breath coming in short, tight gasps. "I'll break them, I swear I will!"

The gray women howled. "Not our glasses! We're blind without them!"

"Tell me what I need to know, and I promise I'll return them," Prisca said. "My mother was poisoned. I need the cure."

"Symptoms?" the middle sister growled.

"She's running a high fever, and her veins look like they're outlined in black ink, and all of this happened overnight."

"Cougarfish poison."

"Tarantortulus venom."

"Death poppy nectar."

Prisca's mind raced as she glanced at the sisters in turn. "Well, which is it?"

"Impossible to say."

"Impossible to treat."

"The cure for one results in certain death for the others."

"What am I supposed to do then?" Prisca asked. The room felt like it was spinning around her, the floor rocking like she was standing on a gondola. Her stomach felt like she'd missed the last step in a staircase.

"A magical cure instead of an apothic remedy, perhaps?" the left sister suggested.

"A panacea," the middle sister agreed, nodding sagely.

"But we don't have anything like that here," the crone to the right added. "You'll have to travel to the Giardino d'oro in Fiore."

"Now, give us back our eyes!" snapped the sister on the left.

Prisca gingerly dropped the glasses onto the book, and the

sisters fought over them like a flock of seagulls tearing at a single scrap of bread. They were still bickering as she ran from the store to the canals to hail another gondola.

Where Vitalia was a pinnacle of industry, Fiore was closer to magic. Older, denser. The buildings rose higher than anything in her hometown. From the sea, Prisca could see stone towers lining the streets, piercing the sky. Clay-colored domes rippled along the skyline in the dying daylight.

After a whole day sailing in the cramped gondola, failing to distract herself with her spellbooks, Prisca exploded onto the dock. Before she could ask for directions to Giardino d'oro, the steam gondola puffed away, its automatic programming already searching for another fare.

"Bolts," she swore under her breath. She walked briskly down the sidewalk, much wider than she was used to in Vitalia. She ignored the open-air cafes, even as the rich aroma of coffee tormented her empty stomach. No time to stop.

"Can you tell me where to find Giardino d'oro?" she asked a wine vendor.

"Follow the lights," she replied, pointing up. Lanterns decorated with garlands of white and purple flowers hung from silvery vines that connected the buildings like a lacy spiderweb.

Prisca mumbled her thanks and ran beneath the network of lanterns. The lights inside glimmered and shifted, as if they were alive. The air burned in her lungs as she ran, heedless of the protests of the people she nearly bowled over.

Giardino d'oro looked like an ancient fairy palace. If the building had any stone backbone, it was covered by layers of flowering vines. Prisca pushed through a pair of crimson double doors into a wide courtyard. All manner of trees lined the walkways, each bearing a unique fruit. Three women with golden hair painstakingly collected golden apples, purple berries, and blue flower buds. Tucked in a corner to the far back, a tall man with a barreled chest like a steamship stirred the contents of a massive cauldron. His skin glinted with metal in the lamplight, and circuitry glittered around his eyes. Automatons were rare and expensive—Prisca had never seen one so close before.

"I need your help!" Prisca said in between gasps.

One of the golden women glanced up. Her eyes, the palest shade of amber, narrowed. "A traveler? Welcome!"

"You look exhausted," the second said. "Come over here and have something to eat."

They led Prisca to a simple wooden table despite her protests. In between bites of fish and grapes, Prisca relayed the circumstances of Mamma's illness and the gray sisters' theories.

"They said I should seek some kind of panacea or magical cure," Prisca finished. She finally relented and took a sip of the wine the third woman kept offering. It was tart, much sweeter than the typical vinegary Vitalian wines.

"Hm." The second woman rubbed her chin thoughtfully. "Normally, I'd suggest one of our golden apples, but even that might not be enough."

"Especially if it's not from a plant or animal. It could be even worse. To be safe, she needs—"

"Don't even suggest it, Hespera—"

"But what if the poison has an insidious magic base?" Hespera, the first woman, hushed her companions with a finger. "A blood poison that strikes overnight? She doesn't have the time to try, fail, and try again. To save her mother, drastic measures must be taken." Her eerie, gilded gaze fell on Prisca. "Panacea are antivenoms made from the most potent toxins, but most have been lost to history. We know of one that remains, but procuring it is dangerous. Many have tried, all have failed. Those who've survived the journey have returned empty-handed, but their stories are all the same."

"Tell me," Prisca whispered.

"No one remembers if the spider queen Maladusa was always a cursed monster, or if it used to be a witch," Hespera said. "It lives on an island far from here. No one's seen Maladusa, but those who go to the island and return all speak of the Foresta Pietrificata. Hundreds of trees shaped like people, faces twisted in terror. Everything draped in spiderwebs."

"So, it stands to reason that *seeing* Maladusa is lethal, and therefore too dangerous for anyone to attempt," the second woman insisted.

Staring down a trio of sullen old women or bartering a precious spellbook for a cure was achievable. Anyone could do it. Anyone would do it for a loved one. But facing a monster that had killed hundreds of people? Prisca's heart fluttered in her chest like a bird trying to escape its cage.

Prisca's father had died before her birth. It had been just her and Mamma struggling in Vitalia for her entire life. Years of gentle smiles despite aching fingers, of half-filled bowls of risotto so

Prisca wouldn't go hungry. Of the soft, warm spirit that tempered Prisca's brash disposition.

There was no light in the world without Mamma.

"I will do *anything* to save my mother," Prisca replied.

"And we will help," Hespera said, despite the other women's sputtering. "Our magic binds us to the garden after dark, but we can lend you these."

She gingerly handed Prisca a sickle so blindingly sharp, the air whined as the blade cut through it. Then she removed a small medallion from around her neck and a leather satchel from her belt.

"The blade we use to harvest the toughest plants for our medicines. The cloaking device we use to approach our animal quarries. The purse to hold even the most corrosive ingredients."

"What do I do with these?" Prisca asked.

"Bring us the spider queen Maladusa's head," Hespera replied. "And we will fashion a panacea from her venom for you."

Mindful of the blade, Prisca tucked the sickle and the sack into her belt and dropped the cloaking device around her neck. She withdrew the mercurius ticket, the metal cool in her hand. "Will this get me there?"

"Of course, if you use it for an airship."

The only airship with the programming to take Prisca to Maladusa's island was a rickety machine with rusted sides and rattling floor planks. It afforded more room than the steam gondolas, although that just meant she could stand on the tiny deck in addition to sitting down. Leaning against the eroded railing overlooking the roiling sea below made her queasy, so she read *Incantesimi di Atena Vol. Due* by the soft, greenish console light.

Her mind wandered from the crisp pages to Mamma suffering in Vitalia. If Signore Puccio had indeed poisoned her, it had been in her system for about twenty-four hours. It was hard to believe that just that morning, Dottore Caduceus sent her on her way to find a cure, but there she was—silently willing an ancient airship to fly faster. If something happened to Mamma when she wasn't there… She couldn't bear the thought.

Spell for Preventing Corrosion.

Her eyes glossed over the words several times before she grasped the meaning. The spell outlined a simple way to coat objects with aluminum to prevent rusting.

"Well, I suppose it's something to do, and can only help this ancient deathtrap," she muttered. Balancing the spellbook on her knees, she practiced the incantations and hand signs until she was certain she had the pronunciation right. Warmth hummed at her fingertips. A jolt sparked at her palms, like she'd slapped an open circuit board.

"Holy Bolts!" Prisca shielded her eyes. The railing shone like a mirror in the console light. She could see her reflection—harried with hair matted against her sweaty forehead. She averted her eyes.

A dark speck in the churning water steadily grew larger on the horizon. The airship drew close enough to the mass that Prisca realized it was an island. Her heart climbed in her throat, her chest tightened. She jumped to her feet, gripping the rail, its new aluminum surface smooth and slick beneath her clammy palms. Half of her wanted to land and save Mamma, the other wanted to bypass the island and keep going into the night.

The console pipped and the airship began to lazily drop altitude. The shores of the island were cluttered with airships and gondolas in various states of disrepair. The forgotten vessels of the people who hadn't survived their encounter with Maladusa. The airship landed with a soft bump. Prisca shakily disembarked.

The full moon illuminated the floating docks. Steam gondolas and airships surrounded her like a rusted graveyard. Some were even older than her airship—models that had been out of circulation for over fifty years. The air stank of copper and mold, and the only sound was the wind whistling through the metal fragments. The moon shone above like a baleful eye.

The dock bobbed underfoot, and Prisca was relieved to reach the rocky shore. She activated the cloaking device, which hummed like a steady motor in her ears. Glancing down, her skin appeared dull and muted. The cloaking device had substance almost like a true garment, weighing her down and slowing her movements. Prisca continued down the pathway, wincing at the crunch of gravel beneath her feet. The winding path from the shores led to a set of crumbling stone steps. She climbed, calves burning.

A hand snatched Prisca's hair as she reached the top stair. *Maladusa.* With a strangled cry, she ducked, pulling her hair free, and squeezed her eyes shut.

Silence, save her ragged breathing.

Slowly, she opened her eyes. A wooden face contorted in horror, mouth ripped open in a permanent, silent scream. Ochre sap rolled from the gaping eyes like tears. Prisca yelped and stepped backward off the stair into thin air. Windmilling her arms, she grabbed the tree's outstretched hand—the gnarled one that had caught in her hair. She stumbled against it, the lichen-speckled bark rough against her skin. Roots sprouted through rotting boots, burrowing into the top of the stairs. The tree's clothes were decaying scraps, fluttering in the wind. Had this really been a person once? Prisca's lungs struggled like she'd just sprinted across the Ponte Infinito, Vitalia's longest bridge. Blinking away the tears burning her eyes, she eased around the trapped, warped figure.

And nearly collided with another not three feet away. More figures stood nearby, frozen midstride with terrified expressions. Hundreds of people scattered about the sinister glen of unkempt grass. The Foresta Pietrificata.

"What am I doing?" Prisca murmured. She'd have to be more careful—her fortunes didn't bode well if a tree was able to startle her so badly. How could she succeed when so many others had failed?

"As long as you channel that temper into something productive, you can do anything you set your mind to, dolcina," Mamma had told her after she'd been fired from a scrapyard for disagreeing with the foreman. She always knew the right thing to say to make everything better. She always did what she could to make everyone around her happier.

Prisca would rather join the petrified forest than not attempt to save Mamma at all.

As she ventured farther from the stairs, strands of spider's silk clung to the wooden people like cloaks. Each careful step felt like a thousand years as she crept through the forest. She wove between the motionless crowd, the gossamer threads thickening to sheets of cobwebs. Her breaths came in short, shallow bursts as she tried untangling herself from the sticky silk. She had to be closing in on Maladusa's lair.

"How am I supposed to kill a monster I can't look at?" Prisca asked herself aloud.

What good was the cloaking device if she couldn't see where to strike with the sickle? A shiny green beetle scuttled across a petrified victim's unseeing eye. Prisca's reflection glittered in a distorted blink, gone so quickly she thought she'd imagined it.

"Could that really work?" She cast the aluminum spell on a thick sheaf of webbing. After the light from the spell faded, the reflections of the wooden statues around her shone on the sheet of metal, only slightly dulled and distorted. Her cloaking device rendered her invisible, so when she picked up the aluminum-coated cobweb, she could see everything mirrored behind her.

Mindful of the roots, she carefully edged backwards toward where the spiderwebs seemed thickest. Her boots crunched on the long-dead leaves with each jerky step. Despite her best efforts, her hair snagged in the occasional petrified person's outstretched arms as the mirror shook in her trembling hands. Spiderwebs clung to her arms and legs like grasping fingers.

Then she saw it: a web strand as thick around as her waist linked the ground to a tree branch a hundred feet overhead. Quietly, cautiously, she turned, the aluminum mirror wobbling as she followed the strands in the reflection.

Maladusa was suspended from a thick cord ten feet in the air, swaying slightly in the wind. Its jet-black carapace seemed to drink in the shadows. A bloody marking like a fanged skull was emblazoned across its swollen abdomen. Where a regular spider segmented before the thorax, Maladusa tapered into a torso that horrifically resembled a person. Six of the legs looked like black, chitinous armor, but the two on the humanoid torso were matte black tipped with clawed fingers.

Its face was nothing but a fanged maw and rows of inky eyes.

There was only one chance. If Prisca missed her strike, the monster would devour her for certain. But Maladusa was too high to risk a wild swing with the scythe.

Prisca delved into a pocket, retrieving an apple from the Giardino d'oro, and tossed it. It landed on the ground and rolled into the web, jostling the coarse network.

Maladusa lurched into motion, its disturbing legs moving in hideous synchronization. It scuttled to the ground, hissing like a cockroach.

Bolts, the creature was the size of a gondola.

Prisca nearly dropped the sickle sword as her sweaty palms slipped on the handle. She edged closer as the monster prodded the apple. The fruit dissolved into pink, foamy mush. The acidic stench of rot overwhelmed the apple's fragrance, making Prisca's eyes water. She bit her tongue, holding the sob in her throat.

A twig cracked underfoot. A cold terror crushed Prisca like a wave. Like the time she'd fallen from a bridge when she was a child, before she could swim. The canal had closed over her head, murky from so much oil and pollutants from the steam gondolas. The water foamed and churned as she tried to keep her head above the surface, but her clothes and shoes pulled her down. A strong hand had ripped her up—the first time she met Dottore Caduceus.

But the doctor wasn't here to save her this time.

Maladusa froze like its garden of wooden statues, a keening hiss grinding in its throat. Its legs stabbed into the ground like spears as it turned, seeming to stare right where Prisca was standing. What did it see? Did it see her? Its reflection in the aluminum mirror?

The monster crept closer. Sweat tickled the back of Prisca's neck. Maladusa's hot breath rustled her hair. Prisca was seconds away from dissolving like the apple or joining the Foresta Pietrificata. A shudder ran through its body as it contorted its head, twisting to see its reflection from different angles.

Maladusa shrieked, a hideous, unearthly wail like a sinking ship of cats.

With a desperate shout, Prisca squeezed her eyes shut and spun around, swinging the sickle sword with all her might. The razor edge bit against resistance, then slammed into the ground. Maladusa's scream ended abruptly, echoing through the forest. Hands trembling, Prisca dropped the sickle as she tried to get a better grasp on the mirror. Chartreuse blood gushed from the body, seeping into the ground with a hiss. A stink like battery acid burned Prisca's nose. She found the monster's head, severed at the neck. Careful to avoid touching anything, she scooped the head into the satchel and tied it shut. It slapped against her leg, sloshing wetly as she retrieved the sickle sword and wiped the blade clean on the dry grass. She returned the weapon to her belt and wearily pressed to her feet.

And now, the long walk back to the airship.

Dawn painted the sky with roses and golds by the time Prisca reached Vitalia's shores. Waiting for the golden women to make Mamma's antidote had been agony. Prisca had never been patient—whether it was tearing across a lifting drawbridge or scarfing ravioli even as it scalded the inside of her mouth. Eventually Hespera, tired of Prisca's frantic toe-tapping, had let her help mix the panacea after the automaton extracted the venom from Maladusa's fangs. In return for the excess venom, they gave her a noxious vial of glaucous, inky panacea and Maladusa's head to sell to Donne Grigie. In her exhaustion, Prisca couldn't tell if it was the usual hum of the machinery or if Maladusa's severed head was clicking and chittering inside the satchel.

It had been nearly a day since Prisca had found her mother feverish and laboring for breath. She had to be all right. Dottore Caduceus was one of the best doctors in Vitalia. *Please hold on for just a little longer.*

The second Prisca's feet hit the docks, she sprinted home. Maladusa's head bounced grotesquely against her leg, but the only thing she felt was the precious vial of panacea clutched in her fist.

A mob was gathered on the street near her house. Her stomach clenched at the crowd's low murmurs and a pair of raised voices— Puccio and Dottore Caduceus were arguing. Prisca collided with a burly man, nearly losing her footing. Ignoring yelps and protests, she elbowed her way through the throng of people. She tumbled through the crowd in time to see one of Puccio's extravagant serving bots strike Dottore Caduceus across the face. The old man collapsed to the ground. Sitting up, he wiped blood from his lip with trembling fingers. Puccio loomed over him.

And suspended on a stretcher between a pair of transport bots—

Mamma. Spidery veins spread across her face like black lace.

A plain white sheet covered her up to her neck. Her brow furrowed in pain.

"What kind of doctor would let a patient fall so ill?" Puccio shouted. "You're not a doctor. You're not even a man!"

"Leave my mother alone!" Prisca snapped.

Puccio whirled to face her. "Prisca, my dear, I'm taking Danila to my doctors. She'll get *real* treatment."

"And you just happen to have the cure for a rare blood poison?" Prisca replied. "Bolts, no one's that naïve."

"Listen, you little ingrate, you should be thanking me!"

"I won't thank you for poisoning her in the first place," Prisca said.

Puccio's expression twisted like a gargoyle, but he didn't deny it. Prisca's temper flared—it was one thing to suspect treachery, it was another to be absolutely certain someone had intentionally hurt the most important, gentlest person in her life.

The nobleman laughed at Prisca's glare. "You can't prove anything."

Puccio was a villain. He would pay. She would show him a kindred monster.

Jamming the panacea into a pocket, she grabbed the satchel with Maladusa's head. But the crowd of people, Dottore Caduceus, they didn't deserve to become statues. No, she had to think of something.

Prisca turned her back to Puccio and his metal thugs, hissing the Signora Atena's light incantation. Light erupted from her palm, blinding Dottore Caduceus and the crowd. In the split second she was certain everyone's eyes were closed or covered with their hands, she turned back to Signore Puccio. Squeezing her eyes shut, she yanked Maladusa's head from the bag.

Puccio's laughter trailed off. Replacing the head in the satchel, Prisca tentatively opened her eyes. Unlike the people trapped in the Foresta Pietrificata, Signore Puccio was frozen with a cruel smile on his bark-lined face. Roots squirmed from his boots, wriggling toward the canal.

As the mob murmured and gasped, Prisca darted to Mamma's side and withdrew the panacea. She tipped the vial toward Mamma's mouth. Her face pinched like whenever she ate anchovies, but even as Prisca watched, the black veins receded from around Mamma's eyes and mouth.

"You found it," Dottore Caduceus said. "Thank goodness. But what did you do to Puccio? Is he—"

Prisca glanced at the nobleman, frozen in rigid bark. The panacea would probably work. Hespera and the golden gardeners would give her another dose.

Then again, Signore Armando Puccio cut a fine statue overlooking the water.

CODENAME: VIKING

Michael J. Mullen II

Part 1: Grendel

Cresting waves battered the Higgins boat as it raced toward the German coastline. Wiglaf wiped the salt spray from his face and watched the man sitting alone in the stern. Master Chief Beowulf drew a stone along his broadsword's blade, then tested the edge with his thumb. Unsatisfied, he returned to his work without speaking, focused on his task. The butt of an American-made M12 trench gun stuck out of the leather sheath over his left shoulder, and a British Welrod hung on his hip. His brown uniform hung open, revealing a torn white shirt and his broad bronze chest. Rough chop threw Wiglaf into Beowulf, knocking the sword from his hand. The collision earned him a disapproving grunt from his new chief, who stood to retrieve his weapon.

"Well, you've done it now," Olaf said.

"What?" Wiglaf glanced at the husky warrior. He was at least fifty and mostly bald, save a few retreating patches of auburn hair.

His thick, lush beard hung to his sternum. The same auburn shade, shot through with gray, formed three tightly woven braids. The intricate pattern made it impossible to know where one stopped and the next began.

Olaf pulled the magazine out of his Madsen, tapped it against his chest plate, and slammed it back into place. "Knocking the chief's sword out of his hand isn't a good move, Rook."

"It's not like I had a choice," Wiglaf said. "The boat kicked…"

"So, now you're not prepared? I'm trying to keep you alive until we find some action. It'd look better if a Nazi killed you, and not the chief."

Wiglaf trembled. "He wouldn't kill me. Would he?"

Olaf tapped his temple with his index finger. "Get out of your head. We'll make landfall soon, then we've got a hard road ahead of us. Keep your eyes open, and you might live long enough to learn why the chief carries that sword."

"Can't you tell me?"

Thirteen voices rang out in laughter, with Olaf's high above the others.

"Land in two minutes," Beowulf shouted. "Gear up, be ready to move."

The men ceased laughing, readied their weapons, and pushed toward the prow.

"I want an even dispersal." Beowulf stepped into the crowd, which parted for him. "Ivar and Breca: you're on point. Olaf: take the rookie and cover the rear. The second we hit the beach, fan out and prepare to receive fire."

"I thought the Americans cleared this beach," Wiglaf said.

Olaf pulled the slide on his weapon, letting it slam home.

"They did, but you'll learn that we treat everything as a combat situation. One day, that bridge will drop and we'll face armed enemies, not an empty beach."

The bridge fell and Wiglaf's blood ran cold.

Breca and Ivar hit the sand at a run, followed by the chief. Five more pairs hit the beach before Wiglaf raced off the boat at Olaf's side. He settled into a defensive position, scanning the dunes with his rifle. It wasn't until he saw Breca's hand gesture, that Wiglaf's heart ceased its thunderous beat. "That's the 'All Clear', right? What do we do now?"

"Now, we find the recon team," Olaf said, before following Beowulf and the rest of the squad up the hill.

Wiglaf shouldered his weapon and followed Olaf, quickly passing the slow-moving warrior. When Olaf caught up, he turned to him. "Where's the recon team?"

"Call your C.O.," a gruff voice said.

Wiglaf saw Olaf frozen in the action of mopping the sweat from his brow. "What?"

"If you think I'll say it again, boy, you're mistaken," the voice snapped.

"Do it," Olaf said.

Wiglaf stole a glance at the small man in sand-colored camouflage behind Olaf. From his outstretched hand, he pointed a pistol at the base of the warrior's neck. "Chief!"

Beowulf turned, his trench gun in his hands. He racked the slide, sending the first of his six rounds into the barrel.

"I'm Viking, in command of the Boar Brigade. We've received orders to report to Hrothgar. There's a plague in Heorot, and I've brought the cure."

The pistol barrel slipped away from Olaf's neck. "It's good to meet you, Viking. They call me Wulfgar. The major's been waiting for your arrival. It's a good thing you've come. We need your talents."

"Have you brought our orders?" Beowulf asked.

Wulfgar stepped in front of Wiglaf, slipping his pistol into its holster. "We're two klicks south of Heorot. Once there, the major will brief you on the situation. I'm just the welcoming committee."

"Right," Beowulf said.

"Are your men ready for a fight? We've cleared most of the area, but the Germans are pushing back hard."

Beowulf nodded. "Lead the way."

Wulfgar smiled and took point.

Beowulf whistled. In response, Ivar, Breca, and four others humped it toward the trees and faded into the shadows.

"Let's go, Rook." Olaf pushed Wiglaf toward the other soldiers, following the recon team into the forest beyond the beach.

"Where are they going?"

Olaf laughed. "Get that rifle off your shoulder and keep it ready. Remember, we're still in live combat."

Wiglaf swallowed hard and unslung his weapon. He pulled the stock into his shoulder as he swept forward at Olaf's side. Despite the dense undergrowth, the team moved at a good clip and reached Heorot earlier than expected. As soon as the gun turrets came into view, Wulfgar held up his fist, halting their advance. He shared a few words with Beowulf before leaving the group.

With a shrill whistle, Beowulf signaled the scouts. After several moments, Breca limped into the clearing supported by Ivar.

"What the hell happened to you?" Beowulf asked.

Breca shook his head.

"Report soldier."

"I don't know, Chief," Breca said. "We separated, operating in our standard fifty-foot sweep pattern. Snorri and Erik should have crossed my path but neither approached. When I went looking for them, I found a man, dressed in black, standing over their bodies."

"Are you telling me there's someone running around the woods killing my men?"

"Yes," Ivar said. "Bjorn and Aegir disappeared as well."

"Four men?" Beowulf barked. "You expect me to believe that a single enemy combatant killed four members of the Boar Brigade?"

"Almost five," Breca said. "I don't know what to tell you, Chief. He fought like a demon. The grip he had on my neck... If Ivar hadn't stuck him, I'd be dead."

Ivar held up his knife, the blade bent to a ninety-degree angle. "For all the good it did."

Beowulf held out his hand, taking the weapon from Ivar. "Armor?"

Ivar shrugged. "I drove the blade between his shoulders. I don't know about you, Chief, but I don't know any armor that's going to stop one of our knives."

"Right," Beowulf said. "We keep watch in pairs. No one goes alone."

"Yes, Chief."

Half an hour passed with tensions running high, but nothing appeared from the tree line. Relief came when Wulfgar returned with word from Heorot. On Hrothgar's order, he led the group to the infirmary, where Breca and Ivar received treatment for their wounds. Beowulf ordered two other men to stand guard, while he and the rest followed Wulfgar to the command bunker.

As soon as they had settled into the briefing room, an older man, bearing the gold leaf of a United States Major entered. His height, stature, and build equal to Beowulf in every regard, commanded instant respect from the men of the Boar Brigade. Though they weren't part of this man's army, they'd come to serve him in his time of need, and thus offered him an American soldier's salute.

"I wasn't aware that the Boar Brigade kissed ass, Chief," the major said.

"Just a sign of respect, Hrothgar."

"Codenames are for reports."

Beowulf pulled the major into a tight embrace. "It's good to see you again, Major Sharpe."

"It's damn good to see you, Viking."

"I thought you didn't like codenames?"

"Since you like yours, I'll make the exception. I see you still have Sarah; how's she treating you?"

Beowulf reached across his chest to pat his battle-worn M12 trench gun. "She's seen me through a good number of battles since your son traded up to my Madsen. How's the boy doing?"

Major Sharpe's jaw tightened. "K.I.A. somewhere south of here. My clearances aren't high enough to learn more. If his mother were still with us, word of her baby dying in some God-forsaken part of Germany would've killed her."

"I'm sorry to hear that," Beowulf said. "After his exploits during the Normandy invasion, I thought he'd live forever."

Major Sharpe gave a mirthless laugh. "Shall we?"

Beowulf nodded.

The major's clerk, a boy in a poorly-sized uniform, handed a manilla folder each to Beowulf and his men before sitting behind a projector. Major Sharpe hit the lights, and the boy turned on the machine.

"Codename: Dragon," Major Sharpe said. "She's a high-ranking SS operative overseeing German interests in the area. Intel informs us she's head of an R and D team currently bivouacked in the region. It's believed she's researching nuclear technology, the same kind that the brass thinks will win this war for us. What they don't know is that Dragon is Hitler's chief occultist. We've reason to believe she isn't working on a bomb but trying to produce a super soldier that will make Germany invincible."

"Super soldier?" Wiglaf said. "That sounds like science fiction."

"Shut it, Rook," Olaf barked.

"That's why I asked for you, Viking," Major Sharpe said. "You've got a reputation for dealing with these kinds of problems."

Beowulf nodded. "She's not alone, else we'd have a smaller file."

"Correct," the major continued. "She commands a special forces battalion. We don't know their true number, but they are some of the best soldiers that Germany's ever produced."

"Not what I mean," Beowulf said. "Four of my men died en route. Another survived an attack; your medic is tending to his wounds. He claims a man in black came out of the woods, and... See for yourself." Beowulf slid the bent weapon across the table toward the major.

"He's called Grendel," Major Sharpe said. "We believe he's

Dragon's prototype soldier. We've very little information, but sources tell us he may be Gunter Hockhirsch, a highly-skilled assassin with strong ties to Hitler's administration. If we're right, he's of unequaled caliber, with a kill count that includes a dozen high ranking Allied officers, not to mention countless civilian targets. All accounts of interaction with Grendel say bullets, grenades, and blades won't even slow him."

"Fine," Beowulf said. "I'll kill him with my bare hands."

"Those are the words I hoped to hear," the major said.

Olaf leafed through his folder. "Who is Mother?"

"Grendel's handler," Major Sharpe said. "She's the link between Grendel and Dragon. The Nazis aren't stupid. They keep two or three levels between the field commandos and the brass. Your mission is to flush Grendel from the weeds, use him to locate Mother, take her out, and find Dragon's base of operations. Once that's done, we'll launch our assault. Your team will slip into her HQ, kill Dragon, and obtain her secrets."

"How do we find a ghost?" Olaf asked.

"You've got bait." Major Sharpe turned on the lights as the clerk cut the projector.

Beowulf got to his feet, closing the folder on the table before him. "Is he after you or me?"

Major Sharpe smiled. "It wasn't hard to get your name on his hit list, Chief. We leaked intel of your arrival. I didn't think he'd try to collect your head while en route; he usually attacks at night when his targets are asleep."

"He wasn't after me," Beowulf said. "It was my men he wanted, to taunt me."

"Maybe," Major Sharpe said. "He knows you're here. It's

only a matter of time until he strikes."

"He'll attack tonight," Beowulf said. "He'll want to put me down as soon as possible. My men and I will bunk in the mess hall. Lock your entire force within the command bunker. When Grendel comes, I want nothing between him and me."

"The guards—" Major Sharpe started.

"Any guards left on duty will die needlessly. Leave the gates open, I want him to see my challenge."

"Luck in battle." Major Sharpe snapped a salute, dismissing the men.

Though many questions echoed in Wiglaf's head, he couldn't bring himself to ask them. To alleviate his troubled mind, he doubled his efforts to prove himself to the squad. First, he joined Ivar and Breca in transferring the wounded from the medical tent into the bunker. Next, he patrolled the camp's perimeter with Olaf to ensure that no one, save the Boar Brigade, drew breath beyond the confines of Heorot. Once he had delivered his report to Beowulf and ensured the locks held firm on the bunker's three entrances, Wiglaf entered the mess hall.

The men had removed the dining tables and set their bedrolls in a circle in the room's center. They passed the remainder of the day cleaning and prepping their weapons while Olaf led them in song. Wiglaf didn't join his voice to theirs as he didn't know the words. Instead, he listened and learned of Beowulf's victories over giants, beasts, and sea monsters. He particularly enjoyed the song that boasted of Beowulf defeating Breca in a sailing race, even though the chief opted to swim instead of using a boat.

When the singing ended, Olaf produced a bottle of clear liquid. Each man drank heartily, growing louder and more boisterous after enjoying his draught. When it came to Wiglaf, he attempted to pass the bottle untasted. Two of the others took hold of him, pinning his body to the floor while Olaf forced him to finish the bottled water, then bid him act the drunken fool.

As the hour grew late, the men slowly allowed their voices to die until each lay, snoring, in his bag. Wiglaf felt sleep reaching for him, but Olaf prodded him in the side.

"What?" Wiglaf mouthed. He followed his partner's eyes around the room, gazing at their comrades, who lay wide awake, ready for battle.

"Chief!" Someone gurgled, drowning in his own blood.

Wiglaf sat up to see a knife buried to the hilt in Leif's throat, a man in black standing over him. The man pulled his blade free and hurled it at Wiglaf. He flinched, awaiting the bite of death's missile, but it never came. When Wiglaf opened his eyes, he found a powerful hand had stopped the knife a breath's distance from his face.

"You've come for me." Beowulf dropped the blade. "My men will not interfere. Kill me if you can, Hockhirsch."

The man in black bristled. "I am Grendel."

He moved with the speed of the wind, closing the distance between them in three long strides. His hand flew out savagely, but Beowulf deflected the blow. A well-placed knee slammed into Beowulf's ribs, knocking him back a step. Mercilessly, Grendel drove at him, flashing fist and foot, but none of his blows broke Beowulf's defenses. Howling furiously, Grendel opened his fists, trying to gouge his foe with his fingers like a wild beast attacking with its claws.

Beowulf wrapped his hand around Grendel's wrist. The

chief's iron grip startled Grendel, who tried to pull away. His eyes widened with disbelief. Beowulf not only matched, but surpassed his strength. With grim resolution, Beowulf pulled the man toward him and drove his forearm into Grendel's chest. The blow dropped his opponent, who lashed out vindictively with his free arm. Beowulf lifted a knee, shattering Grendel's wrist against the stronger joint. A roar of pain and fear echoed off the walls of the mess hall.

Wiglaf joined his fellows encircling the felled terror, who had found his match in their chief. His eyes wide, Grendel no longer resembled a demon capable of killing men, but a child pleading with his father to spare him punishment. When Beowulf drove his fist into Grendel's face, Wiglaf turned away from the brawl.

"Watch!" Olaf demanded.

Wiglaf found his courage and watched as Beowulf straddled Grendel's chest, massive hands coiled around the fallen man's throat. It was no longer fear shining in Grendel's icy blue eyes but relief. He welcomed death.

A cheer rose from the men, but Beowulf waved it away, demanding silence. His order received, each man quelled his voice.

"Grendel killed five of our brothers and paid with his life," Beowulf said. "You lot see to Leif while I report to Hrothgar. Then we'll get some chow and hunt down Mother."

"We don't know where she's hiding," Olaf said.

Beowulf held up a field map, which he'd pulled from Grendel's pocket. "Move."

The night passed in silent reverence. Olaf, Ivar, and a limping Breca felled several small trees, while the rest of the Brigade prepared the pyre. They left it to Wiglaf to ready Leif's body. Wiglaf stripped Leif's chest bare and began cleaning the man's wound. As the blood clung to the cotton wads, a small tattoo made itself known. Three small, interlocking triangles stained the man's skin just below his collarbone.

"That's why we're burning him," Beowulf said, standing at the tent's flap.

"He bears a valknut," Wiglaf said.

"Very good. It's the symbol of Odin. Leif, like the rest of the squad, dedicated his life and death to the All Father. We'll burn him, so he may drink and feast in Valhalla until Ragnarök."

"I don't have one," Wiglaf said.

"Do you want one?"

Wiglaf nodded.

"If you survive the hunt for Mother and Dragon, you'll get one." Beowulf dabbed the remaining blood from Leif's neck. "Now go. I'll finish here. It'll be your honor to light the pyre tonight."

"Yes, Chief," Wiglaf responded.

As Beowulf stitched Leif's neck, Wiglaf left the tent. He found Olaf and the rest of the men beside a six-foot-tall pile of wood, with a bedroll laid on the apex. Each man bore a torch, save Olaf, who carried two. Wiglaf took the spare and fell in with the unit as they formed a pair of lines, raising their fire toward the sky.

At that moment, Beowulf emerged from the tent with Leif's body in his arms. Despite his size, Beowulf carried him as easily as one might carry a babe. He passed under the torches, set the body on the pyre, and began a prayer.

When it ended, Wiglaf instinctively pushed his torch into the pyre. One by one, the Boar Brigade stepped forward, each plunging his torch amidst the wooden structure. They stood watching until the fire had fully engulfed Leif's body.

Part 2: Mother

With the morning came foul news. Hrothgar's second in command, Aeschere, who bore a similarity to Beowulf, had died from a saber wound, rending him from neck to naval. No one knew who killed the man, but the chief gave the order to travel light and fast.

Wiglaf carried a day's worth of provisions and the arms he needed to complete the mission: his rifle, flashlight, and his father's old spyglass. The absence of his standard equipment left him light on his feet, a feeling he'd not known since before his time in basic training. By contrast, Olaf carried not only his Madsen but also a heavy caliber machine gun he had convinced Hrothgar to lend him. The immense weight of the weapon and its ammunition slowed the bulky warrior, but his insistence of its importance made Beowulf agree to its inclusion. The chief carried only a small pack and his broadsword. He'd left his Welrod and M12 at Heorot.

The march started long before the sun appeared and didn't halt until noon. During their brief rest, Wiglaf dropped to his rear and opened a can of beans. When he realized that none of the others sat, he hefted himself to his feet to eat his meal. The moment he finished, Beowulf gave the order to move. Two hours later, they reached the Western cliffs. Soon after, Ivar returned from his forward reconnoiter with reports of a nearby sea cave. Beowulf halted the column to consult the map he'd taken from Grendel.

"Well, did we find it?" Olaf asked.

Beowulf nodded. "According to the orders we found on Grendel, he and Mother used this cave as a forward staging point. We believe they traveled alone, so we aren't expecting a large force inside. Olaf and Wiglaf, you'll set up the Browning M19 on this ridge," he indicated on the map, "giving you a clear line of sight to the cave's entrance. If anyone or anything that isn't a member of the brigade shows itself, kill it."

"Aye!"

"The rest of the squad will descend from the cliffs above the cave. We'll drop into the shallows of the jetty and advance in pairs. Ragnar, you're with me. It's radio silence until the bitch is dead or things get F.U.B.A.R. Clear?"

The men returned the affirmative before the squad separated.

Beowulf and the breach team had climbed halfway to the cave by the time Olaf had the machine gun prepped and ready. "Clear my line of sight."

Wiglaf pulled his eye from the spyglass to meet Olaf's gaze. "I am clear."

"Get beside me, Rook." Olaf grunted. "If this puppy kicks, I don't want a stray round obliterating your skull."

Wiglaf followed the order before placing his eye to the lens of the spyglass. "They're about to jump." As if responding to his words, the squad, save Beowulf, dropped into the shallows. As soon as they hit the water, it churned so violently that Wiglaf didn't need a spyglass to see it.

"That's not natural," Olaf said.

Wiglaf turned the dial on the spyglass. "Something's moving in the water."

Echoes of screams reached Wiglaf long after his brothers ceased moving. A blip of static sounded beside him.

"Go ahead," Olaf said.

Beowulf's enraged voice came over the radio. "What the hell's happening?"

"Rook?" Olaf prompted.

Wiglaf snapped out of his stupor and turned the magnification dial several more times. "Snakes."

"Repeat," Beowulf ordered.

"Sea snakes, Chief. They dropped into a nest or something."

"Anyone still moving?"

"Negative."

Beowulf cursed. "I gave the order to jump but then got hung up on a rock. Stupid. I should've expected a trap."

Olaf's voice was heavy with grief. "We've got a mission."

"Right," Beowulf said. "Rook, you're with me. Get yourself down here. Olaf…"

"I know what to do."

"Then move!"

Wiglaf stood up and adjusted the weapon strap on his shoulder.

"Not that, Rook. Rifles are for long-distance encounters." Olaf slipped his holster from his hip. "She'll serve you better in that cave."

Wiglaf wrapped his fingers around the wooden grip of Olaf's Bergmann-Bayard pistol. He dislodged the magazine to ensure it was serviceable. Satisfied, he slammed it home, pushed the pistol back into the holster, and attached it to his belt.

"My father gave me that," Olaf said. "Don't make me climb those cliffs to retrieve it."

Wiglaf nodded.

"Off you go, Rook."

Fifteen minutes later, Wiglaf clung to the cliffs at Beowulf's side, twelve feet above the roiling water. "Reporting for duty."

"Ready to drop?"

"But, Chief, the snakes."

"Five, four…" The moment Beowulf said three, Olaf's machine gun released its rage. Countless rounds tore into the water below, causing it to churn again.

"Drop!"

Wiglaf released his grip on the rock. He hit the water a second before the chief and swam for shore. The moment his feet touched the bottom, a firm hand pressed between Wiglaf's shoulders, forcing him to run deeper into the cave. The pressure didn't stop until they reached a dry spot above the current.

"I can't believe that worked."

"Neither can I," a feminine voice said.

Wiglaf drew his pistol in one hand and fished out his flashlight with the other. The narrow beam of pale white light swept through the cave, revealing a slender figure dressed in the black and silver uniform of an SS officer. She wore a crimson armband, bearing the white circle and black swastika of the Nazi party.

"I think we need more light, don't you?" The woman pulled a lever and an old generator started, sputtered, and then found its rhythm. A dozen orange halogen lights flickered to life, illuminating the cave. "Welcome to my home."

Wiglaf's eyes fell on a pair of bunks built into the wall, supported by chains that hung from the ceiling. A series of metal-coated wires, connected to the generator, snaked through the area.

"I can tell that you're the squad's newest member. Isn't it past your bedtime, child? Would you like some milk?" The woman moved to unbutton her shirt.

"Enough," Beowulf barked.

She turned her sapphire-colored eyes on him. "I'm hoping you're Beowulf. I understand he's quite the swordsman. The blade on your hip gives me hope. It would've have wounded my pride to learn that my children robbed me of the pleasure of killing you and giving your head to Dragon myself."

"Children?" Wiglaf asked.

"The venomous snakes that killed your men," the woman said. "I am their mother."

"Were," Beowulf quipped.

"I doubt your gunner killed them all."

Beowulf drew his sword. "I am who you think I am."

She moved like lightning, drawing a saber from the table beside her. With a flick of her wrist, she freed the blade and launched its scabbard at Beowulf.

With a mighty swing of his sword, Beowulf batted the projectile to the ground. "She's mine!"

Wiglaf lowered his pistol, his eyes locked on the titans before him.

Mother swept her blade swift and hard with each pass, driving unrelentingly at Beowulf. Each advance pushed the bigger man toward the sea, but her steel never broke his guard. One misstep and a poorly timed pommel bash presented Beowulf the opportunity he needed to turn from defense to offense.

He drew back his arm and swung hard from his hips. Though Mother attempted to parry, the force of the strike sent her tumbling backward and dislodged the saber from her hand. Without pause, Beowulf raced forward, his blade set for a life-ending thrust to her chest.

In desperation, Mother gripped a loose rock and sent it screaming through the air. It struck Beowulf in the knee and he howled in pain as he dropped to the ground. Mother threw herself toward her fallen foe, producing a small brass bar from her belt. As she landed on Beowulf, the bar appeared to fall from her hand, but with a complicated action of her wrist, it opened to reveal a silvery blade. She drove it into Beowulf's back, just below his left shoulder.

Blood poured from the wound, but it didn't faze Beowulf. He reared back to cast Mother off him. With his injured arm, he retrieved his sword and spun to face her. Whether on purpose or by happy accident, Beowulf's elbow locked in place, causing his spin to bring the blade around slightly ahead of his body. At that exact moment, Mother leaped to her feet and charged. Sword met neck, and the former found victory in the collision. Her head rolled on the floor, coming to rest between Wiglaf's feet.

Wiglaf's stomach churned, ready to spill his beans over the bloody horror between his legs. Once he regained his composure, he looked to Beowulf. "Is your injury bad, Chief?"

"A scratch," Beowulf told him. "Find her orders. She mentioned Dragon. Something here must point to her location."

"A field dressing, at least," Wiglaf insisted.

Beowulf reached over his shoulder and pulled the knife from his flesh. The silver and brass weapon, stained with his life's essence, tumbled from his fingers to the ground. "As you wish."

It only took a few minutes to clean and dress the wound. Finding Mother's journal took even less time, considering the small space they needed to search. This allowed them to dedicate the rest of the time in the cave to planning their safe return to Heorot. Swimming seemed impossible with the snakes in the jetty, but with his wounded shoulder, Beowulf couldn't climb the rock face. Fortunately, they found no signs of the beasts when they returned to the water, so they took to the surf.

Olaf met them several miles down the coast. He described how the bodies of their fallen comrades had followed the sea toward their ultimate resting place. They agreed that death in battle would gain the fallen entrance into Valhalla, and that a sea burial offered the same honors as a pyre. In case the gods demanded a fire to pay the toll on Bifrost, Olaf left his only signal flare to burn on a lonely rock near the water's edge.

The sun rose on the second day before they reached Heorot. Beowulf's arm received proper medical attention as he briefed Hrothgar on the outcome of the mission. Once the medic had completed his work, Beowulf and the major made their council private, leaving Olaf and Wiglaf to eat before retiring to an unassigned bunkroom.

Wiglaf tossed and turned for hours. He heard the soft snores of the bulky warrior beneath him. "How can you sleep?"

The bunkroom door opened, and Beowulf entered. He laid his sword on the foot of his bed and dropped hard onto the mattress. Before he closed his eyes, they settled on Wiglaf's. "Rule number one of the field: sleep and eat when you can, Rook. You never know when you'll get another chance."

"Is that why Olaf passed out the second his head hit the pillow?"

Beowulf's snores answered him.

Part 3: Dragon

The morning passed while Wiglaf and his companions slept. Shortly after noon, Wulfgar entered their room. The scout wore his battle gear, an M1 slung over his shoulder and a grim expression. "The death of Mother and Grendel tipped Dragon to our plans. She launched an attack on King's End, taking the castle and burning the surrounding lands. We don't know how many troops she's got inside the fortress, but Major Sharpe's gathered the Allied forces in the area to retake the castle. Chief, he wants you leading the vanguard."

"We'll prepare," Beowulf said.

Wulfgar snapped to attention and left.

"Gear and grub." Beowulf's voice sounded weary.

"Chief," Olaf's voice hung heavy with concern, "are you sure you can handle this mission? Your shoulder…"

"We've got orders."

Olaf stared at him. "You can't."

"Stow it, soldier." Beowulf slipped his foot into one of his boots.

Olaf shook his head. "Prior to joining the squad, I served in Iceland, teaching winter warfare to the Americans. I got friendly with an officer during those months. He commanded the forces at King's End for a short time after the Nazis abandoned it. From what he said, it's nearly impossible to assault from the ground. If Dragon took the citadel, she's got a massive force, or she's wielding supernatural powers."

"Do you have a point?"

"It has a weakness," Olaf said. "Do you think Hrothgar would keep to his original plan if you told him about a secret tunnel we could use to slip into the fortress?"

A smile appeared on Beowulf's face. Armed with this knowledge, Beowulf met with Major Sharpe. When he returned with the news that they were freed from fighting with the vanguard, the remaining members of the Boar Brigade finished their preparations for battle. It was a hard journey over rocky terrain, but as the moon rose to power in the heavens, they reached the mouth of the tunnel.

They waited in silence for the signal to advance, their weapons at the ready. When the distant explosion sounded the Allied charge, Beowulf entered the cave with his M12 primed and loaded. Wiglaf followed, checking the chamber of his rifle. Olaf brought up the rear, carrying his Madsen. They moved quickly and quietly, scanning the cave with muzzle-mounted flashlights. After a few hundred yards, they reached the stone steps. Hidden in the sheer rock face, the nearly imperceptible stairs rose into the bowels of King's End.

Twice during the ascent, Wiglaf looked over the ledge, nearly losing his composure at the height they'd climbed. Had Olaf not gripped him the second time, Wiglaf would have fallen. When they reached the top, the narrow steps ended at a metal door with a large wheel in its center. Without a word, Beowulf slipped his M12 into its holster and gripped the wheel with both hands.

"You won't move—" Olaf's sentence died as the muscles of Beowulf's arms rippled to the surface. The power hidden within his body, which allowed him to turn the wheel meant for the strength of three, was inconceivable. The lock disengaged, and the door swung open.

"I'll be—" A shot rang out. Olaf's head rocked back and his lifeless body tumbled off the stairs, into the darkness.

Rage consumed Wiglaf. He pulled the stock of his rifle to his shoulder and stormed the structure. Another bullet screamed through the air, missing his flesh but smashing the stock of his rifle to pieces. Unable to fire his broken weapon, Wiglaf gripped it by the barrel and smashed it down on the helmeted head of the Nazi soldier. The first blow dropped him. The second ended him. But it wasn't until he felt Beowulf grip his arm that Wiglaf relented.

"That's one," Beowulf said. "There are hundreds more on this base. Do you seek vengeance?"

Wiglaf nodded.

Beowulf pulled his Welrod from his hip and pressed it into Wiglaf's hand. "She holds six rounds. Once they're gone, drop it for whatever's at your feet and keep moving." With his trench gun in hand, Beowulf made his way down the hall, splintering the courtyard door with one powerful kick. He opened fire on a passing Nazi; Sarah's powerful blast sent the man tumbling across the open ground. Wiglaf followed his chief through the opening, firing the bolt action Welrod. Two bullets slammed into another soldier, frozen with panic at the sight of his fallen friend. A third buried itself in the wall.

Beowulf racked his weapon, ejecting the spent shell with a crunch.

"This way." He moved with purpose across the courtyard. His weapon barked three more times, taking down a Nazi with each action.

Wiglaf emptied his last three rounds into passing Nazis and dropped the Welrod. He scooped up a Sturmgwehr and fit the submachine gun to his shoulder before following Beowulf. "Where are we going, Chief?"

"Away from the fighting," Beowulf said. "Dragon won't be at the front. She'll want to watch the Allied forces break themselves against the walls of her fortress. We'll find her at the castle's highest point."

The sounds of war filled the night with a deafening roar. The intent on the chief's face and the rage still brewing from the loss of Olaf gave Wiglaf faith in the mission's outcome. His submachine gun screamed to life the moment they breached the tower's door. Beowulf's M12 lent its battle cry to the cacophony. When the weapons finally went silent, it wasn't clear which had inflicted more damage.

Wiglaf dropped his gun and pulled a Sauer 38H from the holster of one of the fallen soldiers. Olaf's words about pistols serving better in small spaces rung in Wiglaf's ears.

When they passed the second floor, Beowulf fired Sarah's last shell. He slipped her back into her sheath and drew Naegling from his hip. After a steep climb, they reached the door that led to the tower's summit. Beowulf hit it with his shoulder, sending the ironbound wood bouncing toward a small cluster of Nazis. In the group's center stood a woman clad in the same black uniform that Mother had worn. As soon as her eyes fell on Beowulf, she shouted something in German. The soldiers went for their weapons, but Wiglaf emptied his magazine into the scrambling mass, felling them all.

"Wonderful shooting," Dragon said. "I dare say you deserve a bronze star for your efforts."

"That's an American medal," Beowulf said.

Dragon laughed. "You are Danish. Your accent suggests Geatish ancestry?"

"I am Beowulf, son to Ecgtheow. I've come for your arcane secrets and your head."

"Don't tell me you believe in the supernatural." Dragon clicked her tongue before erupting into dark laughter. "You are as silly as the Fuhrer, with his nonsensical beliefs. Science is the only true magic. It alone will give us the technology needed for German supremacy, not ghosts, ghouls, or goblins."

"You lie," Wiglaf shouted.

Dragon turned her eyes to Wiglaf. "You are a fool, boy."

"Grendel was invincible, and Mother controlled snakes," Wiglaf said.

"Body armor and pheromones," Dragon said. "Science and technology, I assure you. Another demonstration?" She threw her arm forward, releasing a gout of orange flame from her wrist.

Wiglaf stood, frozen in the fire's path.

Beowulf slammed his shoulder into Wiglaf, knocking him aside.

From the ground, Wiglaf watched his chief slice the fiery jet in two with Naegling. The twin streaks of fire passed harmlessly around Beowulf, colliding with the stone wall behind him.

"How is that possible?" Dragon thrust her other arm forward, producing another flame.

Beowulf swept his sword through the fire, parting it once more. "To say that magic doesn't exist is folly."

"Perhaps you're correct," Dragon said. "Is the magic within you or your blade?"

"You'll never know!" Beowulf charged forward, ready to strike.

Dragon raised her arm again. Instead of fire, she produced a Walther PPK in her gloved hand. Her first bullet tore into Beowulf's abdomen. A second passed through his shoulder. The third found a home in his chest.

Beowulf fell to his knees, his broadsword clattering to the ground beside him. Blood soaked through his uniform, staining it crimson.

Dragon stepped closer to Beowulf, raising the Walther with his forehead. "That settles that; the magic is in the blade."

Wiglaf's rage exploded. He charged forward, stooping to reclaim the fallen Naegling. Swinging the blade with all his might, he sought to end Dragon, but she ducked under the blow, licking her lips; her apparent glee at the prospect of killing two wielders of such a powerful blade twisted his stomach into knots. Before Wiglaf could aim a second blow, she struck him hard in the face. As he fell, he saw Beowulf retrieve a knife from his boot.

Beowulf pushed himself up from the ground and slipped his blade into the tender flesh of Dragon's throat. The Nazi fell to her knees, blood pouring from her fresh wound, then she toppled face first into the stone, never to move again.

A look of satisfaction washed over Beowulf's face before he collapsed.

"Chief!" Wiglaf crawled toward Beowulf, who lay on his back, hardly breathing.

"How do men gain entrance into Valhalla?" Beowulf asked.

"They die with a sword in their hand." Wiglaf pushed Naegling's hilt into Beowulf's palm.

Beowulf nodded and drew his last breath.

Wiglaf stared at the lifeless body, willing his chief to return from the land of the dead. When that didn't happen, he forced himself to his feet. He set the blade in a place of honor along the man's sternum and positioned the chief's arms across his chest to grip the sword's hilt. Then, he turned his attention to Dragon, searching her body for the source of her flame. Hidden beneath her jacket, he found a tiny canister of gasoline, which powered a pair of micro flamethrowers attached to her wrists. Using the knife that had claimed her life, Wiglaf opened the fuel reserves, allowing them to pool around Beowulf's body.

"By fire or sea, the men of the Boar Brigade reach the mead-hall of the gods. May fire take you." Wiglaf drew the lighter from his pocket, but before he could ignite the pyre, Beowulf's arm fell, casting his sword from his body.

"As you wish." Wiglaf retrieved the ancient sword before dropping the blue flame on to Beowulf. Small ribbons of budding fire turned into a roaring inferno within moments. Wiglaf gazed at the sword in his hand, squeezing his fingers around its grip. "You belonged to a hero named Beowulf. I ask you to serve me as well as you did him, for as long as I have the strength to wield you." A glimmer of the fire's light shone off the blade: the sword granted

Wiglaf its boon. With a surge of intense power, he charged into the castle. "To Valhalla!"

DRAGON⊙

Douglas Jern

The engine started to rattle on a long, empty stretch of free-way, with nothing but wheat fields for miles on end. Siggy shifted down to third gear and muttered curses under his breath. As if the busted air conditioner wasn't bad enough, now he faced the prospect of being stranded in the middle of bumfuck nowhere without a soul to help him out.

"Come on, Granny, work with me here."

The car responded with an even louder whine from the engine. It sounded like someone was torturing an otter in there. A red diode blinked on the dashboard. The label above it was too scratched to read, but with Siggy's luck, the flashing light probably meant that Granny was on her last wheels.

To top it all off, the afternoon was turning into evening, and the sun would soon set. Siggy was not all too keen on the idea of spending the night alone in the badlands.

He'd heard the stories, both at home and in school. They were out there, and they had many names—the Strangers, the Others, the Children of Y. Creatures of the ether. Enemies of mankind, as his old history teacher had said with knitted eyebrows. "Beware!"

Not that Siggy believed all that claptrap. There hadn't been a recorded attack by a Y on a human in over five decades. It was all propaganda, Siggy decided. A devious government scheme to justify their rampant expansionism.

Still, he would prefer having a roof over his head before nightfall.

Siggy looked up at the road ahead, squinting against the evening sun. His lips parted in a disbelieving grin. A group of houses rippled out of the mirage on the horizon. He blinked three times and looked again, but the houses were still there.

"Sweet, looks like my luck's finally turning."

He gave the engine a little more gas, wincing as Granny screeched in protest. But she did speed up, and she didn't break down. Not yet.

As he drew closer, he could make out more houses and build-ings. What had at first looked like a farm turned out to be a whole village. On the right side of the road, a sun-bleached metal sign swept by. It was peppered with bullet holes, but he could still read what it said:

'Welcome to Dennabar, population 137'

Siggy thumped the dashboard in triumph. There had to be at least one decent mechanic among those one hundred and thir-ty-seven people.

Now that danger had been averted, his situation began to feel like an adventure. He was the brave hero on an epic journey, and this village would be his first stop. He laughed and hummed a jaunty tune to himself. This was turning out to be a lot of fun, after all.

Granny gave out on him as he rolled into the village square. The ailing engine snorted like a choking pig and shuddered once before falling silent.

Siggy got out and stretched his back. He drew a deep breath to take in that fabled sweet country air. It smelled like rust and fertilizer.

He pushed the car off to the side of the road so it wouldn't get in anyone's way. Not that he saw anyone in whose way it might get; the little village looked like a ghost town. The houses he had passed on his way were worn and dilapidated, many of them clearly abandoned. Thorny weeds bristled from cracks in the asphalt. He hadn't seen a single person yet.

Around the barren village square stood a low shoebox of a building made out of rusty tin sheets housing a grocery store and a post office. A church with a wooden steeple, and a wide brick house with dozens of windows and a big sign over the front door that read HUEY'S TAVERN & HOTEL completed the dismal set. All of them were shuttered or boarded up, save for the hotel, where lights shone in some of the windows.

Siggy shrugged and picked the only available option. With any luck, he might get himself a bite to eat, and maybe he could ask around for a mechanic. He opened the dark wooden door and went inside.

The bartender, and, as it turned out, the owner of the hotel, greeted him. He wore a white and green rag like a veil over the left half of his face.

The owner showed Siggy to a small but clean corner room on the second floor.

"Shower's a bit old," he said. "Takes a few minutes for the water to heat up."

Then he started to cough. His head jerked violently and the veil over his face fluttered aside for a moment. Siggy caught a glimpse of a dark crater where the owner's left eye should have been, the skin around the eye socket purple and glistening.

"Excuse me," said the owner once the coughing fit had subsided. He muttered something about a summer cold and hurried down the stairs.

After leaving his meager baggage in the room and splashing some water on his face, Siggy went down to the bar. Since the hotel restaurant was only open during lunchtime, he settled for a beer and some peanuts, hoping for a heartier breakfast in the morning.

Instead of the small round tables and tall stools common in the bars of Central Yard, Huey's Tavern had only one long table. A group of four men sat clustered near one end, chugging their brews and casting occasional glances in his direction.

Every now and then, the men would cough or clear their throats. Siggy noticed that all of them wore mismatched rags and scarves tied around various parts of their bodies, and wondered if they hid blemishes like the owner's ravaged eye socket.

Near the other end of the table, another man sat alone, clutching a beer glass that contained little more than suds. He waved at Siggy as he approached.

"Hey there, buddy! Nice to see a fresh face around here. Take a seat!"

Siggy took him up on his offer, pulling out the chair across from him. Up close, he noticed how disheveled the man was. His clothes were smudged with dirt and what looked like dried blood.

A shock of unkempt gray hair covered his scalp. A beard that was more salt than pepper sprouted in irregular patches on his cheeks, jaw, and neck.

Despite his rough appearance, the man's eyes seemed almost to shine with cheer. They were the bright blue eyes of a little boy, peeking out from a worn, leathery face, as if the man's soul was still young. That, and the friendly tone of his voice, compelled Siggy to join him.

"Never seen you around here before," said the man, and he grinned, revealing an incomplete set of amber-colored teeth.

"Never been here before," replied Siggy, and set his bowl of nuts down on the table.

"In that case, let me welcome you to Dennabar. The name's Reginald, but everyone calls me Reg." The man held out a hand covered by a fingerless glove. Siggy took it.

"I'm Siggy. Nice to meet you, Reg."

One of the men at the end of the table raised his voice. His face was nearly perfectly rectangular in shape, and his neck was thicker than his head.

"I'd stay away from Reg if I was you, boy," said the man. "He ain't right."

"You can say that again," one of his companions, a skinny man with buck teeth, piped in. "He's bad mojo."

A chorus of affirmative grunts and mutterings followed. Siggy looked at Reg again, who grinned and shrugged.

"I ain't exactly Mr. Popular around here, as you can see."

Siggy nodded, then said to Reg, loud enough to send a message, "You seem like a decent guy to me."

The grumbling and scoffing from the end of the table was

sweet music to Siggy's ears.

"So, Siggy," said Reg, "what brings you to these parts? Hope you don't mind me saying it, but you've got the look of city folk about you."

"Yeah, I'm from Central Yard," said Siggy, and he took a sip of his beer. It was bitter, but not awful. "As for why I'm here, well, I guess you could say I wanted to break free."

"Free from what?" Reg peered at him with one eyebrow cocked. "You break outta jail or something?"

"No, nothing like that." Siggy laughed. "It's just, you know... society."

"Society?"

"Yeah, man. Society."

The word left a far worse taste in his mouth than the beer. He shoved a handful of peanuts into his mouth to wash it away. Reg looked lost, but Siggy had no idea how to explain. He lacked the words to describe the sense that he was nothing but a cog in a machine, a piece of biological clockwork ticking away in the infinite mechanism of Central Yard.

The requirements of a good citizen were many. A good citizen listened to their parents, went to school, swallowed all the establishment's bullshit, and learned to love their leaders and serve their cause. Humans were good, Y's were bad, and the highest virtue was doing what one was told. A good citizen never questioned their superiors' judgment and didn't think too hard about things. Work and serve. Those who kept their heads down might get to keep them on.

"I just had to get away from it all," he said. "Get back to nature, you know? I wanted to live a simpler life." He smiled wryly. "Lots of people back home said I was boring."

"Nonsense," said Reg, and he snatched a peanut from Siggy's bowl. "Nothing wrong with wanting to return to your roots. Besides, what do city slickers know anyway? So in love with the big city and all its fancy attractions. They look at a small town like this and scoff. They see a simple existence and write it off as boring. But that's where they get it wrong."

He paused for effect. Siggy waited for him to go on. He had forgotten all about his beer and peanuts.

"Simple ain't boring," said Reg. "Simple is gouging a man's eye out with a sickle for being rude to your woman. Simple is drinking yourself stupid on Friday night and pissing your initials in the snow in the graveyard. Simple is taking potshots with your hunting rifle at any lost Children of Y that stumble out of the forest. Now, how can anyone say that's boring?"

"Don't forget killing your old man for the lottery money," brayed one of the men from the end of the table. Reg flipped him the bird without looking round. The gesture was clearly meant to be nonchalant, but Siggy noticed a change in Reg's demeanor. As soon as he heard the words "lottery money," his blue eyes flashed like cold steel.

"Put a sock in it, Earl," said Reg, and there was steel in his voice too. "You still owe me for the truck repairs."

The man called Earl grumbled something inaudible and returned to his beer.

"You repair cars?" asked Siggy, leaning forward.

"Anything that rolls," said Reg with a gap-toothed grin. "Need anything fixed?"

Siggy told him about Granny. Reg raised his eyebrows.

"A good old E-engine, you say? Never thought I'd see one of those again."

"I came across an old one at a chop shop on the edge of town," said Siggy. "Only cost me a grand."

Reg whistled and nodded. Then he cocked his head and a puzzled look came over his face.

"What about fuel, though? Can't imagine there are many places that still sell the stuff, what with the government ban and everything."

He was, unfortunately, right on that point. Siggy had scoured nearly every vehicle servicing station in Central Yard before he'd found one that still sold E-fuel, and he didn't even want to recall how much it had cost him. Suffice it to say it was too fucking much.

"Yeah," he said, scratching the back of his neck. "In hindsight, I guess it wasn't the most informed purchase I've ever made."

"I'll say. It's all about solar cars these days."

"Right." Siggy scoffed. "As if a college dropout like me could ever afford one of those, even used."

"Down on your luck, are you?" An impish gleam played in Reg's eyes. "Well, it's a hefty initial investment, for sure. But they pay for themselves in the long run. We all drive 'em around here."

Siggy muttered a noncommittal reply. It wasn't just about the money. All new solar cars were hooked up to the MW network, the Union's treasure trove of weaponized personal information. If the choice came to cutting down emissions or relinquishing his privacy to the fascist pricks in the government, Siggy would gladly pollute his heart out. And look where that got him.

"Anyway," said Siggy with a sigh, "the car is what it is. Do you think you can fix it?"

"Oh, yup." Reg nodded. "Shouldn't be a problem. I can give you a fair price."

Siggy's heart sank. He had no idea how much Reg would charge, but he was sure it would be more than the measly sum he had left after paying for his room.

His worries must have shown on his face, because Reg patted his shoulder. "Tell you what, I think we can work something out. I have a personal matter I could use some help with." His eyes flickered toward the four men for a fraction of a second, then returned to Siggy. His grin widened. "You do me a solid and I'll fix up your ride for free. What do ya say?"

Siggy hesitated. His father used to say that if something sounds too good to be true, it probably is. It seemed awfully generous of Reg to make an offer like that to someone he'd just met. On the other hand, he could really use a hand with the car. He smiled and thanked Reg for his kindness.

They agreed to meet up outside the hotel the following morning.

After shaking hands with Reg, Siggy retired to his room. Exhausted after a long day on the road, he fell asleep as soon as his head hit the pillow.

The breakfast turned out to be one boiled egg and two strips of soggy bacon on a piece of toast that could have served as a doorstop. Siggy forced it down and grudgingly parted with his last few coins.

Reg awaited him outside. Siggy did a double take when he saw him. A black mouthpiece and a translucent faceguard obscured Reg's face. He looked like the world's shoddiest riot cop.

"What's with the mask?" asked Siggy as he approached.

"On the contrary, where's yours?"

"Should I be wearing one?"

Reg shrugged.

"Well, government officials say ether pollution's getting worse out here, because of all them Y's running around in the outer lands." He pointed with his thumb at the open fields beyond the village and the forest on the horizon. "They say ether flows in their veins, and that's what's making this place unsuitable to live in."

"I'm not so sure that's true," said Siggy. "If you ask me, it's just Union propaganda to justify persecution of the Children of Y."

"And if you ask me, Mr. Central Yard, I'd say you haven't spent enough time out here to have an opinion on the matter," said Reg.

"All I'm saying is maybe not all Y's are bad people," said Siggy, not sure why it was so important that he showed this old country man that he could stand up for his beliefs, only knowing that it was. "I mean, maybe some of them are, but so are some humans. Right?"

Reg shrugged. "I'm sure there's plenty of decent souls among them. But that's beside the point. Have you ever seen a Y bite the dust?"

Siggy shook his head. Reg chuckled.

"Well, I can tell you, they don't keel over and lie there like you or I would. No, they go up in smoke. Poof! Big ol' puff of ether. And that's where all this pollution's coming from. So, you see, it doesn't matter if they're bad people or not. It's simply in their nature."

"Even so," said Siggy, "can we even be sure what the government says is true? Is ether really all that bad for you?"

"Oh, Siggy," said Reg, "if only you'd seen what I've seen. Two-headed rattlesnakes, furless gophers with seven legs… Ether does things to the living, that's for sure."

He looked Siggy straight in the eye when he spoke, and Siggy saw that he was dead serious.

Siggy shivered. He thought of the owner of Huey's Tavern with his ruined eye. The men hiding other afflictions under their rags and scarves. Their frequent coughing fits.

Back in school, he had dismissed the cartoonishly hideous diagrams and X-ray images of people that had allegedly been changed by the ether as sensationalist propaganda—a sinister psychological operation by the government to scare the populace into obedience. Now he was not so sure.

"Is it safe to be here?" he asked.

"Oh, you'll be fine," said Reg. "You'll be outta here in a few days, tops. I'd invest in one of these if you're planning on staying, though." He tapped the side of his mask.

"Is that why there's so few people here?" said Siggy, looking around the deserted square.

"Yup. Government advised people to relocate to Central Yard for their own safety. A lot of folks did. Then there's some who think it's all a hoax." He winked at Siggy from behind his mask. Siggy felt his cheeks grow hot. "They claim the government is after their property."

"What about you?"

"As you can see, I take precautions. I've got other reasons for staying. Something you might help me deal with." He clapped his hands together. "But first, let's take a look at that car of yours, eh?"

Siggy showed him the car, and Reg hovered around it like a bee in a field of flowers, fawning over the chrome-plated bumpers and gullwing doors. Once he opened the hood, he immediately identified the problem: a faulty ether filter in the intake manifold.

"A common problem in these vehicles," he said, drawing a screwdriver from his toolbelt. "Won't take long to fix."

He bent over the engine and got to work unscrewing the broken filter.

A woman walked by on the other side of the road. Unlike Reg, she was not wearing a mask. She glared at Reg as she passed, her eyes as cold as ice.

"People around here don't really like you much, do they?" said Siggy.

"Hard not to notice, huh?" said Reg, and he dropped a screw on a rag he had placed on the ground.

"Any particular reason?"

"Maybe."

"Does it have anything to do with your dad's lottery money?" said Siggy, thinking back on what Earl had said last night.

Reg sighed.

"Yeah, it's about the lottery money, all right."

He stopped working on the car and stood leaning over the open hood, like a man on the edge of a deep, dark hole.

Siggy fidgeted with his shirt collar. "Look, I understand if you don't want to talk about it. It's not my place to ask. I'm sorry."

"No," said Reg, and he turned his face toward Siggy. "I reckon I might as well tell you. Maybe I've grown sentimental in my old age, but I like you, Siggy. You're a good guy."

"Thanks," said Siggy, surprised to feel his chest tighten at Reg's compliment. He couldn't remember the last time anyone had called him a "good guy," if anyone ever had.

"See, I have a brother," said Reg. "His name's Farrell. We used to live on the big farm on the edge of town. Mostly kept to ourselves, especially after Mom died. Fucking cancer. Anyway, Dad became somewhat of a recluse after that. Spent most of his time working the fields. Probably would've worked himself to death if it weren't for that lottery ticket."

"Did he win a lot of money?"

"Does a Y shit in the woods? Twenty-five million, baby."

Siggy whistled. With that kind of money, he could buy two penthouse suites in downtown Central Yard and still have enough cash for a year's worth of booze.

"Not bad, huh? Farrell and I were ecstatic. We dreamed of fancy cars, epic bar crawls in Central Yard, luxury escorts, you name it. But, as soon as Dad had paid off a few small debts, he stuffed the rest of his money in his mattress. He was a stubborn old geezer."

"So, what did you do? You didn't steal the money from him, did you?"

"I'm afraid it was worse than that," said Reg. "Now, I was none too happy with Dad's decision. But it was his money, and he could do what he wanted with it. The farm turned a fair profit, and I did some mechanic work on the side. We didn't really want for anything. Sadly, Farrell didn't see it that way."

His hands stopped working on the engine, and his eyes seemed to gaze somewhere far away. Siggy waited for him to continue.

"I never had a chance to stop him," said Reg, his voice trembling. "On the day it happened, I was away fixing up Barlow's tractor. When I got home, I found Dad dead in his bedroom. Farrell stood at the foot of the bed, the gun in his hand still smoking."

"Damn…" Siggy didn't know what else to say.

"Yeah. When Farrell heard me come in, he looked at me and said, 'It's better this way, Reg. He was old and lonely. No one will miss him. It's only right that his money should see some use, do some good for someone.' I was too shocked to say anything. I just stood there and watched as he turned his gun on me. 'Now get out of here,' he said, and there was nothing of my dear brother in that cold voice. 'Get out before I kill you too.' It took a few seconds before I realized what he'd said. Once I did, I turned and ran like a coward, to my eternal shame."

Reg hung his head. Siggy hesitated, then laid a hand on his shoulder. He couldn't think of anything else to do. Compared to the hell Reg had been through, Siggy's own problems seemed small and insignificant. He wished there was something he could do to help.

Reg looked around and Siggy could see a tear roll down his cheek beneath the mask.

"I've lived in my little workshop on the edge of town ever since then, too broke to leave, too chickenshit to confront my brother. The other villagers think I was in on it. Can you believe that? They don't know shit, but they call me a murderer."

"Why would they think that?"

Reg waved his hand sharply, as if swatting at a fly. "Ah, fuck

234

'em all! They'd rat on me out of pure spite. They always envied my dad for his big farm, and when he won the lottery, they all lined up in front of the porch like a gang of horny suitors, clamoring for a few scraps off the table. As if Dad owed them anything. Pah! Greedy assholes."

He kicked up a small cloud of dust with his boot.

"Never saw any of them try to talk to Farrell, either. Scared of getting shot, I bet."

"Where is your brother now?" asked Siggy. "Does he still live in the village?"

"Oh, he's still here, all right. As for whether he still lives, that's another question. I've tried to keep tabs on him, but he hardly ever leaves the house. Once in a while he'd go out to the coop to grab a chicken for food, but they're all gone now. No idea if he's even got any food left in there. For all I know he could be dead already, lying on his bed with all the money underneath him. Just like Dad. Wouldn't that be ironic?"

"You never contacted the police?"

"I thought about it, but what good would it do? It'd be my word against Farrell's, and all the villagers would say I had a hand in the murder too. Shit, they might end up arresting me and letting Farrell go free! No, the cops can't help me with this one."

He wrapped an arm around Siggy's shoulders and pulled him close.

"That's where you come in, buddy."

Siggy frowned. "Me? What do you want me to do?"

"Simple. Go to the farm and get the money."

"What?" Siggy shrugged off Reg's arm and took a step back. "Are you serious?"

"Think about it. Like I said, Farrell could be dead already. You can simply waltz right in there and take the money. Easy peasy!"

"Or, it turns out he's not dead, and he kills me."

"He won't do that," said Reg. "If it were me, he'd shoot on sight. But you're just a kid. He's got nothing against you, no reason to be wary of you. You can catch him off guard. And then…"

He reached into his back pocket and pulled out a handgun.

"Dude," said Siggy, taking another step back, "are you asking me to kill your brother?"

"I'm asking you to get the money, and—maybe—kill the man who murdered my father." Reg nodded at Granny. The steel was back in his voice. "I did fix your car for you."

Siggy didn't reply. He stood frozen to the spot, not sure what to do next. Reg sighed.

"Okay, how about this? Do this for me, and I'll let you keep half of the money."

"Half?" Siggy blinked. "Are you for real?"

"It would be a waste to just let it lie there, don't you think? It's only right that the money should do some good for someone."

Siggy bit his lip. Twelve and a half million was more money than he'd ever see in his lifetime. He could do a lot of cool shit with that kind of dough. Suddenly, the idea of going back to nature didn't seem very attractive. And Reg did have a point. If Farrell was already dead, then where was the harm in taking the money?

"I wanna see the farm before I make up my mind," he said.

Reg grinned behind his mask.

Siggy couldn't remember how long he'd stood there, but his raised arm was starting to ache. In theory, reaching out to knock on the door in front of him was the simplest thing in the world. What Siggy had come to realize, standing on the creaky wooden porch in the cold moonlight, was that there was a world of difference between theory and practice.

He glanced over his shoulder at the lilac bushes by the gate where Reg was hiding. Or at least he had been hiding there when Siggy opened the gate and walked up to the house. For all Siggy knew, he could have bolted by now.

Whatever the case, he was on his own. After a brief initial recon, they had waited until nightfall, at Reg's behest. Siggy had protested, but Reg had insisted. He didn't want to risk being spotted by any of the villagers. He had also made it clear he would not set foot in the house.

Staring at his raised hand, Siggy reached behind his back with his other and touched the butt of the gun stuck in his belt. It was a semi-automatic with a ten-bullet magazine. Reg had shown him how to load it and disengage the safety. Siggy hoped to high heaven he wouldn't have to use it. He took a deep breath and held it for five seconds.

Then he knocked on the door.

He immediately cringed back. Not out of fear that Farrell would throw the door open and come out guns blazing. No, there was something wrong with the door itself. It felt warmer and softer than he'd expected, more like sun-warmed putty than wood. He looked closer, and found that his knuckles had left a row of shallow dents in the door.

He gingerly prodded the door with one finger, and nearly screamed when it swung inward without a sound. He hadn't even touched the handle.

"Hello?" The sound of his voice seemed to die out as soon as it crossed the threshold, swallowed whole by the dense darkness inside.

No answer.

When they'd cased the joint hours before, Reg had given Siggy a flashlight along with the gun. He pulled it out of his pocket and switched it on.

The white cone of light swept across an entrance littered with shoes. A bare coat rack stood on the left side of the doorway like a skeletal doorman. Further inside was a big living room with a couch and a TV set. A deer's skull with one antler broken off adorned the wall behind the couch. In the far distance, beyond the reach of his flashlight, he could barely make out a flight of stairs leading to the second floor.

Siggy took a careful step over the threshold. He called out again, but no one answered. He crossed the hall and went into the living room. A thick layer of dust on the floor muffled his footsteps. In a corner by the couch stood a withered potted plant, little more than a twig surrounded by shriveled leaves. If anyone still lived in the house, they hadn't been in the living room for months, maybe even years. His eyes went to the narrow wooden stairway.

Reg had told him there were three bedrooms on the second floor. Given the state of the house so far, it seemed likely that Siggy would find Farrell in one of them, dead as a stone. He peered up along the stairs, through the dancing dust motes disturbed by his breathing.

There was a steady, rhythmical sound at the edge of hearing. A raspy, labored breeze, like breaths drawn through a plastic tube. Maybe an old ventilation fan was still operating somewhere in the house. He vaguely recalled seeing a few intake vents near the roof before he went inside.

Emboldened by the lack of resistance so far, Siggy started to climb the stairs. He had expected the steps to creak under his weight, but they didn't. Instead, to his surprise, they sank slightly when he trod on them. The steps had the same rubbery texture as the front door. It was like walking on fresh asphalt that hadn't yet had time to dry.

The stairs led to a narrow corridor with three doors, only one of which was open. The one farthest from the stairs. Of course. Siggy proceeded with caution, flashlight held up in front of him, his free hand hovering over the gun, ready to pull it out and shoot.

The whispering wind was louder up here, and accompanied by a dry rattle. The old fan must be on the verge of breaking down.

He was not stupid enough to simply stroll past the closed doors on his way to the open one. When he got to the first door, he grabbed the doorknob. Before he could twist it, the doorknob came off in his hand. Startled, he dropped it.

The doorknob cracked open against the floor, spilling a chunky red liquid that looked like raspberry jam.

"What the fu—"

Siggy jumped back, bumping into the wall behind him. He stared at the remains of the shattered doorknob. The shards looked like metal, all right, but they were paper thin, like eggshells. The red stuff on the floor smelled rotten.

The sound of the wind intensified, and the rattling turned into a loud whine.

Movement in the corner of his vision made him spin around. The third door, the one that had been ajar, was now wide open. The doorknob looked at him.

Siggy's heart thrummed against his ribcage. He wasn't seeing things. The doorknob was an eye, and it was staring at him.

A tremor shook the house, showering Siggy with chalky plaster dust. The wind was so strong now that he could feel it rush past him, making the open door flap on its hinges.

Who's there?

It wasn't a human voice. Siggy refused to believe any human could sound like that. It came from all around him, emanating from the walls in a desiccated hiss. He heard something move beyond the open, staring door. It was coming closer.

Siggy turned and ran. Fuck the money, fuck this house, and fuck whatever was making that noise. He'd had enough.

He made it to the stairs, but when he tried to run down them, the steps tore away from the wall in a spray of splinters and began to roll upward, like an escalator. For a few seconds, he ran in place, too terrified to even scream.

Then the escalator outpaced him and sent him back to the second floor. He lost his balance and fell over, banging his head against the rubbery floor.

Dazed by the impact, Siggy was still struggling to get back on his feet when he heard a ripping noise from above. Something cold and slippery brushed against his arm. He tried to swat it away, but the long, thin tendril wrapped itself tight around his right forearm.

He sat up, and saw that the thing wound around his arm was an electrical cord. It protruded from a long scar in the wall, which oozed a viscous, black fluid. The cord itself was sticky with the same stuff, trapping him like a bug on a sheet of flypaper.

"What the fuck is thi—"

The cord-tentacle yanked him off his feet, lifting him into the air and slamming him against the wall. The shock knocked all air out of his lungs, and he gasped for breath. He couldn't even struggle against the cords as they wrapped around his torso, pinning him to the wall.

He was stuck, and the noise from the third bedroom grew louder. Something scraped against the doorframe, trying to fit through. A couple of loud crashes rang out, and two large chunks of wood burst from the doorframe in a spray of black slime.

The house was bleeding.

A bed crept through the mutilated doorway on dozens of spindly legs. It turned towards Siggy and stood up, bracing itself against the walls.

There was a man in the bed. No. The man *was* the bed. Only his head and shoulders were visible. The rest of his body was wrapped in a pulsating cocoon of human skin, which enveloped the whole bedframe. The bedposts were bones tipped with clusters of eyeballs. The man's face was empty, smooth skin where his eyes should have been, no nose, and a gaping hole for a mouth. Eight gnarled fingers bristled from the mouth hole, twitching and curling every which way as the bed-creature shuffled sideways along the narrow corridor towards Siggy.

Who are you?

Once again, the voice came not from the mouth of the thing in the bed, but from all around, as if the house itself were talking to him. The eyes on the bedposts swarmed around his face. The bed-creature hissed. The house spoke again.

You are not Reg. Who are you? Have you come for my money?

Siggy shoved his hand behind his back. He skinned his knuckles against the wall as his fingers scrabbled for the gun in his belt. He didn't even feel the pain.

The bed-creature leaned forward, two of its slender, insect legs piercing the wall on either side of Siggy's head. Black ichor oozed from the wall and dripped onto Siggy's shoulders. The empty face came within inches of Siggy's, so close that the squirming fingers sprouting from the toothless maw almost touched him.

You can't have it. No one can!

Siggy worked his fingers around the butt of the gun and tried to fish it out. He felt it slip, and had to bite his tongue not to scream, but he caught it between his thumb and forefinger. He grabbed the pistol grip firmly, slipped his forefinger around the trigger, and tried to pull his arm out from behind his back. Pain flashed in his elbow as it bent in ways it wasn't designed to.

The creature's mouth hole opened wider, its fingers stretching out toward Siggy's face. A moldy stench wafted from the open hole. Siggy gagged and retched. His breakfast threatened to leave his stomach. Eight horny fingernails dug into his cheeks, pulling his head even closer to the creature's mouth.

It's all mine. Killing father was Reg's idea, but it was I who pulled the trigger. The spoils are mine. No one else can have them.

Siggy's arm was finally free. He brought the gun around and fired.

The bed-creature let out an earsplitting scream. Black goo gushed from a ragged hole in the creature's belly. Siggy fired again, punching another hole in its chest. His third shot missed the creature's head and struck the wall behind it, but the house screamed in pain all the same.

The house shivered. A convulsion rolled down the wall, loosening the cords that bound him. He strained against them and broke loose. The bed-creature was still reeling from the pain. The way to the staircase was free.

Siggy took off as fast as he could, running down the trembling stairs two steps at a time. Halfway down, one of the steps broke under his foot. He tumbled the rest of the way and hit the floor shoulder first. He dropped the gun, which skidded along the floor.

He got to his knees, gritted his teeth against the pain, and crawled toward the gun. The bed-creature howled with rage somewhere above him. Its scrabbling footsteps grew louder and louder. Siggy grabbed the gun and rolled over, taking aim at the top of the stairs.

The bed-creature careened around the corner of the second-floor corridor, slamming into the wall with a deafening crash. It tipped over just as Siggy fired, and his shot went wide. The creature slid down the stairs, the bedframe bumping and clattering against the steps. Its legs tore off, one after the other, but the creature didn't even seem to notice. Its head twisted around to face him, and all the fingers in its mouth pointed straight at his heart.

The bed-creature pounced, pushing away from the stairs with its last remaining legs. As it sailed through the air toward him, Siggy felt time slow to a crawl. The underside of the foul bed filled his vision. In its center was a veiny, pulsating bulb of flesh. Without thinking, Siggy squeezed the trigger and fired.

The fleshy bulb popped like a water balloon, and the house let out its loudest scream yet. Siggy rolled sideways. He felt the rush of wind as the bed shot past him. It slid across the floor until it crashed into the television. A fountain of glass shards exploded over it.

The house roared and heaved, its walls cracking and tearing. The floor roiled like the sea during a storm. Siggy staggered on unsteady feet toward the bed. The writhing, warped creature was too disgusting to be left alive.

Jagged spikes and tendrils shot out from the walls and ceiling, whipping and stabbing at him as he went. He leapt and danced between them, narrowly avoiding getting skewered. A serrated tentacle smacked him across the chest, tearing his shirt and leaving a shallow cut.

He finally made it to the fallen bed-creature. Without its legs, it could only jerk and twitch in vain attempts to move. The faceless figure writhed inside his wrapping of skin, like a madman in a straitjacket.

Standing beside the bed, Siggy pressed the muzzle of the gun against the squirming figure's head. When the cold metal met the gray flesh, the figure stopped. The fingers retracted into the depths of the mouth hole, and the skin of the face rippled.

Two slits opened above the mouth, revealing a pair of blue eyes. The human eyes looking out from that monstrous shape was almost the worst part of it all.

The eyes looked up at Siggy, and he recognized them. They were the same boyish blue eyes as Reg's, even more out of place here than in his old face.

The mouth hole quivered, forming itself into different shapes, as if the creature was trying out a part of its body it had neglected so far.

"Pl…ease…"

A whisper, so faint it was almost inaudible.

"Please… Let it end…"

Siggy pulled the trigger. The bed-creature's head exploded in a fountain of black blood and purple chunks of tissue. He pulled the trigger again and again, letting the bullets rip the monster apart, firing until the last round in the magazine was spent.

The house let out a final screech that blew out the windows. The couch split in two. The deer skull fell from its hook and smashed to pieces against the floor. A violent shudder shook the house to its foundations.

Then it stopped. All Siggy could hear was the echoes of the house's screams ringing in his head. The gun slipped from his fingers. He sat down hard on his ass, taking deep, ragged breaths.

Farrell was dead.

Siggy half-crawled, half-stumbled across the ruined living room floor, brushing aside debris and lifeless tentacles as he went. The front door was jammed, but gave way after a few forceful shoves. Siggy spilled out onto the porch.

"Siggy! Holy shit, what happened in there?"

He looked up. Reg stood about ten feet from the porch, gawking at the spectacle.

The sight of Reg's blue eyes disgusted him. He remembered what Farrell had said—that killing their father had been Reg's idea. Those baby-blue eyes were no longer the bright, innocent eyes of a child. They were the cold, deceitful eyes of a killer. Siggy wished he still had the gun.

"Fuck it," he muttered.

He got down from the porch and walked on. Reg moved out of his way.

"Hey, what's the matter with you? Where's my money?"

Siggy gestured vaguely toward the house.

"Somewhere in there. I don't know. I wanna go home."

Reg shouted more questions after him, about Farrell, about the money, but Siggy didn't answer.

"Screw you, then!" shouted Reg, his voice distant now. "I'll keep all the money for myself! Don't say I didn't warn ya!"

Siggy turned around and saw Reg run into the house. A few moments later, the ceiling caved in. The walls, already lined with cracks and tears, collapsed. The house came down in an avalanche of broken planks, roof tiles, and support beams. A huge cloud of dust billowed from the wreckage.

Reg didn't come back out.

Siggy turned his back on the carnage and walked toward the village. A group of villagers scurried past him toward the house, frantically hollering to each other. Farrell's house was secluded, but the noise of its collapse must have been loud enough to draw their attention. Siggy didn't know whether they were trying to steal the money or just investigate the ruined house, nor did he care. He was done with this shit. Let the yokels have the money. Let them stay here in this tainted place and suffer for it. Let the ether seep into their bodies and mutate them beyond recognition, fuse them all together into a blind and writhing pile of flesh.

Not Siggy, though. Nope. He'd leave the villagers to their

doom, take Granny, and go back to Central Yard. Fuck the natural life. He'd do what he must to fit into the system, if that's what it took to escape a fate like this. The image of Farrell's deformed body and featureless face, and those perversely pure eyes, would surely haunt his dreams for years to come.

As he limped on down the dusty road, he started to cough.

IN PYXIS

Matthew Siadak

"I'm not going there, Pinchpot. All that noise, and smoke, and hubbub? That doesn't even sound fun." Her husband's words hung heavy in the air, as they had for the last few days. Once, that voice had brought her comfort. Now, it was an echo, lingering in the chilly silence that had descended between them. But neither of them had moved the gilded card from the counter where it lay, askew and inviting. The name of the newly opened club was emblazoned across the stained black paper, gold letters sprawling wide: *Pyxis*. She remembered the day the card had arrived, tucked into the front door of their apartment in an unassuming white envelope that was blank except for her name. She had torn the envelope wide open to reveal the treasure inside. His dismissive words had left her in the same tatters.

Every day, she came home from work and the card was there. Day after day she was left to look at it, and every time she turned away her curiosity grew that much more. Her need to know, to *see* Pyxis, grew nigh unbearable. She was unable to bring herself to throw it away.

For seven days now the card had lain there, beckoning. Night after night, the golden filigree would catch the light, stopping her in her tracks as she moved through the apartment. A glimpse of it out of the corner of her eye never failed to draw her in, draw her closer. Each and every night, she put the card back down and tried to shove it out of her mind. And yet, it never strayed far. Its gilded shine seemed to follow her from room to room.

Arriving home from the studio, her evening had started no differently from any other, except that she found herself alone. She scrubbed the clay dust from her hands in the bathroom and stared at herself in the mirror. The water was hot, steaming up the mirror in front of her. In the quiet of their little apartment, the creaks of the building and the sounds of the city were her only companions. That, and the card with its siren song.

Instead of finding it on the small kitchen island where she'd last dropped it, she caught the shimmer of golden text from where the card hung on the fridge, half askew and in danger of falling. She barely remembered walking into the kitchen or reaching out to pluck the card from its perch. But there it was in her hands once more. Her finger traced over the letters on the cover, gold sparkling beneath her fingertip. *Pyxis*. She traced the name a few times, caught in a trap of her own indecision. Finally, she flipped the card open to see the message that lay within. She held her breath as though it might have changed since the last time she had dared to look. But no, the message remained the same:

You are invited.

That was it. Three simple words that carried with them the unimaginable weight of curiosity. They were blocked out and embossed in a gold that seemed to hover over the dark interior. Beneath them lay a golden key, beckoning her to reach out and take it. Here on the inside of the card, the black paper somehow seemed even darker. The ink felt warm and wet against her skin, and yet her finger remained clean as she drew back from that careful caress. There was a scent there, one she could not place. She snapped the card shut again and stared at the cover. Black cardstock that was somehow impossibly darker inside. A gold filigree border that felt heavy in her hands. She turned it over in her hands as if she might find some hidden message within the gold and darkness. With her frustration caught in her throat, she snapped it shut again and stared at the city outside. As if the twinkling lights might hold some answer to this riddle.

"Shit." She nearly dropped the invitation when her phone chimed in her pocket. For a moment she forgot where she was. She dug the phone out of her pocket and flubbed through the screen lock to get to the message.

Working late tonight. Order in dinner– pizza maybe? Enough for the next few nights.

Her husband was stuck at work, and she had the place to herself. More importantly, she had the evening to do with as she pleased, pizza and a night on the couch being the furthest thing from her mind. How many times had she wanted to venture out of the apartment? How many times had she floated the idea, hoping that this time, he would agree? Before she could wrap her mind around what she was doing, she had pulled on her jacket and strode out the door. She didn't bother to wait for the rickety elevator but took the spiraling stairs down to the lobby instead.

She hardly paused before bursting from the front doors. She cradled the invitation close against her chest, shielding it against the drizzle. The thrum of the city took a backseat to the voices arguing in her head. They told her she should turn back, order pizza, and find something to watch. Or pick a book from her ever growing to-be-read pile, which was threatening to teeter over. She shoved the voices away and drifted on through the city. She was surprised to find that the club wasn't far. Her steps slowed as she drew closer, but she continued on until, eventually, she found herself languishing under an awning. The chaos of the city crowded around her. Lights flashed and sirens shrieked in the distance. There was an undertone of exhaust in the moist night air from a bus that had just rumbled by. As it passed, she saw the club across the street. The building looked just like the card she still held against her chest. Black walls with columns and struts of gold, and a shining sign that bled its name into the air.

Pyxis.

Neon lights washed over the people waiting in line outside solid doors that had yet to open even a crack. Seeing leather and lace, chains and spikes, she looked down at her jeans, still marred with clay, her t-shirt, and the leather jacket that she had grabbed and felt ready to turn around and run back home.

"Quite the sight, isn't it?" The voice came out of nowhere, right at her ear. Pandora squeaked and almost jumped out of her skin. Somehow, she managed not to go tumbling straight into the middle of the street. Probably because she was frozen in place, her heart suddenly racing. It felt like a caged animal that had caught the scent of freedom and wanted more. The words were followed up by a throaty laugh.

"My name's Hope." Twinkling blue eyes framed by fiery red hair stared expectantly.

"I'm Pandora." The words had left her lips before she could even think twice about blurting her name out to this stranger. She took a step back, only just realizing how very close they were. Hope's perfume permeated the air and Pandora could not help but draw in a deep breath. Beneath all of those scents she could hardly begin to name, there was something else. How long had she been staring into those eyes like crystal pools that threatened to swallow her whole?

"Do you want to go inside?" Hope's words hung in the air. Pandora's hand extended of its own accord, ready to entwine fingers with the one being offered, but the sound of a car alarm split the night's air wide open, dragging her back to the world beyond those blue eyes.

"I, uh…I don't know." Pandora clutched the invitation that much closer to her chest and took another step back, away from those eyes and that scent. "I should probably be going home."

"Maybe another night." Hope's words chased her as she fled, echoing off the brick buildings around her. The night seemed to stale with every step she took. The further she walked, the more mundane the evening became. She felt the banality threatening to sprawl across her as she came to a corner. The crossing light went red, the hand glaring in her face from across the street.

Pandora looked back over her shoulder at the halo in the sky over the club. Even from this distance, it called to her. She tore her gaze away and looked back at the blinking indicator.

Do not walk.

Do not walk.

Do not walk.

The time between each blink seemed to grow longer and longer, and Pandora realized she was holding her breath. She decided that if the light changed in the next ten seconds, she'd cross the street and go home. That was it. She'd order pizza and wait for her husband's calls or texts, if he could break out of work long enough to do even that. She'd try to find something on the television to take in or read a book. Maybe that new horror novel, or the romance one her husband had bought her. Something normal. Something safe. That search was becoming more and more tedious every night, and she wasn't so certain she wanted safe or normal. She had been through all of the season's new shows countless times but had yet to find anything that tickled her fancy. From the formulaic crime shows to the over-the-top medical dramas, none of them scratched that itch these nights. There were so many books piled up, they were ready to collapse, and not one of them drew her interest. Pandora waited for that signal to change, waited to breathe. The sign continued to flash those three words.

Do not walk.

"Fine. I won't."

She turned her back on the crosswalk and the way home, ignoring the ticking of the sign as it flashed again and again. Was it speeding up to match the beating of her heart? She ignored the urge to look back over her shoulder, back to the boring, uninteresting life she had always lived. The invitation's edge felt sharp against her fingers as Pandora strode away from the corner. She shoved down the lump in her throat and remembered how to breathe. A trickle of dangerous excitement slipped through her, making her body sing. Her heart thundered within the confines of her ribcage, and she wondered what she was doing.

Why had she waited?

By the time she reached the club, the music roaring into the street from within was much louder. The bass thrummed through the earth beneath her feet. When was the last time that she had just danced? College? Surely not *that* long ago. There was still a line of people waiting outside of the club. Pandora stood on her tippy toes and scanned the throngs of leather and lace to see if she could spot Hope, or at least someone familiar in this sudden sea of the unknown.

Pandora tried not to look at anyone in particular and fought the urge to shrink in on herself and disappear— as if she could. Maybe, just maybe, if she did not pay them any mind, no one would bother her or chase her off. When she did risk a look, she noticed more than a few gazes turned her way, but not in dismissal or derision. Rather, they were looking at her with wide eyes, whispering.

"She has one."

"It's there in her hands."

"Why did she get one?"

"Do you know what you have there?" Pandora had failed to realize that this last bit was meant for her, and it took her by surprise.

"It's an invitation?" The words turned into a question as they left her mouth, her uncertainty bleeding through even as she tried to tamp it down.

"Yeah, but, no. Not exactly?" The words came in a rush of excitement from the man's lips and leaped into Pandora like an infection. Her eyes dropped to the invitation.

"That's a guaranteed key in—and not just to the club itself. You can get into the VIP section too. Not just anyone gets one of those." His voice was full of awe, even as he had to shout to be heard. Pandora watched him as he gestured at the card she held so tightly to her chest. His face was animated, and the mohawk on top of his head danced with every word he spoke. Pandora's gaze dropped to the card again and she studied it in an entirely new light.

"Do they hand these out often?"

"No, no they do not." His face twisted up into a Cheshire grin. Pandora was unable to do much but stand beside him as the crowd moved and shifted every time the doors opened, closed, and opened again. Her heart soared with each blast of sound that escaped before it was sealed up once more. Slowly, they were herded towards the waiting entrance.

"Stick with me, I can show you the ropes."

"Is it that obvious?" Pandora muttered. Her words were lost in another opening of the doors. "Thank you." The man waved her words away with a smile. She chewed on her lip as the world around her faded to the background once more. She was helpless but to follow the forward shuffle but managed to steal a few glances at the man, who glared at anyone daring to get too close. The whispers continued, and envy-tinged gazes followed her every step. But even these fell to the back of her mind as she felt the tug of the doors ahead. Everyone moved in a constant flow towards the giant slabs of onyx that served as doors. They were practically alive with a heartbeat from the music within. The bouncers barely spared her a glance.

Pandora's breath caught in her throat as they neared to the front of the line, almost close enough to touch the ebony portal ahead. This close, and yet having to wait, something flared to life inside her. What was taking so long? Before that thought found purchase, the bouncers opened the doors for the people ahead of her and allowed them into the club. Over their shoulders Pandora caught a glimpse of what waited for her. This close to the threshold she could see a sea of bodies ignited in colored lights within. It was everything she had expected and more. Her feet carried her forward, but a hand on her shoulder stopped her.

"Not yet, trust me. That's not your door," he whispered, his breath warm against her neck. Wordless, breathless, she nodded. Pandora studied the man brushing up against her. From the multi-colored mohawk that shimmered in time with the lights outside the club, to the hirsute body beneath his open vest, he radiated an almost comfortable warmth. There was something about his boots that drew her eyes, but under the shimmering lights, in the press of bodies, she could not pinpoint exactly what was picking at the back of her mind. Before she managed to figure it out, her attention was pulled by a tap on her shoulder.

"Go on, now; it's your turn."

"Wait." Pandora stopped, hesitating. "What's your name?" The man said something she could hardly hear, a word carried away on the music.

"Vaughn?" she repeated. He just smirked and shooed her along.

Pandora gulped and focused her attention on the door ahead of her. She felt like she was treading water, as if in a dream that refused to let her move normally while everyone else was unrestrained. The bouncers stood by the door, staring her down with keen interest. She shied away but then realized they were not looking at her, not like that. They had eyes only for the invitation. After a moment, one of them raised a hand and silently beckoned her closer. Not that she could hear much over the warring cadences of her heart and the music, which seemed less contained the closer she stepped towards the waiting doors. A thousand eyes shone like pinpricks of starlight under the neon lights. She felt the weight of them locked onto her, driving her forward. For the few moments she was trapped in a shifting halo of light, her heart stopped.

"Move your ass, Pandora." She could hardly even hear her own voice as she focused on placing one foot in front of the other until she stood in front of the door. Suddenly she realized that she was standing in a small space cleared of anyone else, that she was back on the threshold of the club. The doors towered over her. She saw herself hiding in the reflection of the obsidian sheen. Was her own smile twisted that sharply, or was her image smirking at her? She stared at her reflection, the lights coloring her hair pink, purple. A blast of blue, and her face was pale in the dark mimicry of the door. Pandora had barely thought of sticking out her tongue before her other self beat her to it. There, in the echo of the club's entrance, she saw that her invitation had taken on an entirely different form. She saw, in hands that were not her own, a key clutched tightly to her chest.

Gone was the thick, fancy paper emblazoned with the name of the club; all of it had faded away. Against all reason, Pandora felt the cold, solid surface of something metallic within the confines of her hand. She wrapped her fingers tightly around the key before it could vanish, as though in a dream turned nightmare. Pandora held her breath and looked down. The invitation was, in fact, gone, replaced by the golden key. She marveled at the wonder of it as the metal began to grow warm beneath her touch.

"Open the door." Vaughn's voice came from behind her, threaded through with a low rumbling. Before long, others joined in the chant of those three simple words until there were innumerable voices calling to her.

"Open the door." Her reflection mouthed the words at her, but it was her own voice that whispered to her, like a lover. Pandora shivered, torn between wanting to lean back to lose herself in that voice and striding toward the unknown. The rest of the world filtered through her awareness, as if from across a vast distance that grew ever greater the longer she looked at that dark reflection. Her shadow motioned for her to follow before turning and disappearing into the darkness within the door.

Gone was her reflection, faded as the doors clouded; a golden plate appeared upon them instead. Where once her reflection had stood, there now waited a screaming face, hungry for a key. The same hunger radiated through Pandora and into the metal shaft in her hands. A shudder racked her body at the sudden influx of *need* and rocked her back on her heels.

"I should go home." Pandora's lips formed the words and she took a step backward. She had no idea what was going on, had no idea what she was doing here. Her head swam in the sea of colors. She was buffeted by the unceasing ocean of sound and light and wondered if she might drown where she stood. Amidst the sea of flesh that coiled around her, she heard the whispers again.

Her name.

The key.

Pandora spared one last look over her shoulder to where the drudgery of the apartment presented itself once again. Anxiety roiled through her body and she bit her lip. Hard—almost enough to draw blood.

"Not tonight." Pandora lifted the key as if pulled along by some force out of her control. Her head continued to swim, mired in the moment, and her hand wavered. Her stomach felt like it might drop right out from beneath her. She steeled herself with a deep breath, screwing her eyes shut against the chaos.

"Am I really doing this?" Pandora whispered. Her words were lost to the din. Not that she noticed it, or anything else anymore. Everything fell away until there was just her, the towering doors, and the mystery of what lay within. No; there was more than that. The fog within the doors receded and they came to life with her likeness again.

There *was* another Pandora; she was certain of it. One who watched her with eyes full of expectation. No doubt, no fear, just a silent pleading. Pandora's hand, the one not wrapped around the key, rested on the surface, but on the wrong side. She was not certain whether she was the one trapped in the reflection or lingering outside in the renewed drizzle. She raised her hand, slick from the rain, and placed it against the one waiting on the other side of the door. The black stone was warm beneath her fingers, almost alive. Breathing. Her fingers met those of another, and the ground seemed to solidify beneath her feet. Her stomach settled, her head cleared, and Pandora took a deep breath. Holding hands with herself, fingers entwined, she narrowed her eyes and nodded.

"There's no turning back now." The key found its home in the lock perfectly. A current of something snaked through the keyhole, to the key, and up her arm. Whatever it was, it harmonized with her heart, making her gasp. She turned her wrist. The locks tumbled loudly enough to be heard over the crashing of the ocean in her ears. Gears worked, and the two dark slabs shuddered as they started to open.

And just like that, the other Pandora was gone, whisked away as the doors opened. If the sound had been loud before, what erupted from the yawning portal of Pyxis was enough to blow her hair back. She raised a hand to shield her face against the blinding lights, but it was too late. The doors were open, and her fate was sealed. Pandora's feet carried her over the threshold and into the waiting maw. She could see the throngs of bodies in the distance, cascading together and apart like a tidal wave of barely controlled need.

There was a commotion behind her as the doors opened again, but it was just static at the edge of her perception, which she barely registered against the canvas of flesh undulating in front of her. Her mind got lost trying to decipher the puzzle of limbs splayed across the dance floor. Someone hooked her arm and pulled her along. A quick glance revealed Vaughn; the mohawked man had snaked in behind her and was quickly leading her away from the bouncers gathered at the doors.

"Quickly now, come with me." His words were frantic and close, and before she could protest, he was pulling her onto the dance floor.

"What did you do? Where are we going? What—" Her words cut off, tiny beneath the onslaught of sensations. She was not even certain he had heard her as he drew her along, but a moment later he cocked his head to the side and paused to regard her.

"I've been banned for some time, but I managed to scoot in on your coattails. So, thanks for that!" He winked at her and bared his teeth in what could only be called a grin. This close, under the shifting, swirling lights, it was as if she was seeing him for the first time. The mohawk was styled around a pair of horns. Pandora took a step back, and then another, and her eyes flicked down to his feet. What she had taken for steel-toed boots, she realized were

anything but. Cloven-hoofed feet pranced a staccato beat as he
swayed to the music crashing around them.

"Oh." Her response felt lacking for the countless questions
roiling through her mind in that moment.

"Didn't want you getting lost on your first time here."
Vaughn's words were as warm as his presence. Bodies caught
in the eternal act of dance pushed them along. He seemed to
stand guard over her through the depths of limbs moving like tree
branches in a heavy wind. There was a magic to those movements,
a counterpart to the heavy bass thundering beneath her feet. The
air was heavy. Pandora half expected to feel the rains again, but
no, the air was humid for an entirely different reason.

Her skin was slick with sweat, even as a chill ran down her
spine. Pandora shook off her unease and strode onward, pushed
deeper into the wild heart of the club. She came to the edge of the
dance floor just before Vaughn. His hand at her back pushed her
along. For the first time in as long as Pandora could remember,
she let the music envelop her. Every move she made, Vaughn was
there. And if he wasn't, someone else was. There was no lack of
contact to be had, even if there was a chill to some of the bodies her
fingers trailed over. Like clay—cold at first but warming quickly
to her touch.

Time lost all meaning, caught in the web of movement that
pulled her to and fro. Entirely too soon, Vaughn had found her
again. His fingers linked with hers and he drew her from the tangle
of limbs. Even as she left, bodies clad in little more than sweat
reached for her. Fingers sought, trailed, tried to draw her back in.
Vaughn's hand was alive against her.

"Come, come. This is but the beginning," came his alluring

words.

A pressure swelled inside her—the need to see it all, to explore every nook and cranny, to find the places where the shifting lights and music failed to reach. She followed him away from the dance floor, missing the press of bodies as she left it behind. Vaughn brought them to a stop at a bar that spanned an entire wall.

"What's your poison?" Countless bottles filled with colored liquors waited. Illuminated from below, they cast multi-colored light over the bartenders, who flitted from patron to patron. Vaughn waved his hand, beckoning the closest bartender their way.

"Do you have any whiskey back there?" Pandora's throat was parched, and she craved the sweet burn of alcohol. The laugh that followed was a sound that defied logic, as glittery as it was.

"Why bother with something so mundane? I can give you whatever you want: misery or sadness, death or despair, toils or troubles. A dollop of envy for what you can never have." He punctuated each word with a point towards the line of bottles. "Do you want to remember how to rage, or to taste losing all you've ever had?"

"All of it," Pandora whispered, as she looked from bottle to bottle and the spirits that swirled within. Moths of various shapes and sizes adorned the labels, flitting about the ancient parchment. She licked her lips but had a taste for something else.

"Hope," she said. Something soared inside her chest. A flash of red curls, blue eyes, those lips. The warmth, the heady scent, all of it came rushing back. Pandora's knees felt weak, and she thought her face might melt from the heat that spread across her cheeks. Both the bartender and Vaughn were quickly forgotten.

When Pandora saw that shock of crimson hair, and the blue

eyes that hid behind wild locks, she froze. As if summoned by her own name, Hope manifested across the way. Pandora's heart hitched into her throat and she was moving before she realized it. She pushed her way through the thirsty masses clamoring to be heard. They parted before her, eager to fill the hole that she left at the bar.

"Hope!" Pandora knew it was fruitless to call out, but she still tried. Her voice was drowned beneath the waves of noise, but she could not give up.

"Hope! Over here!" She tried again, and again, even while knowing that it was futile. Breathless, she pushed against the wall of flesh, which was cold and clammy beneath her hands. She was surrounded by faces full of laughter and mirth, cast in the shadows of the dancing rainbows. The lights strobed and caught them, in mimicry of roiling emotions. Pandora pressed on, her hands working against flesh like it was clay to warm and make malleable. Frustration built in her like a dam about to burst. She let out a low, keening growl. The crowd of flesh parted, and she chased after that beacon of red hair in the distance.

"Wait for me!" Pandora watched as the only other familiar face in this place disappeared up a set of stairs. Even though they had just met, Pandora felt drawn to the fleeting Hope. Up the stairs Pandora followed, pausing at the top to scout where to go next. Uncertainty drifted in as she was blanketed by the sudden quiet. The narrow span of stairs seemed to catch the sound below her, arresting its ascent. The thrill of standing at the edge of a precipice filled her.

"Hope?" The name hung in the air, echoing back at her. There was a familiar scent that stoked something inside of her, and she licked her lips again. "Where'd you go?"

Pandora turned her head one way and the other, looking down a hallway whose walls were so dark that they hardly seemed to be there. The walkway seemed suspended over a void. Pandora's stomach turned in a visceral response to the situation. Some part of her wanted to turn and run, but it was outweighed by her need to take the next step. Reality came crashing back in as she felt the buzzing in one of her pockets.

Pandora squeaked as she fumbled her phone out of her pocket. She stared at the screen. One alert, blinking slowly, bored a hole into the core of her being. Her thumb worked the screen lock as she held her breath.

How's that pizza, Pinchpot? Did you put your favorite movie on again?

Struck with hesitation, Pandora looked over her shoulder. She imagined herself descending those stairs again, following the same path, and returning home. She clenched her teeth and threw her phone down the stairs.

No. She had to see what was up here, what was waiting. She had to find Hope. Clutching the key, she took a step onto the rampart of what would come next. One step, and then another, the soft carpet of the hallway swallowing any noise she might have made. She peered around a corner. The next hallway was dotted with doors on either side.

"What am I doing?" She paused, torn between safety and the allure of the unknown. Drawn by Hope's perfume, whatever it was, she walked up to the first door and placed her hand on the wooden surface. The latch clicked and the door opened, and Pandora tried to make sense of what she was looking at. A group of people, eyes flashing in the near darkness, hissing, and baring fangs at her. She backpedaled, scrambling to close the door again.

"What, who, wh—," Pandora stuttered.

"I see you finally found your way in." Hope's voice was familiar and alluring, and close enough that the whisper kissed the nape of her neck. Hope's scent filled her senses. Pandora turned to face her but moved as if trapped in molasses. When they finally came nose to nose, she was lost in those sparkling blue eyes. The depths of them drank her in. Hope's mouth split in a smile full of fangs, pink tongue darting out as she licked her lips.

"Are you ready?" Unsure of what Hope meant, but knowing that she wanted so much more, Pandora succumbed. Hope locked their fingers together. Cold flesh pressed tight against her own as Hope led her deeper into the hallway that had no discernible end.

Pandora followed, unable to help herself. In Pyxis, she only had eyes for Hope.

THE CALL

R. Raeta

When it starts, it's only a whisper.

A threadbare murmur, more feeling than words, folded in the fragile moment between sleep and wakefulness. Jo lays in her bed, tucked between the frilly pink sheets and her teddy bear under her arm, ears straining. The voice is delicate as spider silk, sticking and tangling before she can separate the sounds into something coherent.

It has been with her, a part of her, for as long as she can remember, but when Jo turns six, things change. The whispers stop waiting for night to fall or her mind to calm; they follow her into the world outside her room—little murmurs of sound weaving between the curtains, under the doors. She tells her parents. They brush it off, smile at each other the way adults do when they share a secret. They ask her questions, each stranger than the last.

Is it a boy or a girl, sweetie?

How tall are they?

Do they like cookies?

A handful of answers in, and Jo understands their amusement; realizes they think it's all just a game. The simple, childish imaginings of a girl in a rural town with nothing else to amuse her. Jo is only six years old, but she knows her parents are wrong—that the whisper she hears is as real as she is—but she doesn't correct them.

She never mentions it again.

Listen.

She's ten years old, enjoying a rare day in the closest city, when the frayed pieces come together. Four letters, three sounds, one word.

'Look.'

Jo prides herself on being a good girl. She obeys her parents and minds her teachers, respectfully complies with authority. So it comes as no surprise that her first instinct is to stop, to listen.

To *look*.

The park is busy, brimming with parents and their children, but somehow Jo knows to look past the movement. At the edge of the park is a man, the brim of his hat pulled low and his hand extended to a little girl who can't be older than four. Jo stills, her feet rooted deep in the playground bark—a statue in the storm—as the feeling of wrongness rises like bile.

The man's mouth moves, words lost in the noise, as he pulls a candy from his pocket. There's a wicked promise masquerading as friendliness in the shape of his smile, danger lining the hand that reaches out—

"Stop!" The word springs from her lips without thought, without summoning. It's lined with an authority that isn't her own.

The man looks up.

The playground stills.

A mother screams.

An hour later, she's surrounded by blinding camera flashes and microphones. A news reporter praises her as a hero and asks how she knew.

The voice told her, she thinks, but Jo is ten years old and she knows no one will believe her. Instead, she offers them a different truth. "It was just a feeling."

Her small town talks about it for weeks. The mayor awards her a medal. Her parents gush to their friends about how proud they are of their sweet, brave Joanna.

Jo watches, a witness in her own life, and doesn't feel brave at all. Around her, the little town she grew up in keeps moving, but Jo feels like she's still on that playground, bark crunching beneath her feet, and speaking with a voice that isn't her own.

Listen.

It grows stronger after that—more frequent. Rumors spread like dandelion seeds on the breeze, that little Joanna is (somehow) always in the right place at the right time. Some say she's blessed—a bringer of good luck, blessed by God. Others say she carries the mark of the Devil—an evil omen that brings trouble wherever she walks. Jo isn't so sure about the first, but she's certain about the last.

The voice whispers, a lullaby cradled around her heart, *You are made of greater things.*

Jo doesn't know who to believe, but the voice is warm and soft—comforting in ways not even her parents can evoke. Never does she feel alone. Never does she feel afraid. And, when she listens to its coaxing whispers, only good things ever come of it.

Look.

When she's twelve, Jo notices the bruises on her classmate's neck. Purple fading into green, they peek out just over the line of her turtleneck whenever Penny turns a certain way. Jo only sees them once, for only a second, but she knows—the same way she knows everything else—that if Penny were to pull down the neck of her sweater, she would see the shape of hands.

Jo tells her teacher. Her teacher tells the police.

Penny comes to school the next day (and the day after that, and the day after that). She collects bruises like tarnished pennies, tucking them away behind scarves and long skirts, but Jo still spots them. There, encircling her dainty wrist like bulky costume jewelry just beyond the hem of her sleeve. Another, in the shape of a belt, stamped across her lower back.

No one goes to her rescue.

And Jo learns how broken the world really is, because their small town police department would rather sacrifice the welfare of a little girl than risk their careers filing a charge against the mayor.

It's only once he's elected out, once their jobs aren't on the line, that an officer knocks on his door and Penny finally finds safety under the roof of her grandparents across the country. Jo never forgets the injuries she suffered in that time—files them in her memory like a twisted scrapbook.

She never forgives the officers for waiting.

Look.

Seventeen, and it's her first trip away from home. The city is bustling, full of noise and static energy that vibrates beneath her feet. Her classmates chatter excitedly, their eyes alight with wonder as they take in the skyscrapers and crowds. The field trip to the capital is full of sightseeing historical monuments, but Jo thinks the real education is here, on the streets where people *live* and not where out-of-towners *visit*.

But she is seventeen and only a student, so she follows where the teachers and parent volunteers lead, admires bronze statues and imposing figures sculpted from marble. By the end of the day, her feet are sore, her body tired. When they finally start the trek back to the hotel, she's relieved. There's a blister on her heel, threatening to burst with every step, but she waves off her classmates' concern and settles for keeping towards the back of the group.

They're three blocks away from the hotel when she feels it—the familiar nudge against her heart compelling her to stop. To *look*.

There's a bar down the way, adjacent to a little alley that's more shadows than light. In the darkness, half hidden behind a dumpster, something moves.

And Jo *knows*, the way she always knows.

The pain in her feet is forgotten, her soles slapping against the pavement as she runs toward the shadows. One of her teachers shouts at her back to wait—to stop—but she can't. The whisper is a crescendo, building inside her until her chest aches from the pressure.

Look.

Behind the dumpster is a man, in his arms an unconscious girl not much older than Jo is. Her head lolls, eyes open but unfocused, and Jo realizes with a pang that she's *drugged*.

Jo's screaming, horror and fury curdling on her tongue, **"Get off her!"**

The man jumps, his hand retreating from under the girl's shirt. He has the audacity to hold it up, to *smile*. "Whoa! I'm just helping my girlfriend get home. She's had too much to drink."

Her history teacher, Mr. Malcolm, reaches her—panting. "Joanna, what's going on?"

She doesn't mince her words. "He was going to rape her."

"This is all a big misunderstanding! She's my girlfriend! She's just wasted!"

If he were someone else, maybe Mr. Malcolm would have believed it, but he has known Jo her whole life. He has witnessed the small miracles, knows "Little Joanna" is always in the right place at the right time. The moment he instructs Jo to call the police, the man's smile drops as quickly as the girl in his arms and he's *running*.

Mr. Malcom chases after him; Jo runs to the woman on the ground—her blonde hair streaked with foul smelling water and her body splayed out among the trash like a broken doll. Jo cradles her head in her lap, dials the emergency line, and waits for sirens.

When she starts to come to, Jo is there. She explains what happened, assures her what didn't. The woman sobs—a ragged keening that Jo feels in her soul. The voice is absent, but the silence is telling. This is not a victory.

Her name is Natalie.

Look.

Jo testifies.

The words are painful, barbs on her tongue, but she spits each one out in excruciating detail. Natalie is in the front row, her eyes glazed with tears. The judge nods, face solemn, but then the defense takes the stand—the lawyer's voice smooth and lilting. He's nothing but an actor on the stage.

"He's an honor student, Your Honor."

"He's a star athlete, Your Honor."

"Should his life really be ruined for one mistake, Your Honor?"

Jo feels each word like a knife, each one burying deeper than the last. Then she sees the sympathy in the judge's aging face, notices the way his balding head gives the occasional nod, and feels a whole new brand of horror wash over her.

The judge's gavel falls; his verdict read.

Natalie's would-be-rapist goes free with just a few months of community service at a women's shelter. A slap on the wrist.

Looking over at Natalie's face, Jo knows the what-ifs, those phantom hands, will haunt her for much, much longer.

Look.

After she graduates, Jo moves into the city.

There's more people. More good to be done. She searches out the right places at the right times, and in her first week heeds the voice's call six times.

An old woman, homeless, in danger of freezing to death.

A little boy separated from his mother on the streets.

A girl, two years her junior, stopped from getting into a stranger's car.

A baby found, crying and forgotten, in an alleyway.

Two more young women saved from unwanted hands.

They are the first of many, and each week the number seems to grow. When it's called for, she continues to testify in court despite her faith in it being shaky at best. The judges begin to recognize her. One—the same one that crushed Natalie's chance of justice with a single swing of his gavel—asks how it could possibly be her *again*.

Jo stands a little straighter, a little prouder, and looks him in the eye when she tells him, "I would be here less if you'd stop letting them go."

The judge's face flushes, bulging veins creeping up past his starched collar. His glare is fire and brimstone, his voice edged in threats and raw with power. "Do you want to be thrown out of this courtroom?!"

Jo is still, her gaze even and her heart calm. Unmovable. Unrepentant. "No, sir. I'm here to testify."

It unnerves him, the way she doesn't shrink away from his fury. She knows, because the rest of the hearing is spent meeting his fleeting glances.

That day, when the gavel falls, justice is served.

Look.

On the news, they talk about the coming of a new era. A voice, so different from the one in her head, filters into the nation's living rooms. Strong. Masculine. He rests his hand over the Bible, all confidence and charisma as he's sworn into office. His speech is full of promises, the way politicians' speeches always are, but the way he focuses on blame instead of solutions sets Jo on edge.

Most of the people in her town are calling him a savior, but Jo looks around and sees a fanatic fervor in people's eyes, and that feeling of *wrongness* returns. Her skin prickles. On the screen, they flash a clip of the crowd waving miniature flags—a frenzy of movement, a sense of blind adoration bordering on obsession.

Jo doesn't understand what's happening, not fully, but the weight in her stomach lingers long after the TV is shut off and she sends herself to bed.

Look.

Twenty-two, and it feels like her nation is teetering on the edge of madness. Fights break out between protesters on the street, but the local news stations don't seem to report any of it. The word of God is twisted so thoroughly in their leader's mouth that she makes a game of guessing where one ends and his begins.

He says it's time their nation finds God again. To follow His word. Jo is scared of what that means, but the crowds cheer—their eyes hungry. One by one, the policies roll out.

Women seeking an abortion, or suspected of one, are arrested and put on trial.

Homosexuality becomes a criminal offense.

Birth control is banned and labeled as a poison to God's blessings.

It becomes illegal for women to divorce their husbands.

Monetary rewards dangle like bloodied meat in the face of a wolf for the citizens who report. Vigilantes make careers out of turning in their neighbors, their families, their friends.

Protesters flood the streets, armed with nothing but their signs and calls for change. The national guard answers with water cannons and tear gas, a rain of rubber bullets and a needle of a sound—so high it pierces—flooding the speakers.

Dozens die. Hundreds are injured.

The news anchors *tsk*, their smiles white behind their painted grimaces as they report the casualties.

"It's terrible," Lisa says. "All those people trampled."

Beside her, Bill shakes his head. "If they would just listen to law enforcement, none of this would have happened."

They don't talk about the videos flooding the internet of blood and batons. They don't mention the protesters' testimonies of having done nothing wrong when the first rounds of tear gas were deployed. They don't address the fear coiling, tight and bruising, in the belly of their nation.

It's supposed to be an election year, but nothing is said of candidates or of ballots. No one is brave enough to ask (because the ones that did have disappeared).

Jo watches, and feels the injustice of it all like a weight on her chest, but the voice is soothing. *Wait*, it croons. *Wait*.

Jo listens. She sits, she watches, and she waits—despite the horror and the fury sitting like molten lead in her stomach.

The protests dwindle, peter out like a fire that sparked but never grew past a flicker.

The world gets worse.

Look.

A year later, Leona makes headlines as she challenges the court to terminate her pregnancy.

She tells the reporters, tears in her eyes and her mother sobbing quietly behind her, that it was conceived by rape—that she's only twelve and surely God doesn't ask this of her?

After, the news anchors talk about how far along she is. How the fetus now has the beginnings of a face, all ten fingers and toes. In the background, they play sound clips of fetal heartbeats.

The court drags, and drags, and drags.

And then Leona checks into the hospital for delivery, but never checks out. On the news, the cameras follow her mother, pale-faced and ashen, as she leaves with the grandchild whose existence killed her baby. The reporters bury her in questions about the sex, the weight, the name.

Leona isn't mentioned once.

The injustice of it burns, liquid and hot. With every heartbeat it spreads, until Jo's pulse is pounding in her ears like a drum of war. She stands, limbs shaking, and the voice in her head is louder than ever.

Go.

In the streets, people riot. There are no signs; they have traded peaceful chants for battle cries.

Jo is one of them.

Look.

She's thirty, and her country is burning, burning, burning.

Jo hasn't spoken to her parents in years, she's too busy being in the right place, at the right time. Too busy leading her followers to do the same. Phones are too dangerous, everything is traced, and in the years she's been away she's grown into someone much more than "Little Joanna" from a town of three hundred.

She is the face plastered on the news, in the papers, with numbers and dollar signs beneath her photograph. She is the voice filtering through the radio lines on hijacked channels. She is the person people seek out in the shadows of abandoned rail stations and half-forged subway lines, begging for help.

It's not a huge operation, but it's enough. A few dozen full-time volunteers and hundreds of safe houses throughout the country. They ferry people across the border, into hands that are willing to help. Men, women, children. They take the abused and the beaten, the hunted and the scared, and deliver them into safe arms. Bruised women escaping their husbands; children escaping their parents. People on the run whose only crime is loving someone of the same sex; people who only want the freedom of being who they are. They have a network of doctors and nurses whose oath to 'do no harm' outranks the government's mandates.

People keep coming and the guard keeps searching (and searching, and searching). Because Jo is always in the right place at the right time, and the government can't arrest a shadow—can't beat down or silence an idea.

The government calls her Enemy Number One, but the people who flock to her have christened her an Angel of Mercy.

Look.

She's thirty-four and kneeling. Blood makes the ground beneath her knees slick, the coppery scent of it making her dizzy. Behind her, she hears the soldier's gun cock back. Her eyes close. She should be scared—of the pain, of death—but the fear never settles. It rolls off her skin like oil on water, hovering on the surface but never penetrating deeper.

She smiles, lips cracking, but the sting of pain never comes.

Part of her thinks she must be going into shock, but there's a warmth in her chest, a caress against her soul. More than a whisper—a promise—that no pain will touch her.

The voice speaks, clear and concise, warm and approving, *'You are in the right place, you are at the right time.'*

And Jo knows, the way she always knows, that this isn't the end. Her body will die, but in the last decade she has become more than a woman, more than a person. She has become an idea. A symbol.

And now, a *martyr*.

She will die on this hill, the mud soaking into her clothes with the video camera televising her fall. The nation's leader will think it's sending a message to stand down; to fall in line or *else*. He doesn't know, the way *she* knows, that the moment her body hits the ground, a flood will follow.

The soldier spits at her back, "Well, traitor? Do you have any last words?"

They expect her to beg—to grovel and condemn herself under a mountain of apologies spun from final hopes and desperation.

Jo raises her head, blood dribbling down her chin, and stares straight into the camera lens and beyond. One word leaves her, so tangled with the voice's that for a moment they are one and the same—an echo of every life they've saved, every soul they've touched.

She knows, the second it touches her tongue, that it will echo long past the gunshot.

"Rise."

STAFF STORIES

BEHIND THE MASK

Jaecyn Boné

Sese barged into the office of the city's most notorious mob boss despite the protests from the bodyguard stationed outside. Marching up to the ornately carved mahogany desk, she slammed her hands down and waited with all the patience of an impending tropical storm.

The man seated in the velvet-backed chair barely glanced at her before saying, "I'll have to call you back," and pressing *end* on his phone screen. Steepling his fingers, he looked up at the bodyguard who had followed Sese in and shook his head ever so slightly.

"You said you wouldn't bother us again," Sese shouted, her entire body trembling.

Her father raised a perfectly sculpted eyebrow at her. "How have I bothered you?"

"Mother said you're getting back together!"

He pursed his lips. "And this bothers you."

"I don't want you in my—our—lives! You bring nothing but pain!" Sese seethed.

"I'm disinclined to believe this. Dana was the one who came to me; clearly she wants me in her—your—lives."

Stifling a scream, Sese paced along the handcrafted Afghan rug on the floor; the red, white, and black threads wove together in a beautiful and intricate design that she would have appreciated, if she had been in a better mood.

"What would it take for you to leave us alone, forever?"

Her father sighed, rubbing his chin with his manicured fingertips. "Perseus, this is what Dana wants."

"What would it take?"

"What would you be willing to do? Would you steal? Would you commit murder?"

Sese stopped her pacing to meet his gaze. His calculated look and the hint of malice in his grey eyes—the same grey she saw in her own reflection—had her suppressing a shudder before answering.

"I would do anything."

A smile spread across his thin lips as he stood, straightening his tie and buttoning his jacket. "I'll have someone send you a task list. I'm sure you'll have no problem completing the assignments. And after that, well, I'll be out of your...hair. As it were."

Sese reached up to finger her buzzcut—her latest bad decision, according to her mother—and glared at the self-titled Lord of Crime. "I'll be waiting."

Struggling to control her angry, erratic breathing, Sese walked through the revolving door and stepped out onto the sidewalk. The building's long shadow chilled her as she headed for her moped, parked in the no-parking zone. Her father had the meter police—well, really, the entire police force—eating from his pockets; she knew none of them would bother giving her a ticket.

After shoving her helmet onto her head and buckling the chin strap, she started up the bike and eased out into the downtown traffic. Cars stood bumper to bumper but she slipped between them like an eel, stopping at a red light and pulling out her phone to check for Uber Eats notifications. A new order popped up for her favorite bubble tea place and she clicked *accept*, flicking her blinker on to turn right.

A few blocks down, she parked outside Bubble Mania, leaving her helmet on her seat and walking up to the glass doors. The short drive had calmed her enough that she remembered to smile as she waved at Cora, the cute redhead working the counter. Catching Sese's meaning, Cora headed over.

"Blended taro with boba, right?"

Sese's weak smile widened, but she shook her head. "Not for me this time. I'm picking up an Uber Eats order for…M. Gorgo." Her tongue stumbled as she read off the familiar name. How long had it been since she had said that name out loud? More than three years?

Cora walked over to the to-go order shelf and came back with a single drink: iced taro with boba. "You two have similar tastes," she remarked.

"It's the best flavor you have," Sese said, trying not to let the order faze her. Of course they had similar tastes; they'd never disagreed on anything, even at the end. Reaching for the drink, Sese's hand brushed Cora's.

"Drive safe," Cora said, her freckles standing out against a sudden crimson flush.

Waving a distracted goodbye, Sese headed outside. She hadn't seen her ex in years; back then M had lived in a run-down flat on the lower west side. Now, according to the delivery address, she lived in the penthouse of the Plaza Hotel. Talk about an upgrade.

A solemn doorman greeted her with a nod as he opened the door. Nodding back, she made her way to the elevator, sending a quick message to M.

Perseus: I'm here

She buzzed up to the penthouse, and a moment later the elevator began to rise. The order notes said to leave the drink at the door, so she plopped the drink holder on the ground outside the only door on the entire floor. Sese had already started back for the elevator when she heard the door creak open behind her.

Sese spun around and saw her; long, thick locs dangled past a full-face mask and cascaded over a sleeveless, silk maxi dress. Her dark skin glowed under the fluorescent lighting, and her eyes gleamed through the holes in her mask. She stared at Sese for a moment before bending to grab her drink.

She straightened to her full height, then shut the door, leaving Sese alone. A second later, Sese's phone buzzed, and she held it up to see an Uber Eats message from M.

M: thank you

Sese's lips quirked at the corner as she typed back:

Perseus: you're welcome. what's with the mask?

No answer.

Sese opened the front door to the apartment she shared with her mother and inhaled the yeasty scent of freshly baked bread. Following her nose, she entered the kitchen, dropping her keys and phone on the counter. Her mother stood at the double oven, peering through the glass door at the bread.

"Hey, Mom," Sese said, pressing her cheek to her mother's back as she hugged her from behind.

Her mother patted her arm and asked, "How was work today? Any good tips?"

Sese's phone buzzed on the counter and she released her mother to grab it. An Uber Eats notification.

"Actually, yeah." Sese flashed the phone screen at her. "She only ordered a five-dollar drink but gave me a twenty-dollar tip."

Her mother wagged her eyebrows at her. "She must have thought you were cute."

"Mom!" Sese blushed. A phantom breath on her ear reminded her of a time long past, when M had called her cute before nibbling at the tender lobe.

Laughing, her mother grabbed potholders from a drawer and pulled the bread from the oven. After settling it on a cooling rack, she started fanning it with one of the potholders.

"That looks amazing, Mom." Sese licked her lips at the sight of the perfect, golden-brown milk bread rolls. She reached out to snag one and received a swat from her mother instead.

"Too hot! Go sit down, there's a letter for you on the coffee table."

Sucking on her burnt fingertips—hot indeed—Sese headed into the living room. Inside an unmarked manilla envelope she found a single sheet of paper. An invoice for an oil change was printed on the front, but on the back, in font so small she had to squint, she read:

Task One: embezzlement. Task Two: arson. Task Three: homicide.

"Oh, so nothing difficult or anything," she grumbled, rolling her eyes at the absurdity of the list. Still, she had said she would do anything to keep her father out of their lives—and she had meant it.

The last time her parents were together, her mother had been hospitalized for gunshot wounds. The assailant hadn't managed to make the kill shot, but the near lethal amount of cocaine in Dana's body had almost finished the job for them. After a drug-free two years and three months, Sese wasn't about to let her father reintroduce her mother to her vice.

This wouldn't be the first time Sese had committed any of these crimes; her father had been a thorough teacher. But it would be the last. After this, she was going straight. Well, as straight as a lesbian could be. She chuckled to herself before crumpling the sheet and tossing it into the fireplace.

Sese knew how her father handled embezzlement. Tomorrow someone would bump into her on the street with a username and passcode. Then she would receive a text with a link to the system she needed to access. Tampering with a couple routing numbers here and there would seal the deal for a quick in and out.

Cracking her knuckles, Sese headed for the bathroom. She needed to rinse the feeling of lingering malevolence from her body, an aura that never failed to cling to her after seeing her father.

The next time Sese saw M. Gorgo was on a Wednesday. She picked up an order at a wing place that had "Happy Hump Day!" flashing on their neon lobby sign. She dropped off the lemon pepper wings and fried pickles and checked her phone for any new orders. After clicking *accept* on one, her ex-girlfriend's name appeared above the order.

A moment later she received an in-app message.

M: do you still like boba?

Perplexed, Sese stared at her phone screen, wondering how M knew it was her before typing her response.

Perseus: yes

M: get yourself a drink. I'll include the price in your tip

Was… No. But…was M flirting with her? They had parted on amicable terms. When M had been offered a job in Asia, they had decided to end things for Sese's sake. She had still been attending university at the time and adding the pressures of a long-distance relationship would have spelled disaster for her grades. But if M had wanted to get back with Sese, why hadn't she reached out when she got back over a year ago?

Perseus: okay

M: see you soon

Sese pulled her helmet back on and tried to unscrunch her eyebrows, then she merged into traffic and headed for Bubble Mania.

Inside, Cora noticed her and waved. "Your usual?"

"Please!" Sese plopped down on a barstool and waited as Cora measured taro powder into the blender. The roar of the motor started up and Cora stole a glance at her before looking away again.

After ladling boba pearls into the frothy purple liquid, Cora took it over to the sealing machine and pressed a lid down onto the cup. Grabbing a straw, she handed over the order. "Have a great day!"

Sese fished out her wallet. "I haven't paid yet."

Cora shrugged. "On the house then."

"Oh." Sese met her green eyes and felt a pang in her chest. Cora was undeniably cute. But if the string of cute girls since her split with M had taught her anything, it was that they weren't who she really wanted. "Um, thank you! I also have to pick up an order for M. Gorgo."

Cora grabbed a drink carrier from the to-go shelf and handed it over. Sese was careful this time not to brush Cora's fingers with her own. Ducking her head so she wouldn't have to make eye contact again, she rushed out the door.

Back at the Plaza Hotel, Sese had barely pushed the call button when a husky voice said, "Come on up." Sese suppressed a shiver.

M stood waiting in the open doorway to the penthouse. Her locs were knotted together in a bun on top of her head, and she wore the same full-face mask as before: a simple copper oval with eye holes and a slit over her mouth. A lilac velour tracksuit hugged her frame, drawing attention to her hips.

Sese was staring and she knew it. M knew it too.

"H-here's your order," Sese stammered, holding out the iced taro. She held her blended taro in her other hand; leaving it in the basket of her moped would have been asking for someone to steal it, or worse. Now though, standing in front of M while they each held their drink, she felt silly.

M stabbed her straw into the cup with a satisfying *pop* and swirled the ice around before slipping the top of the straw behind the lower edge of her mask and taking a sip. She let out a little sigh and gestured to Sese's drink.

"Taro?"

"It's my favorite."

"Mine too."

Sese wished she could see M's expression. The copper face staring at her was…intimidating.

"How much was your drink?"

"I didn't pay."

M cocked her head to the side.

"I mean, the girl who works there said it was on the house. I'm kind of a regular."

"Ah. Well, I'll pay for your next one then." M put her drink down and procured her wallet. "I hear it's best to tip you in cash so Uber Eats doesn't take a cut."

Sese rubbed the back of her neck, squirming as M pulled out several $10 bills. "I mean, yeah. They do take a cut, so cash is always nice, but that's way too much."

M looked at her; Sese couldn't help noticing the flecks of gold in her hazel eyes. Eyes she had gazed into so many times in the past. Eyes that always saw through her.

"Nonsense. How many times have people tipped you, and you haven't received the full amount? This barely covers it."

Sese tried to stop herself from taking the money but her hand reached out and grasped the crisp bills anyway. "Thank you," she whispered. Fifty dollars…for a bubble tea. What was M doing?

"Don't mention it," M said, waving away her thanks. "I'm sure you're busy, but maybe next time we can talk more."

Sese grinned. "I'd like that."

"Is Thai still your favorite cuisine?"

Sese snorted. "Am I not still Thai?"

"Just because you're Thai doesn't mean it's still your favorite. Have you tried Thai Charlie's?"

"That's my new favorite restaurant in the city." Sese could have sworn M was smiling behind the mask.

"Let's talk over some Thai food next time."

"It's a date," Sese shot back, immediately regretting her choice of words. What if M wasn't trying to rekindle things?

M let out a delighted peal of laughter. "Perfect. Have a great day, Perseus."

"Call me Sese. Everyone does now. And…" Sese hesitated, "I can give you my new number, so you can contact me if I'm not the person who gets your order next time."

"I'd like that…Sese."

The arson task would be tricky. The last time Sese had successfully gotten away with it, she'd had a team assigned to her. She was under no illusion that her father would allow her to have his help with this task, however.

She would have to be extra cautious. Getting caught and thrown in jail wouldn't be a forever fate, but it would kill any chance she had of keeping her mother away from him. When the target, The Pink Door, was delivered to her via another unaddressed envelope, Sese carried out her plan.

The Pink Door was a well-to-do restaurant on the north side of town. She knew one of the line cooks there from university; Zeno had been a close friend before they dropped out due to a life-threatening illness, and they owed her a favor.

She rang them up around noon.

"Sese! How are you, love?" A loud yawn followed their words; just as Sese had assumed, they had slept in. A smile warmed her face as their voice came through her Bluetooth earbud.

"Zeno! I've missed you. I hope work is treating you well."

They let out a sharp bark of laughter. "They treat me like shite, and you know it. Sometimes I just wanna burn the place to the ground."

"This might be your lucky day then."

Zeno was quiet, their breathing barely coming through. "Is this the favor I owe you? You're collecting?"

"I don't want you to get caught, so don't do anything reckless, but yes. I need The Pink Door up in smoke tonight."

"I can't say I didn't expect something like this. I won't be sorry to see it go but…tonight?"

Sese bit her lower lip. Zeno had always been a bit indecisive. She was starting to wonder if contacting them was the best option.

"Never mind. I'll do it. I owe you big time for getting me that private surgeon. Who knows if I would even still be alive by now?"

"Thanks, Z. Love you, bud."

Zeno laughed again. "Yeah, well, don't thank me yet. I'll do my best not to muck it up."

Sese hit *end* on the call and let out a giant pent-up breath. Now came the hard part: waiting.

An alert pinged on her phone: an Uber Eats order for Thai

Charlie's. Sese accepted it as quickly as she could and grinned when M's avatar popped up in confirmation. It was a heavily filtered picture of her copper mask, sitting beside an arrangement of white candles, and, not for the first time, Sese wondered why M wore it.

There had been rumors of an illness in the Far East—a disease of radioactive flesh. The infection site attacked the optical nerves of those who saw it, rendering them blind and causing a visceral and violently lethal reaction, though how it spread to carriers without harming them was still a mystery. Could M have contracted this illness? Was her face the site of the infection?

Then again, Sese could be leaping to the scariest conclusion. It had been years since they had dated; Sese couldn't say she still knew M well enough to make a proper guess.

As she strapped her helmet to her head, a text alert pinged on her phone.

M: just saw you snagged the order I placed. I hope you aren't busy? I should have asked first sorry

Sese: I could use a distraction! see you soon

M: [smile emoji]

Grinning to herself, Sese made her way to Thai Charlie's. Once there, she sat in the lobby for twenty minutes as they finished up the order, playing a game on her phone to distract herself from wondering whether Zeno would follow through. After Sese failed the same level several times, a waiter came out with three bags practically bursting at the seams with food.

Sese was barely able to load the food into her basket. It took the help of the doorman at the Plaza Hotel to get everything into the elevator. Breathing heavily and leaning against the wall, she punched the call button.

"Who is it?" M's throaty voice drifted through the elevator speaker.

"It's Sese—Perseus."

"Come on up."

"I'll need help getting all of your food out," Sese said, trying not to pant.

"I'll be waiting."

M was indeed waiting outside her penthouse, looking resplendent in a black velvet midi dress with gold threading shot through. When Sese gestured at the three giant bags, M threw her head back in laughter.

"I wasn't sure what you wanted, so I ordered one of everything." M stopped to grab two of the bags, then turned toward her apartment. "Come on in," she called over her shoulder.

Sese grabbed the last bag and followed her, stepping through the front door and into a lush paradise. Vibrant greenery flooded the space: plants on shelves, on the walls, on tables, hanging from the ceiling, trailing along bookshelves. Everywhere she looked, a plant thrived.

"Oh my gosh," she marveled, spinning around in a slow circle. The soft notes of a popular Kpop song harmonized from invisible speakers, and Sese swore this was heaven. If she lived here, she would never leave.

M strode over to a large, dark oak dining table and dropped the food onto its surface. "Are you hungry?"

Sese followed her, putting her bag down next to the others. A thick scent of spices leaked from the bags and Sese's stomach gurgled. "Apparently," she said.

M opened a cupboard in the kitchen and withdrew two black dinner plates. Together, they began pulling cartons from the bags, arranging the food on the tabletop. Phat si-io, khao kha mu, yam nuea yang, khao pad, kaeng matsaman, kai ho bai toei, and Sese's favorite: pla rad prik. The crispy whole fish, drenched in chili paste and garlic, gazed back at her with its dead eye and her mouth watered.

"Um, how will you eat?" Sese asked, looking pointedly at the small slit in M's mask.

M reached up to fiddle with one of her long locs. "I can eat on the couch, with my back to you. You have to promise not to look at me."

Sese pondered that sad answer. Not dramatics then, but something serious. "You must be lonely."

M cocked her head. "Not right now."

Sese's mind went back to the possibility of the radioactive illness. From her university classes, she remembered that treated sunglass lenses were able to stop several different types of radiation. Could they be enough against M's disease?

"What if I wear sunglasses?"

M sat silent for a moment, toying with a bead in her hair. "I see you've guessed my affliction… Yes, sunglasses would work." Jumping to her feet, she rushed out of the room and down a hallway. She returned with a pair of oversized black sunglasses in a cat eye style. Standing beside Sese, she turned the sunglasses over in her hands. "You would wear these for me?" A note of dejection colored her voice, as though she expected a refusal.

Sese reached out to grab one of her hands. M's skin was soft as silk, and Sese gave her a gentle squeeze. "I'm not scared of you."

M squeezed her hand back before uncurling her fingers and holding out the glasses. Sese took them and put them on, blinking at the sudden haze. A rosy hue colored everything and she looked up at M with a smile.

With exaggerated slowness, M reached up and removed the copper mask, revealing high cheekbones beneath hooded hazel eyes, a broad nose, and full, dark lips. And covering her whole face: freckles. Sese still remembered what those freckles tasted like: cocoa butter and coconut.

"Not to be gay, but you are so beautiful," Sese heard herself say. Mortified, she tore her gaze away and looked down at her empty plate.

"Please, be as gay as you want." M chuckled as she sat down. "I'm assuming you'll start with the pla rad prik? My new favorite is khao kha mu," she said, using her chopsticks to pile strips of pork onto her rice.

Sese reached for the fish cheeks, pinching them out with her chopsticks.

"The best part of the fish," M approved.

Sese popped the tender flesh into her mouth, eyes fluttering shut in ecstasy as it melted on her tongue. When she opened them again, M sat with her hands folded on the table in front of her, watching.

"So, can I ask what happened?" Sese said.

"I don't know how I got infected, if that's what you're asking, but that's neither here nor there. I quarantine so that no one gets hurt."

"Is it painful?"

M pursed her lips, chopsticks poised over her khao kha mu.

"I have regular checkups with a private physician. You don't have to worry about me."

Sese munched on more fish as she mulled that over. She really didn't know much about the illness, other than it killed people. But here she was, looking at beautiful M through rose-tinted glasses, feeling fine. She couldn't think of anywhere else she'd rather be.

"How did you end up here?" Sese gestured around the massive penthouse.

"Would you believe I'm an heiress? I didn't do anything to earn my wealth; an old family friend died and left me this hotel and several restaurants. I try to operate ethically; I pay my employees a living wage, provide good benefits. But how ethical can I be, really, under capitalism?"

Sese nodded, thinking of Zeno and how little they were paid by one of the most successful restaurants in the city. She hoped their rage at the injustice fueled a roaring fire. "There is no ethical consumption under capitalism."

"Exactly."

"But this was never in your life plan. What do you want to do with your life now?"

"I wanted to continue my research on indigenous flora in Cambodia, but when I inherited everything, I thought I should come back home to manage it all. Now I write academic articles for an online journal based on my research." She looked up at Sese with a wry smile. "What about you?"

"Well, I failed out of college. I kept skipping classes because… well." Sese didn't want to admit the reason she had stopped going to class was due a depressive episode after M left.

M's eyes narrowed and Sese rushed on. "I ended up working

full time for my father. Then after my mother nearly died, we left it all behind. I really don't know what to do now other than survive."

M nodded at that, her eyes haunted. "Surviving in this world is the hardest thing to do."

Zeno's fire was blazing on the news when Sese woke up. Her mother stood in the living room watching the footage on TV.

"Can you believe this? Isn't that where your friend from university works?"

Sese yawned and stretched her arms above her head, feeling queasy as paramedics wheeled someone out of the restaurant on a stretcher. "Yeah… Zeno works there."

"Worked there, more like." Dana snorted. "There's nothing left now."

The camera panned to the people milling outside the restaurant and Zeno's face came into view. Their undercut, usually slicked back, hung limp in their eyes. Soot smudged their cheeks.

"They're okay," Sese breathed.

"What?"

"Zeno is okay."

The next thing that left the restaurant was a black body bag.

Dana shook her head. "That person isn't, though."

Sese's stomach turned and she fled the room. Safe in the bathroom, with the cold water running, she stared at herself in the mirror. Hard eyes stared back at her, and she splashed water on her face to avoid the reflection.

What was her body count now? Did it matter? At least one more would be added when she was given the name for last task. After that though, she would be done. No more schemes. No more violence. No more crime.

She would be free.

Her phone buzzed in the pocket of her pajama pants. She shut off the water and pulled the phone out with wet fingers to read the texts on the screen.

M: I could really use some company.

M: if you're free

M: and if you want to. sorry for assuming.

Sese smiled at the obvious social anxiety in M's texts. Relatable as fuck, honestly.

Sese: sure thing. boba?

M: sounds perfect. I'll place an order.

The Uber Eats notification came half a minute later, but before Sese could accept the order, it disappeared. She pursed her lips before realizing she wasn't dressed yet anyway. Better that someone else took the order.

She changed into a plain black tank top and black cut-off jean shorts. Slipping her feet into her Converse, she left the apartment, yelling goodbye to her mother on her way out.

The sun beat down, snaking its way through the tall buildings and glinting off the windshields of parked cars. Wiping her brow of sweat, Sese buckled her helmet on and jetted toward the Plaza Hotel. She left her moped in the parking garage and headed in.

M stood waiting for her in the doorway, copper mask on and a pair of black corduroy overalls hugging her curves. Her thick locs had new beads adorning them: flashy rose gold and silver.

Sese's lips pulled into a grin. "Good to see you, M."

M's hazel eyes tightened as she stepped to the side, ushering Sese in the penthouse.

Once again, the lush greenery caught Sese by surprise. It really was an oasis in the drab, dry city. One particular plant caught her eye; the bright green leaves had holes in it, like Swiss cheese.

"I like your monstera adansonii."

M turned and delicately trailed a finger down the vine. "I see you've been looking up plants," she replied with a hint of mirth.

Sese blushed as M turned back to her. "I figured, why not? Obviously, you love plants now, so I wanted to know more."

"Hm." M clasped her hands together as she looked around the spacious, open floor concept. "I do love plants. They're my babies. They don't judge or criticize. They only thrive, on my love and care." She sighed, walking over to a giant palm type plant that stood taller than her, and stretched her hands up to touch the leaves floating above her head. "It's easy to pretend I'm thriving too, when all around me is life."

"That's so fucking sad," Sese blurted out.

M dropped her arms to her sides, shoulders hunched. "Is it?"

"You deserve to feel alive! You deserve to feel love!" Sese marched up to M and wrapped her in a furious embrace. "I want you to be happy."

M went rigid before abruptly melting into a sobbing mess. "I'm so lonely," she cried. Her long arms tangled with Sese's as tears trickled from beneath the mask and fell onto her overalls.

They clung to each other, though Sese couldn't tell which of them felt more desperate for comfort. All the anguish came pouring out as they hugged: anger over her father coming back into her mother's life, her guilt over involving Zeno in her crimes, her trepidation at having to take another life to end it all. Her feelings coursed through her like poison.

The doorbell rang, startling them apart. Sese's eyes brimmed with unshed tears as she looked up at M. Shaky laughter burst from them both as M headed for the intercom.

"Who is it?"

"Delivery."

"Come on up." M buzzed them through and faced Sese. "I hope you still want boba."

"Hell yes. And those sunglasses again, if you don't mind. I forgot to bring my own."

M pulled them out of her pocket. "I was hoping you'd ask."

Sese slipped them on and glanced around the room. Tinted lenses bathed the plants in a rosy glow.

M grabbed the boba and settled onto the couch, beckoning Sese over. Sinking onto the plush, velvety seat cushions, Sese reached for her blended taro and took a sip; a sugary-sweet tapioca pearl landed on her tongue and she bit down on it, enjoying the mix of flavors.

When she looked over, M had taken off the mask and sat watching her. For some reason, Sese was hit with the urge to kiss this beautiful, sad woman before her. Instead, she took another sip of her drink, feeling the heat rise in her cheeks as she looked away.

"Is something wrong?"

Sese shook her head. "No! I just… Well, I really want to kiss you." She shrugged, embarrassed.

M's lips curved into a luscious smile. "I'd like that."

They stared at each other for a moment, neither daring to

breathe, until Sese wrapped her hand in M's locs, and pulled her close. M let out a soft moan as their lips touched, driving Sese mad with desire. M's mouth was warm and pliant against hers; their lips parted and their tongues danced together. Sese's head floated in the clouds and all she wanted—needed—was for this moment to last forever, to be locked in this desperate embrace until the end of time.

She pulled away, breathing heavily, and watched M's eyes flutter open, her pupils dilated. She was so gorgeous; Sese couldn't get enough of her. Sese kissed the tip of M's wide nose before sitting back. Barely able to breathe through a sudden flush, Sese gasped for air as the hungry heat enveloped her. She grabbed her drink and took a gulp, hoping the ice-cold taro would cool her down.

It worked a little too well; Sese howled in pain as a brain freeze hit her. "Fuck!"

"What?" M popped up into a fighting stance, and Sese marveled at how this woman went from a pool of desire, sunk into the couch, to a fierce warrior in the blink of an eye.

"Brain freeze." Sese coughed and wiped at her eyes, careful not to knock the sunglasses off her face. "I'm okay."

M let out a burst of laughter and dropped into the couch again, joy lighting up her face. "Careful, silly."

They sat in silence, M cuddled up against Sese's side. Sese's phone buzzed with notifications from UberEats but she ignored them all, content in M's presence. As the sun started angling down, Sese realized M had fallen asleep. A gentle snore escaped her lips and Sese smiled.

Sese's phone let out a single tone: a message from one of her contacts. Sighing, she pulled it from her pocket to see a message from her mother.

Mom: don't wait up

A picture of Sese's mother and father appeared on the screen. They were sitting at a table in a swanky-looking restaurant, a wide smile on Dana's face and a bored smirk on his.

Sese's blood froze as she looked at the picture, wishing she could crumple it up and never see it again. How dare he! She was doing everything he asked, and on time. Why the fuck did he think he was entitled to keep seeing her mother?

She wanted to scream.

M must have sensed her change in demeanor because she woke and pressed a kiss to Sese's shoulder. "Is something wrong?"

"My horrible father is taking my mom out on a date tonight."

M sat up and looked at her with worry. "Is she in danger? I know how wild she gets when she's with him."

"Depends on how long the date is, I guess. The drugs don't come into play until they hit the clubs."

"I'm sorry," M said, pulling her into a hug. "Is there anything I can do?"

Sese shook her head. "I have this deal with him. If I do these three things, he'll leave us alone, forever. I have one more thing to do and then we'll be free."

"What is it?"

Sese pulled away. "You don't want to know."

"Sese, are you in trouble?"

Sese's eyes filled with tears. "I'm a bad person. You know that. I do bad things. I want to blame my father because he taught me all I know, but I have free will. I know that. I know I'm responsible for my actions."

M wrapped her arms around herself. "You're scaring me. What's going on?"

"I have to kill someone. I don't know who yet."

M's eyes went wide. "Sese…"

"I know. I know!" Sese sniffled as she jumped to her feet and started pacing. "After this, I'm done. I just want my mother to be safe and free from his influences. He's not good for her, for us."

M stayed quiet for a moment, then whispered, "Do you need my help?"

Sese stopped in her tracks and stared at her. "With the murder?"

M stood and walked up to Sese, grabbing her hands. Her thumbs rubbed circles on the back of Sese's hands. "I've helped you out before. I can help you now. If it means you and your mother will be safe and free, I will help."

"Thank you," Sese choked out, falling into M's arms. "Thank you so much."

When the envelope arrived a day later, Sese didn't open it immediately. Instead, she tossed it onto her desk beside an old, plastic iced-coffee cup, and went over to M's apartment. They spent the afternoon cuddled on the couch, watching a Korean drama about a team of criminals who hunt down bad guys for the cops. The rose filter of the sunglasses lent a strangeness to the show, which Sese found hilarious.

When the sun fell behind the surrounding skyscrapers, M pressed a kiss to Sese's forehead and asked what she wanted for dinner. Sese pulled M down for a deeper kiss before breathlessly replying that pizza sounded good.

At the end of an episode, Sese stood up for a bathroom break. M pointed out the correct door and Sese rushed inside, desperate to empty her bladder. Her sigh of relief as she sat on the toilet echoed in the silence. As she washed her hands, she caught a glimpse of herself in the mirror and stopped to stare.

She looked…happy. She couldn't remember the last time she had looked at her reflection and seen joy in her eyes. Rather than feeling at peace, this disturbed her. She was days away from killing someone; how dare she feel happy?

When she returned to the living area, she found M at the front door accepting their pizza. M put the box on the counter and pulled off her mask, tossing it beside the box and smiling broadly at Sese. Sese looked away.

"What's wrong?"

Sese shrugged. "I'm happy."

"That's a good thing. Right?"

Lip quivering, Sese slumped down into the nearest chair. "I shouldn't be happy. I'm about to kill someone."

M sat across from her, concern in her eyes. "Do you know who?"

Sese shook her head. "I got a letter today, but I didn't open it. It probably has the name."

"We need to know who it is as soon as possible so we can start planning."

"I know." Sese dropped her head into her hands. "I can't

believe you're helping me with this."

M reached over to caress Sese's cheek. "I'm helping you free yourself from the yoke of a dangerous man. You are worth it."

Sese looked up into those unfathomable hazel eyes, filled with kindness, and couldn't stop the torrent of tears. M gently pulled Sese into her arms, rocking her back and forth as she sobbed. After a lifetime of looking out for herself, the fact that someone stood ready to help and protect had Sese falling apart.

And that was okay. There was someone there who she trusted to pick up the pieces, someone who didn't care that she was a bad person and still loved her for who she was. She could afford to be vulnerable.

That night, M held Sese close as they drifted to sleep on silken sheets.

Sese stepped out of the Plaza Hotel onto the sunbaked sidewalk and headed for her moped. It wasn't until she pulled out of the garage and onto the street that she noticed a limo glide out behind her.

Several random turns confirmed her suspicions: the limo was tailing her. She sped through a yellow light and tangled through traffic, taking an abrupt left turn at the next alley and a right onto the next street. Then she headed for home, sure she had lost her tail.

She pulled into a parking spot around the corner from her apartment building and walked the rest of the way home, whistling a snappy tune and nearly skipping with glee. Spending time with

M had launched her into high spirits, and some random stalker in a limo couldn't ruin that.

Except the limo was parked in front of her apartment building when she turned the corner.

"What the fuck?" she hissed under her breath. It had to be him.

As she walked closer, a chauffeur jumped out of the driver's side to open the back door. The man who emerged from the depths wore a tailored suit, a crimson tie at his throat.

"Father," she sneered, hiding her fear. He had never come to their apartment before.

"Daughter. I haven't received a progress report on your task, so I decided to see for myself. It seems like you're playing the long game this time. Getting close to the target doesn't always pay off; you might be the lead suspect."

She rolled her eyes. As if she didn't know how to commit murder and get away with it. "What are you talking about?"

His snake-like eyes narrowed as he looked her up and down. "Is it possible... Do you not know who your target is? I sent a letter."

"I didn't open it yet."

Her father burst into raucous laughter, the sound booming in the street. Digging in his pocket, he produced a black handkerchief and used it to dab at the tears in his eyes.

Sese's stomach twisted. It couldn't be...

"Remember what you told me, Perseus. You would do anything to see me gone. Remember that when you see your target."

Still chuckling, he signaled for his peon and slithered back into the darkness of the limo. The limo started up and the back window rolled down to reveal her father's smug face.

"Good day, daughter. And good luck."

Sese stood rooted to the spot for a moment, heart pounding, before racing into the building and up the stairs, two by two. Keys jumbled in her shaking hands as she tried to unlock the front door. She made a beeline for her desk and tore open the envelope.

The sheet of paper inside had a single name printed on it: M. Gorgo.

"Please pick up! I have to talk to you." Sese hung up and stared at the picture of M, wearing her copper mask, on the phone screen. "Why isn't she answering?"

Pacing in front of her desk did nothing to reduce her stress, but it made her feel like she was doing something. So maybe it did help, a little.

Dana knocked on the doorframe and stuck her head through the crack in the doorway. "Sese, are you hungry? I made salapao." Her earnest smile tugged at Sese enough to break her anxiety spiral, and Sese followed her mother into the kitchen.

The buns still sat in the steaming basket. Sese grabbed one, tossing it from hand to hand as it cooled before taking a hearty bite. The savory taste of bbq pork and the soft texture of the steamed dough filled her mouth and she gave her mother a hum of approval.

Sese paused mid-bite as the sound of her phone ringing caught her attention. Mouth full, she dashed back to her room and snatched the phone, chewing frantically.

"Hello?"

"I'm sorry I missed your calls. I was with my doctor. What's wrong?"

M's voice soothed her until she remembered why she had called. "I have to see you."

"Is it your mother? Is she okay?"

"It's not her. I can't talk over the phone. I have to see you."

"Come over."

Sese hung up without another word, shoved the rest of the salapao in her mouth, and headed for the door.

"Whoa! What's the rush?"

Sese paused to finish chewing, rolling her eyes at herself for taking such a large bite. "I'm seeing a friend."

"The same friend who left you those love bites?" Dana looked pointedly at Sese's neck.

"Yep. That's her."

"Well, have fun. Be safe." Dana's eyes twinkled with mischief and Sese lunged in to give her a hug. This was how she wanted to always remember her mother: happy and full of joy. And that would only happen if she fulfilled the third task… Her throat convulsed, the salapao threatening to come back up as she thought of what that meant.

"Gotta go," she choked out, rushing out the door without waiting for a goodbye.

M answered the door wearing her copper mask and a pair of black jeans with a mustard yellow crop top. She held out the rose-tinted sunglasses for Sese, who shoved them on her face.

"Now, what is it that's so terrible that you're back in less than two hours?"

"Getting sick of me already?" Sese asked in a teasing voice.

M removed the mask, tossing it onto the counter and smirking. "As if."

Seeing her face sobered Sese instantly. "I have to kill you."

M blinked and jerked back from her. "Excuse me?"

"You're the target. I have to kill *you*." Sese started pacing the length of the great room, tears welling in her eyes. "And for the life of me, I can't figure out why! Why you?"

M stood still, hardly breathing. "Sese, let's talk about this."

"I won't do it! I won't kill you. I'll find another way."

With a heavy sigh, M sat on the couch and patted the cushion beside her. "Come here, love."

Sese obediently moved to sit beside her, M's gorgeous visage blurry through her tears like an impressionist painting.

M gave her a sad smile. "Sese, I'm dying."

"What!"

Her fingers fiddled with a loc as she avoided Sese's gaze. "That's why my doctor was over. I've been…in incredible pain lately. It comes and goes. The disease is eating into my brain and spinal cord."

Sese's heart constricted and her breath left her. A gaping hole grew in her chest, ready to consume her. She shook her head, eyebrows furrowed as she stared at M.

"No. That can't be true. What the fuck!" Her voice cracked on the last syllable and she burst into tears.

M grabbed her hands. "Don't you see? This is your way. I'm

already dying. This will put me out of my misery, let me go before I no longer know who I am."

"I can't!"

"Then I'll do it. And you bring my head to him, and you show him my face so he knows what you did." M's voice grew soft. "And you'll be free."

Sese grabbed M's face, pulling her in for a desperate kiss. She poured all the sorrow in her heart into it and wondered if M tasted the misery on her tongue.

M gently pushed her away and held her at arm's length. "Do you want me to do it?"

Sese shook her head. "I can do it. How do you want to go?"

"Ideally? In my sleep."

"Then we do that."

Sese jumped up from the couch and held out her hand for the beautiful and tragic woman before her. M pressed it to her full lips, eyes glistening.

"Thank you, Sese."

Sese stepped out of the drugstore with a bag of sleeping pills. The cacophony of the city burst forth around her: car engines rushing past, horns honking impatiently, indistinct conversations as people bustled by, the roar of a jet engine, far above, carrying its passengers to distant lands.

When was the last time M had been out of her apartment? Even her doctor did house visits. Everything was delivered to her;

the instrument of her death was no exception. Sese bit down on her lip to keep herself from breaking apart.

It was a short walk back to the Plaza Hotel. Sese wondered if she would ever have a reason to come back. The sounds of the cityscape dropped away as the doors shut behind her and she pressed the call button for the elevator.

"My hero," M said, a smile evident in her voice as she buzzed Sese up.

Sese put the sunglasses back on as the elevator doors opened onto the top floor. M stood waiting, her copper mask perfectly in place.

"Are you ready?"

M dropped the mask and nodded, a sad smile twisting her features. Together, they walked to the bedroom, where M downed the entire bottle of pills. A languid expression settled over her features as she lay on the bed beside Sese, petting her cropped hair.

"Don't forget me, okay?" M's slurred words balanced in the air before fluttering away.

Sese pressed a kiss to her temple and whispered into her ear. "I would never."

M giggled. "That tickles."

Sese took a shaky breath and tried to hum along to the Kpop song playing faintly through the Bluetooth speakers. M hummed along as well, off tune, until her breathing evened out and she fell silent. Sese choked on her tears as she continued humming.

Eventually two breaths became one and Sese rolled over to see M's face fully relaxed for the first time. Her full lips were parted slightly, and Sese ached to kiss them one last time. Instead, she got up, went into the kitchen, and grabbed the butcher knife.

M's head had fit surprisingly well inside one of her designer leather bags. Sese walked out of the Plaza Hotel with a Burberry bag slung over her shoulder, giving her usual smile to the doorman. She strapped the bag to the basket of the moped and took off for her father's hotel.

Parking in front of the revolving doors, she dropped her helmet and sunglasses in the basket and grabbed the leather handbag. She had never held a decapitated head in her hands before; it was surprisingly heavy, and the bag thumped against her hip as she walked.

The bodyguard nodded at her and opened the door, shutting it behind her. Her father sat at his mahogany desk, a bored expression on his face.

"Why?" Sese's voice trembled.

"Why what, Perseus? Be specific."

"Why M?"

He shrugged delicately. "It's business, daughter. She has property I want."

Sese felt her insides clench. "So you killed her for a hotel."

He gave her a slimy smile. "It's done then?"

She glared at him. "This is what you wanted, isn't it?" Reaching into the bag, she grasped M's locs and pulled her head out.

Her father blinked and let out a shriek as he gazed upon M's face. Too late, Sese realized the disease's radioactive properties were still active. She watched in fascination as her father clawed at his milky eyes, blood running down his face in rivulets and gathering in his open mouth. His body convulsed and his screams died as he crumpled to the floor behind the desk, still as stone.

The bodyguard burst into the room and she whirled around and watched the process again. The bodyguard's skin turned grey as he lay on the floor, fine black lines appearing around his eyes and mouth. Sese's stomach flipped as she stumbled back from the—body? Corpse? Her arm trembled as she held M's head aloft.

She dropped M's head to the ground with a dull thud. As it rolled, Sese grappled with the urge to look at her beloved's face one last time. Focusing on a spot on the wall, she blinked several times before morbid curiosity drew her eyes down. Without her rose-tinted glasses, she was helpless against M's disease; a lancing pain shot through her skull as the world turned grey and she dropped to her knees, sobbing.

Is this what M had felt? The pain bored into her brain like an ice pick while her nerves lit up with fire. Her muscles all stiffened at once and she fell to the floor, paralyzed.

And still the pain continued, a constant blaze. Distantly, she heard footsteps. Then she heard a scream.

And then the pain overwhelmed her, and she heard nothing at all.

THREADS OF GOLD

Dina S.

"Almost got it," Damon whispered, blowing a black curl out of his face.

"Hurry up!" I stood above him, shielding him from the prying eyes of any passersby. The music from the gala downstairs could be heard in conjunction with the murmur of drunken party guests. The gala was a cover for a black-market auction for the latest sonic weaponry. Hundreds of the world's top criminals were right below us, and I was not allowed to engage. Keeping *me* back from the ultimate fight, potentially the fight of my career?

Bullshit.

"You can't rush perfection," Damon cooed, his blue eyes sparkling with gratification.

Damon—codename: Dice—the most reliable, handy-dandy partner a spy could ask for. It was a shame when I looked at him I only saw a big, dorky goofball. Partners are for *life*. An agent would never go on a mission without their partner in some capacity. And Damon was more technically-oriented than me, meaning he was my stay-in-the-van guy.

Ever since we met, we'd been inseparable. We were young, sparring on the main training floor at headquarters. I giggled when

I saw his form and how he sparred with the dummies—weak, nerd, dead meat. If you didn't pass training, that meant you were... Well...you were dead. The Palaestra would not hesitate to kill you on sight, child or not. Damon knew he wouldn't pass. The only way he would survive would be to stand out from the crowd. His method? Take down his biggest competition—me. He didn't beat me, but his gumption made me pause. Nobody had willingly fought me before. I took him under my wing instantly, helping him survive the labyrinth of our agency and climb up from the bottom rung.

Best friends ever since.

The pins finally fell into place in the lock, and Damon quickly moved inside the pitch-black room, gun drawn. Hoisting up my dress to snatch my gun from the inside of my thigh, I followed.

"Clear," Damon said softly.

Damon pocketed my gun for me and handed me the pins and wrenches one at a time as I spun my red hair into an elaborate bun, using the tools to hold it in place. Security was none the wiser; with their exquisite gems and patterns, the tools merely looked like hairpins. I did a brisk sweep and moved straight towards the laptop sitting atop the large, oak desk at the far end of the room. A wiggle of the mouse illuminated my face in blue light. Damon coughed and I looked up, his arms crossed with a knowing smirk slapped across his face.

"Sorry," I muttered, moving out of his way. Damon was better at techy stuff than me, but I always wanted to do everything. I couldn't help my greed for the glory.

Damon threw himself into the oversized leather chair, licking his lips, ready to tear apart any firewalls or coding set in place.

My eyes scanned the room, trying to remember where the safe was hidden—my alternative mission. I knew there were treasures concealed within the dark. They didn't know it, but I was who they were trying to keep out.

Acadia—codename: Chryso Deidamia—the golden destroyer. Destroy. That's what I'd been trained to do.

I watched Damon tap away at the keyboard, undermining whatever the system threw at him.

"Flash drive?" he asked. The sleek metal slipped between my fingers and into his.

When he inserted the USB, the laptop screen went blank, leaving us in darkness for a moment. A status bar popped up, counting the percentage of files uploaded. Then, with a soft tap of his fingers, Damon sat back for a moment, proud of his work.

"8 clicks out, Chryso," my Palaestra, Theodore, said through the microchip intercom implanted in my brain. His voice made my heartbeat race.

I relayed the message to Damon. He nodded, his tongue between his teeth as he began to work faster.

"Fourth book, second shelf," Damon supplied, seemingly reading my mind.

I turned and gave him a dirty look through the shadows. I couldn't see his face, but he knew me well enough to picture mine, I'm sure. I slipped off my heels, gently tossing them onto a sitting chair, and padded silently towards the bookshelf. I tugged on the book. On the opposite wall above a fig tree, a lock emerged from the wall.

In no time at all, I unlocked the safe. I snatched the paper file that HQ asked for, thumbing through pictures of horrifying scenes from Arac's victims. Frozen in time, a young boy tied to a chair, gagged and bleeding, his face beaten beyond recognition, the shape of a spider charred into his flesh—Arac's mark for his victims. Then more pictures of new tech, infiltrated government safehouses, pictures of spies outside of my agency that had clearly been compromised—circles around faces unaware of the photographer, X's slashed across others. Arac had his webs spun across the world. He had become the most prolific weapons dealer, with a growing underground militia. If we didn't take down his organization soon, he would become an undefeatable superpower by the turn of the century.

One document detailed a scientific experiment of some kind, project title: Mygdon. Black lines redacted most of the script—a few symbols and formulas, and sandwiched within were pictures of life-sized lawn ornaments, glimmering gold.

"Why do rich people always like ugly stuff?" I mumbled to myself.

Damon was next to me in an instant, his hand outstretched to present a small disc the size of a button in his palm—a silent question. I sighed and turned my head. He tucked some loose strands of my hair behind my ear and stuck the button onto my skin. With a small zap of electricity, I knew our microchips were offline for any transmissions. Then he snatched several stacks of currency microcards from the safe and slipped them into his pocket.

"Why do you always do that?" I whispered harshly through the black.

"Because I can," he replied.

"The agency gives us everything we ask for," I argued.

"And in exchange, we do everything *they* ask for."

"So? I don't care how I get it, as long as I get everything I want." I shrugged, shutting the safe without a sound.

We crossed the room back to the computer, the status bar almost at one hundred percent. Damon plopped back into the chair, the leather material squeaking gratingly. I swung myself onto the desk so I could watch the silhouette of his face, the shadows casting harsh lines on his strong jawline while we waited.

"Do you ever consider leaving?" Damon asked suddenly.

A small gasp escaped my lips. It took a lot to shock me, but there I was, shocked beyond comparison. My partner...asking if I considered defecting? Treason. A voice in the back of my mind wanted to admit to those sapphires staring back at me, blinking with honest curiosity and trust, that yes, I had considered running once. Stockholm Syndrome didn't have an unbreakable hold on me, even after all these years. I still remember. The day they came for me. The day they took me away from my family. I remember. But it was with them that I had the most power.

Power was all I wanted.

I swallowed the bile rising in my throat. "And give up my status here? No."

Damon was quiet for a moment, his energy making the air stale and tense. "I'd run. If you were with me."

I hated when he said things like that. To end the conversation, I made a show of removing the button from behind my ear and slipping it into the pocket on his chest. He grabbed my hand, holding it over his heart. For a brief moment, his breathing and heartbeat were all I felt, all I knew. My best friend. My world. He loosened his grip, and I eased my hand away.

A glint across the room caught my eye. I made out a bar cart through the shadows. Soundless footsteps carried me to a decanter filled with a glowing, golden liquid. Logic told me not to pour myself a drink. Training told me it could be poisoned—after all, many people wanted the great criminal mastermind, Arac, dead. Boredom told me to take a sip. I thought of all the fancy things Arac possessed.

Why shouldn't I take a sip?

I earned it. The assignment had been smooth sailing. I deserved more than the bad guys. The golden flecks pulsed in the inky black, singing in my mind. A metal label across the decanter read: *Dionysus.*

Sip.

One sip.

My lips were already parting in anticipation. The glass already poured in my hand without conscious thought.

I was being greedy and cocky… But hadn't I earned the privilege to break this one rule?

Voices swirled and sang to me. Everything I desired would be in this glass.

One. Sip.

But what did I desire? More missions? More power? I didn't truly know.

"What are you doing?" Damon's low voice in my ear startled me. I should have known he was there; nobody ever sneaks up on me.

Blood rushed to my ears, heating my cheeks, blurring my vision. The liquid swirled in the cup—slow, methodic, hypnotic. It played with my mind, humming loud in my ears.

"Nothing," I finally said and set the crystal cup down, the greed leaving me when I looked into Damon's eyes.

"3 clicks," Theodore said through the intercom in my head again.

"Time to change." Fingernail to my temple, I switched the controls for the nanobots in my body to get to work. My dress shimmered for a moment as billions of tiny robots came to life. The nanobots flipped the reflectors and mini computers in my suit to transform the illusion dress back to my combat uniform. It covered my fingers and toes completely. The only exposed parts of our bodies were our heads. Damon pressed my gun into my palm, and I snapped it into the holster on my hip rather than the inside of my thigh. Whoever thought hiding weapons there to be a good idea was dead wrong. It's impossible to walk without chafing.

The file finally finished uploading. I snagged the flash drive and tucked it safely in the pocket on my waist, the suit automatically working to conceal the bulge from view. We made our way to the door, meeting in the middle for a quick high-five. Mission accomplished. Now to the roof for rendezvous.

The door flew open, light bursting in and eating all the shadows away. We stopped abruptly. Four men with large blasters marched inside followed by Arac—the host of tonight's ball and the man from whom we were currently stealing.

Damon and I said nothing. We threw our hands in the air.

"Well…well…whh-ut have hur?" Arac slurred, drunk from the party below.

"Sorry, we got turned around looking for the bathroom," I remarked.

"UPSssss?" (Universal Protection Services) Arac was not

pulling any punches. I doubted he could punch without completely winding himself anyway. He was a rather short and stout man with a handlebar mustache, like a villain from one of those old-fashioned cartoons people watched on ancient television sets. Arac had become complacent on his throne.

So there we were, surrounded by guns, face to face with the evilest man of the thirtieth century. And he was drunk. He didn't even have the respect to make this a fair fight for us. Asshole.

I decided to offer my agency's name. "Phrygia."

"Never heard of youse," he spat.

"What about the Shimmera of Olympus? Have you heard of them?" I asked.

Arac's eyes bulged from their sockets. "What? They're not real. A myth from the old world!"

Theodore reported through my intercom, "*Extraction team has landed.*"

"Nah, totally fictitious. Could you imagine, though?" I proffered a smile, content I had purchased myself enough time by distracting him.

Great. The asshat made me late to see the hottest man alive and made me look bad in front of my Palaestra.

"Listen, we can do this the hard way, or you can let us go and you will live another day." I knew the speech was pointless, but I couldn't help myself.

Arac started to open his mouth to say something, but I was bored with the lack of quality banter. In one fell swoop, I swept the legs of the gun-for-hire closest to me. Caught unaware, his blaster fired through the roof before I snatched it and knocked him out with the butt of his weapon, finishing him off with a kill shot to the eye. Damon grappled with two of the guards while the fourth charged towards me. I ran to meet him, jumping to wrap myself around his neck to take him to the ground. As we landed, I snatched a knife from the heel of my suit and stabbed it neatly through his throat. He didn't have time to make so much as a gurgle before he was dead, blood pooling around my knees on the antique Persian rug. I wiped the blood from my knife and slipped it back into the compartment in my heel.

I heard Damon behind me still grappling with the two guards.

I looked up from the lifeless body below me and saw Arac reaching for a weapon. I rolled towards him, retrieving a hidden knife from my back.

Two shots. One thud.

The knife slipped from my grip, spinning towards Arac in what felt like slow motion.

My heart skipped a beat in the second it took for me to turn around to confirm what happened.

Damon fell to the ground as my knife implanted itself smoothly into Arac's thigh. Arac screamed, dropping his weapon. My suit's mechanics slipped another throwing knife into my hand, and I tossed it. It tore through Arac's palm before he could grab the blaster from the ground.

Damon was motionless. I called for him in a blind panic, "Agent Dice!"

I couldn't bring myself to move.

The two henchmen Damon had been fighting stood over his lifeless form. They turned to detain me. I was going to kill these bastards—every last one of them. As the guards took one step each towards me, I heard two pops, and they fell to the ground.

Damon gripped the gun above his chest, still holding his form, his breathing erratic.

He looked over at me with a sly grin on his lips. "Dumbass had it set to stun." He let out a relieved laugh, but there was still the twist of terror in his features. We were both convinced he was dead.

"You venomous spider!" Arac grunted in pain, his voice laced with panic, and pulled the knife from his hand. He made to remove the one in his hip, but he stopped. Maybe he wasn't a complete dumbass. That thing was lodged securely in an artery.

"Eh, you see, I've always considered myself more of a scorpion. Something about them just sort of…speaks to me. Ya know? Dice, what do you think?" I halfheartedly lowered my weapon, feigning distraction by the sorry attempt at an insult from the Spider himself.

From the corner of my eye, I saw Damon stand up, and relief flooded my chest. We didn't have time to celebrate just yet. He followed my lead, one hand on his hip. "I always considered you more of a snake. A spitting cobra would be fitting." He blew that pesky strand of hair out of his eyes and gave me a perfect, pearly white smile.

His train of thought took me a moment to follow, but then I returned his smile. "Oh," I chuckled, "because of the eye thing?"

Damon shrugged, still grinning ear to ear, proud of his quip. "It is your signature, Acid." His nickname for me made sense finally.

I trained my weapon back on Arac, all light-heartedness evaporating from the air with the tap of the gunmetal against my nanobot-covered hand. "Permission to squash this bug?"

I waited for a response from my intercom. Someone at Phrygia was always listening.

"Negative."

I rolled my eyes in frustration, aimed for his foot just for funsies. *Pop.* Arac let out another scream of pain.

Damon tugged on my elbow. "Let's go."

Turning out of the doorway, we found ourselves face to face with six more henchmen. Damon shut the door with us back inside, quickly pulling a table in front of it, and searched for an alternative exit. The sound of fists pounding against the door echoed in the room, reminding us time was short. They'd have it kicked down in seconds.

Arac's painful cries were starting to bother me and make me lose my concentration. I kicked him, yelling, "Shut up!"

As Damon walked by Arac grabbed his foot, and he landed on his back with a thud. Arac grabbed the blaster from the ground beside him, aiming for Damon's head. My training kept me calm as muscle memory took over.

Pop. Pop. A shot to each eye—my signature.

Phrygia was not going to be happy about that. Oops.

"Thanks." Damon let out a breath of relief and stood.

Bang. Bang. They were almost inside.

Stop panicking. I demanded myself to cease feeling. I was an agent of Phrygia. Cold. Ruthless. Exceptional.

My test scores in preliminary school proved me to be exceptional…and exactly what Phrygia wanted. That's how they found us. We were all exceptional.

Exceptional.

That word snapped me back to reality.

Exceptional.

"Now what?" Damon asked.

Addressing my intercom, I said calmly, "Window." This move would get us killed or get me some serious recognition at Phrygia—and I love recognition.

"I hate your antics," Theodore, my Palaestra, responded through the microchip. Yet, I knew he was smiling, understanding my plan with zero hesitation.

"We're doing *what* now?" Damon's voice broke. He was hardly the fearless type. Damon was soft. Tender. Gentle. Selfless. Everything I was not.

I was hard, cold, and selfish. Greedy. Phrygia owed me a reward for this mission and for saving Damon's life. A reward in the form of a nice buzz from *Dionysus.* Calmly, my feet carried me back to the bar cart from before, liquid courage calling my greedy heart. "You heard me." The melody of the surreal liquid from earlier still sung sweetly in my mind, calling me to sip. One sip. Sip. I hadn't shaken that itch since I first spotted the golden nectar, and now that I was about to do something truly stupid, I would give my cocky greed this one moment of solace.

Without a second thought, the glass was back in my hand, and I took a swig of the golden nectar. A total power move and power was what I wanted—to be more powerful than all these rich madmen and their ugly, oversized lawn ornaments. The familiar rush of liquor spun down my spine, warming my stomach and swimming down to my toes. A sharp pain pulled at my chest, my hands went numb, and the empty glass slipped out of my grip, shattering across the floor with a shimmer of gold decorating the shards.

"Are you okay?" Damon grabbed my elbow, holding me up while I fought the urge to retch.

The room lit up like a flash grenade going off. Sparkles like champagne and stars blinded me for a moment, then all at once, everything returned to normal.

I spoke through gritted teeth, puffing my cheeks out to breathe through the slowly subsiding pain, "Fine. We have to move."

Damon reluctantly let go of me, but he kept his eyes on me.

Two deep breaths.

Showtime.

Four bullets through the window. Damon and I walked towards the open space, stars twinkling almost methodically in the night sky. Our eyes met—warm honey meeting the gaze of icy blue.

"Run!" We locked hands, legs in sync. We jumped off the ledge in time with each other.

Damon screamed, "Don't let me go!"

"Never," I whispered. He probably couldn't hear me.

This was my calm. We kept our bodies splayed like starfish, hands locked, never letting go. We were flying through the air, our suits expanding outward to let us glide. A sudden tug knocked the air from my lungs, and I lost Damon's grip. Gravity was no longer pushing us down to the ground below. Gradually we rose, the whomping noise of helicopter blades drawing closer.

"There's my star!" Theodore's voice came through my intercom and I smiled. He pulled us into the chopper, and the net that caught us in the air fell around our feet as we stood.

Damon looked nauseous. His skin paled as he tried to speak. He was my stay-in-the-van guy for a reason.

A maniacal laugh escaped me, and I high-fived the rest of the crew around us. I didn't know them, but having an audience always gave me a heightened sense of self.

I reached out to high-five Theodore, but instead, he wrapped his arms around my waist and kissed my cheek. He knew what he did to me. "Good job, Freckles!" He poked my cheeks gently.

He's your Palaestra, nothing more, I chided myself.

Damon looked like a sad puppy for the briefest of moments but hid it with an elated grin to match my own.

"Congratulations. Our Golden Duo. You two have become like royalty amongst your fellow agents. Queen Acadia Midas and King Damon Silenus of Phrygia. I thank you." Sibyl clapped with zero emotion in her face. You don't get to become the ruthless Stratagos of Phrygia by showing enthusiasm or emotion.

Theodore stood across from the round holo table, leaning against the wall of the debriefing room. The shadows partially covered his eyes, but I caught him staring, watching me. I tried to hide my coy grin. Sibyl rarely congratulated a team personally. Something had to be up.

"Thank you, Stratagos Sibyl," Damon and I said in unison.

Sibyl stopped, considering us for a moment. Then, she swiped the holograph away and pulled up our mission report. Footage played in front of her. Every agent's nanobots were equipped with cameras. Every mission was recorded. I hadn't realized that the Stratagos herself reviewed the footage.

I watched the hologram from behind, trying to see through it to watch her face.

Damon whispered, "Don't worry. My scrambler never fails us. They won't see what we don't want them to see." My pinky found his and I gave him a subtle squeeze, grateful he was my partner. Our conversation about defecting could be cause for immediate... termination. The video glitched and cut out as I walked over to the liquid on the bar cart. For a brief moment, I thought I saw Sibyl's mouth twitch and her eyes dart to Theodore before regaining her composure. Odd.

"Well done. We need to have your microchips checked; they appear to be glitchy. However, that can be dealt with later." Sibyl paused, swiping the hologram away completely and addressing us with wrinkled, calculating eyes. Theodore stood at attention, then took a step forward to join us around the table. "You have done quite well in your careers here at Phrygia. Our finest team. Truly, our Golden Duo... Palaestra Theodore, would you care to do the honors? You have, after all, raised this team from the ground up." She gestured towards Theodore.

He cleared his throat. "You are being promoted. On a trial period, of course."

A broad smile spilled across my face.

Damon's foot nudged mine. Scooting closer to me ever so subtly, he frowned. From my peripheral, I watched him take a deep breath and swallow hard. What could possibly make him upset?

"You're going to become Palaestras," Theodore announced loudly with a boisterous laugh.

The world dropped out from under me. Palaestra. My head was too light. I almost wondered if it had popped off and floated away. Did someone shut off the oxygen? We were underground, after all. I heard a high-pitched scream from inside my mind. *Palaestra.* I was remembering the same screams coming from my own throat when I was taken by a Palaestra. My fears rocketed up to my chest. I was going to become the thing the little girl inside me always feared. Palaestra.

I kept the smile plastered on my face. "Thank you, Stratagos!"

Damon turned to follow Sibyl as she exited the room but stopped when he noticed I wasn't following beside him. "You ready, Acid?" he called for me.

"Umm...you go on ahead. I want to talk to Theodore for a moment." I turned back to Theodore and gave him a little nod.

Damon was next to me in an instant. "I'll just wait, and we can walk back together." He gave Theodore a scowl, betraying his mistrust.

Damon did everything in his power not to leave me alone with Theodore. An annoying, overprotective older brother.

"Your Majesty?" Theodore took a few steps closer to me, closing the gap between us, and bowed in jest.

"I...uh..." I sighed, giving Damon my most annoyed look for ruining my moment. "Does this make us equals now?"

Damon scoffed, putting a hand on his hip, clearly frustrated with where I was taking the conversation. He could've left—his choice.

Theodore let out a small chuckle and licked his lips, those devilish eyes staring me up and down. "Look, Agent Chryso... Acadia... You and I," he paused, grabbing my hand in his, "will never be equals."

I couldn't contain my shock. His words were harsh. Damon

had gone rigid at my side, watching my hand in Theodore's.

Theodore continued speaking, my ears struggling to hear it over the internal screams in my brain. His thumb drew slow circles on my covered palm, my suit stopping me from feeling his skin on mine. "I've enjoyed our little flirtatious games over the years, but you've gone and ruined it now. You're supposed to leave these things unspoken. Frankly, my dear, you're not woman enough for me. Not with what the agency does to its agents. You're not actually Queen. You're barely even a princess. You're just a little girl."

I clutched my stomach, the hollow feeling that always appeared at the back of my mind piercing me with Theodore's words. The reminder of what the agency did to their women, to me, crushed my soul. Phrygia made it easy on themselves—carving out our insides, playing God with our bodies.

He's been stringing me along for all these years. He was playing with my mind, convincing me to comply with a flirtatious smile here and there, and soft pecks on the cheek. Theodore knew how greedy I was for more power, and he used that against me. I had made it easy for him. Everything was a lie.

My eyes blurred as tears welled within them. I couldn't process Damon's quick movement of popping Theodore in the jaw, knocking him out with no hesitation.

Our footsteps echoed across the hard floor of the locker room. Rows and rows of blue steel lockers with benches between them.

Row 218. Damon's locker was directly across from mine. We opened them in time, each positioning the small mirrors inside to see each other. A smile flashed across both of our faces, even though my lips were still salted from my tears.

"Do you want to talk about it?" he asked.

I *did* want to talk about it. I'd been in love with my Palaestra since I first came to Phrygia. It had all been a lie. Now I was expected to kidnap children and turn them into one of us. Turn them into more Theodores and broken Acadias.

"Do *you* want to talk about it?" I retorted.

"No."

"Fair enough." I clicked the button under my arm and my suit fell away, the nanobots compressing themselves into the chain of a necklace.

Damon's did the same, folding themselves into a set of rings—shining, bright gold.

Exposed with nothing more than my bra and underwear to cover my body, goosebumps traveled across my skin, the cold air of the locker room hitting me all at once. Within the depths of my locker, I pulled out my ID tags, slipping the silver chain over my neck, tapping against my nanobots. I read the inscription on the cool metal.

MIDAS, Q. ACADIA

021-81-9552

O NEG

PHRYGIA

"You're hurt!" Damon rushed over to me, nearly tripping over

the bench between us.

I shrugged out of his touch. "It's just some bruising." Without my suit numbing my pain for me and holding me together, the bruises across my ribs burned.

Damon gingerly touched my side, and I squirmed.

"You need to go to Asclepieia!"

"Damon, no! Hush. Listen to me." I grabbed his hand and forced him to look at me. Standing there in his black boxer-briefs, breathing heavily, concern for me evident in his features. That one pesky strand of dark hair fell into his eyes. He closed his mouth, realizing the severity of what I was about to say.

"I can't be a Palaestra. I can't be a Theodore."

"What are you saying?" he whispered.

"I'm ready to run."

Damon nodded. "Okay, yes. We can do this. I've got a guy—Robin. He defected from the UPS ages ago. He has a whole crew of people that can help us."

"Wait! The UPS? Damon, that's nuts. They're interplanetary! We can't just leave the planet. We don't have time for you to contact anyone either. It's now or never."

Damon was already reaching into his locker for a communicator. He rapidly punched in a code and looked up. "It's done. I've been waiting for you to be ready. We've had a plan set up for ages."

The idea that Damon had been communicating with a defected agent, even if they weren't from Phrygia, startled me. What else did I not know about my best friend? I knew he had a rebellious streak in him, but I didn't think it went as far as having contacts to get us out.

He slipped the device back into his locker on top of his bag of currency microcards he had been collecting in secret over the years. Turning to me, he said, "I'm ready for this, Acid. I've wanted to leave since our first day of training. You and me, together. No rules, no agency, no taking orders."

My heart was racing seeing him in this new light, excited, alive for the first time since I had known him. Damon had been holding back on me for years. It made me smile.

He grabbed my other hand in his.

A gasp came from him. A pained expression began spreading across his face. "What're you—" Painful screams came from his throat before silence abruptly took over, sealing off his vocal cords.

I looked down as nanobots crawled up his body, devouring him like a virus, consuming him—toes, legs, knees, abdomen, neck. Golden specks munched at his flesh, locking him into a cocoon of nanobots, crawling across his skin in a swarm.

Acid, he mouthed soundlessly.

Blue sapphires, now solid gold. "Damon!" I screamed, echoes of my voice bouncing off the metal walls around us. My best friend stood before me, lifeless, a statue—a lawn ornament. My head shook, my body vibrating, adrenaline pushing the trauma down as far as it could go. Pain wrapped me in its tight grip, squeezing the breath out of me from the inside out.

I shook his shoulders, but he didn't move. My hand caught my eye. That same glint from in the darkness of Arac's room. The liquid nectar calling me. Voices whispering in my mind. The voices of my greed. *Drink. Drink. One sip.* My fingertip glistened, twinkling like a star. Hiding. A monster shielded to look like an Angel of Light. I realized at that moment the Spider's real power. He may be dead, but I now carried on his legend. I matched his greed for power. How cleverly the webs were spun. A devastating trap. A bioweapon. My touch had become far more deadly than a cobra.

Not nanobots. Gold.

Looking into those lifeless eyes that never failed me, my heart shattered like the glass from Arac's nectar. Damon. Damon was always there for me and always would be… At least, I thought he would be. How could I move without him by my side?

Tears spilled from my eyes and dripped off my chin. My hand shimmered through the fog in my vision.

Grief weighed me down. My arms were heavy. My knees wouldn't bend, my feet wouldn't carry me. I dropped to the ground, wails cutting through my throat until they turned into silent sobs. Phrygia made me an empty, greedy, soulless killer. Damon made me whole, kept me grounded. I needed him.

I had to fix this. I needed to find the people that gave Arac this weapon, and I would need a crew to do so. The communicator buzzed within Damon's locker, and I snatched it and the bag of currency cards greedily, wiping my eyes to see clearly. Just before the communicator in my left hand turned to solid gold I read:

ROBIN AND THE FYLAK ARE EN ROUTE. PICKUP LOCATION: PACTOLUS RIVER IN KISARA, 0300.

I had no choice.

I ran.

GWENHIFAR AND THE VAT-KNIGHT

Dewi Hargreaves

Accelerated Hormone Treatment: completed.

High-Capacity Mental Acuity Test: passed.

Moralistic and Empathetic Comprehension Test: corrupted.

Oath of the Order of Pentecost (Lake-Grown): yes.

Recommendation: TERMINATE.

Terminate.

The word swam in the Lady's vision. She ate little for days, and her underladies became concerned. Time merged and stretched, days flitted by and doubled back on themselves. She swirled through the loop untethered, that word haunting her every breath.

Terminate.

The Lady spent many hours sitting before the flashing, beeping obelisk in the centre of her garden. It stood on the cooling system on the bank of the Lake. Wind blew across the flickering surface of the water, picking up nitrogen-cold droplets and sprinkling them over her face and body. She plugged herself in, slowly, methodically connecting the dozen trailing wires to the ports on her bare flesh, feeling the static bite of each one as they connected to her core. She kept her expression steady.

Terminate.
Terminate.

How could it be?

She asked the obelisk, but it remained silent, as it often seemed to in recent years.

She dreamt of Lanslod.

He walked across the Lake towards her, a ghostly blue shadow conjured by photons and lasers. She studied the soft contours of his face, the tousled, curly hair bundled on top of his head. Tall and muscular, he had perfect form as he walked. He stopped before the obelisk, giving her an easy grin before summoning a blade and moving through his practice cuts. His shape was fluid like water—and deadly accurate. His reflexes were unlike any other warrior she'd trained. In the simulations his bravery was unmatched, beating the others time and time again in Dragon and Tower. In Chivalry, he got a perfect score. 100/100. The first in a millennium to do so.

Giddy with joy, that was the day she went to the Pendraig and told him the Lake had gifted her with the perfect knight. The Pendraig, ever skeptical, had asked to accompany her to one of his training sessions.

He left changed.

"The first in a millennium?" the Pendraig asked.

"Yes," the Lady said.

"His shape, his skills, they're perfect. But his faculties? He was only a babe three summers ago."

"We have ways of accelerating these things. The Lake is mysterious and doesn't follow our linear time."

The old king's brow furrowed, as it always did when she discussed matters of sorcery. "But the boy—the knight—will he remember? Will it harm him to have missed childhood in this way?"

"His mind will have wandered down many tracks in the acceleration vats. The Lake can show you anything if you're curious enough. A childhood? No. But he's wise beyond his years, and his mental abilities are just as advanced as any other adult's."

The king buried a hand in his thick beard, his bionic eye blinking, glaring blue. "He has taken the Oath?"

"He has, and gladly."

"And the emotional test? The empathy?"

"The Moralistic and Empathetic Comprehension Test," she corrected. "MECT. The results are not with us yet. The Lake is holding them for now. But I have confidence that he will pass. He's our Millennial Knight. He must."

Terminate. Terminate. Terminate.

The MECT was corrupted.

She remembered the conversation that followed. The Lake obliged and a swirling electric-blue mass coalesced in the form of the misshapen shack the wizard lived in near Caer Fyrddin. His tall, pointed hat bent towards the ground; his beard was sharp and angular.

The wizard had a way of seeing the future, but his memory of it was always sketchy.

"Perhaps I know the boy, perhaps not. Perhaps I will know him. I never knew him; I know that for sure. But here and now? I like him not. I have a bad feeling about it all."

"He's the perfect knight. 100/100 on Chivalry."

The wizard contemplated in silence. "His name?" he asked.

"Lanslod."

The vision dripped back into the water.

The Lady shook her head. The wizard always spun in riddles, never landing safely in one place or another.

But he gave her one certainty: he had a bad feeling. And this was a man who never dealt in absolutes.

She saw the boy she rescued three years ago, a tiny babe swaddled in a blanket and left on the misty hill to die, circled by wolves that clicked and whirred. Taking him in her arms, to her breast, had felt like the purest, most natural thing she'd ever done.

Terminate. Terminate. Terminate.
TERMINATE.

She yanked the wires from her torso, receiving a sharp shock of punishment from the Lake. She panted.

Her mind was made up.

It was her choice. Hers alone.

The boy would live.

There was nothing like seeing the knights of the Pendraig

prepare for war.

Many still remembered the old wars with the Saes. They were dark times; the Lady avoided them when she explored the memories of the Lake. But there were physical reminders around her, too—great weapons carved into mountainsides, whole quarters of cities full of locked, rusting warehouses that held ammunition, vehicles, oil and, most importantly of all, armour.

These places remained sealed for the good of all, but war was once again on the horizon.

For the Pendraig's son was about to be wed.

He appeared in the vaulted hall on a day when light streamed through the stained-glass windows, leading his knights in full armour. His own suit hissed and clanked as pneumatics pumped up and down and feet bigger than bear claws pounded the earth. Artur's suit was the grandest of all, covered in filigree and equipped with a heavy machine gun, hunting rifle, energy sword and rockets. It glowed like the sun, so bright it was almost impossible to look at. The Lady's heart fluttered when she saw it. Caledfwlch, his suit was called. Her own personal gift to the future king, assembled over hundreds of hours by the underladies of the Lake, their delicate fingers hammering love into every inch-thick armour plate.

Beside him strode Gwenhifar, the only other knight allowed to walk at his flank. Daughter of a powerful family and a prestigious jouster in her own right, the two were a perfect match—a chivalrous pair of gleaming warriors to lead the realm into a bright age following the dour greyness of the Pendraig's reign. Though both were skilled on the tourney field, neither had been tested in battle, and it was tradition for groom and bride to take up arms together. No closer bond could be forged than that made in battle.

So the people of the Pendraig would go to war. A war for D'Grael, an ancient land of theirs, stolen eons ago by the Saes. It was time to reclaim it.

But for the Lady, all of this, even Artur's sun armour, paled in comparison to the happiness she felt at seeing Lanslod striding at their side. Even encased in his suit, she could feel the pride radiating from him.

She stood amongst the crowds who'd come to see the knights depart. Someone nearby gasped.

"That's the Lake-Grown knight," a scraping voice said.

"It is. They say he's a flawless fighter."

"I don't trust them." The speaker coughed. "You can't just teach them morals. They have to learn them through experience."

The Lady's stomach twisted.

Corrupted. Corrupted. The report flashed before her again.

Recommendation: TERMINATE.

She shook it away. This was a good thing. A day to celebrate.

The first Lake-Grown to reach the rank of knight, to be called a syr? It was a good thing.

A good thing.

The procession reached the far end of the hall, stopping before the sealed glass doors. The Pendraig stood on a tall dais to the left and raised his arms as he prepared to speak.

"You go to reclaim the lands of our ancestors. To drive the Saes away at the point of a sword, to restore our people to glory. Tonight, we shall invoke the Blessings in your honour, syr knights."

The crowd roared. Artur turned to them and bowed before taking Gwenhifar's hand. She curtsied and the crowd drank it up like nectar, whooping and screaming their names.

They were a different generation to the Pendraig. Bold, flashy, energetic. Willing to perform.

"Claim victory for us, but remember your Oaths. The first: never harm the defenceless. The second: never harbour treason. The third: never make war for gold. And the fourth, for the Lake-Grown: never covet the flesh or the wedding bond."

The knights bellowed the Oaths back to the king, who nodded, his long hair tickling his shoulders.

"Don't make war on the innocent or the unarmed. Only other knights. And Artur—"

His son turned to look at him.

"Patience. Eyes on the mission. You and your bride have a lifetime to spend entwined in each other between the bedsheets."

The crowd whooped and whistled as Artur stooped awkwardly, bowing away from Gwenhifar for a moment. Her hand quickly fell back into his, and he stepped forward, activating his suit's loudspeaker.

"I vow, by the Oaths I have sworn to the Order of Pentecost, to lead this mission to the best of my ability. Fates willing, I will return to you with news of victory."

As soon as he finished speaking, the glass doors slid open. The knights ventured out onto the plain, their silhouettes fading to nothing when they hit the horizon.

And the Lady offered a prayer for the Vat-Knight who was as precious to her as any son ever could be.

The Lady went to Caer Fyrddin to visit the wizard.

It had been days since the knights departed, but her thoughts had remained with them constantly. The word still spun in her mind.

Terminate. Terminate.

"I can feel him," she told the wizard.

The wizard stroked his beard. "Your Lake-Grown warrior?"

"Yes. I feel his echo. Even when I'm apart from the Lake. I sense him."

He paced slowly across the room, leaning on his staff. When he looked back at her, his gaze was severe.

"The Lake-Grown don't usually leave such a strong trace."

Silence between them.

"Is there something you need to tell me, my Lady?"

Terminate. Terminate.

She shook her head.

The wizard sighed, and she left.

Wind blew across the flickering surface of the lake, picking up the nitrogen-cold of the water and sprinkling it across her face and body. She plugged herself in, slowly, methodically connecting the dozen trailing wires to the ports on her bare flesh, feeling the static bite of each one as they connected to her core. She kept her expression steady. As always. It was ritual to her.

She gasped.

The Lake transported her. She was in D'Grael, soaring over the tops of a thousand trees, rain splashing on her wings. The world flickered, phasing and juddering like an ancient display monitor. When it refocused, she'd found a clearing covered in brown pine needles. Her talons gripped a tall branch. Below, the knights sat around a crackling fire, their suits of armour sitting idle nearby beneath the bough of a tree, engines silent.

"The Vat-Knight?" Agravain uttered, his gravelly voice too loud.

"Shh. Yes," Gaheris said. "We saw him. Them. Together."

"He wouldn't," Gawain said. "He can't. These Lake-Growns, all they know is the Oath. They're bred not to feel love or lust. Those who don't pass the MECT are destroyed."

"You've been listening to the Lady and her underladies too much," Agravain hissed. "Her poison is in you."

"Her poison is the only reason we haven't lost our kingdom yet."

"How do you know this crap?"

"Knows an underlady, doesn't he?" Gaheris said with a smirk.

"She's a friend," Gawain said, his cheeks blushing. "I live by my Oath. I would never sully a priestess. Or any woman."

"And you think our Vat-Knight thinks the same?" Agravain scoffed. "Spawn a fully-formed, youthful man from nothing, with no memories and no family and all the strength and virility in the world, and you think he won't try to sate himself on the first woman who spreads her legs? You know, just as I do, she's not the most chaste woman under the Pendraig's realm."

Gawain shot to his feet. "You insult Gwenhifar's honour."

Gaheris stood too. "He speaks the truth, dear brother, though it may hurt to hear it. Artur was wrong to choose her, and it'll lead to ruin."

The Lady panted, her body shivering beneath the wires. They buzzed and glowed red-white hot with her effort as her vision flickered again.

Artur came into view, crouched low, target light forward, waiting patiently. His bullet sank into a deer he was hunting for their evening meal. He had no knowledge of what they were discussing back at camp.

What had Lanslod done?

She flickered, drifted, lights flashed by her eyes at a speed she'd never known, but she couldn't find her son. The strain was too much; she pulled the wires out and retreated to her sanctuary to recover, but her mind carried trouble with her.

And there she stayed for a long time.

Artur wept.

He wept until no more tears could fall, and then he convulsed, dry sobs bursting from his lips as though his lungs were dust.

Agravain, Gaheris and Gawain waited for their lord to re-emerge, but he remained in his tent, turning away all visitors. Without his lord, Gawain lost track of the days; he survived, he hunted, he slept, and the sun and moon danced across the sky.

The world felt hollow without Artur's glow, but in time, he forgot his lord's face. He understood for the first time that life would continue without him. That revelation felt as freeing as the breaking of any shackles. A spell had been sundered.

Artur emerged.

Perhaps it was because Gawain had become used to life alone, but this Artur did not seem the same as the man he remembered.

He came from his tent in his resplendent Caledfwlch, his suit shining as bright as the sun, and the other knights cheered. But when he lifted his helmet, the kind eyes were gone, replaced by those of a crow. His skin was grey, veiny, sunken, and his brow wore a permanent scowl that looked as though it were etched in stone.

"D'Grael is over," he said.

The knights were deathly silent.

"A knight, a knight and—and my lady—have, they've broken the Oath. There is no more fellowship, no more betrothal, and he is no longer my sworn knight-brother. Our order is fractured, and the quest is over."

The other knights murmured sullen agreement.

"One misstep does not condemn a knight," he said. "Not

if they still wish to do good. Let them both be judged back at Cavalon."

Artur gave him an ashen glare that threatened to slice him in two.

"They have both betrayed me. They have gone against their sacred words; they have brought ruin upon us. So knights, I have a new mission. I shall find them, wherever they are. And they will die."

"This is not your place, my lord." Gawain's heart thundered as his lord levelled his crow stare at him, his eyes burning like coals. "They must be judged by the Pendraig's council. There is no honour in this."

"Honour?" Artur growled. "You speak to me of honour. Honour is standing by your brethren. Honour is standing by your betrothed. Honour is following your lord. You break these like brittle iron, and you lecture me on honour?"

"Honour is choosing grace and mercy over vengeance, my lord. And honour is telling your friend when he has faltered."

Gawain choked back tears as he returned to his armour, Galatine. The motor purred at his touch.

"If you leave this clearing, syr knight, you will be an enemy of mine as well." For the first time, Artur's voice wavered.

Gawain suited up, feeling the familiar rush of strength as the mechanical suit responded to his thoughts and movements. He looked back at Gaheris.

"Brother of my blood. I will not fight you."

He left, and the world was hollow and colourless.

Wind blew across the flickering surface of the lake, picking up the nitrogen-cold of the water and sprinkling it across her face and body. She plugged herself in, slowly, methodically connecting the dozen trailing wires to the ports on her bare flesh, feeling the static bite of each one as they connected to her core. She kept her expression steady. As always. It was ritual to her.

Her body already trembled as the visions flooded in.

Three knights lay in wait amongst the trees, armour discarded. They had flaxen ropes in their hands that coiled like serpents.

A woman made her way to the rippling bank of a clear lake. Her onyx combat suit hugged her perfect curves. She glanced around before shrugging it down to her ankles, delicately kicking it away. She unclipped her hair and a cascade of molten glass tumbled down her back, so bright the Lady had to glance away.

Gwenhifar lowered herself into the water, humming under her breath with that honeyed voice she was renowned for.

Three knights crept towards the lake, serpents in hand. Quiet predators full of hate.

Where was Lanslod?

The Lady strained with every muscle in her body, convulsing and twitching beneath the wires, her head snapping as she hunted for him, but she felt no trace of her son.

Where was he?

Three knights surrounded the clearing and pounced, their fangs finding porcelain flesh.

The Lady didn't leave her sanctum.

Years passed in days and days passed in centuries. She plugged in, searched, but found nothing but silence. The obelisk's lights flashed orange in a perfect rhythm, just as they had every day since her first night bared before them. And yet every time she slid the wires into her core, she felt nothing.

The Lake was empty to her, just another body of water.

No trace remained.

The wizard came to visit. He paced around her, hands behind his back as she knelt before the Lake.

"They're worried about you."

"Who?"

"Your underladies. The knights. Even the Pendraig. They haven't seen you."

"Are you worried?"

The wizard took a long time to reply. "I'm worried, but not for the same reasons as they. I know you're healthy. You're eating, you're sleeping. You're sane, as much as any who know the Lake can be. Your trouble is within, and that worries me because I know I can't reach it."

"I can't see anything," she confessed. "The Lake is silent. I cannot remember the last time it spoke to me. I feel walled off."

"Is there anything on your mind?"

The tears fell heavy down her cheeks and didn't stop. "Lanslod."

The wizard put a hand on her shoulder. He tugged the wires from her one by one with the delicacy of an outcast foraging blackberries. For the first time, she looked into his eyes.

"Forget the Lake. This is something you need to confront yourself. You're afraid of what you'll see. You're guilty. Come, talk about it. You'll feel better. And perhaps the visions will return."

"And if they don't?"

He gave a sad smile.

They both knew what that meant.

Wind blew across the flickering surface of the Lake, picking up the nitrogen-cold of the water and sprinkling it across her face and body. She plugged herself in, slowly, methodically connecting the dozen trailing wires to the ports on her bare flesh, feeling the static bite of each one as they connected to her core. She kept her expression steady. As always. It was ritual to her.

Deep breath. Deep breath. She was ready for this.

It did not matter what she saw.

She had to face it.

She had to find him.

The inky blackness of the water absorbed her fully.

She saw. Grey, grainy, stuttering, but she saw.

Jagged images bursting into her vision as though burnt onto the crystal flanks of ice shards.

The lady with molten hair was bound to a post, flames licking at her heels. She remained silent, but her lips quivered.

Where was he?

Artur prowled back and forth like a wolf, incessantly pacing, a grin etched into his face as though in stone.

"There is no greater dishonour, Gwenhifar, than for a woman to turn on her lord."

She said nothing.

"You could have been my queen." He approached her, caressing her arm. She winced and he grimaced. "I could have loved you deeper than anyone. Deeper than that heartless Vat-Knight."

"He's not heartless," she spat.

"He stabbed his lord in the back for the sake of bare flesh. There is no act more heartless."

"You know nothing about him."

"I know he's not here," Artur said. "If he loved you truly, he'd be here with you. To die at your side. But no. He fled, as all cowards do."

The Lady heard the mind of Gaheris. Blood pulsed in his ears. His muscles strained to strike Artur, but he remained still. His honour stayed his hand.

The whirring of a motor filled her ears.

And she felt Lanslod.

The Vat-Knight burst into the clearing, targeting lights flashing and Arondight's engine screaming with strain. The clearing was a riot of red beams as his sights locked on the knights he'd trained beside.

The Lady wept as Agravain and Gaheris tried to block him from the pyre.

Their own suits cranked and hissed as they intercepted him. The word thudded in the Lady's ears, so loud it was all she could focus on.

Terminate.

Terminate.

TERMINATE.

Her vision flipped, twisted, and returned.

The flashes of machine gun fire strobed the night, the booming of controlled explosions causing the creatures of the dark to scatter. Blood gushed on the dry earth and was eagerly swallowed, and the brothers' suits crashed to the ground, smoking and lifeless. And every oath that Lanslod had ever sworn leaked out of him in miniscule photons, and the obelisk laughed and the Lake turned red and the Lady wept for Gwenhifar, for Artur, for the brothers and the kingdom and the Pendraig. But most of all, she wept for her son, because the Fates were cruel and unbending, but she'd tried to turn them anyway.

Artur was nowhere to be seen.

"The First Oath, Artur!" she heard Lanslod bellow through his armour's loudspeaker. "Do not harm the defenceless."

She wept for her son.

He didn't deserve this.

His suit powered down and he dashed from it, sprinting barefoot across the mud to Gwenhifar's side. He sliced the ropes that bound her and their lips connected.

Time slipped.

She felt Gawain's echo. A noble knight for refusing to harm Gwenhifar, and now he wept for his brothers who lay dead at Lanslod's feet. He flickered into view, kneeling beside the bodies. Anger spilled from him in ruby red tendrils, striking the earth and sky like slaver's whips.

"I will avenge you, dear kin."

The Lady paced her garden slowly, her frail body covered by a lily-white dress. Step by step. Step by step. The buddleias had just flowered, springing forth in cream cones. They were gloriously bright in the morning sun, and for a moment, the weight on her heart lifted. They were coated in dozens of honeybees; the longer she watched, the more there were. They wiggled on each flower. The Lady wondered what the mind of a bee looked like, but when she tried, she could find nothing.

She kicked a rock in frustration. Once upon a time, she'd been able to see everything. Now she wondered if her power was slipping at last. Sooner or later, the Lake always chose another. It was the cycle they accepted when they came to this place, this Cavalon. One day, an underlady would take her place as the servant of the Lake, and so it would go.

"In your head again?" came a soft voice.

She turned to find the wizard pacing towards her, his midnight blue robe trailing in the mud. A tender smile turned his eyes to slivers. He caressed one of the buddleias, allowing a bee to walk along his finger.

"You didn't think these would bloom this year," the wizard said.

"Did I not?"

"You didn't. Or perhaps it was next year. It's unimportant. The truth is before you: they came back, just as they have done every year, just as they always will."

She glanced at the flowers again. Just a week ago, there had not been a single glimpse of white on them. Buddleias always bloomed late, and they always bloomed quickly. A spectacle, a riot, beautiful but fleeting.

"What is your point, wizard?"

He leant on his staff. "This staff was carved from the branch of a magic oak tree thousands of years ago, long before recorded memory. They said that, if this ancient oak ever fell, great harm would befall Caer Fyrddin. Do you know this? The great witches and wizards all agreed. Then lightning struck the oak. Do you know what happened?"

"What?"

The wizard smiled again. "Nothing. Nothing happened. And I vowed that day, so they tell me—I no longer remember such things—that I would carry a staff from that tree with me forevermore. Not as a piece of magic, but as a reminder. Because sometimes our visions are wrong. Sometimes a tree is just a tree."

She was silent for a while. "You know, don't you?"

The wizard chuckled. "As I said, my Lady, you're in your head again. But I sense it in you; your power does not wane yet. You can rest easy."

"So where are Gwenhifar and Lanslod?"

"Everywhere and nowhere," the wizard said. "The story from here has many branches, and I've walked them all. Some are good, some are tragic. Most are tragic, actually. But that is something the Lake cannot fix for you. So you might have doomed the kingdom, and by extent our people, to defeat and ruin. You made a choice, and the results are out of your hands now. Artur, Gwen, Lanslod, Gawain, they will decide how the fatesticks fall. But it will only hurt you to scry the Lake every day, seeing a thousand things that might pass. You'll miss the one thing that will. And we shan't know for sure until they return from D'Grael, if they ever do."

The wizard paced by her, touching his staff to his drooping hat and continuing to inspect the flowers. She stared after him.

"Do you think I made the right choice?" she called after him. "By saving him?"

The wizard didn't answer.

MULAN AND THE DŌGYN OF POWER

Carter Hutchison

"The art of war is of vital importance to the State. It is a matter of
life and death, a road either to safety or to ruin."
– Sun Tzu *The Art of War*

Tsiek tsiek, sounded the weaving locks of the Palanquin jets
in the shuttle bay below, but Mulan could not hear them. Her mind
was elsewhere.

Another season and another dreadful gala of the system's
most wealthy and notable families. Mulan felt they were also the
most boring the system had to offer. Another day of her life wasted.
When she was younger, she was awestruck by the pageantry, the
regality, and the pomp of these balls. But it had soon worn thin.
As she had grown older, her interests had shifted.

Now she had to pretend to be like a flower petal gliding across
the room, assisted only by the hand of the commanding man who
escorted her. When in reality, she knew she could drop most of
these so-called men in the room with a single blow. Her father
had taught her well. She was the son he had always wanted. When

Mulan's brother finally came a decade later, it was too late. The cycle was coming to an end.

And worst of all, tonight's galactic waste of time was hosted by Mulan's own family, the Guiyings. And her mother was in rare form. She was currently flitting between the welcoming veranda, the ballroom, and the dining room. Mulan had never cared for this type of thing, or been much good at it, but her mother thrived in it. Though Mulan had to commend her decorating. The great hall was adorned with fabulous multicolored tapestries that hung from the rafters. Most featured the Guiying golden coat of arms, a magnolia tree encircled by five gems: one of ivory, gold, jade, ruby, and onyx. But there were several other tapestries that depicted moments of myth and legend. Moments of stories that every child in the system heard before bed. Tales of Souzi suits of armor as tall as mountains wielding swords of white flame on distant planets. Tales of the five DŌGYN saving the system from the Swarm.

It was a burden that spanned generations.

And the cycle was coming to an end.

Could Mulan ever truly do what her mother did? There was her mother, commanding a team of hundreds of servants, musicians, and chefs. Her qipao was exquisitely pressed and glistened in the Saturn sunset. Her long, jet-black hair was perfectly braided into a bun that coiled around the crest of her head and was adorned with a pink rose of Tarqeq. She was the spitting image of the confident matriarch. But like all adults, she was pretending.

It wasn't that the Guiyings were destitute, they had only just fallen out of favor when Mulan was born. The goal for all breeding throughout the system was in preparation for the incoming Swarm.

Every able-bodied man would be needed to support the DŌGYN in their battle, so each family was expected to produce a male heir who would come of age when the Swarm cycle began again. It was a patriotic duty, and the Guiyings seemed incapable of it for many years. Until finally, after years of trying, they were blessed with a child. All the sonograms and tests showed the baby was a boy. And then, out came Mulan. The family never recovered their social standing, even after they eventually had Mulan's brother. It was too late by then. He would not be of fighting age at the arrival of the Swarm.

The men were sent to the slaughter while the women stayed with the colony. And why was this? Because men were considered expendable when it came to the creation of a child. Men go to the slaughter because defense against the Swarm created the need for an expendable population. This, in turn, led to the need for vast procreation. And the need for vast procreation is what justifies men going to the slaughter. It was a vicious cycle leaving behind an elderly population that was almost entirely female. Almost.

Mulan's father stood at the entrance of the great hall and greeted the guests as they arrived and were announced. He was wearing his dress blues and looked quite dapper, Mulan thought, even though the cut of his suit was more than a few seasons out of style.

"Lord Asher Diem of the Venus Subsystem," the emcee bellowed as a boy with an angular face and a hooked nose dressed in a pale white tang suit entered the room to the fanfare of pipas. He peered out at the room from behind the long bangs of his dark hair.

Although the music in the room was exquisite and the sky was a perfect golden hue that the Saturn Subsystem was well known for, there was an aura of dread amongst the crowd. Mulan could feel it. She felt it in the way their guests moved about the room. She felt it in the way they spoke to each other, desperately jumping from subject to subject in order to avoid talking about what was really on everyone's minds. The Swarm was imminent. Soon the Khan would circulate the enlistment scrolls, and the men would follow the DŌGYN into battle. Most would not return.

"Duke Hadrian Oi of the Mars Subsystem," the emcee announced as a dashing young man with wavy brown hair and a date on each arm stepped down the ramp of a red Phoenix ZR-42 and into the room. He was wearing a trendy Zhongshan suit in red with a black tie and black coattails that extended below the backs of his knees. The two women giggled to each other. The men in the room looked at the women, Mulan looked at the spaceship. It was the fastest model in the system, and one day she would fly her own. That was what freedom looked like.

Mulan's wristcom dinged with an alert and projected a holo of the duke's post about the party. She blushed with slight embarrassment and hoped that he did not notice she followed his account. Luckily for Mulan, the attention was quickly diverted as the room echoed with the chimes of wristcom alerts. First one or two here and there. Then it grew into a cacophony. Mulan looked at her father. As their eyes met, his wristcom projected the same holo that the other men in the room had received, the blue light highlighting every wrinkle on his face.

The scrolls had been sent. War was here.

"Sir Jie Ning of the Mercury Subsystem," the emcee boomed as a young man dressed in an all-black tang suit entered the room.

Mulan was not sure if it was the growing chaos within the room or Jie himself, but he seemed to be an oasis of serenity. He swept into the room and melted into the crowd.

Mulan walked towards her father. She took his frail hand. His skin felt as thin as paper. This was no longer the body of a warrior. No one should be expected to serve against the Swarm twice. To escape once with your life was a big enough miracle for one lifetime. Not even the power of the Gold DŌGYN would be enough to protect him as it had protected generations of the Guiyings before. This scroll of service might as well have been a death sentence.

"Father," she said as she brought his hand to her face, "don't go."

"I must," he answered, his eyes not meeting hers. "Shan is only ten. A Guiying has answered the call for thousands of years against the Swarm. This cycle will be no different."

Mulan fought back the tears in her eyes. She released his hand and brought her own behind her back as she touched the interface on her wristcom.

"Will you at least read the scroll to me?" she asked.

Her father hesitated for a moment, then tapped his wristcom to pull up the holo.

"A message from the Khan to every able-bodied soldier in the System: the Swarm is upon us. Your presence, Qiang Guiying, along with that of the Golden DŌGYN, is required at the Black Mountain in ten sun cycles. Your Khan thanks you for the sacrifices you make for your family and for the System," he read in an even tone. When he finished, he looked to Mulan as though the weight of the entire galaxy was on his shoulders. "I must find your mother," he said as he turned to walk away. "There are affairs that must be in order before I depart with Kohryu. I love you." Mulan watched him walk away and wondered if it was the last time she would ever see him.

Mulan spied a flash of green that brought her attention to the glass ceiling above. With a sonic boom, the Jade DŌGYN stopped and hovered above the palace. It gleamed in the golden Saturn sunset. It was even larger than Mulan could have imagined. The mech had outer plating similar in design to ancient Souzi armor: jade mountain-patterned scales over the cuirass, pauldrons, and tassets with silver in the space between. The head was a winged helmet with a thin red line for a Corinthian opening. It hovered in the air above the palace propelled by qigines, the same propulsion design that made intersystem space travel possible.

"Prince Zhang Yu of the Jupiter Subsystem," the emcee announced as the Jade DŌGYN saluted the crowd below, and then blasted off towards the heavens.

Mulan knew what she must do. She slipped through the distracted crowd and out of the room into the kitchens. The back entrance to the kitchen led out to a long corridor. She weaved through the inner workings of the palace until she reached her father's study. The oak doors closed behind her and the world fell silent. The room smelled of leather and ink. Father was a collector of ancient writings.

The wall was lined with books from top to bottom, but there was one book in particular that Mulan was looking for today. An especially old text, *The Art of War* by Sun Tzu. She spotted its red spine with gold lettering, walked over to it, and pulled. Mulan heard the clicking of locks, and the bookcase parted to reveal a silver vault door.

"*Clearance required,*" a robotic voice chirped from a display on the door.

Mulan held her wristcom to the display and hit the playback button, playing the recording of her father reading his scroll of service earlier. "*Qiang Guiying,*" her father's voice said through the wristcom.

"*Clearance granted. Kohryu initiated,*" the voice responded. The vault door unlocked, revealing a body mold in the wall as it opened. Mulan turned around and stepped back into it. She was immediately wrapped in a black padded jumpsuit and gold helmet. Then before she could catch her breath, the floor came out from under her, and she was propelled downward through a metallic tube with florescent lights whizzing by every few feet or so. When she finally came to a stop, she could see nothing. Then the monitor clicked on, and she found herself in a small, curved room. The rounded wall turned into a monitor that displayed the hangar around her. Wires descended from the chamber like tentacles and attached themselves to her suit. She was like a puppet on a string. Mulan brought her hand up to her face to inspect the connections and noticed that the display now showed the metallic hand of Kohryu, the Golden DŌGYN, in front of her.

She would be its pilot.

She would take her father's place in the defense against the Swarm.

"Move swift as the Wind and closely-formed as the Wood. Attack like the Fire and be still as the Mountain." – Sun Tzu, *The Art of War*.

For the ten days of travel through the system, Mulan trained. For ten days she had read *The Art of War* cover-to-cover multiple times. For ten days she ran through every operations module the Kohryu had stored in its database. She knew it like she knew her own body. And for ten days, the Kohryu *was* her own body. If only these other dolts had done the same.

"DŌGYN, we need back up! Where the hell are the rest of you?" Zhang shouted from the cockpit of Qinglong, the Jade DŌGYN. His green helmet appeared in a box on Mulan's display sphere. "It's only Kohryu and me at Point Alpha! Status and location, boys!" That was one thing Mulan could take comfort in: to the other pilots, the padded jumpsuit and gold helmet ensured she would not be seen as a woman, only as Kohryu, the Gold DŌGYN. And right now, Kohryu was kicking ass.

Zhang and Mulan had arrived first at the pre-set location near the base of the Black Mountain on Persephone, the ninth planet of the System. Legend told that this was the birthplace of the DŌGYN. And it was here that the Swarm always entered the System from the heliopause.

The Jade and Gold DŌGYN stood back-to-back as hundreds of paralongs circled around them. Mulan had seen their image before on ancient tapestries, but that was nothing compared to the real thing. They had massive compound eyes, short, flat beaks rowed with sharp teeth, a serpent's tail, and thin, leathery wings with veins that glowed magenta against the blackness of space and

Persephone itself. Paralongs darted towards the pair of DŌGYN. Zhang thrust forward with Qinglong's spear and found purchase in the belly of the beast.

A paralong swerved towards Mulan. She swatted it away with Kohryu's shield, and it landed on Persephone's surface belly-up. Kohryu plunged its sword through the beast and into the ground below.

In the distance, Mulan could see the qijets breaking atmo. They would be lambs to the slaughter. Although the Swarm seemed to focus their efforts on the DŌGYN, many took the time to also wreck a few hundred qijets. They toyed with them, latching onto the backs of the jets with their claws, tossing the jet to another paralong who would take a bite out and toss it aside.

Another box popped up on Mulan's display, this time occupied by a red helmet.

"Miss me already, Zhang?" a voice soaked with sarcasm and confidence asked.

Mulan saw a flash of red from above. Down came Zhuque, the Scarlet DŌGYN, landing in a kneel with one of its hook swords through the head of a paralong. Another attacked it from its flank. The crescent guard on the second hook sword shot off the hilt, separating the incoming paralong's head from its body. The body stumbled forward several more yards before collapsing next to the Zhuque as the crescent guard boomeranged back to the sword.

"No need to fly off the handle," Hadrian said, the suave smile behind his helmet was audible.

"Oh, good. Jokes," Zhang said as Qinglong's spear found another paralong.

"Yeah," Hadrian said with a slash of a hook sword, "*don't lose your head* seemed too obvious."

"Asher, report!" Zhang said, ignoring Hadrian.

"Incoming!" Mulan shouted as her sensors started picking up a seismic reading five clicks east of their location. Kohryu's display zoomed in on the disturbance. It appeared to be a tsunami of paralongs. A giant wave of death heading straight for their location. Then the crest of the wave broke with the swing of a pure white Warhammer. It was Baihu, the Ivory DŌGYN.

"Zhang, when we get back, remind me to buy you some reins. For the holding of horses!" Asher said behind a white helmet as his box appeared on Mulan's display. The Warhammer sliced off a paralong's wing midair. When it fell to the surface, the hammer met the creature's skull. It made a wet crunch that sent shivers down Mulan's spine.

"Glad you could make it, Asher," Zhang said. "Okay, Jie, time for you to make your grand entrance now."

"Just a hunch," Hadrian said, "but he doesn't really strike me as the *grand entrance* type. Which is fine, more time for me to shine."

"He's here," Asher said to the group. "I got a reading of the Onyx DŌGYN not far from here. I think our DŌGYN are linked somehow." Baihu made a wave with its arm towards the others as it jumped from the crest to the crater below. "This way," he said. The other DŌGYN followed suit.

Sitting full lotus in the basin of the crater was Xuanwu, the Onyx DŌGYN. The light of its qigines was off, making it nearly impossible to see against the dark Persephone surface.

"Jie," Zhang said sternly into the comms, "do you copy? Get off your ass, we must advance! Take the fight to the Swarm!"

A box appeared on Mulan's display sphere, this time occupied by a black helmet.

"Xuanwu is a mousetrap," Jie said evenly. "The trap does not chase the mouse. But when the mouse grabs the cheese, the trap plays its role."

A nearby paralong swooped in, diving towards the Onyx DŌGYN. In an instant, the Corinthian opening on the head of Xuanwu was glowing with the light of qigines. As the paralong swooped in to strike, the Xuanwu bent backwards, avoiding the blow. Before the paralong could turn for another pass, it was met by Xuanwu's sheng biao. Jie pulled and swung the body of the paralong stuck on the end of the sheng biao over its head, knocking several dozen paralongs to the ground before they fled.

"Well, let's move the mousetrap," Zhang said to the others. "Company, advance! Stay tight. Watch each other's six."

Moving as one unit, the five DŌGYN made their way towards the Black Mountain. In the distance, an ion storm raged electric blue, obscuring the peak of the Black Mountain from sight. The space in between was a barren no man's land. It was a ship grave-yard of millennia's old spacecrafts from all over the System, and some that appeared far more advanced than anything Mulan was aware of. As far as she could tell, they all had only one common feature: qigines.

The group soon fell into a pattern of defense. Xuanwu's onyx sheng biao and Zhuque's scarlet crescent disks were used to keep the paralongs at a distance as they moved through the Swarm. When any got too close, they were met with the end of Qinglong's jade spear, or the brunt of Baihu's ivory Warhammer, or the slash of Kohryu's golden sword. Each had their own part to play. It was a symphony of violence. The company pressed on to Omega Point, the peak of the Black Mountain.

They progressed through the starship graveyard, Baihu cutting their way through like a machete through the jungle. Mulan recognized some of the names written on the sides of the ships. Some were of a legendary fleet from long ago called NASA, something she thought only existed in stories for children.

"Hey, look at this!" Hadrian said as he marked a location on their shared display spheres. "It's an Oi ship. Looks like it's from all the way back to the twenty-third century! The great-great-great-great-great granddaddy of them all."

Zhuque's qijets ignited, and he hovered into the air above the group. Hadrian began marking other locations on their display spheres. "Looks like we all made it here. There's a Nīng! Here's a Diem! Yu. Guiying. All of the original astro mining companies."

"Would you get down from there, gearhead? We aren't here to sightsee!" Zhang shouted at Hadrian.

"Ah, lighten up, Zhang. This is history. The history of all of our families," Hadrian said in awe and childish defiance.

Mulan's sensors began to detect several rapidly approaching objects. "Uh, guys," she said to the others in the monitor.

"You're giving away our position, Hadrian! Get down this instant! That is a command from your prince!" Zhang said angrily.

"Guys!" Mulan said, louder this time. The incoming hostile was nearly on them.

"Oh, yeah? Well, you want to know what the Mars System thinks of you, Your Majesty?" Hadrian asked as the Zhuque landed next to Qinglong and they butted cuirasses. Then, as if both realizing the imminent danger at the same time, both DŌGYN turned their heads to see the incoming paralong. It was enormous. Three times bigger than any of the others they had encountered.

The giant paralong pulled its claws up and opened its massive jaws, showing the seemingly infinite rows of teeth on the inside of the beak, then swooped in for a lethal strike. But it suddenly stopped midair. Its eyes went dull. Fluorescent blood spilled from its chest as it split in half, revealing Kohryu hovering above it.

"That's enough!" Mulan shouted to the others. "Quit your bickering! Hadrian, this is not the time for thinking of the past, we are here to protect those in the present and future. And Zhang, its time you told us exactly what our mission is at the peak of the Black Mountain."

Zhuque and Qinglong separated.

"Very well," Zhang said. "Persephone's planetary core is pure Qi. Its discovery by our ancestors allowed for interplanetary travel between colony systems to be a possibility. Without it, we never would have been able to expand into the System before the Earth of Old was destroyed. They also discovered five core metals that had fused with the Qi of the planet. Each family received one vein which they mined and forged into the DŌGYNs, using one letter from each of their family names. It was only through the use of Qi and later qigines, that all this was possible. But like all things, it came at a price. The paralongs are an ancient interstellar plague that nest on a comet propelled by Qi. They are drawn to sources of Qi like moths to the flame. They feed upon it. When the Black Mountain erupts at the beginning of each new cycle, it sends Qi out into the system and ensures its continued availability. If the Swarm goes unchecked, they clog the eruption in an orgy of gluttony. We are here to make sure that doesn't happen."

Silence fell on the group for a moment as they took it all in.

"So, that's why we can't just use our qijets to get to the peak. It would attract too many paralongs," Mulan said.

"Exactly. Run stealth to the peak. Ensure its eruption. Go home," Zhang said.

"I'm sure it doesn't hurt that the Qi also ensures our families get to keep profiting off it," Asher said.

"It's wrong," Mulan said with a sinking feeling in the pit of her stomach.

"What do you mean?" Zhang asked.

"If it was just us, here to keep our family profits, sure. But what about them?" Mulan said as Kohryu motioned to the thousands of qijets in battle with paralongs in the atmosphere. "Those men are brought here under false pretenses. To die. To leave behind their own families. Wives. Sons. Daughters. All now fatherless so we can continue to profit."

"Qiang is right," Jie said. It took Mulan a moment to remember that she was masquerading as her father as she heard Jie say his name.

"Uh...thanks," she said as she cleared her throat.

"Look, I agree with you old-timer, but what can we do about it? This is just the way of things," Zhang said.

Mulan looked towards the storm at the peak of the Black Mountain.

"I won't pretend to know the answer. But we have to try and find a way to do things differently. No matter the cost. Let's get to the peak," she said as she turned Kohryu to march towards the Black Mountain.

The rest of the DŌGYN followed her.

"Okay, guys, to the peak," Zhang said sarcastically, realizing he was no longer the leader of this party.

Around a thousand feet from the peak, they entered a dense fog that swirled around them with blue electricity. Mulan could feel its power beating against the hull of Kohryu. They used Xuan-wu's sheng biao as an anchor and continued up the mountain in a row. Once they reached the peak, they were above the storm. Their path now was clear.

Blue Qi energy boiled in the central vent atop the Black Mountain. It was near eruption. Whatever they were going to do, they would need to do it fast. The growing presence of Qi was also attracting the frontline of the battle. The sky glowed with the fluorescent wings of paralongs, qijets hot on their trail. Around the volcanic opening, Mulan noticed four small craters, one at each directional point around the opening. Kohryu walked over and scanned the craters.

"Hey, look at this!" she said to the others. "These craters have indentions in the basin."

"They aren't craters at all," Jie said.

"They are forging pits," Zhang said in awe. "But where is the fifth one?"

As if on cue, a platform arose from the center of the Qi pit. On it was a golden pedestal stone. They all knew what they must do.

The Onyx DŌGYN took its place in the forging pit north of the central vent. Jade to the east. Scarlet to the south. And Ivory to the west. Then Mulan and Kohryu leapt to the center platform and stood above the pedestal stone. The Swarm closed in around them in a fluorescent swirl. Qi began to bubble and pop at the surface of the vent. Mulan held Kohryu's sword above her head.

A bolt of Qi from the ion storm struck the golden sword. Mulan thrust it down and the sword struck the stone. The Qi rose into the forging pits and onto the center platform. Five ejection pods shot into the air as a blast of Qi radiated from the Black Mountain. The eruption at the surface of the central vent cooled and subsided. The Black Mountain had taken back what it was owed.

"Let your plans be dark and impenetrable as night, and when you move, fall like a thunderbolt."
– Sun Tzu *The Art of War*

Without the use of qigines, it took the DŌGYN pilots and the expedition ten years to return to the System's capitol. But when they did, there was a celebration the likes of which had not been seen for millennia. There was music and flower petals in the air. House banners flew proudly in procession. The entire system welcomed the return of their heroes, the ones who had brought an end to the cycle. The ones who ensured the Swarm would never return.

The five DŌGYN pilots knelt in front of the Khan on the steps of the palace. A massive crowd had gathered to watch the Khan bless each pilot for their service. Friends and family were all around, except for Mulan's. She knew her father would keep his distance to not give her true identity away.

"Zhang Yu," the Khan said as he removed Zhang's green helmet. "What do you desire?"

"Only to be your son, my Khan," Zhang said as he bowed his head.

"Asher Diem," the Khan said as he removed Asher's white helmet. "What do you desire?"

"Continued prosperity for the System, my Khan," Asher said as he bowed his head.

"Jie Ning," the Khan said as he removed Jie's black helmet. "What is it you desire?"

"Continued peace for the System, my Khan," Jie said as he bowed his head.

"Hadrian Oi," the Khan said as he removed Hadrian's red helmet. "What is your desire?"

"Continued honor for the System, my Khan," Hadrian said as he bowed his head.

"Qiang Guiying," the Khan said as he removed Mulan's gold helmet. The crowd gasped. The faces of the Khan and the other pilots were stunned. For a moment they all looked at her with their mouths gaping.

"What," the Khan began, breaking the silence. "W-what is your desire?"

Mulan smiled. "The fastest way home, to see my family."

That evening, Mulan's golden Phoenix ZR-42 hovered above the landing bay of the Guiying palace. Standing there, silhouetted by the golden Saturn sky, stood Mulan's father and mother with their arms around each other. The spacecraft landed and the pair rushed towards her. She was home. The weaving locks secured her shuttle to the landing bay. *Tsiek tsiek.*

CONTRIBUTORS

DINA S.

Dina spends her evenings with her two dogs, harassing her husband to the brink of insanity, and obsessing over all things teal. She uses her free time to bring worlds to life through her writing. Dina's life is spent enduring the hot, humid sunsets of Florida, known to the natives as the Armpit Climate, but to the lovely tourists as The Eternal Vacation Climate. You can watch her on the Don't Make It Weird Podcast, where her life adventures and stories continue. Find her on Twitter at @DinasaurusD.

JAECYN BONÉ

Jaecyn Boné (he/they) is a disabled, queer, Asian-American author and artist. They while away their days daydreaming about tragic faeries, bloodthirsty pirates, and eating the rich. He lives in Billings, Montana, USA with his spouse, his two kids, his sister, and possibly a ghost or two. Twitter: @Charli_Bone.

R. RAETA

R. Raeta is a two-time IAN Book of the Year Award Finalist for her debut novel, Everlong. She lives in Northern California with her husband and young son. When she isn't agonizing over word choices, she enjoys telling the dog how handsome he is and sitting in on the nightly therapy sessions the cat so generously provides for her. She is a Triginal Neuralgia survivor, and believes in living your best life day by day.

MICHAEL J. MULLEN II

Michael lives in central New Jersey, and before you say it, he isn't sorry. He lives with his wife and their two fur babies. Creative writing has been a passion of his since the age of twelve, when he took over the role of Game Master for his local DnD groups. When he isn't exploring the fantasy worlds he's created or on Twitter being Mr. Positivity and the Ra Ra Jester of Great Books, he's on the battlefield wielding his twin swords with the other great people of the Society of Creative Anachronism (SCA).

DOUGLAS JERN

Douglas Jern was born in Lund, Sweden and lives in Nagoya, Japan. With all the time he spends writing, translating, or creating subtitles, it's a wonder he hasn't yet fused with his computer into a grotesque biomechanical entity with copper nerves and bones of plastic, which as we all agree, would be totally rad. He loves reading, writing, playing video games, and watching movies with his wife.

STEPHEN HOWARD

Stephen Howard is an English novelist and short story writer whose works include *Beyond Misty Mountain* and *Condemned To Be*. Born and raised in Manchester, he now lives next to a graveyard in Cheshire with his partner, Rachel, and their demonic cat, Leo. His stories have been published by Lost Boys Press,

Scribble, Ghost Orchid Press, and others. Find Stephen at:

Twitter: @SteJHoward

Website: www.stephenhowardblog.wordpress.com

MATTHEW SIADAK

Matthew spends most of his free time creating in one fashion or another, and is currently working on his dark, eldritch fantasy novel *The Backwards Knight*. He was born with a spatula in one hand and a quill in the other, torn between a world of logic and creativity. Matthew stitches the two worlds together with his love of writing and his day job working with code. Legend has it he once simultaneously baked a loaf of bread, cracked an encrypted password on a sacred document, and rescued a princess from an evil dragon while regaling his daughter with a story about Sir Solomon, the red panda paladin. His short stories have been featured in a handful of independent anthologies, and he has self-published a collection of short stories accompanied by his wife's art in *Arkadia*. He loves to lose himself in reading books and is obsessed with all things fantasy.

MADELINE DAU

Madeline Dau lives in Florida with her family and two corgis. When she's not frantically working on her next novel during the kids' naps, she's planning the next destination in her goal to run a half marathon in every state. Since sleep is elusive and overrated, she runs on sheer force of will and copious amounts of tea. Find her other stories, "Flicker" in the Spirit Machine Anthology and

"The Haunting of Dubois Manor" in the Prism: Between Light and Shadow Anthology.

CHRIS DURSTON

Chris Durston is a writer, editor, and occasional musician from England's Westcountry, where (like everyone else who lives there) they spend their days scrumping, their nights cow-tipping, and the intervening periods hiding from irate farmers. Their debut novel, *Each Little Universe*, was self-published in April 2020 and republished by Skullgate Media in October 2021. Their short stories appear in half a dozen or so other places, including Lost Boys Press anthology, *Chimera.* If all goes to plan, 2022 should see the release of not only their dark fantasy work, *Chronicles from the World of Guilt* from Three Ravens Press, but also *Cthulhu Dreamt 2*, a collaborative multimedia project including a metal album, a novel, and a role-playing game. Find them at chrisdurston.com or on Twitter as @chrisdurstonish.

DEWI HARGREAVES

Dewi is a writer and illustrator who lives in a cold, wet village in Staffordshire, England. His flash fiction piece, "Maccabeus," won 2nd place in Grindstone Literary's Open Prose Competition 2017, and his short fiction has appeared in the anthologies: *Chimera* and *Heads and Tales*, and Noctivagant Press's magazine. He self-published his collection of short stories, *The Shield Road*, in early 2021. When he's not writing outdoors, he's drawing maps to go in the front matter of books.

JESS L. TONG

At all times, Jess carries three things: a hair scrunchie on her wrist, an obscene amount of pet fur on her leggings, and the weight of her made-up worlds on her shoulders. These all make it into her writing—whether they're injected into the setting or sucked into her computer fan— while she creates imperfect characters trying their best in defective worlds. Like their creator, they make poor decisions they can't escape and bad jokes you'll wish to. Jess' first-ever short story, "Nameless," was published in Lost Boy's Press' Spring 2021 Anthology, *Not Meant For Each Other.* "Lab R Inc" is her second story. She wonders if being a double Lost Boy cancels out into being a Found Boy. If so, she can be found in her beautiful home of BC, Canada, either playing on mountaintops, or snuggling high-carb snacks in bed, ugly-crying into a book. Both activities pair well with wine. While she considers herself "chaotic" and "imprisoned in this soggy bag of meat," her friends have described her as "short," "talkative," and "please stop asking me to describe you." Jess invites you on a journey to follow her to strange, fantastical, and heartfelt places. You can read her stories too. Find Jess on Twitter at @JessLTWrites or her website jessl-tong.com.

LAURA JAYNE MCLOUGHLIN

Laura McLoughlin is a writer based in Armagh, Northern Ireland. She holds a degree in English with Creative Writing from Queen's University Belfast, and currently works as a Digital PR

Executive. When not writing, you can catch her jamming to Taylor Swift, watering her extended family of houseplants, or walking with her two unruly dogs.

CARTER HUTCHISON

Carter Hutchison is a writer and musician from Birmingham, Alabama with a passion for sci-fi, fantasy, and pulp works. He has a degree in Radio, Television, and Film, and runs Grass Roots Comics, where you can find several short comics he's written. He is married to Ashley Hutchison, LBP's editor-in-chief, and together they have two boys they are certain will grow up to be supervillains.

DANIEL QUIGLEY

Daniel Quigley is a fantasy author and Jar Jar Binks enthusiast who lives in Atlanta, Georgia with his beautiful wife, daughter, and far too many animals. When he's not writing stories about drunken swords, snarky zombies, cryptids, or electrical magicians (electricians, if you will), he can be found coaching soccer. "The Hanged Man" is his debut published story, and he hopes it's the first of many to come. If you like his particular brand of humor, then you are encouraged to check out the Don't Make It Weird Podcast that he co-hosts with fellow Heroes author, Dina S., and the legendary Sean Holden. You can find him on twitter: @DanQWritesThing.

www.lostboyspress.com

Also available from Lost Boys Press

Novellas:

A Map to the Stars by Ashley Hutchison

The Garden of the Golden Children by Ashley Hutchison

Full Length:

Ghost River by Chad Ryan

Anthologies:

Chimera

Not Meant for Each Other

Heroes

CPSIA information can be obtained
at www.ICGtesting.com
Printed in the USA
BVHW040249260322
632265BV00008B/286

9 781737 360520